A Bone in His Teeth

KELLEN GRAVES

A Bone in His Teeth

*To anyone ever forced to leave their community,
or pressured to stay in one; family is found and chosen.*

*And to Mo, my caller of the sea, my mud witch.
I will always come when you call,
no matter where or when, from any shore.*

"Like wet sand wedged beneath your fingernails, *A Bone in His Teeth* is a gritty, discomfiting queer romance that drags you under from the very beginning, submerging you in its barnacled, seaside settings and ethereal atmosphere. Full of nautical eeriness, this is both a tale of vengeance against the devil you know and finding a home in the devil you don't, delivered with a commanding yet suspenseful pace.

Fans of *Rowan Blood* who relished the vicious details of fey lore will no doubt enjoy the similarly elevated aspects of horror in *A Bone in His Teeth*. Graves' protagonists find themselves trapped by the insidiousness of generational greed and sacrifice, balanced by the reclamation of stolen autonomy with sharp teeth. Readers will encounter plenty of harrowing twists as the novel's gruesome mysteries are slowly unraveled, surgically stripped away layer by layer with thrilling action and poignant, lyrical prose, all of which results in a satisfyingly hard-won conclusion."

—ELLE PORTER
AUTHOR OF *HYACINTH* AND
HEIR TO THE AUTUMN COURT

"Romance and horror blend in this tale of seaside folklore where love is both tender and terrifying, A BONE IN HIS TEETH is a must-read for all fans of queer monster romance!"

—K. M. ENRIGHT
AUTHOR OF MISTRESS OF LIES

CONTENTS

Content Warnings   xi
Epigraph   xiii

Chapter 1   1
Chapter 2   10
Chapter 3   21
Chapter 4   32
Chapter 5   42
Chapter 6   51
Chapter 7   57
Chapter 8   71
Chapter 9   83
Chapter 10   94
Chapter 11   103
Chapter 12   111
Chapter 13   118
Chapter 14   134
Chapter 15   145
Chapter 16   167
Chapter 17   180
Chapter 18   190
Chapter 19   207
Chapter 20   225
Chapter 21   235
Chapter 22   250
Chapter 23   262
Chapter 24   274
Chapter 25   285
Chapter 26   302
Chapter 27   313
Chapter 28   317
Chapter 29   329

Chapter 30   338
Chapter 31   350
Chapter 32   362
Chapter 33   374
Chapter 34   387

Acknowledgments   393
About the Author   395
Also by Kellen Graves   397

A BONE IN HIS TEETH is a Dark Fantasy-Romance with Horror elements for an Adult audience. It contains tropes commonly found in that genre, including but not limited to:

- graphic descriptions of violence, gore, death, specifically including gun violence
- descriptions of human decomposition as well as desecrating the dead
- themes of mental, physical, emotional abuse, and trauma surrounding them
- language used in a sexual context to describe the anatomy of a FTM trans man which may be dysphoric to some readers
- brief themes of SA described in a character's past (no actions described in detail on page)
- alcohol use, smoking
- rough but consensual explicit sex
- descriptions of the grief of losing a loved one

The ice was here, the ice was there,
    The ice was all around:
    It cracked and growled, and roared and howled,
    Like noises in a swound!

At length did cross an albatross,
    Thorough the fog it came;
    As if it had been a Christian soul,
    We hailed it in God's name.

(....)In mist or cloud, on mast or shroud,
    It perched for vespers nine;
    Whiles all the night, through fog-smoke white,
    Glimmered the white Moon-shine.

'God save thee, ancient Mariner!
    From the fiends, that plague thee thus!
    Why look'st thou so?' - With my cross-bow
    I shot the albatross.

The Rime of the Ancient Mariner (1834)
Samuel Taylor Coleridge
via poetryfoundation.org

Chapter 1

Alba never knew the name of the town where his mother came from; he did, however, know that should he ever return to an empty house in Welkin, he could go there to find her. She'd said as much, every time they had to hug goodbye after another single night he was allowed to visit between long stretches at sea. *Should you ever return to an empty home, don't believe anything they tell you. You'll always find safe harbor under the moon.*

He assumed there was a reason she was never specific, he assumed she would leave a note telling him where to go if the day ever came. But the rainy, cold morning he limped through the door, smelling of sweat and moldy straw from the journey by train, the house was as silent as his ringing ears. Only his hands dragging along the old, familiar wallpaper made any sound. His heavy footsteps, having to shuffle his aching hip as it still hurt too badly to put weight on. The grunting breaths of the chaperone who followed behind him with every step, knowing to not let Alba out of his sight while inside.

The only sound left to assure him that house had once been his, was the jingling of his mother's chimes from the kitchen window, tousled by the wind and whistling lightly every time air passed through the notches carved in dangling silver tubes.

Some things remained in their places, but Alba knew not to trust them. He knew it was likely that no one had been back to that house in at least a week, maybe two—exactly as long as it took him to get back home with his injury.

Edythe Marsh left behind her nicest shirts and dresses—but her work clothes were missing. The shoes she wore to church remained on the shelf by the door—but her walking boots were missing. Creature comforts like her favorite perfume, hair brush, hand lotion, face powder were exactly where they always were whenever Alba came to visit—but the hair clip he'd once gifted her, one she wore every day, adorned with pearls and plate-pressed with the image of a mermaid, was nowhere to be found.

Alba knew better than to mention it to the man who followed on his heels between each room. Reminding himself what she'd always said. *Don't believe anything they tell you.*

He searched high and low for any sign of where she wanted him to follow, where exactly on the sea he should search to find her. He had a limited amount of time at his fingertips, pretending everything he did was done to gather his small number of allotted belongings to take with him to Belmar, every now and again inciting a grunt of warning from the man who hovered in the doorway while Alba rifled through his mother's nightstand. Alba never responded, focusing his entire being into keeping calm. Knowing he wouldn't get a second chance once he left the house behind.

They would clear out his mother's things, a new family would move in. It would be as if Edythe and Alba Marsh had never existed in that little house with the old wallpaper, flowers painted on the ceiling beams overhead, broken windows patched with newspaper, jars of candles in the cupboards, his childhood bed carved with ocean waves and smiling fish and a cluster of mer-people who swarmed around his pillow like a halo of protection against nightmares. That's what his mother always told him. *They appreciate the color of your hair every night while you sleep. Oh, what they wouldn't give for a piece of it!* Stories told to him long before his legs were ever long enough to tap his feet against the footboard. He could only just count the number of times he'd laid beneath the carved mer-people since then on two hands.

Perhaps the new family who took their place would have someone small enough to lay in that bed and dream of the sea, too. They would hope the same things Edythe and Alba's father once had—that a job with the Warren Sailing Company would be life-changing.

They would find where Edythe had tracked Alba's height from when he was a child, notched into the post in the kitchen cupboard. He wondered if they would consecrate a stone and jar of sea water in the back yard as an altar to a sailor lost at sea, just like his mother had; set for Alba's father, starved to death on a northern ice-locked ship then eaten by crew mates who inevitably died right alongside him.

Alba used to shudder at the thought; but since returning home years prior knowing what it was like to fear for one's life on an ice-locked ship in the north, knowing what human flesh tasted like on his own tongue, he'd realized to die first was actually a blessing.

THEY DID NOT GIVE him a cane to aid in walking, even when it became clear Alba's hip might never heal enough that he'd be able to wander without a limp. Some days were better than others, some days the injury felt more like a dull ache while others hurt as badly as the first time he hit the deck from the height of the mast.

He could usually count on it by the chill in the morning, the sight of storm clouds coming on the horizon, the groaning chorus of fellow once-sailors made redundant by similar injuries or age or other circumstances as the sun rose and the work bell rang. Alba was hardly the youngest amongst them; he counted himself lucky to still be able to limp his way down the stairs at all. It meant he would have an early chance at breakfast, at least. A cruel weight added to the pressure in his limbs, making them creak with every movement, to have to put himself first in order to keep living.

Welkin was where families lived while their husbands, fathers, brothers, sons worked on ships set out to sea; built in the trees a two-hour wagon ride from Belmar on the shore, which smelled of rotting fish, seaweed melting to slime on the seawall where barnacles grew, tangled with decaying flesh of anything unfortunate enough to be caught there rather than in a net. The fish and crab Alba gutted morning to night behind the counter of Maggie's stall were lucky, he thought. Reminded with every slice of the knife through wriggling undersides.

So often, he gazed down at the sharpness of that blade and thought how it might feel to be sliced so smoothly, so effortlessly. He wondered if he would writhe with eyes bulging, gasping silently at the air until finally giving up and letting death come for him, accepting there was no other chance.

Every time he'd been faced with it, himself, there had always been the slightest chance, a reason to get himself free. Nearly drowned, stabbed, robbed in a port town—how many times had Alba lied there beneath a gloved hand, knife sharp and prodding at his belly, staring at the sky, compelling death to keep its distance because he wasn't ready to go? There was someone who would miss him. Someone back home would grieve him, would curse death and all its messengers. The small braid woven behind Alba's ear always said so. The grim knew it every time it coiled ghostly fingers through the plait and understood to keep its distance.

His mother used to always tell him, the sea rarely took someone who would be noticed gone. Someone who bore the mark of a protective braid behind the ear, especially when given by someone who knew the old magic of the sea. Alba never believed her, until he'd visit home once a year and she would insist on pulling out what he'd been so careful to keep knotted. In those few hours without the tightness on that patch of scalp, he never felt more vulnerable to the deadly fancies of the world.

Ever since those townspeople found him, weeks prior, dumped on their dock with a note pinned to his back, telling whoever found him to ship him back to the Warrens in Belmar for a reward—he hadn't felt the tug of the protective plait under his ear. Perhaps that was why he couldn't figure out where his mother had gone.

At the very least, Alba not knowing where to find her meant the Warrens and their dogs might never, either.

The knife in Alba's hand, morning and night, would continue to tempt him even when splattered with viscera from the day's catch, speckled with scales and splintered shells, reminiscent of all the times he stood on the edge of a ship deck gutting the same offerings while the sea tore beneath his feet, only a rope around his waist keeping him upright. Whispering apologies with every stripped spine tossed back into her, knowing it wasn't what she wanted, knowing why she rolled with such a bitter rage. Water that was always clear and blue so far from shore, muddy and brown with blood and vomit and rot in the shallows where Warren ships docked in comparison. Where men returned to land either on their feet or carried on their backs.

Water that lapped at his feet when he wasn't behind Maggie's stall gutting fish, shifting beneath where he hung scraping barnacles from wooden hulls, or polishing the visages of mermaids carved into wooden bows. Dark water hungry for anything not already dead. Beckoning him back, as if wondering why he no longer visited out where she was her most tempestuous. Teasing him with constant promises only he heard—whispers from the depths that if he gave himself to her tide, she might take him to where his mother was hiding.

You'll always find safe harbor under the moon. He ruminated on those words endlessly while staring at the ceiling where he slept, while his hands busied with grimy work, while standing on the cold workhouse roof at midnight when the ache in his hip made it impossible to sleep. Cigarette smoke filling his lungs, staring at the bright moon in the sky instead of allowing himself to think how easy it would be to jump and hit the dirt at the bottom. Knowing it might not actually be high enough, considering how being mastheaded only left him limping on land.

You'll always find safe harbor under the moon. The more the days waned on, the more Alba hated those words—until the morning came when his normally-empty telegram box contained a single card. A card he removed too quickly in the early rush, nearly dropping it to the floor.

```
Moon Harbor Telegram Office; Whitesand
Cove, 051724-016.


TO: SEA PRINCE ALBATROSS MARSH.


MESSAGE: WICKIE. BLUECASTLE. FULL MOON.
```

Something struck him again and again in the center of his back. He turned to look, but it was only his own pounding heart thundering against his insides.

He swiftly tucked the telegram into the inner pocket of his jacket. Not sure what else to do, only knowing that he didn't want anyone to see. To ask. An instinctive, protective motion. A telegram from his mother, he was sure of it. The thing he'd been waiting for. Proof she was safe. A hint of where to find her. He was sure of it.

He touched it through his coat again and again as he left the workhouse and punched his timecard. As he approached the fish market, then Maggie's stall, claiming his seat at the worktable. As he took the carving knife and went about gutting the catch of the day.

He could leave after clocking out. Not sure exactly which direction to go, but—it would be a full night's head start. They wouldn't notice him missing until at least the next morning. They would have no idea where he went. He would figure it out before they did. He would figure out Moon Harbor. Whitesand Cove.

Bluecastle. He only had to get out of Belmar, out of Welkin, out of the woods that surrounded them.

The thoughts circled endlessly in and out of the front of his mind as he worked, hands acting on reflex as every pale fish was the same beneath the knife. *Moon Harbor Telegram Office. Whitesand Cove. Wickie. Bluecastle. Full moon.* Perhaps that was why he didn't notice when the perpetual cacophony of the market quieted down into whispers, tension growing as bodies shifted to step out of the way of something moving through them. Someone smelling of rich perfumes and donning dress shoes and a fine coat had come to pay a visit, and Alba only noticed once he heard the voice speak his name.

"Heard you got a telegram today, Albatross." Josiah Warren leaned against the edge of Alba's worktable, careful not to stain the fabric of his coat. His dark brown hair was slicked back with pomade, beard cleanly trimmed and collar starched to stand straight. Flicking away a piece of fish meat with a leather-gloved hand, he laughed when it stuck to Alba's cheek. Alba ignored him, wiping it away without another glance and continuing his task.

"No such thing," he answered.

"Don't be coy. A handsome man like you is bound to get letters from all the hearts you broke in the north, hm? Was it a message from some lover missing you dearly? Some whore in a brothel crooning about how much they hope you'll come see them again soon? Come on, show me."

"It was a mistake," Alba insisted as plainly as the first time, though his movements with the knife stiffened. He took the next fish on the pile, skirting the blade down its scales before cutting it open and unthreading its spine from the meat. "Meant for someone else. No whores from the north callin' on me."

"Postman said you tucked it into your pocket."

"The postman is a liar." Alba spoke before he could close his mouth, agitation rising as clearly as his nerves. Josiah's eyes never left him, still sitting perched on the edge of the table. It wasn't the first time he insisted on being a pest—Josiah took an interest in bothering Alba any chance he got ever since they were children—but that morning was different. He wasn't only there to tease; he knew it, Alba knew it. They both knew Alba was lying, they both knew Alba wasn't about to give in so quickly.

He forced his mouth to remain closed. He reached for another fish, but that time Josiah grabbed his wrist. He squeezed it hard enough that Alba may have flinched, had he not grown so used to aching all over in the past weeks. Still, Alba finally met the man's eyes, surprised at the intensity of them. Despite the calm veil over his expression, Josiah's gaze was edging on frenzied, like he thought that would be his only chance to get Alba to speak. Like he knew, the moment the end-of-day bell rang, Alba would be long gone before anyone could try and stop him.

"It's none of your business who is sendin' me telegrams," Alba finally conceded, knowing there was no more point in trying to pretend. "S'not gonna get in the way of my work, neither. I know my place."

Josiah knew Edythe Marsh had fled. He knew Alba would run to join her the first chance he got, and getting her back where she could be used to ensure good behavior from him was likely high on Josiah's priorities, despite Alba being nothing. Despite Alba being no one, really. Josiah simply didn't like not being in control, even of the smallest rats in his fleet. He had something to prove as the last Warren son since his brother's passing, and Alba was easy to wrangle.

But while Josiah sat comfortably in manor houses drinking spirits and tracking Alba's worth in ink on paper over years of hard labor, holding his mother's wellbeing over him if he ever dared a thought to argue or run away for an easier life—Alba learned how to sail. He learned how to fistfight. He learned when to bow his head to a threat and take it, or when to turn and strike back.

Every one of those instincts, always folded and tucked away like old clothes in a trundle drawer whenever he returned to land, surged back to the surface the moment Josiah grabbed him again. As Alba's arm was shoved out of the way, allowing Josiah to reach into Alba's inner jacket pocket in search of the telegram.

Those survival instincts flared—and Alba did not hesitate to slam the carving knife straight into Josiah Warren's leg. Nor did he hesitate as Josiah stumbled back screaming obscenities. Alba leapt to his feet, kicked the stool away, turned the table over, and ran.

No one tried to stop him—they all just watched. Wondering if he would make it, wondering how far he would get before someone shot him in the back. Alba didn't turn to look.

He pushed through the splitting pain in his leg, his hip, up his side into his ribs, until it spread throughout the rest of him and diluted beneath the fire of adrenaline sparking his blood.

He sought the road; the trees; the moon; he sought his mother's promises of mer-people who would admire the color of his hair while he slept and grant him whatever wishes he could think of.

Alba would run for them until he finally dropped dead, or found the safe harbor she always promised existed.

Chapter 2

Alba stowed away in the back of a fishmonger's cart, surrounded by stinking barrels of cod and halibut, all the way until they passed a sign for a town called Findley. A town Alba had heard mentioned in passing while in Welkin or Belmar, a place he'd never been on his own. A staunch reminder that he'd barely been anywhere at all outside of where he was allowed to wander. A staunch reminder that running away, in many ways, wasn't easier than staying. Having to wrap his arms around himself to resist the urge to lunge from the wagon and race back to where things were familiar, even if terrible. Forcing himself to focus on how familiar didn't mean *good*. Familiar didn't mean *safe*.

Pulling up into a seller's market, the wagon driver swiftly uncovered Alba's hiding place, grabbing him by the back of the collar and throwing him to the street. Cursing at and kicking him until satisfied. Alba barely felt it. He barely even perceived the whispering onlookers huddled around, just pushing himself up at the first chance and dragging his aching body away, down the first quiet street in view.

Slumping against a brick wall to catch his breath, he pressed a cold hand to his swelling cheek and checked over his shoulder to see if anyone followed him. No one did. Without the sight of any Warren dogs sniffing around, Alba took it as proof they had no more idea where he was headed than he did. It didn't mean he was scot-free, as there were always recruiters traveling between towns to entrap naïve sailors into contracts as torturous as his own—but just the briefest thought he'd evaded them was enough to make him grin, then laugh, though the sound quickly puttered out again as he attempted to stretch his leg and put some weight on it.

Before anything else, he had to find a walking stick. He wasn't going to make it much further without one.

There was a wad of cash still in his pocket from the day's sales at Maggie's stall, enough to buy a slender cane carved from a pine branch from the general store, then a cheap meal and a bath at the tavern. When asked if he wanted a place to sleep with it, Alba shook his head, just eating as fast as he could.

He couldn't stay in one place for long, especially not in a town like Findley that was only a few hour's wagon ride from Welkin. Josiah's men would be out looking for him, he knew. They'd probably already added the stolen money, the ruined fish, the mess, Josiah's doctor's fees to his longstanding debt, and Alba wasn't eager to know what they had in mind for him to work it off if caught. Not that Alba would feel the added weight of it on his conscience—he never knew what the original number accrued by his father even was, even while sailing, supposedly working it off bit by bit. Having learned years ago that no matter how hard, long, steadfastly he dedicated himself, that number would never go down enough for him to earn his freedom back. What was a little more added to an impossible fee?

Thanking the tavern owner, stacking the bills in a way the man wouldn't notice Alba had stiffed him a dollar from the price, Alba asked one last thing before getting back on his way.

"Can you tell me which way to Moon Harbor?"

The man raised an eyebrow, before shaking his head and taking Alba's practically licked-clean plate. "Never heard of it. Try takin' the fork east up the road, though, assumin' it's on the water."

That was good enough. Alba grabbed his jacket and hurried out, glad for the help of the cane that quickened his pace as the man called out for him about the missing cash.

HE MANAGED to hitchhike his way to Clearshore next, a wet little down on a stack of cliffs overlooking the sea that reminded Alba too much of Belmar. Smaller, smellier, air hazy with the plethora of steam ships sailing in and out of her port and crowding the docks.

He'd never seen so many in one place—the Warrens insisted on utilizing traditional sails for their trawlers, though rumors claimed they simply didn't want to, or even couldn't afford the investment in steamers. Alba couldn't help himself from wandering up and down the busy dock platforms to gaze at each and every one of them, not minding the smell, if anything finding it a strange comfort after even that short amount of time in strange places on land. He wasn't used to going so far on foot; to be close to the water again was a reassurance that nothing in the world was completely unfamiliar.

Between the ships, nets dumped whole sea's-worth of fish into barrels and buckets on the wooden planks, mostly groundfish and crab. So much at once that many were left to rot, forgotten or unneeded, tipped back into the water to make room for fresh catch coming in. Surely in a place like that, Alba thought he would find a single sailor who knew the name *Moon Harbor*, but most just waved him away when he approached. Insisting there was no work for him, to move along.

He followed the smell of food to the town's inn, ordering their cheapest meal and something to drink, as well as however many cigarettes he could get with a dollar. It stank of sweat and aged salt in the large eating area, humid and hot with a burning fire in the corner and reeking of talking mouths full of unbrushed teeth. A good place to blend in—while equally knowing that was exactly the sort of place Josiah's men would think to look for a missing sailor like him. He would make himself scarce after a few bites, just enough to quell the hungry raking of his stomach.

"Heard you asking 'bout Moon Harbor on the docks," a stranger grunted as he claimed an empty stool alongside where Alba sat. "What's a good lad like you wantin' with a cursed place like that?"

Alba recognized so many of his crew mates, captains, water-logged seamen in the stranger's face parched by decades in the sun, wiry hair matted beneath a cotton hat with a narrow rim. Aged tattoos peeked out from beneath the collar of his shirt, the cuffs of his jacket, many matching Alba's own.

"Cursed place?" he asked, motioning for the bartender to refill the man's beer to hopefully keep him talking. Having no intention of paying for it when they were done. The man threw back half of it before continuing.

"Aye," he breathed. "Won't catch no fisher who knows a thing trawlin' in or outside those waters. Not anymore."

"Not anymore?" Alba asked. "Protective of their waters, or something?"

"Yes and no." The man shook his head, taking another drink. "But even if'n you manage to catch somethin' without them noticin', don't reckon you'd be eager to keep it. Things in that water grow wrong. Curse any man who eats anything from 'em. Shame, heard it used to be such a pretty place."

Alba couldn't help but smirk. He'd heard enough stories just like that one, old myths around hunting grounds, reasons why a captain refused to go into one area of the sea over another, some even willing to add two days onto a journey to fully skirt around a particular spot on a map.

But knowing how secretive his mother had been with even just the name of the town his entire life, something told Alba such rumors were more likely passed by people of that town, themselves, to keep sailors from poaching what was theirs. To keep unwanted strangers and the trouble they might bring far from their shores.

"Well—can you tell me where to find it anyway? I have some business there—"

"Find work some'ere else, lad," the stranger grunted, finishing his drink, then motioning to the plate of food in front of Alba to silently ask for one of his own. Alba sighed, nearly calling the bartender over—before two figures stepped into the crowded bar behind them.

He couldn't see faces beneath the brims of hats, but didn't need to. Sliding what remained of his own plate to the man, Alba grabbed his coat and left out the back before the bartender—or anyone else—could notice.

ALBA LINGERED near the docks another hour, asking anyone who passed by if they knew anything of Moon Harbor, Whitesand Cove, before knowing it wasn't safe to hover any longer than that. Especially as the sun set and darkness came, bringing with it chilly air and rain and a growing ache in his leg, Alba had to find somewhere to go. Somewhere that wasn't there, not with two dogs sniffing around.

Following a crowd of people carrying bags and clutching their jackets close, he overheard a name that caught his attention—*Bluecastle.* Bluecastle Township, located a few miles away; a name mentioned in his mother's message, one he hadn't considered might be a town. He went straight for the wagon boarding to head in that very direction, barely buying a seat just before it headed off.

Bluecastle Township was bigger than Alba expected, hesitating near the cart as the rest of the passengers disembarked behind him. Knowing a room at the inn would cost more in a place that bustled so loudly, where streets were lit by rows of kerosene lanterns rather than flickering wicks like in Belmar.

He only had a few dollars left. He didn't want to waste them. He still didn't know where he was going or how much it would cost to get there—or even why his mother's note had mentioned Bluecastle in the first place. He might have thought her there waiting for him, had the telegram not come from Moon Harbor directly.

Pulling the message card from his coat, careful to shield it from the rain, he gently cursed her for being so intricate in her riddles. He never liked them as a child, either.

It was the last thing he wanted to do, knowing it would leave a mark of his whereabouts should anyone ask the teller about messages sent from their clicker, but Alba sought out Bluecastle's post office. He had Moon Harbor's location number on the telegram in his hand, he could send a message asking for help. He would sit and wait for as long as it was safe. He only needed one more clue. Anything.

But as he approached the post office doors, there on the notice board right outside, he got one. A single clue, clear as day. Practically laughing at him for losing his patience just a moment too soon.

SINGLE WICKIE NEEDED. WHITESAND COVE. LIFETIME CONTRACT. $30/WEEK. NO PRIOR EXPERIENCE NEEDED. CHECK IN WITH POST CLERK.

Alba tore the flier from the board with a shivering hand, a funnel of rainwater spilling from the eaves overhead and drenching his already soaked coat. *Moon Harbor. Whitesand Cove. Wickie. Bluecastle.*

He raced into the post office, shaking off the rain like a dog and hurrying to the clerk. Showing the flier, they handed back a single envelope through the grated window, and Alba took it eagerly. Finding a bench out of the way, his eyes flashed up constantly with every pedestrian who came and went, though the office was hardly busy at such an hour. Knowing to let his guard down for even a moment might be the last of him.

Inside the envelope was a crisp two-dollar bill, a ticket for the river ferry, and a note instructing where to go from the third stop up the river.

"Careful with that one, boy," the postman grunted as Alba leafed through the contents, making Alba jump. The man leaned casually on one elbow as he spoke, newspaper spread on the desk in front of him as there weren't enough folk to keep him busy so late at night. "Wages are high for a reason."

"What do you mean?" Alba asked, glancing at the water-specked advertisement again. He'd barely skimmed the dollar amount the first time.

"Someone's in here putting up a flier for the same tendin' job every month, like clockwork. Must be a reason so many wickies leave despite the pay."

"Lighthouse keepin's not an easy job," Alba answered without thinking, glancing down at the note again. The post-teller's attention flickered to Alba's cane, looking like he wanted to say something about it, before rolling his eyes and going back to his newspaper. Alba didn't say anything else, either, focused on how the telegram from his mother poked out from where he'd tucked it down the cuff of his jacket to keep dry.

None of that mattered to him—he wasn't going there to take a job.

He tucked the note, the ticket, even the telegram back into the envelope, then used the two-dollar bill to bribe the teller to let him sleep there for the night. It wasn't comfortable, but it was warm. It was safe, so long as no one came looking for him before the sun came up. He prayed as much. Not when he was so close.

.   .   .

THE FERRY STATION was located alongside the post office, both buildings perched on the edge of the canal and smelling of rich, sweet water once the rainclouds dissipated and the sun came with morning. Alba didn't sleep particularly soundly, but it was still a welcome rest, filled with thin dreams of smiling fish and pretty mermaids swimming in circles around him, calling out how eager the were to meet him and finally take an offered piece of his hair. He smiled back at them. He laughed when they tousled fingers through his braid, loosening it until the red strands were caught in the wind, then the waves. Beckoning him to come faster, they were eager to meet. Eager to grant his wishes in exchange for a few strands. When he finally woke again, he was sure he tasted saltwater on his tongue.

Alba was the first person on the platform so early, claiming a seat near the front to be the first on board when it was time. It would be another few hours before the boat came, which meant he was free to listen to the birds as they shivered off a night-long rain; to breathe in the smell of the fresh earth and the canal, intermixed with faint hints of the city at his back; to eavesdrop as pedestrians passed by on the walkway opposite the ferry station's breezeway.

He wasn't completely unequippped to navigate unfamiliar towns, especially port towns, especially after so long traveling from place while sailing—but after so many years developed sea legs accustomed to the constant rocking of waves, he wasn't sure he'd ever get used to the solid flatness of the earth. He found himself unconsciously swaying to and fro while waiting for the ferry, as if the bench treaded water where he sat.

Even closing his eyes, Alba could smell the frigid, salty air of the north. He felt the constant wavering of leaning against one of the trawling reels. The voices of a slowly-gathering crowd at his back were the men he sailed with; the lapping water of the canal was the sea kissing the side of the ship as if inviting the boards to split open and spill their contents into the water to be devoured.

But Alba wasn't on a dogger, he wasn't in the north. It was

the prior night's rain that dampened his hair, not snow or frost blown from the sheer edges of glacial corridors on either side of them. He was on solid land. He was on his way to find his mother in Moon Harbor, where they might escape the grasp of the Warren Sailing Company once and for all.

Despite being nowhere near the ships and the sea that once framed his entire being—upon opening his eyes, there was still a face Alba recognized in the morning light. Hovering in the throng of people filling the ferry station, as the vessel itself finally trundled up to the platform. Alba blinked in hopes it was only his imagination, but the face remained—and the man's eyes landed on Alba the exact moment the ferry bell rang out for boarding. They stared at one another for only a moment—before Alba's instincts came alive, and he leapt to his feet.

It took only a split second of his cane tangling in a stranger's luggage for Marco to catch him, grabbing Alba roughly by the collar and yanking him back. Alba nearly fell, caught at the last moment and spun around as if it was all just some sort of misunderstanding. A hand found the small of his back, guiding him toward the road as he scrambled breathlessly to gather his bearings.

"There, there," Marco whispered. He was a tall, burly man, one of Josiah's closest associates after working alongside his older brother Herman Warren for years before his death. Skilled in as many tricks of sailing as any other, but none more than sniffing out lost sailors like Alba.

Far from the first time Alba had been snatched by him, he knew it would certainly be the last if he allowed himself to be lead away any further than that. The moment they left the crowd on the platform, there would be others. There would be hands all over him, grabbing and tying and throwing Alba onto the back of a horse, into a wagon, wherever they could get him. He would never get another chance to run again; Josiah would make sure of it.

Alba pushed through the petrifying, nauseating sensation of

the large hand on his back. Knowing its strength from the first time he was touched like that, thirteen-years-old on the street in Welkin. Called over, then walked to the wagon at the far end of town. Beaten and gagged when he realized what was happening. Kicking and screaming, crying out for his mother, taken into Belmar where they threw him in the brig of a ship right as it set sail. No chance to say goodbye. To tell his mother where he was going, that he'd never asked for it. It was a whole year before Alba was allowed to return and apologize to her.

Not again, not again—he wouldn't be taken away from his mother again.

Lacing his cane between Marco's legs was enough to make the man stumble, and Alba's foot slamming into the crook of his knee made him drop. Just enough for Marco to throw his hands out, enough for Alba to twist away and stumble into the nearest cluster of pedestrians.

They swore at him, shoving him in return, but Alba's ears only rang with the sound of the ferry bell; with Marco's voice behind him shouting *'stop!'*; with a decade-old memory of that same voice laughing while throwing him, bruised and bleeding and subdued, into the back of a wagon. Telling him *'you're not going anywhere, little prince.'*

Alba shoved through the crowd toward the ferry, using his cane to clear a path, shouting for all of them to get out of his way, deafened by the sound of Marco chasing after him.

The ghost of fingers trailed through strands of his hair just as he barely leapt onto the rear platform of the ferry already pulling away from the platform.

The ticket-man gave Alba a bewildered look, half a second from tossing him right back into the canal, but Alba quickly produced his ticket.

He glanced over his shoulder as his ticket was checked, meeting Marco's eyes one last time. A predator narrowly missing its prey, Marco's eyes were cold, sharp, and Alba knew that likely wouldn't be the last time they saw one another. Not if he wasn't careful.

But he would be—he'd be careful. He'd find his mother and leave with her. They would go somewhere safe to live, to make a life, where Alba could finally be a good son and take care of her like she was meant to be cared for. Somewhere no one would ever find them. He only had to reach Moon Harbor, first.

CHAPTER 3

ONLY ONCE ALBA WAS ALREADY AN HOUR'S WALK DOWN an empty road, following it as instructed by the note after disembarking the ferry, did he realize how little sense the directions made the further he went.

Follow the dirt road at the edge of Willowswort south for one mile. At the wooden signpost, turn east toward Mardston. You will find a stone marker three-hundred feet past that. Follow the footpath north for one mile. You will find the road into town past the creek.

Alba muttered curses the whole time he walked, smacking ferns and roots from his feet, pine trees and dangling branches from his face. Constantly checking the instructions again, growing more and more agitated the more worried he grew that the place he searched for wasn't Moon Harbor at all. *Whitesand Cove* could be anything, any place. For all he knew it wasn't a town at all, and he was walking into some sort of depraved trap where they would rob then strip him naked before sending him back into the wilderness. Or worse. Stranger things had happened to those lost in the woods, and Alba was not well prepared.

He might know how to recognize a siren's song on the sea, but he would have no idea what to do if he accidentally crossed paths with something else equally nefarious and ancient in the trees. He wasn't sure he'd be less willing to cross those paths than for Marco to catch up to him again, though.

His nerves heightened once he spotted what he assumed to be the mentioned stone marker off the side of the road—an aged, moss-covered tablet donning a carved mer-creature nailed into a tree, easily missed if he wasn't looking for it.

Making his way down the footpath on the other side, the rainy sky festered overhead and made his hip throb, sky growing dark enough to nearly make him think the sun had set early. He lit a cigarette to warm himself, to quell the nervous rattling of his bones, telling himself to get a grip. He still couldn't help but glance over his shoulder every time something moved in the corner of his eye; he couldn't help but stop short whenever he was sure he heard a voice somewhere in the trees, only to sigh and hurry ahead once more. At least the landmarks appeared as claimed by the note.

Reaching the road at the end of the muddy path, he could only wonder why that perfectly good thoroughfare was hidden from the main one, deep enough in the trees that there was no chance a cart would roll by that he could bribe into giving him a ride. Detesting how he was being forced to walk it on foot, one hand clutching his cane with every step while the other shakily drew the cigarette to and from his lips. His mother wouldn't be happy if she saw him, if she smelled the tobacco on his clothes, hating the habit he picked up from his crew mates. By the time Alba found the town where he hoped she waited for him, he would have smoked all ten of them in his pocket.

He was sure he would walk that road for an eternity, never finding the end, his penance for a worthless life spent dedicated to lining the pockets of those who deserved it least—but the sound of singing came before he fell to his knees to pray for deliverance. He still nearly did, stopping short so fast the cigarette tumbled from his mouth, bouncing on the hard dirt road and skittering away.

Slowly bending to pick it up again, he watched as a group of five white-dressed spirits passed by just on the other side of the trees. Not noticing him, too busy with their melancholic song, baskets balanced on hips and hands scattering what Alba could smell to be rock salt.

A cold breeze shifted what looked like crowns of dangling white pearls in their hair. Pearls and minuscule shells, thumbnail-sized bells tinkling with every movement to accompany their voices, fluted silver tubes whistling on their belts with the movement and reminding him of the ones that hung from his mother's windchime back home. The sound captivated him more than the sight, like sirens of the land, and Alba couldn't help following their movements as they passed by.

It was only when one of them suddenly lifted their eyes to meet his that he realized—the song was familiar. It was undeniably similar to one Edythe used to hum when Alba was restless as a child, unable to sleep, afraid of the dark things that lurked in the woods on the other side of the window.

He put his hands up innocently as the salt-scatterer paused, still holding his gaze. Patting his hands up and down his chest, Alba finally produced the envelope stuffed full of instructions to reach the town, holding it up for them to see. The woman looked at him a moment longer, then nodded, then pointed in the direction he was already headed. None of the others so much as paused, and the woman went about her task the moment her indicating hand lowered again. Alba returned the envelope to his coat, adjusted his cigarette, and watched a moment longer before continuing on his way.

Five white-clad maidens, both men and women, singing and salting the earth along the only road into Whitesand Cove, accessible by a footpath only noticeable if one knew where to look. Perhaps that man at the bar in Clearshore was right when he said Moon Harbor was a cursed place—clearly enough that the residents were forced to cleanse the land with salt from baskets.

Alba pulled out another cigarette, knowing he was going to

need it—only to jump and drop it, too, when a sixth white figure suddenly stood at the edge of the road, watching him. Naked, hair cropped short, lingering slightly behind a bush like it was just as curious about him as he'd been about the others.

The paleness of its skin made it appear bloodless, like flesh petrified into bone, and Alba almost thought it a marble statue before it blinked and tilted its head. Alba cleared his throat, offering a polite nod of greeting, pausing a moment longer before taking another step forward. It watched him go, not unlike he'd watched the others. Silent and curious.

THE TREES finally gave way to the open sky, and Alba smelled the sea before he saw her. He quickened his pace, sighing loudly at the sight of her rich blueness drowning the horizon, lapping against a ribbon of dark beach that kept her at bay from the town sprawling tightly at her feet.

Stone-brick buildings huddled close to one another, snaking down the steep hill toward the water, barely expanding across the wide grassy clearing more than a few blocks. One road led in and out, being the same one Alba followed. In the distance, the light-house needing a keeper stood proudly on a cluster of dark rocks, a second taller, listless tower silhouetted alongside her in the ocean fog. Fishing boats spotted the water around them, keeping within the embrace of stony cliffs that extended from the mainland like embracing arms to force the edges of the cove. Natural breakwaters that should have left the water ripe with fish, crab, things to catch and eat and sell.

It all hit him at once, unable to resist grinning. Knowing no Warren dog would find him there so easily. Finally understanding exactly why his mother always knew that town would be the safest to go to once there was no other choice.

Alba carried the envelope in his hand upon approaching the outskirts of the clustered buildings, not wanting anyone to think he was an unwelcome stranger. Not sure yet how forthcoming he would be with announcing he was, actually, a personally-invited stranger. Had his mother already told them about him? Perhaps they would expect him. Perhaps they would see and know him right away, welcoming him, offering him a meal and somewhere warm to sit while they fetched Edythe from wherever she was staying.

When he wasn't keeping an eye out for townspeople—of which there was a surprising few wandering around—Alba was instead taken with the surroundings. From the furthest point at the mouth of the road, the cluster of buildings appeared as quaint as any other small fishing town—but upon closer inspection, Alba saw the age in her structures, foundations cracked and cobblestone streets worn down in disrepair, more mud puddles than walkways. Windows were caked in a thin layer of brine from the sea spray, some decorated with sporadic designs like from a bored child taking their time walking to school.

Doors and exteriors were hand-painted with scenes of people fishing on boats, mermaids under the water, fish and crab and other creatures filling nets with plenty, many of the scenes over-looked by a bright, silver-leafed moon in the sky, full and radiating with beams of light like other artists would paint the sun. Some doorways were permanently shuttered, hinges petrified by a thick layer of coarse salt as if mortared in place intentionally. He couldn't help but wonder if the town had been victim to a plague at one point, reminded of the disease that briefly spread through Welkin, then Belmar, then across Warren ships only a few years prior, some houses still locked tight with bodies rotting inside to that day.

The air was filled with the sound of musical wind chimes not unlike those tied to the belts of the salt-scatterers in the woods, or his mother's back home. The humming song mimicked distant singing voices, and Alba finally spotted silver flutes lining the walls of the buildings that whistled when caught by the wind just right.

He paused beneath one, impressed by the size and intricacy of the pipe, as long as his forearm, some notched more than once as previous holes were clogged by years of salt and rust. Listening as they whistled and hummed, he almost fell victim to recognizing words in the sound. Reminding himself not to seek such magic out, knowing it would only claim his soul in worse ways. His mother used to say as much when he was a child wandering the woods alongside her searching for mushrooms and roots to eat; hardened sea-captains used to say as much while stuffing cotton in their ears when the first sign of something amiss on the far horizon made them perk up.

Alba wondered what their purpose was to those people, whether to keep negative spirits away, or perhaps to attract pretty things into their harbor. His mother had always insisted the reality of mermaids, just like those painted on doorways he passed. He'd never seen the type she described from girlhood while on the sea himself, but something like anticipation pinched the back of his neck as if he might finally have his chance.

Following the road all the way down to where the dock separated the town from the water, Alba read the signage for each doorway as he went. A tavern, doctor's office, undertaker, general store, fishmonger, post office, harbor office, even an inn, though it looked far from patronized.

Reaching what he assumed to be the conservatively small town center, he paused at the dry fountain in the middle, appreciating the stone carving of a mermaid perched within it. Rather than water spilling from the pitcher tucked between her breasts in webbed hands, she was caked with thick layers of salt and long-dried barnacles, not unlike the rest of the buildings. As if that town had been built beneath the sea, only appearing on land when the tide went out morning and evening.

But the people of the town milling around him seemed as land-born as he was, and he noticed how they kept their distance once they finally noticed him in full. Whispering, throwing glances before hurrying away, they seemed to all realize there was a stranger amongst them at the exact same time. Sneaking glances from open doorways, tucking one another behind their backs, most blended in with the surroundings as they wore clothing as faded as the facades of the buildings—clothes worn down and gray from use, but adorned all over in shining jewelry, hair clips, silver embroidery on the cuffs of their sleeves and collars of their shirts.

Many pulled shawls over themselves as stark white as fresh snow, as if caressing heirlooms hand-washed obsessively to keep the color so pristine. Many wore shimmering powders on their eyelids and crimson on their cheeks, though it hardly did anything to hide the dark bags under their eyes or the pallid color of their faces. Alba noted the lack of children running up and down the streets, suddenly aware of how deadly silent that place was of any signs of life aside from the waves against the dark beach and whistling song through the pipes on the walls.

Not knowing where to start, considering the strange looks he received from those crowding around the tavern and against the surrounding buildings, Alba opted for the post office to make his inquiry. A familiar place, one he knew of what to anticipate upon stepping inside. No matter where he went, on foot or by sea, every bar, port, post office, cemetery were all exactly the same.

Inside, the lobby was dark, the counter unmanned, though Alba thought he heard movement from behind a cracked door on the other side of the room. Rather than calling out to the clerk, he opted first to search the labeled post-boxes on the wall, quickly skimming the names under each cubby to see if his mother's happened to be there. He even checked the box for non-residents, but there was neither letter nor telegram inside.

He searched the outgoing box last, moving quickly so no one would spot him and think him up to no good, though it was as empty as the rest. More than empty, he realized, upon removing his hand to find it coated in a layer of dust. Essentially dormant.

Pulling the original telegram from his pocket, Alba double-checked the location information, even confirming the origin number engraved on a sign over the resident boxes. He wouldn't put it past his mother to sneak into the telegram office and send something without anyone knowing, but that only sparked more questions in the back of his mind. Mainly—*why* she would have to do something like that in secret, if she really was as safe in that town as he'd assumed from the start. If the words *SEA PRINCE* weren't included with his name on the message, he might have even had a moment of doubt that it was his mother to send it at all—but that diminutive was all the proof he needed.

The bell on the office door clanged, and Alba jumped, turning quickly to find an older man stepping inside. He held a shotgun tucked behind his leg, partially in view. Wanting Alba to see it, but not to threaten him right away.

"Can I help you, lad?" He asked. Alba quickly slid the telegram into the envelope of the work request, hiding the motion beneath rifling through the papers.

"Is this Moon—erm, Whitesand Cove?"

The man grunted in lieu of replying, never taking his eyes from Alba. Alba took that as a yes.

"I'm—looking for someone who told me I might be a good fit for this job posted in Bluecastle Township. Her name is Edythe?"

The man's tense stance relaxed at the sight of the job posting. He looked Alba up and down more than once, eyes lingering on his face the longest, and Alba wondered if he could see the resemblance he had to his mother. Her blue eyes, sharp nose, narrow jawline, round lips. Last, the man's eyes lowered to the cane Alba leaned on, and he cocked an eyebrow.

"Never heard of no one called Edythe," he said first, given in a way that implied he wouldn't be taking any argument from Alba about it. A way that made Alba fight the frown on his lips, sensing something else unspoken under the words. A lie, perhaps a half-truth, he didn't know. Perhaps it was only the instant knife of cold disappointment in his chest. "And that flier's askin' for a wickie, y'know. Tower's got 150 steps in 'er."

Alba answered on instinct, ignoring the man's first comment about knowing nothing about anyone with his mother's name. For all he knew, she'd asked them to lie about knowing her, since

Warren dogs would be sniffing her out as much as Alba was. He decided to play along, a thousand decisions forming in his mind at once. The need to not reveal too much right away, the need to find a way to stay in that town a little longer, until he could figure out what his mother had planned for them. He extended his foot slightly to prove he was still able to walk as well as anyone else, the cane just helped him along.

"I've got at least two years combined experience tendin' to a lantern," he insisted. "Makes up for my leg. Really only bothers me when it rains, anyway."

"It's always rainin' here," the man responded, but it wasn't combative. He added: "Where at?"

"Northeastern coast."

"Warren lighthouses?"

Alba forced himself to remain calm at the mention of that name. Considering the number of Warren-owned lighthouses lining the northern coast, it wasn't strange to ask. To assume. "Sometimes. A few different companies."

"Got any work papers?"

"No, sir. You're welcome to hold my wages 'til I prove myself competent, though."

The man's eyes narrowed, but Alba didn't show any insecurity in his expression. It wasn't a lie; the Warrens never wrote up work papers as they never planned on letting anyone contracted to them work anywhere else.

"Don't pay wages until after the first month," the man countered. "Most don't last that long, anyway."

Alba recalled the post clerk in Bluecastle Township saying something similar, how there was a new flier on the job board every month like clockwork. He almost asked why that was, but decided against it, not wanting to come across as someone eager to stick their nose into others' business right away.

Something told him he'd have to prove himself harmless, trustworthy before those people told him anything about where his mother was hiding. She must have been somewhere truly safe, protected by her childhood flock, and Alba wouldn't press it too soon if that was the case. He internally thanked them for it. He wouldn't let himself wonder why they were so surprised to see him, why his mother hadn't ever said anything about him coming.

"No complaints from me, sir."

The internal conflict on the man's face remained for a moment longer, before he adjusted his knitted hat and combed fingers down through his white beard. Alba saw peeks of tattoos on the palms of his hands, his fingers, worn down at the knuckles and skin thick with callouses.

"I can work on fishin' trawlers, too, if you need any hands there," Alba went on, just in case.

"You seem a little young to have so much experience in lighthouses and doggers both, lad. If you don't mind me sayin'."

Alba smiled like he was in on the joke. "I've been sailing since I was a teenager. Got shanghai'd when I was barely thirteen."

"Sorry to hear it."

"Taught me how to work," Alba answered like a promise.

In the doorway, a handful of skeptical faces leaned inside, more hovering through the salt-fogged windows. Clutching their white shawls close, whispering to one another like Alba was a ginger-haired cursed come upon them. He silently prayed they weren't the type of town to kill the likes of him on sight, the type to worry his presence alone would sour their secluded fishing spot. They might have been even more eager if they knew he'd been born like a woman, too.

"Aye, you can tend to the lantern and prove yourself, if y'like," the man finally said with a nod. He put out a hand to shake, and Alba took it right away. "Name's Eugene Michaels. I'm the Harbor Master of this place. Don't got no mayor or elected officials, so I'll be the one you come to if you've got any problems."

"Alba Marsh," Alba answered despite knowing how risky it was to offer his real name. Hoping it would spark some kind of realization in the man's expression, that maybe after all was said and done, he'd hurry off to where Edythe was hiding to let her know. Eugene Michaels' hand in Alba's only flexed slightly, jaw clenching for the briefest moment before relaxing again into a polite smile.

"I'll get a pack put together for your first couple days out there, then row you out myself, Mr. Marsh. You're welcome to a drink and a meal at the bar until then."

"Appreciate that." Alba folded and tucked the work request back into its envelope, sliding it into his jacket pocket before anyone could ask for it back. Before anyone could see how his hand trembled the moment he was released from the handshake. Stemming from a growing apprehension rooted deep in his being, having to tell himself again to trust what his mother had planned.

Chapter 4

While it made Alba itch to put down even temporary roots anywhere for long, he would trust whatever his mother had planned. The distance from shore and the high vantage point of the lighthouse's lantern room would help him see what was coming, at least, should Marco or anyone else sniff him out even in a place as remote as that.

"You'll be the only keeper out here for a time," Eugene said as they approached the lighthouse rocks, floating in a small boat that wobbled with every swell of the water. Overhead, rain broke through the thick clouds, and Alba was grateful for the chill in the air. He was sweating under his coat, either from the warmth of the drinks from the bar or the anxiety bubbling under his skin. "Can't leave a boat with you 'til we get another crafted, neither. Last storm wiped out a handful of 'em against the rocks. But someone will fetch you once a week or so to come into town and stretch your legs and get supplies."

"Alright."

Eugene Michaels worked the handles of the oars with knowing strokes, with strength that betrayed the age of him. Alba's eyes lingered on his worn knuckles and aged tattoos again, wondering what the man saw when looking at Alba in return. If

Alba gave off the appearance of an experienced sailor like he claimed, or more like someone spinning tales for a chance at the impressive wages offered for the work.

He knew some parts of him proved he didn't lie about his time at sea, but there were other unavoidable ones that always drew unwanted curiosity when stopping for the night in random northern ports. His unlucky red hair, the narrowness of his shoulders, the shape of his brow, the indisputable lack of even a shadow on his jaw that he often worried betrayed his claim to manhood. He'd learned long ago that avoiding eyes was the simplest way to avoid those words he hated so much, but couldn't blame in their curiosity. *You sure you're a sailor? Somethin' about you looks more like a lass.*

Instinctively, Alba wrung his fingers around his wrist where a white woven bracelet used to hang, decorated with pearls his mother once said would bless him to grow into the masculinity he wanted. *They're magic bits from the sea. They'll make you as much a man as anyone else so long as you keep wearing it. Save sprouting a member, but a cock never made a man anyway. Should even keep your blood away if you're consistent.*

It'd been only a few months since it snapped off and disappeared into the sea, though Alba was surprised it lasted even that long.

"Place needs some work, too. Last keeper did their best, but didn't stick around long. Disappeared like the rest of 'em." The man chuckled as he said it, like he knew exactly why his wickies ran off before ever getting paid. Alba knew as well as anyone else how plenty of lighthouse keepers vanished in the night, either from madness or loneliness or disillusionment, sometimes clearly running for greener pastures or simply ceasing to exist by morning.

He glanced over his shoulder at the approaching rocks, watching as the shadow of land emerged from the frothing water. Moon Harbor, Whitesand Cove, whichever name they preferred, indeed had two lighthouses like he noticed upon first arriving, emerging from the dense fog like titanic creatures looming out of the sea.

At their base emerged a modest single-level structure with a peaked roof and shuttered windows, likely the keeper's living quarters, no bigger than the Marsh home back in Welkin had been. It was accompanied by a handful of surrounding out-buildings that Alba could guess the purpose of without having to see up close. He wasn't lying when he said he'd tended to lighthouses in the past. Wouldn't even need a tour, if the old man didn't offer one.

"The taller one—the older sister, we call 'er—retired ages ago. Lantern wore out," Eugene explained while slowing their approach to the waterlogged rocks. "Use 'er belly mostly for storing goods and things for the town, now. The smaller one, the younger sister, is the one you'll be tendin' to. Don't bother thinking you can fix up the older one, neither. Don't need another wickie crackin' their head open 'cause they don't look for the gaps in the stairs. S'the reason I hold on to the only key, so don't poke around all by yourself."

Alba grimaced. "You don't have to worry about that from me, sir."

"Young'un's lantern is brighter than the older one's ever was, anyway. Does all the work with less fuel. Got a new oil basin in 'er, too, so you only gotta fill 'er once a night then mind the counter-weights. Needs windin' every two hours on the dot."

"Gears need wettin'?"

"Not her. She's a special sort. The fuel we use drips down from the mantle and greases her up as she turns. Special stuff from a manufacturer up the coast, don't rightly know what it's made of. Whale fat and some extra science."

"Sure." Alba managed a genuine little half-smile. Eugene Michaels was definitely a sailor if Alba ever knew one.

"Don't get a lot of ships comin' in and out of the harbor, neither..." the man added as the dingy reached what Alba assumed was the rocks' promise of a dock, though it was hardly more than a few metal loops hammered into the stone and blocks of wood pressed into the steep cut of the muddy shore. Eugene paused as Alba clambered out over the slippery stone, and Alba bit back a throb in his hip while focusing on remaining upright. "...so don't worry about loggin' the ones that come and go. Weather doesn't change much, neither, 'cept once or twice a month, so don't worry about tracking that, either."

"What's the purpose of keepin' a log book then, sir?" Alba asked, half joking. Eugene's response was as serious as ever.

"S'pose it's better suited for things out of the ordinary."

Alba grunted as the bag of supplies was tossed into his chest, nearly losing his footing and dropping his cane.

"Out of the ordinary like what, sir?" he asked with a wheeze.

"Don't let your imagination run wild now, boy," the man chuckled, grabbing the oar and shoving off from the rocks without another moment's hesitation. "If you've truly spent time at sea like you've said, you'll know what I'm talkin' about. Nothin' any stranger than that happens 'round here at all. Suppose it's mostly to keep 'ya sane while trapped on this here rock."

"Oh," Alba said. Wanting to add more, knowing there should be more, but he could think of nothing. By the time anything came to mind, Eugene Michaels was already disappearing into the fog back toward the shore, and Alba was alone.

The lighthouse rock's living quarters were smaller than those he'd lived in while tending to Warren-owned lighthouses, but better-kept.

Straight through the front door opened into a small kitchen, a staircase to the sleeping loft above on the right, a door to the washroom to the left, and a handkerchief-sized sitting area alongside that. A single table sat in the middle of the kitchen with two chairs tucked neatly into it, a thin layer of dust coating the surface just like it did the counter, the sink basin, the floorboards.

Eugene mentioned they'd been without a lighthouse keeper for at least two weeks, and the light dusting of missing inhabitants in every part of that house proved it. Alba had almost asked how the lighthouse continued to function without anyone out there to wind the weights and trim the wicks, but decided not to prod in the moment.

Regret tingled the back of his throat as he left his sparse things at the foot of the stairs and took a closer look around. The constant clanging and humming of turning gears from the lighthouse filled the back of his ears once he paused to listen, both unsettling and comforting in its predictable rhythm. Eugene had also mentioned her newer oil basin, and perhaps it wasn't so out of the question that they'd rigged some sort of automatic reel to wind the weights. But such a thing would never last forever, hence the need for a keeper.

Either way, Alba sighed. Closing his eyes for a moment, he traced back through the events of the previous few hours to recall if there was anything else he should have picked up on sooner. Frustrated with it all, relieved with it all. Unsure how he felt to still not know where his mother was—to not even know if he was *in the right place*, despite all signs pointing to *yes*.

He pulled his hair from the braid keeping it together down his back, shaking out the strands and running fingers back through it. Sweaty and stiff from the long journey, knowing the rest of him likely smelled the same way. He would wash off as soon as he was done gathering his bearings. He didn't want to look so bedraggled when his mother came knocking, whether it be later that night, in the morning, or... sometime. Just, sometime soon. God, he hoped she really would.

The sitting room was sparsely-furnished with smoking chairs, bookshelves, hand-washing basins on side tables, a moth-eaten rug spread over the floor; in the kitchen there was a single copper sink basin and butcher-wood countertops, dinner table barely big enough for its two rickety chairs underneath. The cabinets were well-organized but empty of anything that didn't have a perpetual shelf-life, which he was used to.

The simplicity of the kitchen reminded him too much of home, especially with every small repair he picked out during his observation. His mother had always been a simple, no-frills sort of woman, even in the things she wore, the way she pinned up her dark blonde hair, whether it be to scrub the floors or replace shingles on the roof.

Asking for help risked adding on to the debt they owed to the Warrens, who owned the livelihoods of every family in town while their loved ones toiled away on ships. Every time Alba was graced with a night at home, the first thing Edythe did was proudly show him all the things she'd fixed up while he was away, oftentimes taking hours as she rambled on and on about how difficult something was, how she had to ask Agnes down the road to borrow some tool or another to get the job done, how she had to chop her own wood or collect sap for makeshift glue. He hoped she'd have more of the same to show him of wherever she was hiding.

Limping his way up the stairs to the lofted bedroom at the top, Alba tossed the bundle of supplies onto the farthest of two wooden trundle beds, stripping off his jacket next and throwing it over the head of the bed frame closest to him. The room was smaller than the kitchen below, two beds separated by only a few feet against opposite walls. Stormy blue light came in through the window at the mouth of the A-frame ceiling at the end of the room, cracked open to allow the chilly fresh air inside. A door leading to a cramped closet hung cracked next to the foot of the opposite bed, though Alba wondered how anyone was meant to store anything inside of it. It explained the single trunk tucked in the corner.

He collapsed face-first into the nearest bed when the wind whistled particularly hard through the window. The frame squeaked and groaned under his weight, and he groaned back, allowing himself the briefest moment to close his eyes and pretend like he had a chance to drift off to sleep. But even there, on that rocky spit of land obscured by the fog, a mile from the shore where such a secluded little town sat untouched by visitors in what he guessed to be at least decades—Alba felt nerves prickle the back of his neck every time the house leaned against the weather picking up outside. Nerves fueled by the anxiety of being found, the anxiety of being in the wrong place altogether.

Anxiety made sharper by the fact he'd just taken a job known to be physically demanding and wholly exhausting, even for two or three wickies overseeing a single lamp. He might die of exhaustion before his mother ever came to see him—and she would never forgive him for it.

After unpacking the bundle of supplies, tucking the plain work clothes away in the trunk, storing the temporary foodstuffs in the cabinets, Alba went to seek the cistern in one of the outbuildings—but stopped when the front door clattered loudly upon pulling it open. A string of pink and white seashells dangled from a piece of twine on the exterior knob. Right away, he searched for who might have left it, but saw no one. Pulling the clattering string away, he looked a little more closely.

"Hello?" He called out next, but no answer came. Deciding he must have simply not noticed them upon first arriving—not thinking too hard about how he wasn't sure how that was possible—he left the string on the coat rack and made his way back out again.

Scanning the rocks for a visiting boat, listening for chattering voices, Alba couldn't help the newest pinch of apprehension at the back of his throat. Just swallowing hard against it until it finally released and let him get back to the task at hand.

Checking the brick rainwater cistern on the side of the house, Alba was relieved to find it still relatively clean of mold from the last wickie who'd stayed there, dumping in a scoop of chalk from the dry-box under the eaves for good measure. Returning to the house, in the bathroom, it took a number of cranks on the iron hand pump before water spluttered into the polished-steel washtub, brown at first before clearing up, smelling like rain and mildew in a way that reminded Alba of home as much as everything else did.

He worked the pump until a few inches of fresh water lined the bottom of the tub, finally kicking off his muddy boots and stripping off his sweat-stiff shirt when something rattled beneath the floor, startling him.

For a moment he was sure the storm was about to sweep the house away, then prodded at the pump handle to see if it came from the pipes. Leaving the washroom, he paused as the rattling continued, then followed the cacophony, the vibrations beneath his feet, to the opposite side of the kitchen where a door lead to what he assumed to be a storage pantry.

There, he found the source of the noise, raising an eyebrow and crouching down for a better look. Flattened beneath a heavy crate full of piled trawling nets, overcast daylight beamed between the cracks outlining a trapdoor cut into the floor. The hatch itself rattled violently, seemingly even more so with Alba's attention. He could only imagine some sort of crazed gull or a harbor seal trapped in the cellar underneath.

Not wanting to deal with a hole in the floorboards or the stench of something dead and rotting, he grabbed a broom from where it leaned against the wall, pushing against the crate blocking the opening until the netting inside spilled and the whole thing toppled over. The rattling subsided in an instant, and Alba paused another moment in waiting. Sure he must've frightened whatever animal was trapped underneath.

When nothing came crashing through, he searched for the latch to heave the door open—only to find the metal beaten within an inch of its life, pinning the trap door locked shut.

There was no way of knowing if the latch was bent from age, or a previous wickie going mad and hammering it to hell in an attempt to stop similar rattling, but Alba's curiosity compelled him back to his feet. He limped around the room, searching the sparse shelves for anything he could use to pry the hatch open.

Settling on a rusted iron chisel and hammer, he knelt back to the floor to whack at the bent loop.

After a few strikes, it gave way, metal ring flinging upward—and the wooden cover snapped up with it, nearly taking Alba's head off. A cyclone of wind blasted through the opening, whipping Alba's hair back before settling again, allowing him to lean over and peer inside. A swirling inlet of seawater greeted him down below, making his mind spin trying to recall what the keeper's quarters looked like from the outside.

Leaning slightly more, he draped his head through just enough to get a better look, finding that that small leg of the house sat on raised stilts over an edge of rocks that curved inward from the shore. He hadn't noticed from the direction they arrived, but the immediate realization that he could fish and dump crab pots from right there next to the kitchen was enough to make him practically cry out and praise god.

The wind whistled up through the hole to tangle his hair as if in agreement. The water churned in its narrow inlet as the tide pushed and pulled against the rocks, tempting him to jump in and feel how refreshing it could be. But Alba knew better than that; he knew how to tell a trick from the sea.

Pulling himself back onto solid ground, Alba thought back to the other out-buildings, wondering where he might find crab pots or fishing line, perhaps netting that wasn't as unwieldy as the trawling nets piled there in the storage room—only to pause as his hand touched the edge of the hatch a second time.

The underside of the wood crunched with a layer of barnacles that blinked at him like a thousand eyes, wondering why their world had been suddenly turned upside down—but they weren't the reason Alba stopped. They weren't the reason his lungs squeezed his heart, making it stutter. With deft movements, he pinched between a cluster of the wriggling creatures, holding his breath when he realized.

Throughout the barnacle nests, some flaking off with the

movement, others encapsulated, grown into the thick shells—
were chipped human fingernails.

Chapter 5

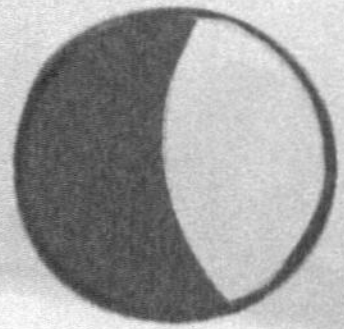

Alba bathed in silence. Mind racing, gazing down at his hands any time there was a pause in scrubbing his skin. He'd definitely only imagined it. It was only the exhaustion weighing heavy on his eyes.

He focused on cleaning the sweat from his skin, his hair. He drained the shallow tub and dressed in his new work clothes, then forced himself to return to the storage room with the trap door. Pulling it open, his heart pounded in the back of his throat—but whatever he thought he saw, he reassured himself with proof to only be the hard petals of barnacles. No fingernails. Nothing of the sort. Alba only needed a good night's sleep—and he grimaced at knowing it wouldn't come until morning, after his first night of tending to the lantern.

He left a note on the table stating where to find him, just in case his mother came while he was away. His handwriting trembled as he struggled to hold the pencil still. In anticipation, in anxiety, in hopes she would.

With an oil lantern in hand, he stepped into the darkening evening light, pausing to listen, gazing up at the gallery of the younger sister lighthouse. He'd already grown accustomed to the constant sound of her gears while in the house, only hearing them again as he gave them thought. Just loud enough to rumble over the wind, over distant stormy thunder, the waves against the rocks. But, to his curiosity, there was no gleam of light from the lens at the top of her tower.

Perhaps the fuel basin had run out, despite Eugene's promise. Alba grimaced at the thought of the amount of wear on the gears without anyone to keep an eye on them, limping through the rising storm toward the base of the shorter tower.

Through the door, the tower's belly was dim, walls lined with boxes of scattered replacement parts and other supplies. Overhead, Alba could see the floor of the platform beneath the gallery, two long ropes of counterweights hanging like the discs of a grandfather clock waiting to be wound.

Unmoving, despite the constant noise. His curiosity turned to frustrated confusion, forcing himself to continue as normal, anyway. He'd already imagined one strange thing while not paying attention, he wasn't eager to be another wickie gone mad before even the first night was over.

He'd expected to be hit with the smell of whale oil, that less-than-appealing waxy stench that always left a bad taste in his mouth—but instead, a fresh, minty scent clung to the air like herbs drying in the sun. He recalled again what Eugene said about their lighthouse using a special kind of fuel brought from the city up the coast, searching for the storage containers, eventually gazing down into a drum filled with solidified oil like in other lanterns he'd worked.

It was indeed far different from anything else he'd ever seen—white, pearlescent, silky under his fingers unlike the slippery, smelly residue left by whale fats. The sweetness of the aroma even tempted him for a lick, somehow sure it tasted like sugar, but he resisted. He wasn't going to go mad so quickly.

Using a spatula to scoop a bulb of solid oil onto the hot plate next to it, Alba melted down what he needed to fill the tin bucket on the floor, screwing the lid on tight before facing the height of the stairs. Sighing, he adjusted the grip on his cane in his hand, tapping the end against the bottom-most step as if to reassure himself the way was sturdy. The sound echoed off the curved walls all the way to the top, warning the lantern he was on his way.

THE INITIAL HIKE took longer than Alba expected with the stiffness of his leg, but at least once he made it, actually tending to the lantern came naturally. Summoning habits from so many lonely months tending to similar lights up and down the coasts in the north, sometimes with a crew of men, sometimes all alone as a form of punishment. He even found a strange comfort in trimming and lighting the wick inside the massive, domed fresnel lens, appreciating the way the cut glass warped the outside world into ribbons of color from inside.

He wound the dangling counterweights, watching the gears on the lantern table creak to life and begin rotating as the weights dipped slowly to the floor far below. Alba greased the gears between their teeth, next; he walked the circular floor of the gallery to gaze through the glass at the dark horizon outside, noticing the attention to detail from the previous tender when wiping them down. Even the vents overheard were brushed clean, which meant he wouldn't suffocate on fuel and mercury fumes by sticking around too long. Another relief, as he wasn't sure he'd actually be able to make it all the way back up the stairs again if he returned to the ground floor. He opted to stay where he was for the remainder of the night, making a note of amenities to bring with him the next time.

He tried not to look out the weatherglass too much in search of someone rowing their way through the dark water to see him. Someone with dark blonde hair pinned back in a familiar pearl and mermaid-plated pin.

He tried to focus on the work, on finding things to busy his hands and his mind.

He wiped dust from the lantern as it slowly turned, keeping

his eyes lowered so the beam wouldn't blind him, warmed by the heat of the glass from the flame inside.

He oiled the crank of the counterweights to subdue the high-pitched noise with every turn to reel them back up again.

He sat on the metal floor beneath the gallery, leaning back against the stone wall and allowing himself just a few moments to close his eyes. The counterweight dropping to the full length of the cord let out a loud *clang* each time, so even if he did accidentally fall asleep, it would never be for long.

Finding the previous lighthouse keepers' log hidden beneath a pile of cleaning rags, Alba smirked at the words *Moon Harbor, Whitesand Cove Lighthouse* printed on the front in faded gold ink. Final proof that he was at least in the place where his mother's telegram was sent from.

Flipping through the most recent pages, Alba found further proof of what the Bluecastle Township clerk and Eugene himself had described—the constant churn of lighthouse keepers over the course of years, one right after one another with none ever staying to see the start of a new month.

To Alba's disappointment, none ever wrote of anything to hint at what made them so eager to leave, except the occasional mention of strange shadows in the corners of the house, the sound of singing from far off at sea, one even writing long diatribes about how tending to the lighthouse at Moon Harbor was akin to trapping a rabbit in a cage, lured by dandelions and fed to evil clustered in doorways that refused to let anyone leave.

The last entry from the most recent keeper made his breath catch. His fingers trailed over the written words, delicate but practical. Not the pen of a charm school graduate, but still a nib held between thoughtful fingers. The style reminded him—of his mother. Had there been any indication of a name, or even initials beneath each dated entry, he would have known for sure, but whoever they were, they left notes as vague as all those before them.

An itemized list of supplies in the cupboards and store rooms.

Mentions of things like shadows and a strange wind; finding a dead fish in the rainwater cistern; how gulls tried to fly into the house through the storage-room trapdoor they kept tightly shut from the first day they arrived. They mentioned how surprised they were at the lack of life in the harbor, how they'd expected to find so much more from what they knew of the last time they were there. Alba tried not to see too much into the words, but he couldn't help it.

If the lighthouse had been where his mother was hiding before he arrived, where had she gone?

Was she the one who draped shells on the doorknob while he was inside? Why would she hide from him? Were there other rooms he hadn't found in the house, yet? A cellar? A loft in one of the out-buildings? But Eugene himself said the last lighthouse keeper ran off like the rest of them...

The closer he looked at the list of supplies, the more he realized they seemed more like the scribblings of someone preparing to leave. Not on impulse, like all the others, but on purpose. Writing down how much money they had on hand. On another page, a list of the best choice of foods for traveling, and how they needed new boots that were better suited for the wilderness. Lists scattered throughout other standard information logs, checklists and small notes to prepare for what would come, only for the final note to come the morning before the full moon.

Alba's heart thumped. He dug into his jacket pocket, removing the telegram, as if he hadn't already memorized it.

FULL MOON. His heart sank. Had she—already gone? Did the message take longer to reach him than she expected? Did he take too long getting there to meet her?

Had he really—missed his mother entirely?

He slammed the log book shut, tossing it away. He stared down at the telegram, grinding his teeth together in a mix of frustration and the childish urge to burst into tears. But he wouldn't cry. He had work to do, and he wouldn't cry, and he wouldn't lose all the hope he'd collected over a decade in a single moment of something he might have been making up from strings he didn't know were even meant for him written into a logbook with no proof of his mother ever being there at all—

Pressing his palms into his eyes, he pushed hard until colors and lights popped in his vision. He held his breath until he couldn't, long enough to wipe every thought from his mind except the need to inhale.

He re-wound the counterweights. He wiped down the hot lens again. He threw down dirty washrags from the top of the stairs so he could launder them before the next night.

His mother hadn't left him. She wouldn't have left him so quickly, without any warning, without even giving him a chance. She would not have gone anywhere without a hint of where he could follow. They always promised to meet in Moon Harbor, damnit, even if he only recently learned its name—and she wouldn't have grown impatient after only a few weeks of waiting for him. Not after an entire decade of waiting for him before that.

The writing in the log book could have very well been anyone. He'd come to the right place, and he knew it, and he was imagining her in places she'd never gone because he was so eager to see her again it practically deluded him.

She hadn't left him. Or if she had—she would come back. She would come back for him. Or he would go looking for her. The full moon—yes, the full moon. If he found nothing else before then, he could do as all the lighthouse keepers before him and vanish the night of the full moon to return to the road and continue searching for Edythe Marsh.

He would search for her in that town as much as he could until then. He would be patient and he would wait. He would seek out clues in all the places she might have left them. He would search every corner of his mind, his memories, for anything he might have missed that would be so obvious once he realized his mistake.

He would not give up hope. There had been so many other opportunities to give up hope, times it would have made far more sense, and that was not one of them. He would not give in to distress. He would not be driven mad by strange winds or shadows in the corners of rooms or fingernails caught in barnacle nests under trapdoors.

Alba tucked the telegram back into his jacket. He continued the rest of the night's work, allowing himself hardly another thought.

EDYTHE MARSH DID NOT COME LOOKING for him in the lighthouse while he tended to it. While new discoveries should have made that an unfortunate possibility, Alba could still barely swallow the disappointment.

As the sun rose, lightening the sky to a dull blue and indicating the end of his shift, he let the weights unwind and doused the lantern before staring at the little town clustered on the shore a mile away. The beach was hardly more than a black ribbon from so far away, so high up. He realized the irony of it being called *Whitesand Cove*, though couldn't summon even the tiniest twitch to the corner of his mouth in amusement.

Making his way down the stairs, he double-checked the lid on the oil container before stepping out into the crisp morning air. Eager for a chance to sleep and nothing else, there were few things that could make him pause before heading straight for the house —and it was the sound of humming coming from somewhere so nearby it made goosebumps flush his arms.

He nearly bolted on old sailor's instinct—but forced himself to think, first. The sound of the hum wasn't drawing him anywhere, wasn't any more tempting than the aroma of warm bread on a cold day. Grounding himself into that reassurance, he took a step forward, then another, then moved swiftly to search the exterior of the house, finally finding what he hoped to be the source.

Fluted pipes, just like those on the buildings in the town. They whistled loud enough to pierce through the melancholic fog hanging over his mind, and he gave in to a different sort of temptation to get a closer look.

The craft of the instruments was stunning, delicate and intricate, silver metal inlaid with thin swirling motifs up and down the shafts. Even the bolts securing them to the wall were shaped like seashells. He didn't know how they, or any of those in town for that matter, created such a nuanced sound with only the wind to play them, but he'd never been one who understood instruments or music much more than to simply enjoy it. His mother knew how to play the flute, always saying it was the best way to summon a mermaid, but Alba had never been keen on learning, himself. Likely for the best, as he later learned even a passive whistle while sailing could very well doom every soul on board. Perhaps because the sound might summon sirens, no different than his mother promised.

He couldn't help a little tune that tweeted between his lips, cracking a smile as the wind answered through the pipes as if complimenting him. He whistled further, and the wind responded, distracting him from the pit in his gut, harmonizing with the sound as if it knew exactly what notes he would offer before he did—until a third song joined them, and ice flooded his veins.

Turning, Alba searched the outside of the house, then the narrow corridor of beach grass between the quarters and the rocky edge of the land. With a sinking feeling, he dared himself to search the horizon last—and out in the dark water, a white spot lingered amongst the endlessly cresting waves.

Hair like silvery spiderwebs swept gracefully in and out on the water, swirling around a pair of equally pale, broad shoulders, while the continuation of its humming song combined to make it impossible for Alba to look away. Still—he managed a step back. He didn't know what it was, too far to see clearly—he only knew he had to turn his ear away. The creature seemed to realize, to sense Alba's resistance—because it suddenly extended two arms and dipped forward.

Toward him. It was swimming toward him.

Alba's body flared hot, moving on its own, stumbling backward before whirling on heel and rushing for the house. As soon as he did, the song of the sea-creature found him again, more intensely that time, gripping him over every inch. Like a net cast over his being, it hooked the bends of his arms, his knees, the nape of his neck, and pulled. It tugged at the back of his throat, the base of his spine, his navel, attempting to draw him back. To lure him to return. That thing in the water was singing out to him—and for the first time in his life, Alba was tempted by it.

Fear crashed through him. Bright and sharp enough to make his ears ring, to break the spell just long enough to stumble around the corner of the house and toward the door.

He slammed it shut behind him, locking it, breathing sharply with his hands pressed to his ears, until the pull on his body faded enough that he was sure he crouched on dry land. The floorboards of the house. He was not in the sea, he had not only imagined his own escape from Belmar. From Josiah Warren.

His hands remained fixed over his ears as he hurried on crouched feet into the kitchen, yanking open the cupboard beneath the sink and searching rapidly through the contents for something, anything he could stuff into his ears. Knocking over jars of candles, packets of garden seeds, a bucket of seashells and pearls and fish skulls, he finally unearthed a roll of cotton bandages. Tearing two pieces away, he shoved them into his ears deep enough that pain bolted up his temples.

He'd never been enticed by the sea before. Not once. To finally know what so many sailors heard before giving in to the call that tempted them—and for it to happen to him while all alone, isolated, with hardly a soul knowing where he was—

It was nothing but beauty—and dread—and heartbreak, at forcing himself to ignore it. Gut-churning, soul-rocking heartbreak, distressing enough that Alba burst into tears with how badly he wished to turn and race back out to hear it again.

CHAPTER 6

IF EDYTHE MARSH CAME WHILE ALBA SLEPT, HE WOULD not have heard it. She would have found him, though, he knew. She would have pulled the cotton from his ears, shaken him awake, flicked his nose then pressed a finger to the tip of it so he'd pay attention to the list of chores she had for him.

Instead, he woke alone to the early afternoon sun through the window. The first time he'd ever woken up alone, he realized, which perhaps was why it took him so long to pull his ghost back into his body and recall where he was.

He laid there disoriented for a long while, first by the overcast blue sheen on the air, then by the swollen dryness in his mouth. His lungs felt like they cracked with every sharp breath, dry as chalk and heavy in his chest. Groaning, he finally attempted to roll over, blinking a dozen times before slumping off the side to his knees on the floor.

The wash basin below the window was still empty, so he had no choice but to drag himself down the stairs to the kitchen, where he cranked the water pump with a chorus of miserable grunts until clear water finally spurted out. He drank greedily from the spout like a feral animal in the woods, having to pump more and more and more as he couldn't get enough to quell the desert festering in his stomach. Only after swallowing enough that he thought he might burst did he finally straighten up again and wipe his mouth, reclaiming a few of his senses from the swirling exhaustion clouding his thoughts.

The effort had made a mess of the water, a puddle of it gathered on the floor under his feet and soaking his socks. He grabbed a hand towel to wipe it up—only to realize the water was more than a puddle at his feet. It was a trail, dripping in a scattered path of movement from the bottom of the stairs, to the sink where Alba stood, to—the door of the storage room, where it disappeared beneath the crack.

His heart thudded. He hesitated a moment, before limping stiffly to the door. On the other side, the hatch sat wide open, something heavy in the water below clanging loudly against the rocks as if the tide no longer wanted whatever it was. But the question of the object was nothing to Alba's ringing ears, staring only at the trenches carved into the edge of the wooden floor.

Claw marks of something heaving itself from the sea into the house, its trail of water the only indication it'd ever gone back again.

Alba kicked the lid shut with a *bang* and a clatter of the metal ring. Breathing heavy, he stared down at it for another moment, before closing his eyes and pinching the bridge of his nose. He turned and closed the door behind him, stopping again to gather his bearings.

He first thought his heart pounded loud enough to ring in his ears, before realizing it was the rhythmic clang of the lantern turning overhead. Just like the day before—only that time, he was sure he'd put her to rest that very morning at sunrise. She shouldn't have made a single sound.

Another *bang* crashed from the storage room, making Alba shout and stumble back, tripping over one of the chairs and hitting the floor. Another bang, and the storage room door flew open—revealing a crab pot with what appeared to be catch inside, slammed through the closed hatch and dribbling water in every direction over the floor.

Alba could only stare—trying to remember if he'd missed seeing any crab pots the night before. In the water or in the storage room. He was sure there hadn't been, he was sure he'd even looked. He was—*he was sure of it*. Wasn't he?

Moving slowly, he approached the pot with his heart racing. Nudging the front gate open, he risked a glance, then carefully tucked his hand inside.

A single crab waited for him—but as Alba pulled it out, his stomach knotted when he realized it was mostly empty shell. The meat had been carved out, or perhaps rotted away, revealing the polished cavity inside. Its outside was printed with lines of seaweed stuck fast to the toothy exterior, barnacles petrifying one of its claws in place. Legs sprouted in every direction from the same holes in the sides, more growing like fingers from the joints of others.

Despite resembling a desiccated corpse—the creature hissed a bubbling sound, pinching at Alba with a claw donning a third joint. Alba yelped, dropping it in surprise, a few of its malformed legs snapping off as if made of brittle sandstone—and continuing to writhe against the floorboards. He kicked them back into the water, followed by the rotten crab itself, heart pounding in his ears.

There was something else in the pot, but Alba didn't risk thrusting his hand inside with the same courage as the first. What waited at the bottom was not a crab at all, but what remained of the flipper of a harbor seal, stringy viscera dangling from the detached end. The flesh between the bones hidden inside was thin, nearly translucent against the dim light coming through the hole in the floor—and Alba quickly tossed it back as well the moment he realized why it unsettled him so much. The joints resembled a hand, webbed and rotting and terrible.

Kicking the pot away, it skittered across the floorboards and plunged through the trapdoor back into the water. He threw himself against the door again, slamming it with a deafening sound before grabbing the kitchen table to shove against it. Outside, the wind picked up, howling through the open hatch on the other side, whistling through the flutes on the house. He closed his eyes, pressing his hands back over his ears again.

He wouldn't lose his mind. He wasn't a wickie driven to sea-madness after only a single day alone.

The trap door banged shut, making the floor shake and muffling the wind. He pressed his hands harder into his ears, until they rang as loud as gears turning on the lantern in the pitch dark of night.

He would not go mad. He would not go mad. He would be patient, he would wait.

His mother used to scold him for always being in a rush, telling him *'take that bone from your teeth; good things come to those who wait.'* And he would. He would wait for her. For the first time in his life, he wouldn't be in a hurry. He would allow his fate to come for him, he would give his mother time to find him.

He would not go mad.

Alba didn't realize exactly how many days had passed of maintaining a strict routine to keep himself from spiraling—sleeping, tending to the lantern, ignoring any strange sights in the corner of his eye or the back of his ears—until the clouds parted in the sky for the first time since arriving, and a bright moon beamed down at him as if eager to finally say hello. He knew right away by the size of her—a full moon. He'd been tending to that lantern for an entire week, already, despite barely recalling how a majority of the time passed.

He tried not to get his hopes up. He tried to prepare himself for disappointment. But Edythe's telegram haunted the back of his mind as he went about his work, and soon he couldn't help but hope and hope and *hope* the FULL MOON mentioned on the telegram was, in fact, a promise that she would return for him after all. Perhaps even that night. Perhaps he'd get his chance to leave that cursed place before the sun rose.

Alba burned away at his jittery impatience by wiping down the weatherglass for the hundredth time that night, when something moved on the dark water below. A tiny flicker of lantern light caught his attention, barely illuminating a rowboat. Manned by a single silhouette, heading straight for the lighthouse rocks.

His nervous heart sprang to life, fighting to keep the rush of emotions at bay, though being quickly crushed beneath them. Who else could it be? Who else would row across the full moon's high, angry tides in such a small boat, just to see him? In the middle of the night, with no one else around?

Alba wanted to hope. He wanted to believe it. He couldn't fathom what else it could possibly be.

Hurrying a little too fast, his foot caught in the ladder leading down to the gallery. He crashed into the metal with a deafening *clang* and a grunt, but barely felt it.

He wound the cables of the counterweights to buy some time.

He wouldn't wait for her to find the note he left on the table every evening.

He wanted to see her for himself. He wanted to hug her. He wanted to see her and know she was alright, and prove the same for himself. Would she be surprised? Would she be relieved? Would she swat him on the back of the head and call him foolish for what he'd done to find her?

He didn't care—he grinned the whole time he descended the stairs, wishing he could move faster. Wishing his damn leg wasn't so eager to lock up, nearly sending him tumbling all the way down to his death.

Throwing open the lighthouse door, the wind nearly swept him off his feet, but he braced against it. Unable to help another smile splitting his face at the sight of a little rowboat banging against the rocks. He grinned even as the flutes on the house rang out shriller than ever, loud and piercing enough they nearly cut into him like knives.

The sea was high with the constant wind, tide rising higher and higher with the draw of the full moon, waves crashing against the rocks with sprays higher than Alba was tall. No one in their right mind would have chosen to row that far out unless—unless it really was—

He hurried against the wind, the storming water, fighting the slippery ground and how the grass tangled in the foot of his cane in his hurry. Not realizing he held his breath until he made it to the door of the house, hanging open with lantern light from the other side trickling through the crack.

"Mama?" he gasped upon stumbling inside. He searched for her in the dimness, deafened by the shrieking flutes, the roaring waves, the endless pounding of the hatch in the storage room—

The man standing in his kitchen turned. Alba didn't have to know his face to know who he was, where he came from—why he was there.

One of Josiah Warren's dogs had finally found him.

CHAPTER 7

Alba didn't see every moment as it happened, unfolding too fast. The lantern snuffed with the sound of breaking glass as it was knocked off the table; one of the chair legs snapped as Alba was thrown into it before being pinned to the floor. Hands found his throat, but didn't last as he shoved his good leg into the man's stomach and pushed him off.

He moved on instinct just like every other time he'd been cornered in port alleyways, behind bars, on the ships where he sailed. He knew how to fight, he knew how to break noses and defend against a person twice his size if he needed to.

At least, back when he had the muscle strength and stamina, he could—and while it was a little sloppier that time, Alba still managed to get that man on his knees. Grabbing his head and slamming it against the edge of the countertop. Again and again with fingers knotted in his greasy hair, until no more sound came from his mouth except guttering life on weak breaths. Alba slammed it once more, even then, before releasing the heavy heap and letting it slump to the floor.

Hearing every sound in the house with ears sharpened by hot blood, he was inundated with the creaking floorboards beneath all the movement, the wind outside, the waves, the whistling pipes, the trapdoor that slammed and rattled like a growling creature in the store room. But Alba just stared down at the fresh body at his feet, unblinking until his eyes burned, empty of anything until he was flooded with everything.

Realizing what he'd done wasn't what made the heart-wrenching sob bubble up the back of his throat—it wasn't even the first time he'd killed a man. No—it was the embarrassment. The pure, venomous mortification of allowing himself to get his hopes up so easily despite how silly it was to think what he had. To hope what he had, without question, letting his emotions get ahead of him. What was he, a child? Disappointment was bitter, syrupy-thick in the back of his throat as he beat back the emotions that wanted to invade him like a hand into a glove. He forced his mind to remain clear. There wasn't time for embarrassment.

He couldn't keep a body in the house. He couldn't just toss it over the edge, either, unless he wanted it to linger on the surface and haunt him.

He didn't even have the strength to drag the man all the way across the kitchen and out the door, across the grass, the rocks. He couldn't lift and carry him—

"Enough!" he shouted, whirling around and throwing the storage room door open as the trapdoor slammed and slammed. "I said *enough!*"

The hinge halted halfway. Hovering as if held up from below, but there was nothing. He glared at it, chest heaving with breath, sweat making him shiver against how tightly he clenched his muscles. He watched as the hatch door shuddered, then slowly opened the rest of the way, bumping against the hinges with maw gaping open into the dark, sloshing water below. Inviting him in. Inviting him through.

No—not him. Alba looked back over his shoulder to the body piled motionless on the floor. Sweat dripped into his eyes. His breath shook in his throat, finally closing his mouth and holding it in. Moving without deciding. Knowing if he let himself think too much about it, nothing would get done.

Picking his cane up, Alba left it on the table. He went to the door, searching the edges of the dark rocks outside and locating the man's rowboat where it bumped and scraped against the stone. No thinking, only doing.

He crossed the wet grass, at the whims of the storm as much as a bird in the sky, but managed to keep his footing. Never feeling the throb of his hip, the limp he dragged himself along with, before jumping into the thrashing dingy. No thinking.

Kicking off, Alba used the oars piled at the bottom to navigate around the treacherous edge of the rocks. He followed the direction of the rotating lantern light, the ribbon of white foam where water crashed against land, around to where the inlet beneath the house would open up to him.

He expected to see all sorts of shadowy creatures clambering in and out of the open hatch, though wasn't particularly relieved when nothing of the sort was visible upon rounding toward it, either. No thinking.

Positioning the boat beneath the hatch door, Alba searched for somewhere to loop the anchor rope off, settling on a mostly-rotten beam stretching across the floor overhead. The space was just high enough for him to stand, though with a sharp hunch in his back, and he ignored the new pain throbbing in his hip as he worked at the awkward angle. Even punching his leg a few times and cursing at it to *quit*.

Stepping from the unsteady boat to the sheer muddy edge, Alba bit back more discomfort while clutching at the long beach grass to crawl his way to flatter rocks by the water, praying he wouldn't be swept away before finishing. Barely managing to scramble to safety before exactly that happened, a few more noisy waves chased after him as if laughing. Promising to get him next time.

He hurried back to the house, cursing the new rain that speckled the back of his neck. Cursing his leg. Cursing the wind, the water. And then—cursing the sight of two more rowboats heading toward him. Making him duck down and cling to the side of the house as nervous sweat dripped down his spine.

Rushing inside, he closed the door behind him a little too loudly. His hands shook as he locked it, wasting no time getting back to the man's body and grabbing an arm to begin the work of dragging it to the open hatch. His foot slipped in a puddle of blood, crashing to the floor with a groan before crawling back to his feet and getting back to it again. No thinking. No thinking. Except—

It had to be more of Josiah's men on their way. They must have been waiting for the first on the beach, to help subdue Alba once they made it back to land. When their friend never did, they decided to investigate. Alba couldn't take on any more than he already had. He was exhausted. God—he was so exhausted, only wearing down faster as the man's body weighed twice as much in death.

Sweat continued to sting his eyes, drenching the front and back of his shirt by the time he reached the open hatch. He barely had the man's thick legs scooted into the opening when a knock came at the door, making Alba's blood run cold. He risked the quickest glance, heart pounding in the back of his throat at the faint glow of lanterns through the window, how it was definitely a small huddle of men on the other side. He could hear their voices. He could sense them.

Kicking the storage room door shut behind him, Alba gave the corpse one last shove through the open hatch, grimacing when it landed in the rowboat below with a sickening *thud* and crack of bones. The front door opened right as he slid down after, pulling the hatch shut behind him.

He scrambled for the oars. Kicked the body's arms out of the way, finding the best way to sit, even if it was uncomfortable. He pushed off from the rocks, straining every muscle in his arms and shoulders to row in the opposite direction of where those men would have docked on the other side. Waiting for him. Looking for him. They wouldn't find a damn thing except a puddle of wet blood on the floor. They would have to leave again before morning, else risk someone from town spotting them. They might even go all the way back to Welkin and tell Josiah there was no sign of Alba there at all.

Silent tears of overwhelm, relief, fright, adrenaline spilled from him, and that time Alba let them. His hands were too busy rowing into the darkness to care to wipe them away, too busy *not thinking, only doing* to properly process any of it. To consider what he would do, next. How, with a boat of his own, there was nothing stopping him from rowing back to shore by himself. Disappearing just like all the previous lighthouse keepers who came before him. Just like he once teased to himself.

The thought made tears burn hotter, wetter in his eyes, though he didn't know why—except how bitter it was to know there was still work to be done. He couldn't rest, yet. No matter how tired he was.

DECIDING he'd rowed far enough when he could no longer hear the waves against the rocks, the rhythmic hum of the lighthouse's gears, the whistling pipes on the house, Alba drew the oars back into the boat.

Tensing the muscles of his legs to keep from capsizing, he carefully maneuvered the man into the center, grateful for all the experience he had dumping bodies over the side just like that. Knowing which parts to move first, where to lift them over the edge, where he should lock his knees and when to heave to keep the backlash from sending him over the opposite side. He'd never had to do it by himself before, but—his mother would have been proud. He couldn't wait to tell her. Maybe over drinks, in a warm bar somewhere, a plate of potatoes and corned beef and bread and gravy in front of him. Laughing about all the nightmares of the lighthouse, all the nightmares they'd suffered while Alba was sailing and she was trapped in Welkin.

Laughing about where they would go next, how they would

avoid getting caught. Until they found a place to settle down, where Edythe could grow old without a worry and Alba could take care of her well into her age. Like a son was meant to do.

More useless tears flooded his eyes, dripping down his cheeks. He ignored them, letting them do what they wished. No thinking.

The man's legs wheeled over the edge and into the water with a final thrust, and Alba tumbled backward with a grunt. The need for urgency clawed at him right away, commanding him to get back to his feet, to keep moving—but the moment his hands found the oars again, he groaned, collapsing back into the belly of the boat for just a moment.

Not long enough to let the exhaustion sink all the way to his bones. Just enough to catch his breath. To live in the ease of such a warm, happy, colorful fantasy a moment longer. The draw of rowing himself to shore and leaving without a word grew more tempting, especially as the night wore on and there continued to be no sign of Edythe coming to find him. Why not?

He glared up at the sky through arms crossed over his face, not sure if he resented the clouds for only parting on his last day in Moon Harbor, or thanking them for the view before he had to go again. He'd never seen stars so bright, like pricks of diamond; he'd never seen a moon so full, so fat, so beautiful, like she really did favor that miserable little rot of a town like Edythe used to say.

Well—good for them. Alba wasn't impressed. The moon had her reasons, and he didn't care enough to question them.

The sound of gurgling brought him out of his haze, closing his eyes and sighing. Was that the sound of the man's body sinking? He wanted away from it. He wanted to be back on shore. It was decided, he would leave that cursed rock for the next lighthouse keeper to come and clean up after him. They could have his clothes, his coat, his cane, the puddle of blood on the floor. God, Alba didn't give a shit any longer.

Sitting up, Alba rolled his shoulders, stretched out his legs, then his arms. He bent over to grab the oars off the bottom of the boat—only for the water to suddenly churn beneath him, something massive suddenly hurtling upward from the depths and flipping over the side.

Choking on a shout, he stumbled back at the sight of the man's waterlogged corpse draped over the front half of the boat. Around him, the water thrashed as hard as it did against the lighthouse rocks, nearly knocking him off his feet as he braced and fought for the edges to hold onto.

The sound filled his ears, mixing with the wind, with the heavy pound of his heart, but he didn't dare look away. There were bite marks on the dead man's face, trenches dug through his chest and bleeding dark, thick blood.

"I prefer pretty redheads like you."

Alba didn't move. He didn't blink, eyes petrified on the body. That voice, low and rumbling, hoarse with vocal chords saturated by salt, gurgling beneath the sound as if from a throat clearing water. A voice with the same warm, velvety tenor as the one that sang to him days prior.

The boat jostled again, and Alba lurched back into his body. Leaping to his feet, he nearly lost his footing a second time as it wobbled sideways.

He frantically searched the foaming water encircling the boat, careful not to shift his balance one way or the other, but there was nothing. There was no one, nothing, nowhere that voice could have come from. Like the musical pipes on the house, in the town, that mimicked the sound of singing with the blowing wind —Alba had to wonder if he'd only imagined it.

"Show yourself!" He commanded the darkness nonetheless, feeling foolish as he did.

There was no one. He'd only imagined it. It was only him and the dead body at his feet, proven by the resounding silence that echoed in reply. The water's thrashing even faded, until only bubbles kissed the sides of the boat.

Forcing himself to breathe, Alba moved again. He searched the man's corpse, finding a knife tucked into his belt. A hand pistol in a strap on his shoulder. He pocketed both, not sure why he didn't do it first back at the house. Hell, his hands quickly dug through his pockets in search of anything else he could pawn, too, because it suddenly felt like the right thing to do.

He couldn't stop shaking. He tucked away a handful of dollars and a silver pocket watch, deciding that was the reason the sea spat him back out. A gift after tricking him with who he thought was his mother. Wanting him to get everything he needed from the man before returning to shore and escaping that terrible place. That was definitely it. Definitely all.

Alba made sure to thank her before throwing the body back in, that time stretching his neck over the side to watch it sink. Waiting to see if it would rush back to the surface again. It didn't.

He reached for the oars again, plunging them into the water—only for both to suddenly jerk from his hands, vanishing into the darkness. He didn't make a sound—just stared. Forgetting how to breathe. Something, that time, waited for him to notice.

Only a few feet from the boat, strikingly pale against the dark water, the creature had the features of a man. Two eyes, a sharp nose, mouth mostly obscured beneath the surface. Sub-dermal lines accentuated the shape of its brow, high cheeks, strong jaw. It shined in the moonlight, minuscule scales over its cheeks shimmering slightly, hair a shade of silver as if woven from silkworms bred in the moon's beams, darker as it was soaked through. Pieces floated in an arch around where it tread the surface, glittering with strands of pearls and shells as large as Alba's fingernail, interspersed with slender braids to keep front pieces from spilling over its face. Its skin was as pale as its hair; its eyes were as silver and bright as the moon. Practically luminescent from where it gazed at him, like shining torchlight through a glass jar in the woods at night. Like a predator watching from dark bushes.

Immediately, Alba knew it was something to be afraid of. Every one of his most innate human instincts told him to get far away by whatever means necessary—but then something else draped like a warm balm over those warnings. Muffling them. Seducing them.

Until all Alba could think—was how beautiful it was. How his mother had told him stories of such things, how a part of him always knew exactly what he would find in the waters of Moon Harbor if he ever had the chance to look. Suddenly drunk with wanting nothing more than to know, to hear its voice again, that time promising he would appreciate it properly as the sweetest thing to ever grace his ears. He would give anything to be the creature's object of attention for just a moment, a moment longer, as every thought he had melted through his fingers and all he knew was the moon-kissed creature in front of him.

"You're a mermaid of Moon Harbor, aren't you?" He asked, voice quiet, like he was embarrassed to be so grating in comparison. "My mother... used to tell me stories about you."

The creature didn't respond. It just watched him, silent, unblinking, for what felt like an eternity, until Alba thought he might unravel with need to hear its voice. When its mouth finally emerged from just below the surface, lips round and perfectly shaped, points of sharp teeth shining in the bright moonlight when it spoke, what remained of Alba melted with the rest.

"You shouldn't have run from me before."

Alba leaned toward the edge of the boat, putting his hands on the wood. His heart sank. Had he? He couldn't remember.

"Is it true you make wishes?" he asked, touching his braid, messy and nearly undone from all the excitement. Recalling his mother's stories. Thoughts hardly more than flashing colors and honey and innate desire. "In exchange for a piece of hair."

"Is there something you'd like?" The creature glided slightly closer.

Alba's heart pounded in the back of his throat. Choking him. It was so ethereal up close, like nothing he'd ever seen, nothing he could ever possibly imagine. It turned his thoughts to smoke, sweet perfume, incense that tickled his brain, his spine, trickling down into the rest of his body until he was paralyzed by the mere beauty of it. Until a swirling in his gut festered to life, making his thighs clench, tingling below his navel.

Alba nodded—though he suddenly couldn't think of anything but the desire curling like choking vines around his hips, his throat. Just staring at the creature's mouth.

Pressing his lips together, he exhaled a small breath. Fighting to gather his bearings. Something beneath the soft, cottony layer on his mind was thrashing, trying to get his attention.

"There's something I want as well," the mermaid said, voice pitching slightly deeper, so alluring, so honeyed that Alba physically shivered as his insides writhed in growing heat.

He leaned slightly farther over the edge. The boat wobbled beneath his weight. The mermaid smiled, and Alba nearly lost himself to it. He would give that creature anything so long as it kept speaking to him, seeing him.

"Promise me you won't leave this town until you give it to me," it said. Smiling gently, lovely and handsome and enchanting. Like Alba was a gift, a treasure.

Bubbles swirled beneath where the creature floated; something dark whirled around where a long white tail tread the water. Alba barely noticed, wholly captivated by the face in front of him. He nodded before thinking.

"I promise—"

A black mass erupted from the abyss, hellish shrieks erupting from its lungs as claws thrashed out and attacked the mermaid. Alba gasped, nearly lunging over the side of the boat to reach for it, to help—but the moment the mermaid and undersea demon collapsed back into the water with nothing but thrashing bubbles and whitecaps in their wake, the spell sloughed off, releasing his mind.

Alba threw himself back, gasping another ragged lungful of air, barely biting back a scream of horror as every withheld instinct rushed him all at once. But there was hardly time to do anything else as the mermaid suddenly lunged from the water again, that time clawing at the edge of the boat and heaving itself inside.

It moved with surprising speed, a webbed hand slamming Alba back against the bow post by the throat. Alba choked, clawing at its scaly, slippery skin. He kicked his feet, attempting to knock the monster off balance—but it stood on a bend of its snakelike tail, out of reach, like a viper poised to strike.

No longer hidden beneath the water, no longer whipping his thoughts into a sweet, empty lather, Alba was forced to witness the creature's striking human features up close without any of the drunken, sweltering worship directing his thoughts. The shape of its jawline and neck decorated with slitted gills; broad shoulders and masculine chest rippling with strong muscle and draped in a collar of dangling pearls and shells. The tight muscles in its arms flexed as its hands tightened around Alba's neck, making it impossible to think clearly, seeing only that the creature opened its mouth to speak, perhaps to sing and cage his mind again.

Alba's hands frantically groped at his belt, pulling the dagger stolen from the man and slicing an arch across the creature's chest. Black blood spewed from the wound, splattering across Alba's shirt and forearms, the mer-creature hissing and snarling and crashing backward in shock. When it lifted animalistic eyes back to Alba, its nose wrinkled in a snarl, before throwing itself back over the side. The vessel rocked violently with the weight, and Alba barely managed to keep himself upright.

There was no chance to inhale a single breath of relief—as the boat suddenly lurched to the side, dumping him into the sea.

Plunging into the deep darkness, king tides pushed and pulled by the moon tore him in every direction, and his instincts kicked in properly that time. Instincts from years at sea, from falling overboard in worse storms than that. Kicking his legs to right himself, following the trail of bubbles blown from his mouth to the surface, his only other thought was to keep his grip tight on the knife.

He barely crested through the surface again, tearing at the air with his lungs, before something grabbed and dragged him back down. He moved fast, swinging the knife to slice at whatever gripped him—but the creature didn't flinch, even when Alba was sure the blade made purchase.

Reeling back, he stabbed again, again and again and again at the fleshy, slimy shadow that clung to him, all the while thrashing and fighting for his freedom. The demon that attacked the mermaid was taking him somewhere. He couldn't tell the direction, it was too dark, the tide was too cold and too unpredictable, unable to discern if he was even right-side up or not.

The salt burned his eyes as he clawed at the thing, but only thick, gelatinous residue scraped off with his fingers, like plump seaweed. Something knotted under his nails like hair, but he was sure he felt bone where a face should have been. It was hands that dug into him, distinguishing enough in the blurry darkness to be sure it was a humanesque creature that dragged him off—even wrapped in fabric like clothing; gripping him with stiff, bony fingers.

He could only hold his breath, though the thing bobbed to the surface at random as they went, allowing him a gasp of air each time. He fought whenever the creature's grip faltered, continuing to sweep the knife out hoping to catch it off guard, but never resulting in release. He opened his eyes against the cold, salty water whenever they no longer burned, searching for any sign of where it took him, any sign of the moon-kissed mermaid that'd attacked him first, until the very last thing he expected to feel grazed the backs of his fingers, and his body jolted as if struck by lightning.

Sand—it was sand. The creature had dragged him back to the black shores of Moon Harbor. New, blinding hot adrenaline exploded in his veins, shoving against the thing that clutched him, managing to wrench himself away—only to be crushed back into the water, against the muddy bottom by a suffocating weight coiling around him with sudden ruthlessness.

The knife tumbled from his hand. He swore he heard the

rotting demon-creature shriek, thought he felt it rush to claw at the mermaid that'd caught up to them, but the moonlit creature's tail lashed out, slamming the monster into the sand before hands grabbed Alba by the back of the shirt and wrenched him back to the surface.

Gasping, Alba clawed at the earth. He kicked his legs, digging the toes of his shoes into the land and fighting with everything he had to climb up the shore's incline, wanting to get as far from the water as he could, not wanting to drown when he was so close—but the weight of the mermaid was too much, flattening him until his breaths were hardly more than rasps.

"Not so fast, light-keeper," it hummed into his ear, voice laced with disdain, with reserved fury, though still threading Alba with magic woven from desire. "You already made your promise, don't forget. You won't be stepping foot outside of this town until you do as I say."

"Please—" Alba choked, cut off when a sharp hand scooped under his chin, arching his head back and forcing him to meet the creature's gaze. In the far distance, the moon kissed the horizon. Preparing room for an incoming sun. Giving the sky barely enough light for Alba to witness the seething hatred in the creature's silver eyes as it continued speaking. Ignoring him.

"You will go into Moon Harbor and ask what has come of the merrow who once filled these waters," it said, sharp nails pressing into the soft skin of Alba's throat. "Only when you have an answer that satisfies me, will I lift this curse. You shall not walk anywhere you cannot hear the sound of the waves, else you crumble into a pillar of salt to be tousled into dust by the wind."

"Please—" Alba begged again, voice hoarse—and the merrow answered by jerking Alba's head to the side, burying teeth into the crook of his neck.

Alba jolted, biting back a scream, clawing at the sand as his eyes bulged toward the sky, pain crashing through him from where the merrow's teeth dug deep enough that blood bubbled from the seal of its lips and dripped down Alba's back. Only once it was satisfied did its jaw unhinge and pull back, letting Alba fall to his stomach.

"Blood for blood," it spat, crimson residue from its mouth splattering the sand by Alba's head. "Now—do as I say. Should you step foot in these waters again without an answer, I won't resist feeding you to things worse than I."

The weight slid off him. Alba barely had the strength to turn his blurry eyes to look, to search for that piece of the moon, to see if it really left him with those final words—but it wasn't the merperson that moved in his vision.

Down the beach, blending with the foam of the constant waves, barely visible from where they hid just beneath the water—Alba swore a dozen pale, bloated corpses gazed back at him in pity, just before the exhaustion made him slump back to the shore.

CHAPTER 8

ALBA WOKE AGAIN WITH SAND AND SALT IN HIS MOUTH. Coating his tongue, gagging him. He dug fingers into the sand, wondering why it didn't have the bite of frost. Why his fingernails didn't scrape against ice like cold glass, why his cheek didn't lose a layer of frozen skin when he finally lifted his head.

He wasn't in the north, he hadn't gone overboard—he was face down in Moon Harbor's black sand, and every inch of him *hurt,* like a sheet of ice carved through by the bow of a steel ship. Cracked in every place there was a fragment of weakness to snap.

It took a few attempts to push himself up, groaning each time, gasping, clutching at the thick scab of caked blood on the gash in his shoulder. Unable to move more than to drag of his pitiful corpse as his leg locked up every time he tried to bend it and kneel.

Eventually a cluster of townsfolk noticed, rushing to grab at him, pushing hair from his face and sand from his mouth, checking to see if he was alive. Demanding to know what happened, how he ended up there, as if it was a crime to wash up on shore with air still in his lungs. As if they'd seen the drowned faces in the waves, too, and had to know if he really was alive or just another reanimated corpse. Even he wasn't sure.

He had no explanation to offer as they roughly pulled him to his feet, dragging him down the length of the beach toward the steps up to the road. Into town. All while Alba's world spun, his body aching as badly as the day he fell from the mast and crashed to the deck below.

THERE WAS ONLY one doctor in all of Moon Harbor, and Alba was left to shiver on the exam table in the single exam room meant to serve an entire town of people. Waiting for the doctor to come.

If he wasn't so cold, so weak, so exhausted, he might have had the time to wonder how such a thing was possible when fishing resulted in so many cuts and breaks and gruesome injuries day over day. But he was cold. He was weak, he was exhausted, so he just stared up at the plain ceiling while what had to be two dozen voices chattered on the opposite side of the door.

The room smelled distinctly of old fish, aged salt, like they used it as an overflow for the fish market when no one needed a checkup. The cabinet against the wall was packed with old books and rolls of surgical tools in leather satchels; a hand-drawn poster on the wall indicated parts of human anatomy; bottles of varying liquids labeled with handwriting too scratchy to read lined a shelf by the window, covered with a pair of heavy curtains; an icebox with a padlock on the front sat in the corner, smeared with what looked a little too suspiciously like old blood someone forgot to wipe up after tending to a wound. Another curtain separated the room in half, only a peek of the other side visible through a crack at the end, and Alba swore he saw a peek of fins and fish scales piled in a tin bucket on a shelf. It would explain the smell.

When the door finally opened and the doctor stepped inside, she was followed by a handful of townspeople on her heels, including Eugene Michaels. The remaining dozen faces clustered in the doorway, like the state of Alba's being was the most impor-tant news that morning. As if they all had a vested interest in their lighthouse keeper, the first one to survive into a new month seemingly in years. Ah—perhaps that merrow had eaten all of the others, too. Perhaps Alba was simply the first to ever survive.

He had to get the hell out of that place.

Forcing himself to sit up, the doctor approached to offer a more thorough examination than the initial *dead-or-alive* check, asking Alba to open his shirt, extend his arms, perform the same choreography he always did when getting exams for eligibility to sail. And, like all those times, that morning Alba said nothing about his aches and pains, new and old. The doctor would see what was obvious; anything else was none of her business.

She seemed determined to know every inch of him, however, eyes moving as her hands did. Alba was briefly captivated by her tan eyelids and cheekbones dusted with shimmery powders, complementing her lips dabbed with rouge, thick hair pulled back into a tight bun and decorated with a seaglass-adorned pin. She wore dangling earrings that made Alba think of iridescent abalone shells, though the color was paler than anything he'd ever seen before.

An assistant wiped the dry blood from his shoulder while the doctor locked the rest of him over, eventually asking what happened. Alba told her only as much as he thought necessary to be convincing, though admittedly not sure why he had such a sudden urge to withhold some details. Perhaps carryover from what he'd witnessed of other men brought to shore for madness from sea, how they were sent off somewhere never to be seen again when it gripped their minds too hard to be useful for work.

And despite the clear depictions of mermaids throughout that town, from the paintings on their walls to the statue in the center, even the endless stories his mother told him growing up— Alba wasn't sure exactly what kind of relationship the towns-people had with the real thing, if any. There were endless stories and myths and warnings about mer-people, no matter where one went—like how sailors whispered about sirens, or even how the Warrens had sea-maidens carved into the bows of their ships for good luck and full nets. But that didn't mean those people looking at him would believe claims of seeing one in person—let alone to claim having been attacked by one in their own harbor, where they fished day in and day out.

Alba opted to withhold any more information that necessary —just in case. Just until he had a better idea of the townspeople and their relationship with the mer-people alleged to live in their waters.

"I got swept off the rocks during the storm last night. Must've got caught on something," he said, motioning to his shoulder as the assistant continued dressing it. "Foolish of me to be out there in the middle of it, but I couldn't believe how big the moon was. Won't happen again."

A completely believable story, but the doctor didn't react. No one in the room did, like they all knew beforehand what the truth was. Like it was some sort of test, like they truly were waiting for him to ask about mermaids in the water. To admit what he'd seen. Something about that only made him more hesitant to be so forthcoming—as if an outsider like him wasn't supposed to know of the merrow of Moon Harbor at all.

"Think I just need a rest now," he prompted, not liking how quiet the room had gone, how it almost felt intentional to get him to keep talking. Edythe used to do the same thing when trying to get the truth out of him as a child. "Probably won't get in the way of tendin' to the lantern tonight as normal."

"I haven't finished my evaluation yet," the doctor answered, authoritative and dismissive. Her assistant stepped behind the center curtain and returned with something folded in butcher paper.

Those crowded in the doorway mumbled to one another, seemingly annoyed, enough that Eugene turned and gave them a look to be silent. Alba noticed all of it, every tiny flicker in their expressions, how they watched him with a curious mix of mistrust, disdain, even a sort of—disappointment.

The doctor unwrapped whatever was folded in the paper while Alba's eyes glazed over the townspeople, and he jumped when something slippery and cold pressed into his skin. His wound immediately tingled, skin stiffening beneath whatever was spread over him. Only then did he panic, wondering if the gash resembled two sets of sharp teeth, though neither the assistant nor the doctor mentioned it.

"We use what we have on hand, here," the doctor said instead, using a brush packed with horsehair to smooth the bandage against Alba's neck. "You might find it alarming at first, but we're simple folk. Don't think us brutes when you look in the mirror later, alright? Now, one last thing..."

Alba didn't know what she could have meant by that, but didn't get the chance to ask when she took his wrists and extended his arms again. The curtains were pulled open from the window by the assistant, allowing a surprisingly bright stream of sun to spill over where he sat. Only when so brightly illuminated did he realize what the doctor was trying to show him.

Spread across his skin like spilled ink over parchment, splatters of black intermingled in and out of his tattoos. He stared at them in confusion, even attempting to rub his hand over a streak and frowning when it didn't smear.

"Do you remember how you got these markings?" She asked, brown eyes flickering up to meet his. The way the sun beamed through them made the gaze more intense than if it had been another dreary, overcast day. Enough that Alba's breath caught, realizing his instincts were right. Those eyes—they expected a specific answer. Like they already knew.

"I..." he started, mind racing. Not sure what to do. If they already knew of that merrow in the harbor, why not tell him so? Why ask him? The fact they waited for him to answer, rather than asking outright if the mermaid was who Alba had seen—something about it kept his words further at bay. "I don't know, I'm sorry. I don't remember."

He lowered his eyes back to his arms, his skin, unsure what exactly discolored them, but knowing from the way the doctor asked that it had something to do with the mermaid who'd attacked him. A blanket of cautious understanding draped over him, closing his mouth again. Forcing his words back.

There was a reason Moon Harbor hid itself in the woods, on the shore; why the people there blocked off their roads and made themselves so hard to find. Perhaps there were many reasons their wickies went missing so regularly, but suddenly Alba had to wonder about that as well.

He remained quiet, until the audience of onlookers started muttering amongst themselves again. Growing impatient. But Alba wouldn't speak. He'd learned early on to never volunteer information unless asked directly—and those rules applied on land as well as they did on the water.

"Let the boy get some rest now, doctor. A few days of goin' back to normal may refresh his memory," Eugene Michaels finally said, stepping forward to plant a hand on Alba's shoulder. "Sea never keeps a man's mind for long once he gets back to work on land. C'mon then, lad, we'll get you some supplies before rowin' back."

Alba didn't wait for another invitation, pushing himself from the exam table. Wincing as his leg wobbled beneath him, swiping a walking cane from the coat rack by the door on his way out. No one said anything to stop him, the crowd even parting to let him through.

"You've got a two-dollar credit to get what you need for the week, be it food or anything else," Eugene told him as they exited onto the street. "Just tell 'em to withdraw it from your wages. I'll leave you to it, meet me at the dock in about an hour, will ya?"

"Alright."

Alba watched Eugene shuffle off, before turning on heel and heading down the nearest alleyway without looking back. Bypassing the shops, the main roads, heading straight in the direction of the trees.

Breathing heavy by the time he reached the top of the incline, he returned to the main road to give a break to his legs. Forget his coat, his small collection of personal belongings. He wouldn't stay any longer—he couldn't. He would find his mother another way. Just like he decided the night before on the water, before ever meeting the eyes of the streak of moonlight beneath the surface.

Except he barely made it within the embrace of the trees when a bitter, nauseating rush of brine flooded his mouth, making him wretch.

Stumbling backward, he attempted to spit it out, but his tongue dried into dirt under a hot sun. His eyes blurred, parched as if he had no eyelids to blink; his skin ached and itched, and he swore he felt the start of his nail beds splitting over bone. All in an instant, all of it fading just as quickly again when he stumbled back out of the trees.

A vague memory stumbled into the back of his mind, spoken in the harsh words of that creature pinning him against the sand—

You shall not walk anywhere you cannot hear the sound of the waves, else you crumble into a pillar of salt to be tousled into dust by the wind.

"D-damnit," he croaked, voice hoarse as his insides fought against the internal salt that ransacked him. He lifted his eyes to the road again, heart pounding in the back of his throat.

Whether he liked it or not any longer, Alba was trapped in Moon Harbor's miserable embrace. Until, as he blearily recalled— he learned what happened to the rest of the merrow that once filled those waters. A promise made at the request of a merrow all the same, who had had a taste of Alba's blood.

ALBA STARED across the water as it passed them by, crawling at the speed the old man could row. In his lap he held a bundle of provisions, three boxes of cigarettes, chalk for the cistern, mortar for cracks in the lighthouse's exterior, a handful of castile soap chunks for bathing and washing rags. Eugene was even kind enough to look the other way when Alba clumsily hid a bottle of whiskey in the bag, both of them knowing it was practically treasonous for a wickie to drink on shift. Also knowing it was a staple for the work to get done.

Alba was already buzzing from a handful of drinks thrown down at the bar while waiting to cast off. It was only his second time being rowed out to the lighthouse rocks, and both times his blood had been warm with alcohol.

"You collect the cards that come in them packs?" Eugene asked as Alba opened one of the cigarette boxes and knocked a stick out, begrudgingly offering to share one, secretly glad when the old man shook his head no.

"Used to," he answered, lighting a match and inhaling the flame into the end. "Lost a few dozen of 'em one night when I forgot they were in my pocket and a wave hit me. Nothin' but ink and mush after that."

"My son has a collection going," the man countered with a wink. "Doesn't get out much anymore, but likes the pictures on 'em."

"He live in town?"

"All his life. Almost got out a handful of years ago, but fell ill, then his fiancé left him 'fore he could. Never had any desire after that."

"Sorry to hear it."

"Don't be," Eugene shook his head. "Selfish of me, but I never liked that lover of his. A right troublesome man, for him and this town both."

It took Alba a moment before realizing what Eugene meant— *His son, his son's fiancé. A troublesome man.* Rather than commenting on it, he let out a short, breathy laugh, then hooked a finger back into the cigarette box and slid the collectible card out.

"Here, then," he said, briefly glancing at the advertisement for a luxury coffee brand printed on the back before handing it over. He almost asked, wanting to know more about the fellow man-loving-man in town, but sucked on the tobacco in silence instead. It wasn't his business; it wasn't their business about him, either. At the very least, it was a strange relief to know Eugene wasn't the type to judge such things, especially should he ever learn some of what Alba kept close to his own chest.

Eugene took the cards with a small nod, saying nothing else as Alba turned to stare back across the water and inhale as much smoke into his lungs as he could. Thick clouds clustered off in the distance, signing the approaching end of the sun. Perhaps the moon was only strong enough to pitch light through the indefinite gloom when she was at her fullest, brightest.

Perhaps her merrow servant only had the audacity to attack when she was beaming in the heavens like that, too. He took another drag, thinking what he might do the next time he saw the creature bobbing in the water within view—though such a gruesome fantasy would surely make his mother scold him.

Alba bathed in only a few inches of water, not having the strength to pump any more than that. Not so pathetic to ask Eugene for help, though the man said he'd be happy to check around the rocks for damage after the previous night's storm while Alba got some rest.

Alba should have insisted he leave on that offer, too, but he was too damn tired. Tired, sore, bloody, irritated—not to mention the massive blood stain on the kitchen floor that Alba wasn't sure yet how to explain. Admittedly, a single nap might be the difference between calmly watching over the lantern at sunset, or burning the whole thing down.

Scrubbing relentlessly at the black marks on his skin like lines of splattered smoke, Alba grew more agitated the longer he thought about all those people crowded around the doctor's office looking at him. Waiting for an answer when the doctor asked what they were, how Alba got them. Eyes full of knowing, just waiting for Alba to *say it*. Whatever *it* was.

What would have happened if Alba had been more forthcoming? Would they have accused him of being mad, like it was a claim other sailors made regularly? Would they have gutted him on the spot in order to keep their town secret? His mother used to speak so openly about the mermaids in the harbor, they couldn't be so naïve to think there wasn't another living soul outside their town who knew.

He scraped at his skin until it was red and swollen, but just like the ink of his tattoos, there was no rubbing the dark streaks away. Only as he scoured his memory trying to remember anything that might explain them did he finally make a connection, recalling how that merrow's blood splattered across him when cut with the knife. It'd even said something about '*blood for blood*' while pinning him to the sand as dark as its own blood had been.

The realization filled Alba's mouth, his insides with a rotten taste. Another reminder of what he had to deal with, now, before he could flee that horrible place. Given a chore by that beautiful, awful, finned moon-creature; forced to sit and wait for his next orders like a child, like he'd sat and waited his entire life for one assignment on a ship to another, one assignment to another, then another; waiting and waiting for when it would finally be his turn for a night back in Welkin to visit his mother, only to be back in line waiting for assignments in Belmar the very next morning. Waiting and waiting and waiting—

"*Damnit!*" he shouted, throwing the soap into the tub with a hollow *bang*. "Damnit, *god—damnit!*"

He wasn't going to do what he was told without question. No more. Not any longer, never again. He wasn't going to bend over backwards like he was told and hope it would be gentle. He was no one's object to boss around, not any longer, he would kick and thrash and fight and tear as much as he had to—!

The trap door banged from the store room, stopping Alba short. Holding his breath, he stared at the bathroom door, heart pounding as he swore he heard footsteps, next. Whispers, the scratching of nails on the underside of the floorboards. He thought of those bloated faces he was sure he saw in the waves before going unconscious on the beach; he thought of that rotting flesh that grappled for him in the water and swam him back to shore faster than should have been possible.

Moon Harbor was a cursed place. The people knew more than they let on, and that merrow surely had something to do with it. Alba didn't care where the other mer-people who that once filled the waters went—he was too busy trying to find where his *own* kin had gone, when all signs pointed to Edythe Marsh disappearing from that terrible place as much as the mermaids apparently did.

Alba closed his eyes. He scratched at the aching wound in his shoulder, grimacing when the bandage flaked off under the movement. Pulling away to look, he expected to find cheap fibers under his nails, instead rubbing his fingers together at the sight of—fish scales.

Frowning, he stepped from the bath and limped to the mirror, wiping grime from the surface and staring in shock at the shiny sheet of white scales plastered to his skin, keeping the wound closed. It explained why the doctor said all those strange things in the exam room, about how the people did what they could with what they had. How she hoped Alba wouldn't see them as brutes when he saw his reflection later. *Brutes.* They were brutes, all of them. Including that creature in the water.

He didn't know what to do—and the reality of it crashed down on him all at once, nearly buckling his knees and sending him to the floor. He braced his hands against the edge of the washbasin instead, arching his back, hanging his head, clenching every muscle just to remain upright. Standing there, naked, shivering, miserable as the wind beat on the house and the sun crept closer to the horizon outside the windows.

He couldn't leave. He couldn't stay. He would die either way. The merrow in the water would kill him first, unless the townspeople killed him first, unless Josiah's men came back and killed him first, unless whatever driving him mad on those haunted rocks killed him first.

Trapped. Stuck. Hopeless. No different than being isolated on a boat in the north, nothing but water and shelves of glacier ice in every direction, knowing there was nothing he could do but sit—and wait—and pray—and consider death as the only way out.

He let out a long breath through his nose. Always in a hurry. *Take that bone from your teeth.*

The townspeople wanted something from him. The merrow wanted something from him. Even Josiah's dogs wanted something from him.

If he couldn't get out of that place on his own, if there was nothing he could do but wait—then, perhaps, so be it. Alba was good at waiting; that was all fishing ever was. All sailing ever was. All his life ever had been.

He would take his mother's advice and *wait,* on his own terms rather than someone else's. He would take the bone from his teeth. He would sit anchored until the water around him no longer frothed, like a shipping boat anticipating the arrival of its catch. Eventually, something would come. Alba would capture it then.

CHAPTER 9

Singing rang out from the water as early as that same evening, as soon Alba headed to the lantern for the night. Almost as soon as Eugene Michaels took his boat back to shore and left Alba alone.

Alba stuffed cotton in his ears as he went about his work. If the merrow wanted to negotiate further, it would have to come to him. He would not be lured. He would tell himself it was only the pipes on the outside of the keeper's quarters.

He could wait for an eternity for the creature to come to him, first. He would not be forced to bend against his will.

It felt like an active rebellion to ignore the singing for one day. Then an absolute mad thrill to ignore it for two. Doing his chores out in the open all while knowing pale eyes bore into him from somewhere on the water. He never turned to look. Not once.

Not even when the faintest singing crept past the plugs in his ears and made his insides tangle sweetly. Sweetly, but not enough to lure him. Barely enough to make him tingle all over, to tempt him into touching himself while alone in the lighthouse or after retiring to bed, just to ease the rooted desire spawned by the magic of the sea.

The merrow didn't need to know that. It never would. Alba

wanted the creature to believe the wickie it accosted on the shore was so unintimidated and unbothered that he forgot all about it by the time the sun rose. The thought alone was enough to make Alba smile madly and laugh under his breath all day long.

He minded his business. Minded his wounds between tasks, icing the swollen bruises on his face and body; grimacing every time he was reminded it was the skin of a fish on his shoulder, though admittedly intrigued at how what was once a gaping tear in his flesh healed over to hardly more than a faint scar in an impossibly short amount of time.

He slept with a knife under his pillow, the gun he'd stolen off that man's corpse tucked between the bed and the wall, as well as a few gulps of whiskey in his blood for the sole purpose of actually being able to drift off. Cotton remained jammed in his ears, making it impossible to think over the ringing.

He fixed the shingles on the roof without turning his eyes to the horizon, even as song beat against the cotton blocking his hearing; he attempted to trap something to eat off the side of the rocks rather than through the hatch, though caught only more warped creatures that resembled that impossible hollowed-out crab. He cleaned the cistern, washed the windows, painted the outside of the lighthouse, smoked while watching harbor seals snap teeth at laughing gulls swooping down on them.

Never once did he remove the plugs from his ears except when he bathed, which for the first time in his life, he indulged in more than once a week. Dunking his head just beneath the water, letting his ears fill with it, was a sweet respite from the scratchy fibers. More than once he nearly fell asleep in the tub's embrace, simply wishing for rest. A single moment of peace from the deluge of calling song.

He didn't know exactly when the luring magic ceased, only that a gust of wind while walking from the lantern to the house blew the cotton from one of his ears, and he didn't notice until all the way through the front door. It made his heart race in a panic, thinking of what might have happened had the merrow been out there watching, waiting to pounce—before risking another listen.

Realizing it was finally silent, except for the distinct sound of the pipes. He shakily pulled the cotton from his opposite ear, even, though stood ready to plug them back up again if a single note rang out from the sea. When nothing did, he even risked going about a few chores with reclaimed senses. Aware of every single sound that came, anticipating when the song would return.

For the rest of the early morning, it never did. Even into the afternoon, then the evening, all night long until sunrise, Alba never heard the merrow's song again.

He briefly thought it might be another sort of madness, feeling more agitated and anxious than ever with suddenly not a sound coming from the horizon. He soon searched while smoking rather than avoiding it. He stood on the edge of the rocks amongst the harbor seals and laughing gulls, staring out across the water as his hand trembled on the cigarette. Not remembering the last time he actually got a good night's rest, whether stuffed with cotton or while hearing nothing.

He swallowed back half of his bottle of whiskey that morning after finishing his post-tending chores, enough to force him to sleep. A little too much after rationing for the week prior, not realizing how quickly his tolerance had plummeted. Having to practically crawl up the stairs when it was time, laughing whenever he lost his footing and nearly tumbled back down them.

Collapsing into his cot, Alba didn't know exactly the moment he sank into the reaching hands of exhaustion, only that the dreams came quickly after.

He hadn't dreamt in so long, he nearly forgot he could—not expecting the eroticism that greeted him on the other side of closed eyes. Swirling with panting moans and roaming hands, pale merrow eyes bright like the moon while holding his gaze, smiling gently, handsomely, the softest hum emerging from the back of its throat as Alba leaned over the rocks to try and get a closer look. Hands that touched his chest, between his legs, until he was naked on his back in the grass, spread for ocean waves to lap against. Joined by a tongue, warm and slippery, against the inner parts of his thighs. He rolled his hips against the sensation, throwing his head back and tangling his fingers in silver-white hair upon groping for whatever it was eating him alive—

Alba's eyes snapped open, finding that very creature looming over him in the dim late-morning light.

Despite the alcohol still hooked in his muscles, he managed to lash out his arm, slamming a closed fist into the creature's perfect nose.

The merrow stumbled back with a snarl, giving Alba just enough time to reach for the knife under his pillow. He prepared to gut it open, but the merrow was faster, lunging and twisting the knife from Alba's grasp, both of them tumbling from the bed and crashing to the floor.

Alba braced to be crushed beneath the weight of a monstrous tail, straining his tired eyes to see where it coiled, only to be met with two naked, human legs, instead. It caught him off guard enough that the merrow managed to grab and slam him to the floor, making Alba wheeze, colors popping in his eyes as he flattened back with a gasp.

"What did you tell them, you little rat!" It hissed, voice deep but smooth, lacking the same honeyed enchantment of what Alba remembered from the first time they crossed paths. Still, Alba's insides fluttered, only for a moment, as if tousled by singing magic just through spoken word—but the lure wasn't strong enough to make his mind spin. The creature's fury poisoned its own charm. "There are traps all over this harbor now—tell me what you said to them!"

Alba couldn't help staring drunkenly at the moon-kissed face hanging over him, contorted in such rage there was practically icy fire burning in its eyes—and he suddenly burst out laughing. He didn't know why—perhaps if he wasn't so drunk, he would not have found any humor in being pinned beneath the same hands and mouth that already once tore his throat out—but he couldn't stop. It only made the merrow angrier, baring its teeth, but Alba just laughed more.

"You left your mark on me!" He finally said, thrusting out his stained arms to illustrate. "I didn't say a thing about you! But you left your mark on me! Took a bite out of me! You think they wouldn't notice?" He attempted to shove the merrow off, but the creature was stronger, heavier, and Alba was drunk, so his palms just smacked against clammy bare skin. "You wanted me to ask them about the rest of you—you mermaids, as if they would be expectin' you—yet you're surprised they've put out traps? Have you been feastin' on their fishermen? Or are you the reason all their wickies keep vanishing?"

"I was not the one dumping a body into the harbor only a few nights ago," the creature snarled back, taking a handful of Alba's hair, making Alba yelp before chuckling again. "If there is anyone they should be laying traps for, it should be you!"

Alba's evident lack-of-intimidation clearly bothered the merrow enough that its jaw never loosened, hissing every word through clenched teeth. Never realizing its poor timing as Alba would have been far more rattled any other time he didn't have half a bottle of whiskey in his stomach. Alba also didn't know how to say that he'd hoped the merrow would come, and had even been waiting impatiently for that very moment—though soon forgot all of that at the sight of a cock waving around between the mer-man's two legs. Far less intimidating than the tail from their first meeting. In his warm, floaty haze, Alba even reached down, nearly grabbing it and making the merrow pull back in surprise.

"You clearly have two strong, workin' legs," Alba said with a sarcastic smile, slurring his words slightly. "More than I've got. Why not go into town yourself and stop botherin' me?"

"You think I wouldn't have done that already if I could?" The mer-man hissed back. "You have no idea what will come if you make an enemy of me, so I suggest—"

Alba burst out laughing again. It took him a moment to gather his bearings back, shaking his head.

"An enemy of *you!* The likes of you! Please—I've met arctic seals more frightening than you. *Erk—*" he wheezed when a hand found his throat, pressing down, but the smile never left his face. "This—doesn't frighten me—either. You ever been—mast-headed? That's how I—broke my hip in the—first place. What about salted—after a floggin'?"

The merrow stared at him with a look of—disbelief. Like he truly could not fathom how Alba showed not a single flicker of terror even when pinned beneath him.

The merrow's handsome lips hung slightly parted as if on the verge of asking what the fuck was wrong with him—but instead, he just sat back. Straddling Alba's hips, he kept his hand on Alba's throat, the weight making Alba flinch for the first time as his bones shifted uncomfortably.

"What do you want?"

Alba gave the merrow a look, rubbing his sore neck, scales from the bandage on his shoulder flaking off under his fingers.

"What?"

"I said—" the man's jaw clenched in and out, muscles flexing in his cheek. "What do you *want?*"

Ah—that was what Alba had been waiting for. What he wanted. That shift in the tide, ebbing toward him rather than out of reach. That merrow, despite everything to say otherwise—was no different than any man.

"Lift your curse on me."

"No."

Alba expected that.

"You only want me to ask about them? Your missin' merrow kin? What makes you think they'll tell me anything? I've only been here a week. They'll answer me like any other tourist who's heard the stories—if they don't kill me for tryin', first."

"What stories?" the merrow snapped. "Don't tell me you yourself know where they've all gone—!"

"What? No!" Alba groaned, finally writhing as the hand returned to his throat. "Of course not. I only—know anythin' because my mother grew up here. Told me lots of things about the lot of you. God, you're heavy—"

"And what sort of things were those?" the merrow's eyes widened, a wicked, exasperated grin spreading over his face. "Clearly not enough, 'else you wouldn't be tempting me like this, wickie."

"Told me you were beautiful and stupid!" Alba snapped back. "Seems at least one of those things is right!"

The merrow's smile stretched as his hand tightened around Alba's neck again. Alba managed to thrust a knee up, smashing the bare cock between the creature's legs and making him wheeze. He nearly managed to kick the mer-man off entirely, but he recovered quickly, grabbing and shoving Alba back to the floor again.

"Why don't you tell me where she is too, hm? I'll give her a story to tell."

"If I knew where she was—I wouldn't still be here!" Alba shouted, flooded with emotion he didn't realize was tucked away so tightly. The words burst from him like igniting kerosene in a lantern too small to contain the heat. "Fucker—! If I knew where she was I wouldn't still be rottin' away in this shithole, would I!"

The merrow smirked, dark and satisfied with Alba's outburst—before it twitched, slightly. His hand remained pinning Alba on his back, for the first time pausing to look him up and down. From his red hair, to the tattoos on his skin, to the front of his shirt pulled open in the quarrel and exposing his chest. Clammy, sharp fingers trailed down the center of it, before his pale eyes flickered back up again.

"Then perhaps we share some common ground," he said. Calmly. Even a little bit tempting without so many words, but Alba knew, even in his inebriation, that there was merrow-magic at play when he spoke. Singing to him without song; luring him to listen. He did. He was too overwhelmed with other emotions to defend against it. "Were you supposed to find your mother here?"

Alba tried to keep his mouth shut—but the temptation to answer was too strong. Tugging at the back of his throat with the same luring draw as the tongue in his dream.

"Y-yes."

"Are you sure she didn't send you as a sacrificial lamb instead?"

"Yes!" Alba lurched up, but the merrow shoved him back down again.

"Well, then," he purred. Alba's heart raced at the sound, staring unblinking up at him. At his long silvery hair draped with pearls on strings, more adornments hanging down the front of his humanesque chest and back. In such a form, wearing such magic, he looked as human as any other man Alba had ever seen—but still breathtaking. Unsettlingly handsome. A beauty sailors crooned songs about, a creature to avoid lest they be tempted into drowning, even with two legs.

"If—Maybe if I can find out about your kin—will you help me find out where she is?" The words rushed out of Alba before the merrow could speak first. The merrow shoved a hand to Alba's mouth, silencing him before he could utter anything else.

"And how am I supposed to do that?" He asked. "I don't know anything about you or your mother."

"But—one of your kin might," Alba insisted against the pressure muffling his voice. "You could ask them—for me."

The merrow furrowed his brows like he had something to say to that, but didn't. His lips parted slightly like the sentiment sat right there on the tip of his tongue, but it was another long moment before he finally spoke. Still keeping his hand pressed to Alba's mouth.

"Perhaps."

Alba groaned, collapsing back to the floor in frustration. The merrow grit his teeth in annoyance, like he'd expected Alba to cry and rain gratitude down upon him with such a simple agreement. He added in a bitter tone:

"There are many things I don't know about this place any longer—but who knows who or what information will be found once someone starts digging. Me in the water and you on land. Be it my kin, or your mother who claims to know so much about us. Perhaps one of us may be able to find something for the other."

Alba sighed, but nodded. Realizing—perhaps that was all he'd be able to get without exchanging his life for more. And despite how thin that promise of help was—it was, at least, a promise of help. No matter how small, Alba was willing to accept anything he was given by that point of hopelessness.

"I'll even keep the drowned from bothering you any longer if it means you won't look so... *wild* the next time you go into town," the merrow went on. "If it'll help you earn the trust of the people there."

Alba should have argued the real reason he'd looked *wild* when last carried bleeding into the doctor's office—but something else caught his attention, first.

"The—what?" he asked breathlessly, a line of spittle trailing off his lips as the hand was finally pulled away. Though even as he asked, he thought he knew. He recalled that corpselike thing that'd attacked the merrow the first night they met, which then swept Alba into its arms and dragged him all the way back to shore. "Do you mean—those people in the water?"

"*People,* yes and no," the merrow muttered. He finally stepped off of Alba's body, and Alba reckoned with the height and size of him.

Broad, carved with distinct muscle over every inch of his anatomy, legs and torso and shoulders and arms all flexing with every movement. Had he not been so enamored by the merrow's face and hair and physique, Alba's gaze may have even lingered on the prominent length dangling between his legs, eyes only flicking back up again as the mer-man went on:

"Humans who die at sea take on many forms—sometimes sea

birds, sometimes wailing spirits, sometimes drowned corpses. By the sailor art on your skin, I would've thought you knew that already."

"How do you intend on keepin' them away?" Alba asked while sitting up, losing his train of thought as he scrambled for anywhere else but the man's body to look. Still tempted to scour every inch further out of curiosity. He was definitely too drunk to manage such a thing with grace. He was definitely too drunk to think he was capable of averting his eyes in the first place.

His face flushed again with inebriation and hot blood once fully upright, room briefly whirling around him and making him press a hand to his eyes to keep from being sick. He only glanced over his shoulder again at the sound of a heavy weight collapsing onto the squeaky bed where he himself had just been sleeping.

"I stay here, with you."

"Oh—absolutely not."

But the reclining merrow-man was already making himself comfortable, leg crossing over a knee, arms bending behind his head. Closing his eyes and relaxing naked on the blankets, hair spilling in a halo over the pillow and long enough to drape off the edge to curl on the floor.

"Do you have a name, at least?" Alba tried again. Wanting to maintain whatever grasp of control he had on that arrangement quickly slipping through his fingers again. The merrow sucked on his teeth, as if in consideration, eyes cracking open to gaze at the ceiling.

"Eridanys."

"Like the stars?"

Eridanys looked at him with a slight twitch in his brow, like it was impressive for Alba to know. Alba rolled his eyes, suddenly wondering how little a merrow could possibly know about the life of a sailor.

"Yes," he answered nonetheless. "The river, specifically."

"Well, I'm Alba," Alba answered. Eridanys pressed his lips together, parted them, then closed them again as if he wanted to *argue*, but then thought better of the effort. Perhaps by the way Alba looked at him with tempered annoyance. Still trying to digest exactly everything that'd come to pass since being forced awake by a naked stranger in his house.

Eridanys, the merrow who could sprout legs, but could not cross onto Moon Harbor's shores, perhaps because of the traps placed for him. Who might be able to learn information about Edythe Marsh's whereabouts if Alba was able to find where the other merrow who'd once lived in that harbor had gone. It was a long shot—but Alba didn't have much choice. He didn't have any allies, he didn't have any other leads or clues of where else to look.

None of that taking into consideration how the same merrow making himself at home in Alba's own bed had cursed him to remain in Moon Harbor until he did as he was asked.

"Eager to start?" Eridanys asked as Alba collected his work pants and shirt from where they were folded at the foot of the bed, braiding his hair over one shoulder and grabbing his cane.

"I'm not goin' back to town for a few days," he said. "You can stay until then if you really want to. For now, I might as well get to work for the day. I'll be in the lighthouse once the sun goes down later. Please don't eat any of my provisions in the pantry."

"What do you mean, won't be going into town for another few—! Come back here!"

But Alba was already hobbling down the stairs. No longer listening. Flushed with lingering whiskey and relief and silent gratitude to his mother for all the times she insisted patience would lure what he wanted to come to him. Perhaps the merrow Eridanys thought he'd caught Alba off guard—but Alba was just thrilled to finally have even a sliver of hope to cling to.

Chapter 10

ALBA DID NOT ACTUALLY EXPECT ERIDANYS, THE merrow, to still be in the loft overhead when he returned hours later for something to eat before retiring to the lighthouse. He especially did not expect to find him still fast asleep where he originally reclined.

He even paused at the top of the stairs, waiting to see the merman twitch, for his eyes to flicker open before sitting up and flipping his hair and accusing Alba of being so naïve to think he would let his guard down so quickly—but he didn't. The merrow —the man—remained motionless where he rested, save for the rhythmic rise and fall of his chest with each breath.

When Alba was sure Eridanys truly was asleep, he risked a closer look. Once again both impressed and off-put by exactly how beautiful he was; hair shiny and silvery, skin as smooth as an aristocrat's, though Alba could pick out the tiniest flickers of scales just beneath the surface. Especially over his cheeks, his jawline, even down to his collarbones and strong shoulders.

God—strong shoulders. Taut muscles over his chest, trailing down to additional ripples in his stomach. Alba's eyes traveled further, unable to help himself—before forcing his eyes forward again. At ease, at attention, as if called by his captain. He could not imagine a worse fate than the merrow waking to find the lonely wickie looming over him with eyes wandering a little too far.

He almost couldn't believe how easily the man rested, breathing deep and steady, eyelashes twitching like he dreamed. Eridanys was either so sure of himself that he felt completely safe closing his eyes and drifting off right there, naked, defenseless, in the home of someone whom he had no reason to trust—or, Alba realized as he picked out faint dark circles beneath the man's eyes, perhaps he was simply as exhausted as Alba was. He'd mentioned traps set around the harbor, after all. He'd mentioned looking for his missing kin, which Alba knew from his own experience to be draining. Physically, emotionally, mentally.

Alba pressed his lips together, exhaling a puff of breath to knock a clump of hair from his eyes. How ironic, for someone of the land and someone of the sea to meet in that same miserable place. Searching for those who were meant to be there waiting. Missing. Not a trace to be found. As if Moon Harbor had swallowed every one of them whole.

Leaving Eridanys to rest, a part of him sure the man would be long gone by the time the sun rose, Alba made his way back out of the house with a lantern in hand and a book tucked under his opposite arm.

He paused on the edge of the rocks to light a cigarette before cordoning himself off in the tower, breathing in a long drag of tobacco and sighing it back out into the evening sky. A sky as dark and cloudy as the morning and afternoon that came before it. It might really be all the way until the full moon again that he would get a chance to see the stars, to see the sun in the sky. God, what a miserable place.

As if to argue, the town's distant musical pipes spoke up, singing all the way out to where he stood on the rocks. The water lapped rougher against the stone, splattering the toes of his shoes enough that he frowned and took a step back.

He waited for the gust of wind to reach the lighthouse like it always did—but the smoke from his cigarette remained vertical toward the sky. Not a breath to disturb it. Alba glanced back toward the town, to the yellow-orange lights of their streets illuminated as the sun set. Alba inhaled another drag. The singing from the dark shore continued.

The smoke from his cigarette never moved.

ERIDANYS WAS STILL asleep in Alba's bed when Alba returned the following morning, dripping water on the floor from the rain that'd soaked him through on his way back.

It continued heavily against the roof as he climbed the stairs to the upper loft, shivering and eager to strip the cold shirt and pants off so he could crawl into whatever empty blankets he could find. Eridanys had promised to keep the *'drowned souls'* from bothering him so long as they were in agreement, and while Alba wasn't sure he believed it, he was just exhausted enough to try.

Unbuttoning his shirt, he couldn't help but let his eyes linger on Eridanys again, who hadn't moved an inch. Alba cleared his throat, kicked his boots off with excessive noise, but Eridanys still didn't stir.

For a moment, he genuinely thought the merrow might be dead, finally reaching out to touch his shoulder. Then to shake him a little more aggressively, only to yelp when a pale hand suddenly lashed out and grabbed his wrist, nearly breaking it in half.

"Easy!" Alba snapped, yanking his hand away as the man blinked away his disorientation. "You haven't moved in some twelve hours, you know. Do you need to be watered? Like a beached whale?"

Eridanys narrowed his eyes, but said nothing. Moving his feet over the side of the bed, he stood, stretching tall, elongating his chest and stomach, nearly sending Alba reeling when he caught himself staring.

"Christ—if you're gonna be stayin' in the house with me, you need to put some clothes on."

"Where have you been?"

"Tendin' the lantern. Like I already told you."

"And what will you do now?"

"*Now?* Now, *I'm* goin' to sleep." Alba finally pulled off his wet shirt, then decided if there was no qualm around nudity with the merrow, then neither was there for him, kicking off his pants and damp undergarments while he was at it.

He crawled into his own bed finally left empty, blankets chilled and slightly damp from the creature curled up beneath them prior. Unable to help the quiet sigh of relief through his nose to just be off his aching leg.

"Until when?"

"Afternoon," Alba exhaled, closing his eyes.

"What should I do until then?"

Alba glared over his shoulder. He'd left Eridanys to sleep like a corpse for practically an entire day and night, not a single question or comment from his mouth the entire time.

"Anythin' you like," he answered flatly. "Except eating my food and bothering the lantern. Oh—and killing me, in case you get bored."

"I wouldn't wait for your permission to kill you."

"*Christ.*" Alba muttered, returning his head to the pillow. Tired enough to not actually care if Eridanys decided to kill him. So long as he was deep enough asleep to not feel it, he wouldn't even notice. There would be nothing to grieve.

Before drifting off, Alba was aware of Eridanys hovering at his back. Just within reach of the bed, lingering for another few minutes before finally making his way down the stairs. Down the stairs, and out the door.

Alba listened to see if he could hear the sound of splashing, but he was already being taken by the tide of his own exhaustion to notice. Sinking into the smell of sea salt and rain and rich clay on his pillow.

. . .

It was the deepest Alba slept in a long time; deep enough that when his eyes finally opened again, he thought he was back in Welkin. He always slept so deeply, peacefully, on those rare single nights back home, knowing he was safe. Deep enough to help him survive constant restlessness until the next time came to treat him. Whenever that would be.

He never should have slept so soundly with a bloodthirsty mer-creature wandering around in the house, on the rock, wherever Eridanys went. A part of him even briefly thought it all to be a dream, but breathing in deep lungfuls of the unique scent on his pillow, his sheets, reassured him otherwise.

With every reminder, Alba ruminated a little more on why the merrow was so eager to come to such a swift agreement. Hardly any debate, hardly any real argument. Then to insist he remain in the house even while Alba worked; to even resist killing Alba while he slept, despite everything else saying he never should have had eyes to open again.

It had to be desperation. Alba knew. He knew how such a thing looked on a face, even one as inhumanly handsome as Eridanys'. Desperation that guaranteed Alba's safety, his ability to sleep soundly even with a demon of the sea wandering in and out of the shadows. Nothing, no one so desperate would kill the only thing they thought could save them.

Crawling from the warm bed with a groan, Alba pulled on his spare clothes. He carried the still rain-damp shirt and pants downstairs to drape over the steel bathtub to dry. He cut a piece of stiff bread, spread it with butter, and snagged a single piece of bacon from the cold box to fry in lard on the stove.

He made a pot of coffee—with a dribble of whiskey, to settle his nerves—all the while checking over his shoulder to see if the mer-man would come back through the door demanding something to eat for himself. Alba didn't know how he would answer, though it would probably sound something like *"go fetch your own food from the sea, like a dog."*

He stood over the sink to eat, watching rain speckle the glass, ears buzzing as wind made the distant flutes of Moon Harbor hum. Like the night before, nothing nearly as notable came from the ones on his own rock, making a mental note to check them for plugs. Maybe a seabird nested over them, maybe they were clogged with decades of brine to be chipped away. Maybe the storm had torn them off and thrown them into the sea.

A sweep of wind made something flicker from the side of the window, and Alba leaned forward to see for himself. His breath caught, spotting Eridanys standing naked on the edge of the rocks, gazing out over the water. His long white hair drifted behind him, swaying gently when it wasn't being whipped by the salty wind like a bride's veil; like something out of a sailor's warning. To see the shadowed cuts of muscle down his back so distinctly, Alba's face burned.

Just like it always had when his gaze lingered on some handsome crewmate drawing in pots alongside him on a boat, arms straining and jaw clenched in focus. Or when one would come up from behind and grab at a rope Alba clung to, arms encircling him, thinking nothing of it while Alba's entire body lit up like a lantern. Watching handsome mouths move when they chatted away in a bar, how lips parted over the rims of glass mugs. How tongues curled around fishbone while repairing nets on deck, holding the needles in their mouths while strong hands tightened knots over their laps.

Alba closed his eyes, shoving the rest of the bread into his mouth and forcing every thought out of his mind.

Christ—he really should find that man on the rocks some goddamned clothes.

Though—perhaps to test his own strength of will, to prove to himself he could keep on just fine not distracted by the mer-man's nudity—Alba decided to check the pipes on the house as his first chore of the day.

He braided his hair over one shoulder, pulled on his boots, then his jacket. Double-checking for the box of cigarettes in the pocket, he stepped out into the light rain, groaning internally when the air was more frigid than he anticipated. Lighting a cigarette helped, inhaling deep lungfuls before leaning against his cane with a sigh. The rain always brought throbbing to his hip, but the good night's rest helped ease the ache some. Helpful, especially that morning, with the ground as slick as it was.

He made his way around the house, pretending like he never noticed Eridanys perched on the rocks, scowling when he found the house's flutes and realized they weren't any more plugged up than the first time he heard them sing. They even weakly hummed as he approached, wind not strong enough to summon anything more profound. As if avoiding him, the lighthouse rocks, taking preference with the town and her music instead.

Despite his best intentions to ignore Eridanys entirely, Alba couldn't help but wonder if the man himself didn't know where the sound came from. Especially with how he stared out toward the foggy ocean rather than the town where Alba knew better. Watching him for another moment, Alba inhaled another drag, before sighing the smoke out of his nose and limping over.

"It's notched pipes on the buildings in town," he said, a sudden gust of wind grabbing his coat and flaring it out behind him. Eridanys barely glanced his way, before turning back toward the water. Alba insisted: "The wind makes them sound like singing."

"Why?"

"What do you mean 'why'?" he answered, holding the next inhale of smoke in his lungs before letting it drizzle from the corner of his mouth. He hadn't exactly questioned it any more than that initial thought when he first arrived. Just seeming like a strange quirk of the town, nothing more. "Maybe there's no reason. It's just a pretty sound, you think?"

"You must not be a sailor after all, if you think such things are *pretty.*" Eridanys said it with a wry smile, but still never looked Alba's way.

"Aren't they?" Alba grumbled. "I assume you're talkin' about songs of the sea, despite me never mentionin' them." He sucked on the cigarette in agitation. "I can be a sailor and still say the singin' of the sea is pretty. That's the point of a siren's song, isn't it? To be pretty. A merrow of all creatures should know that."

"A siren's song isn't supposed to *sound* like anything," the merrow argued with surprising conviction. "Sailors who hear it are meant to *feel* it, not *hear* any part enough to decide if it's *pretty*. That's what makes it so tempting."

"Sure, yeah. Same thing."

Eridanys looked at Alba like he thought he was something made just to be insufferable. Alba raised an eyebrow back, inhaling another drag and shrugging.

"I've never *felt* anything with a siren's song. Only ever *heard* it, far enough away to not do anythin' to me. And it was always just *pretty*. Maybe I just wasn't ever their type, hm?" He added sarcastically, but Eridanys' nose wrinkled in irritation.

"Their type of *what?*" he asked, argumentative as ever.

Alba shrugged again, not eager to get into the details of it with someone so keen on being contrarian. Knowing sirens with big breasts and pretty faces always drew the attention of men with the most neglected peckers. And while Alba was always equally neglected as the rest of them—it wasn't breasts he was interested in. He wasn't quite sure how to explain that to the mer-man next to him, though Eridanys seemed to come close to realizing on his own when he said: "You reacted to my song once. I saw it."

Alba stiffened. It was his turn to stare out at the sea, pretending to be lost in thought. Eridanys was right, but Alba wasn't going to let the mortification show on his face.

"Is that what that was?" He finally mumbled, flicking ashes over the edge. "I don't remember."

Eridanys scoffed again, ego bruised, having no idea the sort of thoughts Alba had been fighting since he arrived the night before.

Sleeping in Alba's bed and strutting around with his cock and ass and every other perfectly sculpted part of him on full display for someone as starved as Alba to see. Even the dream before that, and the constant fondling himself while resisting the song singing out to him in the days leading up to it—vowing then and there to never utter such embarrassing truths out loud.

"Can you hear it while in your lighthouse?" Eridanys asked next. "The sounds from the town."

"No, not really," Alba answered, more of a rasp than a full sentence.

"Then I'll join you up there."

Alba choked on an inhale, coughing up smoke that burned his throat. "Excuse me? That's not somethin' you—"

"It'll drive me mad otherwise," Eridanys said matter-of-factly, turning away. Toward the tower, where he went and stood to wait for Alba to join him. Alba could only wonder—how something as harmless as whistling pipes could *drive him mad.*

CHAPTER 11

Eridanys stood silent in the gallery while Alba wound the counterweights and prepared the wick. Staring out over the sea just like he had from the rocks, though that time not stark-naked as Alba had managed to dig a pair of old clothes from the house before meeting him at the lighthouse door. Knowing he wouldn't be able to function properly otherwise. Absolutely loathing how, despite the wool pants and linen shirt being slightly too big for him, they were still plenty flattering on Eridanys' frame.

"If you're gonna stand up there, at least be useful," Alba called out, amused by the look of disdain Eridanys threw back at him.

Handing the merrow a cloth, he explained how to wipe down every edge of the lens, even the parts that already looked clean enough. Despite the scrunched look on his face, Eridanys took the rag and did as he was told. Like he knew Alba would only nag him about something else if he didn't.

"You said I wouldn't have to hear the sounds from up here!" the man snapped after hardly a minute of hard work. "But I hear them clearly as ever—!"

"Wait until I light the thing, damn!" Alba argued in response, busy lubricating the gears and crank on the counterweights. "You won't hear a thing 'cept the clangin' of metal. Just be patient."

Eridanys scoffed. All he ever did was scoff, and something about it that time made Alba laugh under his breath.

He continued his own regular tasks wordlessly, until the silence itched at him, opening and closing his mouth a few times before finally deciding to take the risk. Figuring there wouldn't be any harm in asking.

"You... want me to find out what happened to your kin, that used to live in this harbor... Right?"

"Yes," Eridanys answered, hardly allowing Alba to finish speaking.

"Did there used to be a lot here?"

"Why would I ask where they'd gone if there hadn't been?"

Alba huffed, throwing Eridanys an annoyed look, though the merrow's back was turned.

"What makes you think the townspeople have any idea?" He went on anyway. "How do you know the mermaids didn't just go live somewhere else?"

"Mermaids," Eridanys muttered like it tasted bitter, but didn't offer an argument to Alba's statement right away. Long enough that Alba lifted his eyes again to look, seeing only tense consideration on Eridanys' expression as he thought about it. "If they chose to go live somewhere else, the townspeople would know."

"They must have had a pretty open relationship with them, then," Alba implied, reconfirming his own previous suspicions that the town was very aware of the mer-people in their harbor, and may even be protective of them. "Tell me again, if they're familiar with the merrow already, why you can't just go ask them yourself?"

Eridanys' silence returned. Alba gave him all the time he needed to concoct an answer.

"They... might recognize me," he finally muttered. Alba

raised an eyebrow, watching as Eridanys shook his head to himself, then ran fingers back through his long white hair. As much as Alba wished to ask why that might be an issue, he decided against it. It was unexpected for Eridanys to respond with any sincerity at all.

"These black marks on my skin, they're from your blood, aren't they?" Alba went on, not waiting for an answer as he'd already figured it out for himself. "When I was sittin' in the doctor's office after you attacked me, she asked if I knew where they came from. But the way she asked... well, I thought if I answered honestly, they might kill me on the spot. Anythin' to say about that?"

Silence again, but Alba watched Eridanys' face as he aggressively polished the lens. Brows furrowed, jaw clenching in and out in concentration.

"Perhaps you have the survival sense of a sailor after all," he finally admitted.

"Is that a compliment?"

"It might be best you don't admit to knowing about me outright," Eridanys went on, ignoring Alba's comment. He glanced sharply back to Alba, eyes narrowing. "Or that you've heard stories about the merrow who used to live here, either. Earn their trust and get them to talk to you about it first. And once they do, *do not* tell them where to find me, either. I'll be sure your curse stays so long as I'm alive."

"Implyin' they'd try and catch you if they knew?" Alba read between the lines. Eridanys' handsome mouth pressed into an annoyed line, turning back to his rag on the lens. "I assume that's why they put out the traps."

"A sailor's intelligence, too. An infant could have deduced that."

"Oh, *alright*," Alba sneered. "You really don't have to be such a prick all the time. You'll get wrinkles on that pretty face of yours."

"Why would my face wrinkle?" Eridanys snapped back,

animalistic, alarmed. "I'd never let you close enough to skin me in the first place—"

"Jesus *Christ, what?* Alright, I'm sorry, it was just a tease. I have no intention of skinnin' you." The thought made him subconsciously run a hand over the fish scales used to cover his wound, finding most of them flaked off. "They already know you're here, though, since there's merrow blood on my skin. I can keep tellin' them I don't remember how I got it, but who knows how long they're gonna believe it."

"Ask them yourself what the marks are, then."

"I suppose that's an idea. I'll be goin' back into town by the end of the week, so I'll see if I can learn anything while I'm there. Might see if they have any historical records, too, if I have the time..."

"Do you think they would have documented where my kin went?"

"Oh—maybe? I hadn't thought of that. I was mostly thinkin' how... they said they didn't know anyone by my mother's name when I first got here, but she was born here, like I mentioned to you before. Surely someone would have recognized it with a town so small... Thought it was strange for them to pretend like they didn't... and you haven't been here a while, either, which is why you don't know where your kin went, so you probably wouldn't know her yourself, either, would you?"

"Probably not."

Alba nodded, strangely disappointed despite already assuming that much.

"Good to know," he muttered. It was tempting to ask why Eridanys left in the first place, long enough for the other merrow to vanish without him, but again decided against it. Counting himself lucky once more to hold even a little bit of conversation without so much contention and snarling as previously.

Finishing his work with the gears, Alba dropped the oil brush into the bucket by his feet and pulled himself up the ladder into the gallery. Nudging Eridanys out of the way, he passively complimented the even polish on the lens, pulling the glass open to light the mantle inside. Eridanys watched in silence over his shoulder, shifting on his feet like he wanted to see better, even like he wanted to ask something, but never did.

Alba lit the wick, closed the panel and returned to the platform below to release the counterweights. The clanging of metal echoed throughout the tower, and the thing Eridanys wanted so badly finally came: the rhythmic grinding, clinking, heavy sound of the lantern coming to life, rotating and spilling her light over the sea, the dark beach, the town and trees in the distance.

Alba let her turn a few times before calling out *"how's that?"*, though no response came. Rolling his eyes, he went about making himself comfortable rather than insisting.

It was easy to lose track of time after doing it so many nights in a row, thoughts rich and swimming with all the things he'd seen and learned in such a short amount of time. Tempted to scribble it all down in the keeper's log just so he wouldn't forget, just so he could be sure he recalled every single detail to one day share with his mother. He could already imagine her face when he told her about it all, how she would grin before declaring *'of course it's true! Did you always think I was only making it up?'*

Too easy to lose himself in those thoughts, in imagining how those conversations with Edythe would go when they eventually found one another again. Easy enough that he didn't realize the first two hours had passed without a word from Eridanys until the counterweight banged at the end of its rope down below. Alba jumped, quickly closing the book in his lap and hurrying to rewind them, only then questioning what in god's name the merrow could be doing in the gallery for so long without a sound.

"Eridanys?" he called out, waiting a long moment before adding: "Answer me or I'm comin' up."

Nothing. Alba felt a sudden flash of concern, limping to the ladder. He announced Eridanys' name one more time, then pulled himself up the rungs and thrust his head through the open hatch to squint against the blinding light.

A few feet away, where Alba had first left him, Eridanys stood. Motionless, even as Alba said his name again, even as Alba reached to tug on the cuff of his pants. Eridanys stood still as a man turned to stone, staring thoughtfully into the rotating light.

"Eridanys!" Alba called again, before heaving himself all the way inside, using one arm to shield his eyes from the light and reaching for Eridanys' hand with the other.

The man barely shifted, only moving because he was touched, head remaining angled straight at the bulb. His eyes never moved, never blinked. It wasn't until Alba got all the way to his feet and put his hand out, fully covering Eridanys' eyes, that the merrow's ghost finally slumped back into his body. As if every inch of his muscles were tensed to the brink of shattering like glass, and only when the focus broke could he finally relax.

"What the hell are you doing!" Alba shouted over the noise, finally able to yank Eridanys toward the hatch. "You'll go blind in a minute! If it doesn't cook you alive first, you walking fish...!"

The words carried off. Eridanys didn't reply. He still hardly moved, except to obey Alba's tugging hands toward the opening in the floor. It forced Alba to bite back his annoyance, another pinch of worry plucking at the back of his neck when he considered something might actually be wrong. All the old stories of wickies going mad with charred eyes and bubbling skin rushed him, moving his hands and feet with more urgency as he guided Eridanys down the ladder. Telling him calmly to watch the steps, to move slowly. Eridanys obeyed. He did everything Alba said without complaint, without a word.

When Alba could no longer keep his hand over Eridanys' eyes, needing it to climb down himself, his breath caught at what greeted him from the depths of the merrow's pupils. A dull light glowed in the back of them, pulsating slowly in and out, an occulting light with the same characteristics as the lamp turning over their heads. Flashing like an animal's caught in the beam of a lamp, all while the rest of him remained motionless. Unresponsive. Dazed.

Alba stared at him in confusion, in more than a pinch of worry, whispering Eridanys' name as he didn't know what else to do. He swallowed back the new wave of concern, focusing on the task at hand.

Getting the man down the stairs. Back to the house. Somewhere he could lay down and close his eyes and rest, if that was what he needed. Creature of the sea or not, Alba didn't like the sight of it—like nothing he'd ever seen before, even in all his years on the water.

"C'mon," he said calmly, pushing those thoughts off. He put a hand on Eridanys' back, then moved it to his shoulder, then down his arm to cup under his elbow. "C'mon, come this way. The stairs are right here."

Eridanys' eyes lingered on Alba the entire time they went, expression lax, never scoffing or smirking or even sighing. Just watching him without seeing—being guided without knowing he ever followed.

On their way down the steps, for a split second, Alba grappled with the idea of how easy it would be to—what? Throw Eridanys over the railing? To kill him? To put an end to that nightmare almost as soon as it started, breaking the curse keeping him in Moon Harbor, to finally take his leave? It might be his only chance, with how subdued, pliable the merrow had suddenly become, hypnotized and obeying every command Alba gave him. All the way down the stairs, never taking his eyes away. Never taking his hand away. It would be so easy, and Alba would not have lost an ounce of sleep over it when all was said and done—

But his legs continued walking them out of the lighthouse, one hand holding his cane, the other holding on to Eridanys. They walked him through the dark rain outside, back to the house. Not to the rocks, not to where he'd tucked the handgun into a crook of the coat rack. Not where he'd hidden the dagger in the seams of the wall in the bedroom loft.

It would have been so easy; it wouldn't have been the first time he'd taken a life to save himself, even in that same house—but the thought of killing someone who clung to him with such blind trust, whether they were aware of it or not—made Alba's heart twist until he could hardly breathe. As if, should he look back another time, he would see his mother at the end of his arm.

Chapter 12

Like the first night he slept there, Eridanys hadn't moved when Alba returned the following morning. That time, though, Alba didn't know if he was truly just resting, or something else. He didn't know much about medicine, only what he'd gleaned over the years from watching other people, just briefly touching the merrow's forehead to check for a fever. Only somewhat sure that the clammy chill against his palm was normal.

He nearly pinched one of Eridanys' eyes open to check for the glowing light in his pupils again, but stopped at the last second. Not sure he wanted to know. Not sure if he'd only imagined it the night before. Not sure of anything, except how he hated feeling so useless.

How many people had he visited with his mother around Welkin growing up, struck with a fever or some other ailment that she eased so easily with herbs or just friendly company? *You can't rush someone into getting better,* she used to say. Just like she would've said to him in that moment, as he stood over his silent companion like a looming reaper. The thought made him hurry back down the stairs as fast as his cane could take him.

A storm brewing on the horizon left the sky dark enough that Alba needed a candle to light his way around the kitchen. He double checked the latches on windows, doors, even the hatch in the storage room that had been admittedly silent since Eridanys made his promise to keep the hauntings away. He had never been so unsettled by the stillness, the silence as much as that stormy morning. Even with the wind howling outside, making the flutes sing wildly, Alba couldn't help but feel restless in the quiet.

He went about his chores despite the weather, nailing the shutters closed on the windows just in case, climbing the stairs to the top of the lighthouse to fasten the vents shut so rainwater wouldn't spill over the lantern, checking the cistern and scowling when he found a dead gull floating inside. Fishing it out, he stared at the waterlogged creature for a long time, at its legs that were a little too long, at the bulge in the side of its neck that puckered with what looked like a cluster of young barnacles beneath the feathers. He carried it to the edge of the rocks to throw into the sea rather than leaving it to rot in the grass, then dumped all the remaining chalk he had left into the cistern to clean the water meant for bathing and drinking and cooking.

He didn't want to think about it, didn't want to dwell on how a gull found its way through the metal grate into the basin in the first place. Didn't want to think about how something similar had been mentioned in the lighthouse log books by a previous wickie. Perhaps Eridanys could only keep the haunts out of the house.

Alba checked on the silent merrow often between chores, sometimes calling his name from the bottom of the stairs and listening for a reply, sometimes climbing up to the loft to see for himself. Eridanys' eyes never opened, he never moved from how Alba first set him down on the pillow. Alba had to constantly remind himself that a chest rising and falling with breath meant even a catatonic person was still alive; and if Eridanys really was just sleeping, if he really was resting, that would be best for whatever had happened. Surely.

Just like all the times Edythe had put Alba to bed promising he would feel better by morning. No matter what kind of pain he was in. Did she also pace back and forth on the other side of the door, stepping in and out, listening to his breathing, whispering his name, again and again and again until the sun went down? Alba hurried back down the stairs when he realized he was no different, acting so foolishly for someone he had no reason to worry about so much.

Unable to sleep himself, Alba searched high and low for things to keep him busy until the sun went down. Until he could trudge off to tend the lantern and have no excuse for checking on the merrow asleep in his bed.

He was in the process of sorting through the thin offering of books on the shelf in the sitting room, checking for mold and tossing away any speckled with black spots, when he swore he heard a sharp breath come from the loft. It made him stop, straining his ears to listen, before getting to his feet and grabbing his cane to hobble to the stairs. He didn't have to call out that time, heart thumping when he spotted the top of Eridanys' silver head where the man sat up in bed.

Hurrying up the stairs, Alba barely managed a relieved *"It's about time!"* when the merrow lunged at him, shoving him down so fast it knocked the cane from his hand and sent it tumbling down the steps.

"Hey—!" He attempted, grunting as Eridanys slammed him back against the floor, fists gripping the front of Alba's shirt with impossibly tight hands, white hair tumbling over the man's shoulders and forming a foggy curtain around them. Alba's ears rang, still trying to gather his bearings, all while Eridanys' demands repeated clearer in his mind—

"What did you do to me!" He snarled, lifting and shoving Alba back against the floor once more. Alba clawed at his arms, fighting to find his mouth in all the confusion. "Tell me what you did to me before I rip your throat out!"

"Nothing!" Alba finally shouted back, managing to get a grip on Eridanys' arm with one hand, the other grabbing the front of the man's shirt to keep him pinned away. "I didn't—do shit to you, damnit! Get off me—before you break my leg again!"

He braced to be slammed back again, only cautiously opening his eyes when it didn't come. Eridanys still had him caged against the floor, unmoving, and while Alba expected anger on his face, fury that matched his voice—instead, the man's expression was tight with apprehension, with skepticism, eyes flickering over every inch of Alba in search of a lie. Wild confusion, like an animal waking in a trap and not knowing how to set itself free. But as the shock wore off, Alba saw past all of that, lurching upward suddenly and grabbing Eridanys' face as a surprise to both of them. Eridanys roughly shoved Alba back down with a hand on his chest, forcing the words from Alba's mouth:

"Your eyes are back to normal!" He exclaimed. Eridanys frowned in new confusion, furrowing his brows and shaking Alba by the front of his shirt as if he was talking nonsense. But Alba just threw his hand out again, grabbing a fistful of Eridanys' hair and forcing him to stay still so he could get a better look. That time, the merrow didn't snarl back in protest, just glared at Alba in annoyance.

"Thank god," Alba groaned, keeping his grip on Eridanys' hair but slumping back to the floor with a sharp laugh of relief. "I had no idea what I was gonna do if you were gonna be like that forever. Damn you!" He tugged on Eridanys' hair again, glaring at him, summoning a muted growl from the merrow in response. "What the hell were you thinking, starin' into the light like that! I've heard of men boilin' alive while even farther back! What in god's name were you thinkin'!"

Eridanys grabbed Alba's wrist before it could yank his hair again, but his eyes remained forward, boring into Alba as deep as the light had glowed in the depths of his own. Searching him, as if still convinced Alba was hiding something. Like he was trying to decide whether or not to answer—though the longer it took, the more Alba suspected even Eridanys didn't know what had happened to him.

Something about the rotating light was mesmerizing, Alba knew that much and would admit. The first time he tended to a lighthouse at sixteen, even he'd been prone to staring into its glow, especially after long stints without any sleep to keep his mind sharp. Perhaps Eridanys simply never had the wherewithal to know the dangers of letting it burrow into his vision and lay hooks in his bones.

"I dreamed the entire time." Eridanys surprised Alba instead, voice flat, low, like he didn't realize he spoke. Alba raised his eyebrows in question, finally pulling his wrist from Eridanys' grasp. Eridanys continued looking straight at him, a thousand miles away. "It took me back there, to that place where I... I thought all of this had been a dream, my finally coming back here... Boiled Neptune, what a relief, even to wake up to your ugly face..."

Alba scowled, finally sitting up and pushing Eridanys away. He almost said something equally insulting, but the words caught when he saw how Eridanys' hands over his knees trembled. Despite it, the man's expression hardened back to the same icy blades Alba had come to know, and Alba could only roll his eyes and turn away. He used the nearby bed to pull himself up, sitting on the edge of it.

"Can you still see?" he asked next, waving a hand in front of Eridanys' face. "If not, that's fine, I can help—"

"I'm fine," Eridanys growled, turning away and getting back to his feet. He brushed himself off, running fingers through his tousled hair before rubbing palms into his eyes. "I said I'm fine! Stop looking at me like that. I don't know what sort of dark magic that was, but I never needed your help, and I certainly don't need it now."

"You most certainly did need my help, and I gave it to you freely," Alba snapped back before considering if it was worth it.

Eridanys sneered, tearing his fingers through a tangle in his hair with clearly growing agitation.

"And what do you want in return, then? Since humans always demand repayment."

Alba frowned, then scoffed, then shook his head. He got to his feet.

"A 'thank you' would've been nice, but I see even that might be too much for a miserable creature like you. But you know what? The disdain you hold for the thought of me helpin' you is sweet. The next time you do somethin' stupid and need me to hold your hand and walk you out, I'll even do it again. Bastard."

He attempted to limp by, but Eridanys' hand lashed out, grabbing Alba's arm hard enough that Alba hissed.

"I do not take kindly to being baited," he growled. "Tell me what you want in exchange. I will not owe a debt to the likes of you."

Alba stared at him in disbelief, before yanking himself free and hobbling to the stairs.

"Pull your head out of your ass. That's enough for me."

"My head is nowhere near my ass!" Eridanys shouted back, but Alba was already making his way down the stairs, searching for where his cane had landed at the bottom.

Eridanys followed close behind, enough that he stepped on the back of Alba's heel, making Alba trip. He would have crashed to the floor below had a pale arm not lashed out at the last moment, hooking around Alba's waist and yanking him back upright again.

Breathless, Alba's heart pounded, muscles flooding with adrenaline as even that brief sensation of falling made memories rush past his eyes. Wavering at the top of a cold mast, beat by the wind and then a strong wave. Losing his grip, nothing to grapple for as gravity hooked into his ankles and tugged.

He clawed at Eridanys' arm, clinging to reality, before jerking away and hurrying to the bottom of the stairs where there was no more risk of falling at all. Eridanys watched him without another word, though Alba barely noticed. Avoiding eye-contact as he reached for his cane, hating how his hand shook, voice following suit despite his best attempts to keep the growing discomfort at bay.

"If—if you're feelin' as fine as you say, I have some other things you can do f-for me before I have to tend to the light. Or you can fuck off and leave me alone, if you like that better. I don't need your help either, y'know—"

"Then why ask—"

"Because I can't stand someone like you!" Alba shouted, finally spinning back to look at him. "Because you insist on stayin' in this house with me! And sleepin' in my bed! And gettin' in the way! If you can't even sacrifice a 'thank you' for how I kept an eye on you, then you can fuck off from the rest of what I've let you have! Either earn your keep or get out!"

Eridanys glared at him, muscle twitching in his jaw, tendons flexing in his neck.

"I could have let you fall," he said. "Just now. You would have broken your neck had I not caught you."

"Yeah," Alba answered. He said nothing else, leaving out the door for the fresh air. Tainting it with the acrid taste of cigarettes, three in a row as he leaned against the wall, letting those words echo in his head as he beat back whatever it was that made his whole body shake.

Considering all the things he could have snapped back in return, all the ways he could have killed Eridanys himself the night before, choosing instead to baby him—Alba learned his lesson to never do such a thing for anyone ever again.

CHAPTER 13

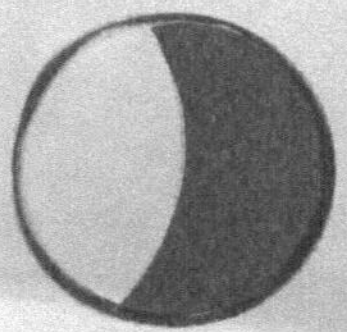

Eridanys was nowhere to be found by the time Alba returned to the house that next morning, and stayed gone for three days following.

On the first day, Alba thought *good riddance,* even as he laid awake swearing he heard gargling, disembodied voices whispering from beneath the floor. Even as shadows caught in the corner of his eye when he wasn't paying attention. As if the drowned souls surrounding the lighthouse rocks emerged more eagerly than ever the moment the merrow who'd kept them away was gone.

On the second day, Alba's annoyance reached a peak as he stewed over how insufferable the merrow-man could be, beginning when he found a string of pretty shells hanging from the lighthouse door upon leaving in the morning. Made worse when a fat fish was unexpectedly thrown into the storage room from the hatch, slicing Alba's hands with a thousand little cuts as he attempted to grapple it, still flopping, into a basket. Then the additional crabs tossed over the rocks into the grass, which he knew with certainty were from Eridanys by the additional strings of shells tying them together. Alba would have gladly thrown them right back if his stomach didn't growl so greedily the moment he had them in his hand.

By the third day, Alba's anger had subsided, leaving room for embarrassment over getting so emotional to start with. Eridanys even seemed to harbor similar feelings as the sea-gifts continued, manifesting as more strings of pearls, more fresh fish and crab, then a new cane that looked suspiciously stolen straight from someone on shore. Admittedly, the thought of some poor old sailor walking on the beach being robbed of their cane by the sea made Alba laugh, but he still tossed it back while calling out for Eridanys to take it back.

On the morning of the fourth day, Alba waited on the edge of the rocks for Eugene Michaels' boat to reach him. Hoping that's what the signal light from the harbor office the night before meant, knowing he was going to run out of food soon enough even with Eridanys' occasional offerings.

"If you think standing there looking pathetic will get me to ask what's wrong, you're mistaken."

Alba jumped, searching the water until he found a moon-white face scowling up at him. He raised an eyebrow in question, before realizing what the merrow meant.

"Oh," he said. "I'm not here waitin' for you."

Eridanys scoffed, rising out of the water to rest his elbows on the rocks.

"You don't have to lie. What other purpose would you have to..." he trailed off, following Alba's finger as it pointed toward a distant rowboat headed their way. The merrow's long tail swished under the water in agitation.

"Why bother! You know you can't leave the town—"

"I'm goin' for supplies. Remember? I told you about—"

"Why haven't you been eating what I brought you?"

"I have. It's not enough. But thank you for the offerings."

Eridanys scoffed again, just like Alba expected him to, making him smirk in reply.

"S'not so hard, see? Sayin' thanks."

Eridanys' white tail thrashed a little more, making the water bubble.

"You should thank me for keeping the drowned souls away even while I wasn't there."

"Thank you." Alba decided not to mention how some still got through.

That annoyed the merrow further, for some reason only god knew, muttering and avoiding Alba's eyes.

"When will you be back?"

"Around sunset, probably."

"Then I will watch the house while you're away."

"Alright. Thank you."

More agitation. Like he'd emotionally prepared for a bigger fight. Alba teased a little further, adding: "I'm sorry for snappin' at you the other day, by the way. Was childish of me."

"Good!" The tail whipped back and forth hard enough to make the water lap against the rocks. "And I am sorry for leaving!"

"Alright. Thank you—"

"And I am sorry for not being more grateful! For your help! *Thank you!*"

"You're—"

But Eridanys plunged into the water, making Alba choke on a sharp, surprised laugh. He watched the faint glow of the moonlit creature roll and writhe deep underneath, swimming fast in a dozen circles before surging back up to the surface again. Looking more agitated than ever, like uttering a single one of those words made bugs crawl under his skin.

"I would like to sleep in the house at night again!"

"Alright."

"And I will earn my keep! Like you insisted the last time."

"Sure—"

Eridanys dove back under, swirling around a few times before emerging again.

"I will wait for you in the house while you're away. Until sunset. I won't argue about it."

"Alright."

"And I'll do as I please while I'm in there."

Alba narrowed his eyes. "You will not."

"I'll do as I please," Eridanys snapped. "I'll crawl out of the sea and rip your head clean from your shoulders if I wish to!"

"Get a move on, then, if you really want an audience."

Eridanys glanced toward the arriving boat a second time. His jaw clenched tight when he turned back again.

"In the general store, if you find something called 'licorice,' bring it for me."

"Wh—Excuse me?" Alba balked. Ignoring the fact a merrow had just asked him for candy, he was more put off by how Eridanys would ever think he'd be willing to do a favor for someone so goddamned insufferable. "I'm not using my already-limited change to buy you some overpriced sweets. Especially when I already know you won't be grateful."

Eridanys hissed at him, tail fin splashing again in the water. "After everything I've been through for you—!"

"You've done nothin' but be a pain in my ass!" Alba snapped back. Eridanys' face contorted in fury, tail thrashing like an agitated cat. Alba glared back at him just as long, before finally rolling his eyes. Sighing.

"I'll bring you a snack if I get a chance, alright? Don't get your hopes up. You better thank me later if I do, too."

"Then do as we agreed and learn what you can about my kin as well, will you? Unless you insist on being a useless—"

"Another word and I'll fry you."

Eridanys grumbled something in retort, but swam off anyway. Alba scowled the entire time, all the way up until Eugene rowed into reach. He asked what the look on Alba's face was for, but Alba shook his head. It was only the sea driving him mad.

Alba didn't miss how Eugene's eyes flickered to his arms more than once while rowing back to shore, though he never once mentioned the marks first. Alba almost wished he would, especially after the conversation he had with Eridanys in the lighthouse.

Warned to not mention outright he'd seen a merrow in the harbor, warned to not be too forthcoming with anything he knew, all the while knowing he couldn't pretend to not know anything forever. Especially if he wanted to figure out where his mother was, if she was coming back, if the people there were only pretending not to know her for any reason other than protecting her while she hid from the Warrens... None of it having anything to do with the newest merrow-shaped burden on his back.

God—Alba needed a drink. Maybe the bar was the first place he'd start once they arrived.

"Oh," he said upon remembering, patting around his coat pockets to find the cigarette cards he'd been holding onto. He handed them to Eugene, who raised an eyebrow in question, but still politely accepted them. Alba cleared his throat. "Erm—for your son. Last time you said he collected them?"

"Oh, right!" Eugene laughed, and Alba relaxed slightly. "'Scuse me, mind's not quite what it used to be. That's awful thoughtful of you, lad."

Eugene went back to rowing, letting Alba's mind wander as he watched. Letting the rhythm of the boat sedate him, breathing in the fresh air, losing himself in the sound of the water lapping against the boat.

He would never admit it to Eridanys, especially after the snide comment that morning, but Alba actually had scribbled down ideas for where he might find information about the merrow that used to fill that harbor, as well as where he might find information about his mother. Town hall, where there might be birth records, or at least some sort of family record, as well as historical town documents; around the shipyard, or perhaps in the bar, where some fisherman or another may be willing to chat about the town stories or myths in exchange for a drink.

If all that failed, then perhaps giving Eugene Michaels all of his spare cigarette cards would be enough to earn good favor and a history lesson, or even just to question if the old man knew anything about the marks on his arms. *'I've sailed a little more than a decade and never seen anything like this, what do you think it might be? Some kind of seaweed? Squid ink? I know some jellyfish stings can leave a man marked for the rest of his life...'*

It sprinkled rain as they reached the dock, and Eugene hobbled off to tend to his own errands after agreeing to meet again later that afternoon. Alba, meanwhile, lingered, silently counting the boats that floated in place compared to the vacant spots he was sure he'd seen occupied upon first arriving. Fishing boats, trawlers, doggers, dinghies that likely left at the crack of dawn, where they'd stay working on the horizon until the sun set.

He wondered if they often caught the same sort of deformed catch he'd found in those crab pots, or if that curse was isolated to the lighthouse rocks—and upon spotting a group of people seated by the dock, he realized that was as good a place to start asking questions as any.

"Where can I buy some fresh catch?" He asked the cluster of old folk sitting on a circle of barrels off to the side of the dock, repairing a haggard net using fishbone and spun fibers. Interspersed were silvery threads as white as their own long hair piled into bundles on the backs of their heads, clearly in no mind to pluck out any of themselves that fell victim to the working circle.

All four of them looked up as Alba asked, but only one woman bothered to answer. The reply came with a scoff.

"Don't think you could right afford it, lad, even with that hefty wage Mr. Michaels offers 'ya."

"What d'you mean?"

"Anythin' pretty caught in a net goes straight to bein' packed up and shipped off for sale," she spat. It was unclear if the vitriol was meant for Alba or something else. "If'n you want a fresh fish dinner, you either catch it yourself or barter for scraps."

Alba let those words linger.

"Sorry to hear that," he said. A few eyebrows quirked in

curious reply. "Waters get overfished? Can't even pot a good crab out at the lighthouse."

"Somethin' like that," another muttered, given a look by his neighbor.

"S'nothin' to be done about it," the first woman said with a sense of finality. "Go'n shop the general store like the rest of us. They've got plenty to eat. Chopped fish in a tin, too."

"Thanks," Alba said, though didn't turn to leave right away. Over the heads of the netting circle, a row of silver pipes hummed against a mild sea-breeze, and a different member of the circle noticed him looking. Her face was gentler, rounder, hair draping in a long white braid down the center of her back and pinned from her eyes with clips donning misshapen pearls.

"Don't mind the pipes, lad," she said, voice friendly. "Nothin' more than an attempt to lighten the mood in this dreary place. Keeps overzealous fishers from goin' too far out at sea and gettin' lost, too. Always know which way to come back home."

"Oh," Alba said with a smile. "Definitely a prettier sound than foghorns. 'Cept when they sound like singin' voices out at the lighthouse; reminds me of when I was sailin' up north—"

"Ain't no singin' in this place," another man grunted. "A good sailor knows better than to chatter about sea-songs this close to the water, too. I'd mind myself better if I were you."

Clearly meant to end the conversation, salty enough to make any other young person clam up in embarrassment, Alba just kept his polite smile.

"Considerin' that fountain in the middle of town, I thought you folks would be more welcomin' to singin' mer-folk. Aren't they supposed to be good luck? Grantin' wishes and all that?" Said as innocently as he could conjure, in the tone of any other tourist who wasn't trying to stir trouble, who didn't know any better than the common stories told about mermaids and fisher-men. The old man grunted, none of the rest of them saying anything else at first, though all shifted uncomfortably between one another.

"Big difference b'tween sirens and merrow, lad," the woman with the kind face finally responded. "Never met anyone who did dealin's with either and won out in the end, though."

"That's enough, Elena," another one nudged. "Don't go fillin' the boy's head with fantasies."

"Bad luck to chat about merrow close to the water," the man who warned about the singing reiterated.

"Sorry," Alba interjected again. "Not tryin' to bring misfortune on you. Just bein' friendly."

"Go on and get friendly with the store b'fore they sell out of tinned fish."

That was the gentlest insistence Alba was going to get, he knew, a part of him also reassured that learning anything about the merrow of Moon Harbor without drawing too much attention was going to be as difficult as he originally thought.

He wouldn't push his good favor, nodding and wishing them luck with the net. A chorus of mumbled goodbyes answered, and he had to swallow the sigh at the back of his throat as he turned to limp away.

Alba got the drink he wanted at the bar, then a second one, then had enough alcohol-induced charisma to smile a little too big at the tall, rugged, broad-shoulder bartender who just gave him a wary smile in return. Had Alba not already had a list of things to do while on that side of the shore, he might have stuck around to ask where the keeper got such nice alcohol from. How he kept his arms so big. If he heaved kegs and crates of rattling bottles all by himself. It'd been a long time since Alba had let himself swirl in thoughts about a handsome stranger, only clamping his mouth shut again when he nearly bragged about the big, strong fish staying with him out on the rocks.

Thankfully, the tiniest part of him still sober swiftly scruffed the nape of his neck and compelled him off the barstool, toward the exit before he said anything truly idiotic.

He channeled his nervous energy into wobbling over to the modest town hall across the road. Inside, a single attendant sat behind a desk, looking surprised, then suspicious, when Alba stumbled in. Alba spoke with more confidence than even he expected, asking if there were any historical records for the light-house as he wanted to know which parts made up the mechanisms in case he needed to order any spares. The man working the desk looked him up and down, perhaps seeing his flushed cheeks and slightly wavering balance, finally exhaling an exasperated breath and motioning toward a back room with a hand-written label reading *records* over the door. Alba thanked him, limping his way in and closing the door behind him.

Knowing he shouldn't be too liberal with the amount of time he took, Alba searched the single long bookcase running the length of the wall. The room was hardly more than a broom closet, moody daylight through a window in the ceiling offering just enough visibility to finger through the volumes.

Historical building records; shipping registers; fishing license records. When he finally thumbed over one labeled '*Births, Deaths, Marriages*', he pulled it free, only to groan internally when the names inside resembled handwritten parish records more than actual organized documentation. Without anything in alphabetical order, he was forced to skim lines as they were writ-ten, having only a general idea of when his mother was born.

Not knowing Edythe's maiden name, Alba could only go by her first name, though quickly came up short. There were a handful of births associated with parents either too faded by time to read or intentionally scribbled away, which made Alba uneasy, though he did everything he could to avoid falling down a drunk mental-spiral of why his mother's might have been one of them.

Flipping back another number of pages, a different name surprised him, making him pause and smile to himself: *Edward Marsh*. Alba always knew his father was also from Moon Harbor, that he and his mother had run away together after being sweet-talked by the Warren Sailing Company to move to Welkin and work under their flag. But that was the first time Alba had seen anything in writing that proved the man ever actually existed. More than just someone Edythe talked about while Alba laid in bed, under the the headboard painted with smiling mermaids who watched over him while he slept.

Seeing Edward's name gave Alba another idea, flipping to the *marriages* section to see if his mother might have been mentioned there, instead. When he did find Edward Marsh's name on a line —Alba's heart thumped in confusion when, sure enough, Edythe had been freshly scribbled out right beneath him.

A knock came at the door, and Alba slammed the book shut in surprise. He took only half a second to recompose himself before shoving it back onto the shelf, gathering his cane and going to the door. He didn't meet the man's eyes as he hurried by, just thanking him for his time. Wanting some fresh air. Trying to outrun the spinning confusion that nipped at his heels on the way out.

He nursed another two drinks at the bar, then did as he was meant to and bought foodstuffs and other supplies at the general store, including a shoulder bag to stuff it all in. Also including three more boxes of cigarettes, already tapping one out of the box before he even made it back out the door.

Alba wouldn't think about why they would have scribbled Edythe Marsh's existence from their town records. He wouldn't wonder whether she'd been purged before or after she tried to return, and whether or not it really was a lie when they said they didn't know anyone by her name when Alba first asked.

Maybe they truly didn't. Maybe they were the ones who struck her from the page.

He wouldn't let himself dwell on something else that hadn't occurred to him until that moment, either—that, despite how vague Edythe always was with revealing where she came from, there was likely some record, somewhere, of her and her husband

Edward first being recruited for the Warren Company. There was a chance someone, somewhere, would think to check Edythe's hometown to look for her, or Alba, or the both of them.

How, even if Moon Harbor had gone to such lengths to hide itself away, there might still be one recruiter or another who remembered how to find it. How that might have been how the first of Josiah's dogs ever thought to check the lighthouse for Alba at all. How, though they seemed to have left after that night, the other handful of men who came after would know how to get back and possibly where to find and surprise him again sometime in the future.

Christ—Alba burned through his cigarette in record time, swiftly lighting another right after it. Hoping it didn't ignite the thick vapors of alcohol on his breath with every inhale.

Closing his eyes, Alba wiped a flush of nervous sweat from his forehead. Perhaps he needed to be a little more honest with his merrow companion when he returned to the lighthouse; to tell him the extent of the danger he was in. How there was a very good chance if Alba was found and swept up off the road, he'd turn to salt in the woods by Eridanys' own curse without it ever being his fault. That wasn't fair. Eridanys would see how that wasn't fair, wouldn't he?

Considering the man's apparent obsession with debts and gratitude and apologies, Alba might have to take him something to offer in exchange for the plea of leniency. Anything, even the licorice he previously asked for, would be better than nothing.

Pushing off from the wall, Alba wasn't paying attention, and nearly walked straight into a new bride passing by—before realizing it wasn't a bride at all, but one of those people he'd seen spreading salt in the woods when he first arrived. They muttered a stiff apology and hurried away to catch up with three others making their way up the road, a basket of salt under each of their arms.

"They never stop anymore, why not?" One of them asked under his breath as they went, adjusting the opaque veil draping from pins on the back of his head. The basket of salt over his arm overflowed, sprinkling along the road behind them, and Alba's interest piqued. He waited just a beat longer before taking silent pursuit, salt-bearers none the wiser to the ghost on their heels

"... Mother said... traps... wickie washed up... marks," another answered, words muffled by humming flutes as they passed by. "Says... singin' for... out there..."

When one of them glanced over their shoulder, Alba halted to gaze into the window of what appeared to be an abandoned book-shop, though there was nothing through the dirty glass to the other side. The salt-scatterers didn't seem to realize, though Alba's curiosity ticked higher. Replacing the previous panic with thoughts of salt, singing, the mention of traps only he knew were for Eridanys.

Alba's heart thrummed. He waited for the salt-bearers to continue up the way, before following again. Not eager to make the climb on his stiff leg, but curious for what else he might learn.

The return of sprinkling rain dampened Alba's hair as he breathlessly reached the top of the hill, far enough behind those salting the earth that they forgot all about him. Fog rolled over the road from the wall of trees ahead as if to keep him from going too far off course, chilly breeze nipping at him under the cuffs and collar of his coat and making him shiver.

Turning off the main road, he didn't want to be noticed poking around anywhere he had no reason to be, while also keenly aware that he'd eventually reach the edge of Eridanys' curse and buckle into salt if he wasn't careful.

The worn footpath he followed through the grass and up another muddy incline eventually led to the gates of an old ceme-tery, and he stopped to catch his breath while peering inside. Headstones emerged from the rain-saturated earth like crooked teeth, most leaning to the east as if it was the wind's preferred way to blow. Long, tangling sea-grass carpeted most of the area, swal-lowing some headstones at the base and completely obscuring others that were flat markers rather than upright slabs. It was impossible to see exactly how far the cemetery stretched over the clearing, though Alba could tell by the distant sound of water that it must have halted suddenly over the edge of a cliff to the sea. He had no intention of wandering that far.

Pulling open the squeaking gate, Alba whispered a polite greeting to any souls who'd noticed his arrival, not wanting to catch them unawares. Not needing any more restless spirits following him back to the lighthouse quarters where he was already being harassed enough.

Searching for another path that would take him back toward the trees, he focused on the sound of distant bells, listening for the singing he recalled from the first time he witnessed the salt-ritual while arriving on the main road.

Eventually he found what he was looking for—a path that cut through the cemetery toward the woods, though he was surprised with how eagerly it shot straight into the heart of the forest. A single string of bells on rope dangled across the pathway at the entrance, dancing back and forth in the breeze as if inviting him for a closer look.

Fully aware of the moisture in his mouth, determined to turn back as soon as he felt the first sense of his tongue shriveling, Alba approached the jingling garland. In the distance, he caught the sounds of the salt-spreaders' chorus, closing his eyes to picture them. Wondering again what the purpose was of salting the forest, wondering if Eridanys would know, wondering if mentioning it would be enough to satisfy the merrow until Alba was able to return to town again in another week. A part of him knowing it really wouldn't be.

Alba bit his lip. He turned his tongue over in his mouth, determining he still felt completely normal. The merrow's curse hadn't taken hold of him, yet. He could step a little further in, to see if he could spot the salt-spreaders. He could faintly hear their song, after all, which meant they couldn't be too far.

He took a few steps, then a few more. Moving carefully, keeping every sense focused on his tongue, his hands, waiting for the moment he felt the first tingling of the curse taking hold. He walked to a tree flowering with white clusters of petals, pausing alongside it. Glancing over his shoulder, realizing it wasn't nearly as far as he first thought, he breathed a sigh of relief. The string of bells was still close enough that he could hear it in the breeze. The humming of the fluted pipes in the town were still rich and crisp in his ears.

He went a little further, stopping alongside a fallen tree speckled with mushrooms growing from a carpet of moss. Over his shoulder, he still hadn't gone much farther than he thought. He felt fine. No curse plucked at his insides, yet.

He went a little farther. Following the distant singing, searching for white-veiled ghosts salting the earth. Still hearing the whistling pipes, the sound a welcome companion between the trees. Urging him farther with its reassuring closeness. A little farther. A little farther.

"What pretty hair you have."

"Too bad about the color."

Alba turned quickly, but there was no one. Only the trees in every direction. His heart thumped at the base of his throat, trying to decide if he'd only imagined it—when something trailed up the nape of his neck into his hair. He whirled back again, holding his breath when still nothing was there to greet him.

"Who—?" The word raked painfully up his throat, tongue suddenly swelling dry and thick in his mouth. He stumbled backward, turning quickly to take a few steps back in the direction from where he'd come—but instead of the hard path behind him, he tripped over an upturned root, crashing to the ground.

Gasping, he clambered backward, kicking out his legs and only tangling himself further in roots and thorny brambles. He was—in the trees. Deep within them, far deeper than he thought, thick enough to block the rain and light overhead.

Searching for the path—it was gone from where he'd only just seen it. Searching for the mouth of where he'd entered—it was barely a spot of light in the distance. All the while, he nearly crumbled into dust as the merrow's curse clutched him hard and fast. But he—he hadn't—

The path had just been there behind him. He'd seen it, he'd watched it the whole time—

His ears rang. Musical laughter sounded out around him, filling him with the same sickening lure that Eridanys' voice first did, realizing with a twist of his gut that he could no longer hear the salt-scatterers in the distance.

Sweat broke out on his skin, shirt clinging to his back as he attempted to rush back to his feet, only to get caught in the loamy earth and dragged down again with the twist of his leg. Gasping, mouth dry and breath dusted, he threw out his hands, groping the undergrowth in search of his cane, giving up in favor of crawling. Desperate to escape to where there was just the smallest peek of the horizon through the trees. Impossibly far away. For him to have walked that far, without feeling a thing, without realizing, listening to the song of the salt-bearers—

Salt-bearers, he realized with a thud of fear, that may have always been too far away to hear all along. Fluted pipes that were too far away to truly be heard so clearly all around him—pulling at his insides in a nauseating mix of horror and temptation, nearly the same as what he felt with cotton stuffed in his ears against Eridanys' song. Insides squirming with the faintest desire to be taken and touched, caressed, fondled by any hand that may emerge from the trees, not unlike all those times left flushed and itching for touch on the rocks—

A song from the woods—a song of the sea—

By some miracle, Alba reached the end of the path of his hands and knees. He tumbled out of the trees just as unseen hands groped at him, grasping at his hair, the back of his shirt, attempting to drag him back before he could go.

There in the grass—was his discarded cane. Never in his hand, despite how sure he was of it as he walked. No—as he was lured. He was lured, no differently than a man lured by the sea—

Clutching the cane into his chest, Alba knew he had to move

faster, further, lest that song hook into him again—but Eridanys' curse was only just loosening in his chest, allowing him to breathe, to piece thoughts together—

Whispered invitations, soft laughter emerged from the trees again. Cooing at him. He risked a strained glance back over his shoulder.

Speckled between the shadowed trees, an audience of pale faces peered at him with expressions ranging from curiosity to disappointment. He may have thought them only ghosts—but every single one shared a resemblance to the ethereal, moonlit beauty of the stubborn merrow who haunted the waters around the lighthouse.

Something deep in the reaches of Alba's subconscious knew even before the thoughts pieced together—that those pale visages might have been exactly who Eridanys was looking for.

CHAPTER 14

ALBA SLIPPED IN THE MUD MORE THAN ONCE ON HIS way out of the cemetery, down the footpath. He finally reached the top of the road and hurried into town dirty with wet grass stains and sweat and his ears ringing loud enough to practically deafen him.

"Mr. Michaels—!" he exclaimed upon stumbling into the harbor office. Hoping to return to the lighthouse as soon as possible—but every word slipped from Alba's mind as he met the old man's eyes where he stood behind the desk just inside.

Eugene had been interrupted by the door thrown open, mid-conversation with a stranger who had their back turned to Alba. But even without seeing his face—Alba knew. Alba didn't have to see. Just like every other threat he could recognize by the mere proximity of them, he knew. Though that threat, in particular, made his blood freeze in his veins.

Blonde, bearded, broad. With a smile that would chill Alba's blood from miles away, freezing him where he stood, not even jackrabbit instincts kicking in despite the urge to bolt. Alba knew better than that. He'd been trained better than that.

The only thing to surprise him was how even Marco appeared caught off guard as he turned, looking Alba up and down while his surprised smile never faded. Clearly not expecting to find a familiar face in such a remote, isolated place. Confirmed when he spoke, tone as arrogant as ever.

"Well," he said, "would you look at that. Never thought I'd cross my lost little pup while running errands."

"Don't bother the lad," Eugene attempted, and Marco glanced over his shoulder with an eyebrow raised. Silencing the man in an instant.

Eugene offered Alba the briefest look, though Alba didn't know if it was in question or pity. Alba never took his eyes from Marco long enough to see it clearly. A part of him wasn't even convinced it was real—wanting nothing more than to blink the man away. Only his imagination. Perhaps to blink himself awake —only a nightmare. But no matter how many times he tried to will Marco away, the man never vanished.

"This the one you've got tendin' your light?" He went on, nodding his chin toward Alba.

Eugene didn't answer outright again, just stammered a few words, foolishly confirming without meaning to. Marco smirked again, stepping from the desk suddenly to grab Alba by the arm and yank him toward the door.

Alba jerked back on instinct, petrified instantly with the look of warning Marco gave in response.

"You and I need to have us a chat, little prince. C'mere."

Alba was ashamed to freeze up, trying to find any of the courage he once had in Belmar's fish market, at the ferry station when he broke free of Marco's grasp the first time—but even without thinking it, he knew. There was nowhere to run in a town that small, with the water on one side and a forest rife with singing voices and a curse of salt on the other.

He stumbled when his cane tangled in his feet, dragged from the harbor office and around the side. Down the muddy alleyway alongside the neighboring building, where Marco shoved him into the wall and took a step back. Pulling a box of cigarettes from his pocket, he lit one, before glancing Alba up and down.

"What are you doin' here?" Alba asked before he could stop himself. Marco quirked an eyebrow, before nodding toward him in expectation.

"Take off your coat."

"What?"

Alba flinched when Marco raised a hand to backhand him. He quickly shirked off the jacket without another word.

"Push up your sleeves."

Alba did. Marco grabbed his arm with a rough hand, turning it over, leaving Alba to wonder in apprehensive silence what he could possibly be looking for. Eventually, the man inhaled a long drag of tobacco, then plucked the cigarette from his lips and pressed the hot end into the underside of Alba's wrist.

"Mr. Michaels said the new wickie had some strange marks show up on them," he said with a curt smile. Alba's heart thumped nervously, eyes flicking down to the merrow bloodstains between his tattoos. "Says you don't know where they came from, either. But you know better than to lie to *me*, don't you, Albatross?"

Alba did know that—but his mind was too busy spinning, wondering whether or not even Marco knew what they were, or if he really was asking. He nearly risked a made-up story about an ink squid or residue from repairing shingles on the roof—but then recalled another thought he'd had hours earlier. Just before following the salt-scatterers up the road. Before finding himself lured into the trees without realizing what sang to him.

That realization after finding his father's name in the town's register, knowing he was recruited to sail for the Warrens by a nameless, faceless pair of recruiters that went town-to-town just like all the others. How there was likely someone, somewhere, who knew Alba's mother and father were both from Moon Harbor, and it wouldn't be so out of the question to search for both Edythe and himself where she had been born and grown up.

But more than that—depending on who knew what, there was the additional chance someone apart from Alba knew the stories of merrow in Moon Harbor's waters, too. And if there was anyone working for the Warrens who would know such stories—it would be Marco. Josiah's closest confidante, who had once worked alongside Josiah's older brother Herman Warren before his death. For Herman Warren, who oversaw the company when Edythe and Edward Marsh were lured from Moon Harbor to Welkin not unlike those singing spirits had just lured Alba into the woods.

When Alba didn't respond fast enough, Marco's hand tightened around his wrist, smashing a thumb into the burnt skin left by the end of his cigarette. But Alba barely flinched. He barely felt it. Recalling Marco's tone when he first mentioned the marks—and how it resembled the doctor's tone that once asked the same.

"C'mon, now, Albatross," he said, pushing Alba into the wall. "If there was ever a time for you to try and persuade me to be gentle, it would be now. Even Josiah doesn't know I'm here over any other town collectin' debts. Doesn't know you're here, neither. Yet. I suggest you think 'real hard 'bout how you want to play this, hm? Answer me. Truthful."

Alba swallowed back on the lump in his throat. There were many things he knew, many more things he could only guess, but nothing that would help him in that moment except one: Alba could not outrun Marco a second time. He could not overpower Marco even a first time. But—

But he knew someone who could. He knew someone who even might, if Alba asked nicely.

He knew where, if he could get Marco there, alone, he might be able to get away with it. Without anyone else seeing. Without anyone on the outside ever knowing Marco stepped foot into Moon Harbor in the first place.

"Y-yeah," Alba finally managed, averting his eyes and attempting to speak clearly. "Yes, Marco, you're right. There's... somethin' I think you should see. Just you, no one else. Erm— somethin' I think might even interest Mr. Warren, in favor of my debt, maybe..."

Marco's smile twitched with interest.

"That's a good boy. Why don't you lead the way?"

Alba didn't know how much Marco knew about the merrow —clearly enough to know the marks on Alba's arms were nothing to scoff at—but Alba wasn't going to ask. It didn't matter how much he did or didn't know, what he really thought Alba had to show him. All that mattered to Alba was ensuring the man never took another step out of Moon Harbor to tell Josiah about it. To tell Josiah about *him*.

"It's at the lighthouse."

"Let's go, then," Marco said with a tenderness that made Alba's skin crawl, like a man whispering sweet things to a lover in the privacy of the alleyway. It wasn't helped when his arm wrapped around Alba's waist, leading him with a hand on the small of his back toward the docks.

Alba didn't miss how so many townspeople stopped what they were doing to look, either—as if they all knew Marco and who he worked for, too. He'd mentioned something about being there to collect on debts, no different than any other shithole town that owed money to the Warrens, and Alba felt the briefest pinch of pity on those people. Perhaps the Warrens were who the circle of people mending the net when he first arrived meant when they said all their prettiest fish went to paying off debts.

As they reached the dock, the man's gentle arm around Alba's back hooked suddenly around his neck, possessive, controlling. Alba clawed at his arm with one hand, barely keeping up with the long stride without tripping or losing his cane in the process.

Grunting against how roughly Marco handled him, Alba barely managed to use his cane to point at the old man's row boat tied off to the dock. Marco wasted no time, unhooking his arm and shoving Alba off the edge, where Alba crashed into the dingy with a groan and a clatter of his cane.

He barely lifted his head as Marco pulled the docking rope away and tossed it, hopping down to join him with boots planting on either side of where he lay on the bottom. They'd only floated a few feet from the dock before Eugene came running, red in the face from the effort, though clearly choosing his words as carefully as Alba had.

"Sir, is this really necessary—!"

But Marco flashed a handsome smile, saluting him like a soldier to their captain.

"I'll bring her right back soon, Mr. Michaels," he promised, referring to the rowboat. "Mr. Marsh and I just have some personal business to discuss over at your lighthouse. Won't be long. Will pay you for the lease when we get back. Double for the trouble."

Eugene clearly didn't know what to say—and even if he did, wasn't sure he could. Wasn't sure it mattered. Alba might have been able to tell him as much, but didn't have any mental energy to spare for the old man whose boat was being stolen with Alba prone on the bottom of it.

Once they left the safety of the dock's reach, Marco grabbed the back of Alba's shirt, pulling him upright and onto one of the seats. He tossed both oars to him, and Alba didn't protest. He took the worn grips in his hands, placed them through the iron hooks on either side of the boat, and went to work. Neither hurrying nor taking his time, both wishing for more time to think and to arrive there as fast as possible.

He didn't know much—there wasn't any room in his head for extra considerations—only that Marco wasn't going to leave the lighthouse alive. Alba would make sure of that, if anything else. He would leave as a bleeding corpse or, perhaps—eaten by the hungry merrow Alba hoped still lingered close by like he said he would.

"You look well, all things considered," Marco complimented with a smile from where he sat so casually opposite Alba, never taking his eyes away. His arms draped over the edges of the boat, legs crossed casually in front of him.

"How is Mr. Warren holdin' up?" Alba asked in return, barely trying to sound sincere. Knowing that small flicker of bitter vindication in his chest at the thought of what he might get away with was a dangerous assumption to make. "I assume he got his leg looked at right away."

Marco's smile tightened slightly. Keeping his cool, but less than thrilled to see Alba so comfortable speaking so sarcastically of his employer.

"Sure did," he answered nonetheless. "Right away. Everyone was so worried. You're going to have quite a mess to clean up when you get back. Unless whatever you have to show me is particularly impressive—perhaps even enough to quell Josiah's ire with you."

"You'll be impressed," Alba replied. Hardly skipping a beat. Accustomed to facing down men as wild as that one in his fancy coat and shiny shoes and trimmed beard. "You asked me where I got the marks on my arms—I intend t'show you."

Marco reached into the inner pocket of his jacket, pulling out another cigarette and lighting it. He tossed the still-flaming match into the sea, snuffed with a tiny sound. Alba breathed in deep lungfuls of the second-hand smoke as he rowed, inhaling through his nose, refusing to let the growing ache in his body show through even the smallest gasp of his mouth. Even though his chest and shoulders began to throb from the effort, even though the smallest beads of sweat built on his forehead. He was already exhausted from the hike to the cemetery earlier that morning, the events of being drawn into the woods—but he wouldn't let that man see any hint of any of it.

Barely managing to tie the boat off once they reached the rocks, Marco grabbed Alba by the braid and hauled him up the muddy steps. Alba stumbled after him, cursing and clawing at his grasp, only to be shoved down into the mud and his arms pulled behind his back. Marco tied them using rope from the boat, smashing Alba's face into the dirt again for good measure before heaving him back to his feet. Alba could taste blood from his nose as they approached the front door, mind racing, just hoping—hoping—Eridanys was hungry.

"Is this really better?" Marco asked as they entered the house, hand gripping the back of Alba's neck to keep him docile. "Better than the workhouse? Better than sitting on your ass carving fish all day?"

"I'd prefer sleepin' in the gutter over bein' on the receivin' end of Josiah's breath another day—"

The hand on Alba's neck clawed at his hair, slamming him face-first against the countertop. He choked as blood from his crushed nose rushed down the back of his throat, pulled back and shoved into the cabinet doors next with enough force to crack one of them. Marco pinned him there as the world spun and more blood dribbled from Alba's nostrils, filling his mouth with the taste of rust and salt.

Marco looked at him with disappointment, the same look so many captains had given him over the years, men who didn't enjoy beating their disobedient sailors senseless, but had no choice if they wanted to maintain control. Alba needed to be brought back down to reality. Alba, who was smaller, skinnier, practically made frail since being kicked off the ship where he'd built his physical and mental fortitude after a decade of having no other choice—and Marco seemed intent on reminding him of exactly that.

"I wouldn't speak so poorly of Josiah in front of me, Albatross. You know my temper," he said, smiling at Alba for another long moment before yanking him back from the cabinets. His hand returned to the back of Alba's neck, making him hunch. "Now—show me what you brought me all the way out here for."

Blood dripped to the floor from Alba's nose as he was pushed through the kitchen, fingers digging into his nape as he limped, every step a fight to remain upright. Alba still didn't answer, sweat drenching his brow as he searched all over, strained his ears to listen, tried to find any sign of Eridanys where he could call out to, praying the merrow hadn't gotten bored and gone back to the sea when Alba actually needed him.

When something splashed from the washroom, followed by

the squeak of the steel tub, Alba released a breath of relief—only to be shoved in the direction of the doorway as Marco heard it, too. The man's grasp on Alba's neck firmed, and Alba winced, but remained silent. All the way to the washroom door, which he opened before Marco pushed him in.

In the bathtub pumped so full of water it overflowed with every movement, a long tail draped over one end and coiled along the floor. Attached to the surprised, handsome merrow, who had been combing his hair with a spindly shell dredged from the bottom of the sea before being interrupted. The sight was something out of a storybook, and Alba couldn't help the little laugh that bubbled out of him, splattering some of the blood that dripped from his nose.

As he did—Eridanys just stared at him. Never once did his eyes flicker to Marco, not even for a moment, unblinking and locked on Alba's pitiful state.

"Said—I'd bring you a snack," Alba managed, voice wavering, before Marco shoved him to the floor. Without his hands free to catch himself, Alba crashed to the wood with a miserable sound, instincts telling him to kick away before his mind ever caught up.

Luckily for him, Marco lost all interest in anything but the merrow in the tub. His eyes shone in desire, gazing at Eridanys with a mouth that practically watered. He took a small step forward, reaching for the knife tucked into his belt. Despite the new threat, Eridanys still only stared at Alba.

"So this has been keeping you company all this time, little prince?" Marco asked, approaching with another step. Alba held Eridanys' eyes, silently begging him to do something. "Stunning, just like Herman always described... Oh, Alba, this is a gift, indeed. Mr. Warren may even wipe your slate clean."

Eridanys' eyes finally moved to Marco. Imperceptibly fast, sharp as knives, enough that Marco halted his slow approach.

"Warren?" he repeated the name, and Marco grinned like it was astounding for a merrow to be able to speak at all.

"You really must be one of the last of Moon Harbor, then.

We're going to take such good care of you, you lovely thing. Have many fish returned to this desolate place since you came back? I hear swarms are drawn to things like—"

Eridanys moved even faster than Alba's eyes; he moved as fast on land as he did in the water, so much that Alba didn't see exactly how it happened—only that, once the water in the tub settled again, Marco was writhing on the floor with his throat torn clean away, flesh clenched in Eridanys' jaw between sharp teeth. On the other side of the house, the trap door in the storage room suddenly slammed open then shut again, making Alba jump, straining to look—but there was nothing except his own fast, heavy breaths, and the wet moaning of Marco's life slipping out of him.

He didn't see exactly when Eridanys' tail gave way to legs again, but suddenly he was there, scooping Alba off the floor and carrying him to the tub. Alba had no chance to say anything before Eridanys tossed him like a rock into the overflowing basin, bursting back out again with a gasp and spluttering curses. Eridanys already had his back turned, though, trap door slamming impatiently as the merrow grabbed the nearly-dead Marco by his arms and started dragging him out of the washroom. Into the kitchen, toward the banging hatch, leaving a streak of blood in his wake. Alba called out for him to wait, not knowing why, straining against the ropes still binding his arms and clambering from the tub the moment he pulled himself free.

He made it just in time to watch as Eridanys clutched the obnoxious hatch and heaved it open, gazing down into it for a moment. Alba heard the water thrashing below, churning in the inlet right underneath, as if frenzied with hungry sharks. His own feet remained rooted to the floor, not wanting to get any closer to Marco's body as he had to—but whatever was there caught Eridanys attention. Long enough that Alba finally said his name in a rasp, jumping when Eridanys' sharp eyes snapped back to him.

"Thank you," the merrow said, nodding to the body. "I actually was getting hungry."

"You'll come back?" Alba blurted. Eridanys cast him another look, smirking briefly to himself like the question was amusing.

"Once I take care of this."

He pulled the body closer, shoving it through the hole—before diving in after it. Alba did nothing at first, petrified, listening as the treacherous water beneath the house finally quieted again—only then lunging forward to slam the trapdoor back shut.

Chapter 15

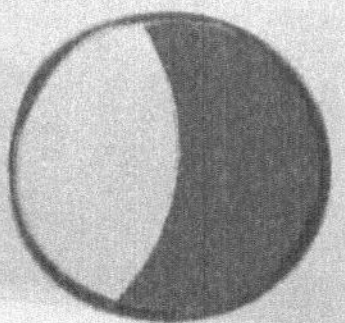

Eridanys said he'd come back, and Alba wanted to believe him. He only wished the mer-man would come sooner, unsettled by every sound the house made while there alone. Aware of every boat that went in and out of the harbor as he watched through the window while not distracting himself with chores or keeping to the lantern.

Fearing someone else would come. Clearly, someone else would come. Someone already had. There would be a third. Then a fourth, and a fifth. And Alba just wished his feral sea-creature would come back and be ready to gut anyone who did.

He was left alone to dwell in his thoughts for far too long. Drowning beneath feelings of relief and pure glee at the death of Marco right in front of him, combined with the pain of scrubbing the man's blood from the floorboards.

He avoided any sight of his reflection, whether in the washroom mirror or the weatherpanes in the lantern room while wiping them down, embarrassed and disgusted at the sight of his own swollen and bruised eyes and split lip. All the while ruminating on curses he hoped strong enough to trap Marco's soul in the harbor just like all the other reanimated corpses who bothered him so much whenever Eridanys wasn't there. Combined further with the growing frustration of simply wanting to tell Eridanys what had happened to him in the woods on the edge of town. Thinking of those pale faces as often as he thought about the sound Marco made after having his throat torn away. Dreaming about both whenever he closed his eyes. Waking up choking more often than not, either from his windpipe ripped away or his own tongue swelling until it cut off his air.

It was only two nights Alba sat alone in the lighthouse, one afternoon between them where he tried to sleep but couldn't. Two days during which plump crabs kept appearing tossed over the rocks. Sometimes thrown haphazardly through the trap door again, where Alba would have to chase them down without losing a finger. Proof that Eridanys was, at least, somewhere close by.

On his second afternoon attempting to sleep, he nearly blew Eridanys' head off with the pistol. Glad he realized before pulling the trigger, having lurched from the bed and turned faster than a storm whips a weathervane at the sound of footsteps climbing the loft stairs.

Eridanys just scoffed at him, frowning in a way that said '*go ahead*' like he thought Alba was a coward. Alba wasn't. Alba wasn't going to admit his relief to have his tentative companion back either, though, especially when they dripped water, standing naked, all over the floor at his feet.

When Alba spotted the decorated clamshell in one of Eridanys' raised hands, he asked:

"What's that?"

"I knew your face would look like shit after everything that happened," Eridanys said, popping open the top of the shell and raking fingers into a mass of slimy muck inside. Without saying anything else, and before Alba could protest, he plopped it over Alba's swollen eye, then down the side of his face, over half his mouth and bruised jaw. Alba jerked away on instinct, opening his mouth to swear at the man in annoyance, but the taste of muddy, minty seaweed infiltrated his tastebuds first, making his tongue tingle and swell along with the rest of his skin.

Eridanys smirked like he enjoyed watching Alba choke on it, dropping to a knee in front of where Alba sat on the edge of the bed and smearing more mud on him. Alba averted his eyes—but not before becoming acutely aware of how close the man suddenly was. Smelling of the sea, briny and fresh and crisp. Skin shining slightly with dampness and highlighting every line of every muscle as they moved. More than aware of the mer-man's bare cock hanging between his legs all over again. Alba would not look. He did not look.

He—only looked a few times, and only for the briefest of moments.

"Even the sea-mud gets enchanted where merrow live," Eridanys went on, and Alba pursed his lips in frustration, but didn't try to argue again. "The mud, the seaweed, the fish, the rocks... this mixture will help heal your face in a few days."

"Why does it matter to you?" Alba couldn't help it. Eridanys scowled.

"A 'thank you' would be fine, too."

Alba almost punched him. But the smallest hint of sincerity in the offer admittedly made his tense feelings soften some. Allowing himself to watch how Eridanys' own face moved as he concentrated on dabbing the mixture on all parts of Alba discolored by Marco's hands. His eye, his mouth, jaw, nose, around his throat, his ear that still rang faintly.

The mention of merrow-magic reminded him of something else, hand traveling to his bare wrist and running fingers around it in silent consideration. The bracelet his mother gave him as a child, with the promise it would make him a man. Silver and braided with pearls, made of ocean magic as Edythe claimed. Alba never questioned it; Edythe was always saying strange things like that, was always mixing up some strange concoction or another, wrapping Alba up in strange rituals involving white fish and the moon and burning candles while playing her flute and sipping on sea water. He never questioned it as anything more than his quirky mother—but the more he learned about that place where she came from first-hand, the more all of it made sense. In a way that made him grieve how little he'd paid attention during those years. Heavy with how much he missed her in that moment, and still could only pray that, wherever she was, she was safe.

"What are you thinking?" Eridanys must have seen the wandering behind Alba's eyes. "Better not be that you're still going to shoot me."

Alba scrambled for anything to say that wasn't the truth. "Thinkin' about how... maybe it's no wonder the townspeople worship mermaids. Erm, *merrow,* so much. Or why they're so protective of even the mention of you, I s'pose. If you livin' in their harbor even made the mud special."

Eridanys smiled mischievously that time. Like it was a point of pride, like he was the sole reason for any bounty that ever existed in those waters. "Moon Harbor never saw fishing as rich as when my kin lived here."

Alba nodded. Marco had said something like that, too, hadn't he?

"Guess it's no wonder the town looks like absolute hell now, with all of them gone," he replied. Eridanys' wicked smile spread wider. Satisfied to hear it. "Were your kin this generous back then, too?"

"Oh, am I generous now?"

Alba rolled his eyes. "First with ripping out Marco's throat for me, and now smearing sea-shit on my face."

"Neither of those things were for you," Eridanys said like a promise, before adding: "Though I've never seen anyone as ugly and pitiful as you when you stumbled into the washroom. Makes my stomach turn just thinking about it."

Alba laughed again, weaker that time. "Doesn't surprise me that merrow appreciate beauty."

"It doesn't?" He said it in a way that could have either been a prod for compliments, or genuine confusion. Alba bit his lip, but decided against it. He didn't want Eridanys' ego to get any bigger than it was. There wouldn't be any room left in the house if it did.

"Are you still hungry?" he asked, instead. "Or did you eat Marco whole?"

"I did," Eridanys answered without flinching. "His meat was greasy and bitter. Like alcohol."

"That doesn't surprise me, either." Alba pulled hair over one shoulder as Eridanys' muddy hand trailed down to run into the crook of his neck. "Well, I still have those crabs you kept tossin' over the rocks. And through the hatch. I was gonna cook them tonight, if you want some."

"I didn't throw any through the hatch…" Eridanys muttered, furrowing his brows, before shaking his head. "Whatever you say. If it's your way of repaying me, then so be it."

"Oh. I didn't realize we were still acting that way."

"What way?"

Alba smirked, flipping his hair back off his shoulder and getting to his feet.

"Nothin'. Glad you're keepin' track of debts owed to one another, because I'm not."

Something about that bothered him, because Eridanys scoffed again, making sure to stubbornly wipe his muddy hands all over Alba's bedsheets before getting to his feet to follow him down the stairs.

ALBA FELT like a starving animal watching the crabs boil in the pot, rolling his tongue over in his mouth as the hunger clawed at his insides and Eridanys' healing mud-mixture made his face tingle. Eridanys soon joined him from the stairs, wearing the same shirt and pants Alba had once found for him, Alba having insisted he put something on before getting anything to eat. He watched the mer-man as he made his way to the table and taking a seat like any other dinner guest would.

Despite seeing it all before, there was still something strange about Eridanys' feigned human-ness, long hair damp and pulled back out of his eyes, legs crossed and fingers strumming the table as if waiting for his serving of food to be offered. What a stark difference from the creature Alba first met the night of the full moon, looking handsome as ever in the low firelight of the stove. The dim, late-afternoon light coming through the window over the sink. Handsome, but that time, not in a frightening way like Alba first thought. Perhaps because he kept being reminded of the sea-mud on his face—and how Eridanys never had any obligation to bring him such a thing. Yet, for some reason Alba still didn't totally understand, did.

"Have you ever eaten boiled crab with butter and herbs?" The merrow spoke first.

Alba gave Eridanys a look he clearly didn't expect. He thought it was a joke—but the look on Eridanys' face said otherwise.

"Butter? What's that?" he couldn't resist. Eridanys attempted to explain something he himself clearly only vaguely understood —that being where butter came from—and Alba had another thought: "How do *you* know about butter on boiled crab? Or *licorice*, now that I think about it. Since I don't think either are a merrow delicacy. Doubt you milk sea-cows like we do land-cows."

"You really think you're the first human I've ever known well?" Eridanys answered, and Alba shrugged as an answer. "You're not even the most interesting."

Alba frowned, unexpectedly embarrassed, but not on that last comment.

"I guess you're right. It didn't occur to me, seein' as you very clearly resent every moment with me."

Eridanys frowned, like he was annoyed the jab didn't cut as deep as he'd hoped.

"My previous human partner used to cook for me occasionally. More than just fish and crab, too," he said, sticking the sharp end of a fingernail into the tabletop and tracing a line down the wood fibers.

"You had a human partner?"

"Once. He died."

"Oh," Alba trailed off, self-conscious. "Sorry to hear that."

His eyes flickered to the merrow, then back again. Eridanys was looking right at him, as he always did, though that time with a sense of waiting. Waiting for Alba to say something else, maybe to ask more questions. But Alba wasn't sure how to respond to something like that, especially when Eridanys said it so casually.

"Don't be," he finally spoke again, still calm as ever. "He deserved it."

Alba still said nothing, though he also didn't flinch. Instead— he nodded silently, eyes remaining on the pot. He didn't know how much time passed with those harsh words hanging between them before Eridanys continued:

"Was it something I said?"

Alba looked back at him. Looking at him. *Looking at him*, as if he thought it might change his reaction. Perhaps someone else would have been shocked, or at the very least inhaled an off-put breath. But Alba felt nothing about the words, or the implication that Eridanys felt nothing about the death of someone he called his partner.

"Does that make you uncomfortable?" Eridanys insisted, and the tiny smile at the corner of his mouth told Alba what sort of answer he wanted to hear.

"Why would it?"

Eridanys' smirk turned curious. "Most folks would at least ask why I felt that way."

Alba furrowed his brows at the crab pot again, before shrugging. "After all the sorts of folk I've met—I think there are some people who aren't worth grieving. Not that anyone *deserves to die*, but—I've met plenty of folk I wouldn't personally go out of my way to save, either. People who wouldn't be mourned if somethin' happened to them."

"An interesting moral dilemma. You say it like a practiced speech."

"I don't know anythin' about you or your partner, why would I scold you for sayin' he deserved it? It's none of my business, anyway. Besides... it's not like my hands are clean in comparison."

He scowled at the thought of the man he'd killed right there where he stood only a few weeks prior, before shaking his head and adding: "Sometimes... you have t'make choices if it's a matter of survivin' in a world that'd throw you out first if it could. If you say your partner deserved it, whatever happened, who am I to judge the circumstances?"

"How many times have you had to do something to survive?" The merrow asked. Alba could hear the sarcastic smile on his voice without having to see it, as if he didn't believe Alba was capable of such a thing. Despite having seen it for himself. Alba just continued frowning down at the pot of crabs.

"Enough."

"What was the first time?" Eridanys continued, that time with genuine curiosity. Alba just wished his dinner would cook faster so he could focus on stuffing his mouth rather than speaking. Trying to decide how much he really cared to share. Wondering if it really mattered if he was honest. Wondering if merrow like Eridanys really cared about the politics of sailing as a lad or a lass. Or a lass who was a lad.

"Is it true what men say about ladies on sailin' ships?" Alba started. "That they bring bad luck, misfortune, from the likes of you and other sea-monsters like you? That Poseidon stirs up whirlpools and rogue waves and tempests in a fury at the discovery of two tits on his waters."

Eridanys grinned in a way that told Alba he was readily familiar with those tales. He couldn't help but smile back sarcastically.

"Poseidon is prone to furies like all of those, indeed, though there isn't a man alive who could actually explain the cause of a single one. Though two breasts on the open sea—I can assure you, he would only attempt to sink her ship because he wants a taste of them for himself."

"Good to know," Alba smirked. He couldn't help it. "Well—sailors really believe it. Some would even be so willin' to throw the poor lady overboard to become a siren to sink another ship on their tail than risk their own misfortune.”

“Not at all how sirens are made, but go on.”

“Well...” Alba gazed out the window, watching the way the suffocating sunlight cast the faintest dull glow even through such thick clouds. Without thinking, his hand lifted to his chest. He trained his palm over the flatness where a breast should have been, but never was.

“I was born like a lady,” he finally said, unsure how else to explain the complicated emotions tangled around such words. Words that made his pulse pound harder than admitting to killing anyone ever would. “Even now, if you looked at me naked as the day I was born, you’d think so. By what everyone else says a ‘lady’ is, at least. But I grew up to be a man. It was never a problem at first, ’til I was snatched off the street to sail for the Warrens. I knew I had to be careful, of course—there were plenty of men who wouldn’t give a damn, even a few who confided that they were like me, but a woman.

“But for every man who wouldn’t bat an eye, there was another who might throw me over; or worse, leavin’ me wishin’ I had been. The man who deserved to die... who I killed, the first time, was like that.” Alba could taste the bitter chill on the air. How the harsh wind pulled at his braided hair, wet and whipping and making it hard to breathe. He focused on his moving tongue to remain where he was—two feet on the ground. Warm in front of the stove. “There was still another three months left on our contract, and I was not about to spend it havin’ to choose between lettin’ him do as he wished to me to keep my secret, or tellin’ the captain, which would get me stranded, or...”

“Worse,” Eridanys finished for him. Alba nodded, squeezing the flesh of his flat chest one more time. He let out a breath that trembled slightly, pushing the memory, the discomfort away and hoping Eridanys didn’t sense how it made his blood race. How he could feel the shift of a tossing ship beneath his feet. The needles of icy spray prickling his cheeks, when larger waves didn't attempt to sweep him into the black water on their own. Insides sweltering with a mix of rage and fear. Staring at that man leaning over the railing, searching for the root of a tangle in the nets before the storm tore him from the boat. Every time a dark wave spit over him, Alba hoped it would take him. Every time he remained despite it all, Alba whispered prayers for another to come. But again and again, no wave was strong enough to knock that seasoned sailor off balance.

"So I pushed him," he whispered. Another confession, to himself, to Eridanys, to whatever god might be listening out of curiosity, though he'd lost hope any paid attention long ago. "I cut that bastard's safety line and I let the sea decide what to do with him. He was swallowed up before anyone could even call out anyone'd gone overboard—and we were so busy tryin' to save the nets, it didn't matter. They didn't bother. Somethin' I always feared would be my own fate—to fall over and no one bother—for just a moment, was my saving grace."

Alba's ears were ringing when Eridanys' voice cut through the memory, thick and heavy and choking not unlike those frigid waves had been. When Alba finally jolted back to the present, he had to ask Eridanys to repeat himself.

"The sea feasts most enthusiastically on the land's most unwanted offerings," he said. As if quoting an old poet. Alba gazed at him in quiet intrigue, before laughing weakly again.

"Never swallowed me up, though, no matter how many times I fell in. Always spit me right back out to be fished with the rest of the day's catch."

"You must have had someone on land who would have grieved a little too loudly. The sea can always tell."

Alba smiled to himself, not expecting the amused warmth that bloomed in his chest. He absentmindedly touched the roots of his hair where a protective braid used to tug. "My mother used to say somethin' similar. She would have raised hell like the sea had never seen, I think. She, erm... named me after a seabird for that reason, you know. I was named after my father at first, but after he died when I was only a baby, she changed it. Said she didn't want me to have the same fate. Maybe not knowing that namin' me after a sea bird meant I was destined to end up there one way or another..."

He trailed off. He didn't know what he was saying.

"Albatross," Eridanys reiterated. "The prince of the sea. Little prince. That's what that man called you, isn't it?"

"Yes," Alba sighed. "My mother used to call me that, too. He only did it because he knew that."

"I'm glad to have torn out his throat, then," Eridanys responded with a little lick of his lips. Alba was surprised, the sentiment coming off almost like a misguided offer of camaraderie. Like he did it because he knew it was something that bothered Alba, despite having no motive to care what Alba thought about anything. Though the merrow's next comment shed some light on his true sentiments: "Although, to be fair, any man who works for the Warrens deserves that sort of fate."

"Not all of us had a choice," Alba mumbled bitterly. "How much do you know about the Warrens, anyway? You reacted to hearin' the name like you knew them."

Eridanys drew more lines in the table with a fingernail, thinking before answering. Alba wondered if he'd have to buff out scratches when the night was over.

"They take young workers from Moon Harbor regularly. Or used to, anyway, when I still lived here. For their boats, I assume."

"That's what happened to my parents." Alba nodded. He wondered again if Eridanys had known either of them while living in the harbor, but stopped himself from asking. Instead looking the mer-man up and down, wondering if merrow aged at the same rate humans did.

"An evil family," Eridanys went on, not noticing Alba's lingering eyes. He carved more lines into the table, like the reminder of it all was enough to nearly send him into a frenzy. Alba wanted to ask more, wanted to know what else Eridanys had to say about it, but instinct pricked the back of his throat, urging him to hesitate. Not wanting to push the merrow over the edge of anything that might make him explode; not wanting to push so hard that Eridanys refused to continue.

Even more—speaking of his parents, of the merrow in the harbor, Alba suddenly remembered there was something he'd needed to tell Eridanys since the last time they saw one another.

"Speakin' of, there was—! Erm, that is..." He didn't know how to say it, tongue tangling in his mouth as he turned fast enough to make Eridanys jump. "There was something I found while I was in town last. That I didn't have a chance to tell you with all the bloodshed. You see—well, you know all the singin' we've been hearing? I said it was just the pipes on the buildings, but... now I'm not so sure. I think... I think it's actually singin'. And it's coming from the woods on the other side of town."

Eridanys straightened up, though hesitation painted his expression.

"Did you see who was singing?"

"Well, sort of, but not clearly—they lured me deeper into the trees than I thought, only realizin' at the last moment. Nearly dropped dead from your damned curse because of it, too," he added sourly. "Thank god I came to my senses and crawled back out before that could happen. But then there were just... faces. A whole audience of pale faces lookin' at me, who... Well, I thought —who looked like you. Erm, I mean, just in how pale they were, and their eyes, and... they didn't have long hair like yours, I think it was all cut short, but I swear it was the same pretty moonlit color..." he trailed off. Not realizing how long his eyes lingered on Eridanys' hair at the thought. Eridanys certainly noticed, however, stroking the braid with his hand and only then making Alba realize he was staring.

He quickly cleared his throat, adding: "They definitely looked more like you do in your human form, too. Didn't have the strange ears or tails... I mean, I assume, since they were on land instead of in the water... Obviously there's no proof it was your kin, since I don't know why they would be in the woods, but...I also heard some townsfolk talkin' something about how 'salting the earth' wasn't satisfying the spirits anymore. That could mean anything, though, I suppose... Could be some other kind of evil spirit hauntin' the place... Wouldn't be surprised..." he rambled, unable to help it as Eridanys only stared at him. Wishing the man would say something, do something.

"You said they... lured you?" He finally asked. "Was it with their song?"

"Well—I don't know. I don't remember. I was bein' careful, only walking in a little bit at a time, tryin' to follow the people throwing salt, but then I was just suddenly... much deeper in than I thought. The path was gone behind me, even though I was sure I followed it. I'd even dropped my cane and never noticed. I just... don't know how it happened."

"And here I thought you said you'd never been tempted by any song of the sea."

"Well..." Alba frowned. Knowing as well as Eridanys did that he had been, once, by the same mer-creature sitting there at the kitchen table. "Maybe I just wasn't expectin' it. Not often you get lured into the woods by a bunch of tree-sirens."

"There's no saying the things in the woods are sirens," Eridanys corrected. "Siren songs are different from other creatures, even merrow."

"Oh?"

"Both sing to draw something in, but usually for different reasons." He smirked. "Merrow lure humans to trick them, to offer a granted wish, to make a deal or ask for something for themself; sirens sing to feed. They prey on a human's physical desires of the flesh, in order to draw them close enough to drown. You say you've never been tempted by sirens while sailing though, so do you not...?"

"I'm—I enjoy—*physical desires of the flesh* just fine, actually," Alba said, speaking the words a little too fast.

"It's perfectly alright if you don't"

"I enjoy them! At least—I think I would. I don't know, I've

never..." He had to look away again when he found Eridanys gazing at him with a new kind of intensity. One of curious hunger. Like a beast trying to determine if Alba's skin-and-bones existence was enough to sate it for a night.

"Never what?" The man encouraged. His sly smile remained. Like he knew what Alba meant to say all along. "Perhaps you've simply never given in to the call of something you would risk it all for?"

For him to say such a thing when Alba knew better than both of them exactly how that same mer-man's song had reduced him to a flushed, tingling mess in private—Alba almost couldn't keep the mortification off his face.

"Perhaps so many years sailin' just made me numb to them," he finally said. "Like their magic wouldn't work on me no matter who sang for me to hear. Merrow or siren or anythin' else. I don't know what happened in the woods, but—but I definitely wasn't being drawn in because of... of... *physical desires of the flesh...*"

Eridanys regarded him like he was more interesting than he first thought. Or perhaps he simply enjoyed watching Alba stumble over his words, which only made Alba more wary. He wasn't usually so tongue-tied when talking about sex, about intimacy, let alone about resisting the song of sirens—but he'd never been forced to navigate such topics with anyone like Eridanys, either, who looked at Alba like something to eat. Like, despite saying otherwise, was perfectly aware of how his own song once tugged at the nape of Alba's neck. The base of his hips, his navel, arousing and tempting enough to leave Alba flushed and frightened and barely clinging to his senses on the kitchen floor.

"Have you ever wondered?" Eridanys asked, smiling as he did. Alba sensed it to be a trap. "What would happen if you ever gave in?"

"Like you just said—they eat their prey. What else is there to—"

"Don't you wonder how they might pleasure you, first?"

"Oh, I..." Alba trailed off. His ears felt hot. "They don't actually pleasure their prey before killin' them, do they—"

"And what if the siren enjoyed the indulgence of you so much that they decided to let you live?" Eridanys continued, unraveling his hair over a shoulder and stroking it in a way that emphasized the elegant length of his fingers, his hands. "To instead mark you as their own, death fall on any others who try to take you for themself?"

"That would never..."

"Wouldn't it? Plenty of creatures in the sea would love a human plaything. Even merrow used to do the same with chosen mates here in Moon Harbor," he said with a hint of implication. Alba's thoughts swirled back to the start of their conversation, though didn't quite hook on what Eridanys was referring to as the man's handsome mouth curled into a smile somehow even more captivating. "Though they gave it a poetic name, tried to pass it off as something other than simply indulging in the pieces of warm flesh they wanted all to themselves. Didn't want their own desires compared to the barbarity of sirens, perhaps."

"You keep sayin' 'they' as if you aren't a merrow, yourself," Alba said. He didn't like how Eridanys kept smiling at him, like he had a secret. Like he was getting to the real point of everything he was sharing, if only Alba would be patient. "What was the poetic name?"

"They called their chosen humans *shore-callers*," the man continued as if Alba hadn't interrupted. "Special humans who, when chosen and properly mated, wouldn't ever fall for another creature's luring song again. Only ever made victim to their own merrow's call."

"Oh..."

"And who, in exchange, could call their merrow mate in return. Even allowing them to cross onto protected shores and walk freely amongst them."

"That's not real—" Alba started, surprised at how the words popped out of him like air escaping a canteen. Not realizing how tightly he held his body, how focused he was on watching Eridanys' mouth as it spoke, heart racing and skin prickling with warmth. Words spoken as if sung; teasing his insides with the sort of passive sea-magic he had no defenses against.

"It very much is real." Eridanys folded his arms, smiling wide enough to show his sharp teeth. "Why would I lie to you about such a thing?"

"What does all that have to do with—with sirens? In the woods or otherwise?"

Eridanys curled a piece of hair around a finger, never taking his eyes from Alba. "I suppose I wonder if that sort of mating ritual would still work the same even if I was technically no longer a merrow, myself."

Alba's mind spun. Starting to piece together what, exactly, Eridanys had been hinting at since the start.

"Sirens are just merrow cursed to hunt for their own food and companionship," Eridanys continued, and Alba jumped when the man suddenly got to his feet, joining him at the sink where the pot of boiled crabs sat draining into a basket. Claiming one, he tore a leg free, crunching into it shell and all. "Made savage by the waves. Driven mad with hunger, enough that it warps their song, changes how their magic hooks into the minds of prey. Merrow thrive when raised within a familial kinship—so to drive one out, alone, into the vastness of the sea, understandably forces it to resort to its most base instincts to survive. Both hunger and... otherwise."

Alba looked at him for a long time, specifically his mouth, teeth sharp as they crunched through another leg of crab. Only then did Alba realize how close they stood to one another, as effortless as how he'd been drawn into the trees by magic he didn't know he could hear. Magic he didn't realize was hooking into him, as Eridanys said. Making his insides writhe in want for something he didn't know, making his heart race, until he almost couldn't keep Eridanys' sharp gaze any longer.

"Then—you're a siren? Driven mad by—by eating humans?"

He stammered while getting the words out, hating to utter such a sentence out loud, feeling like such a thought was more taboo as someone who'd once been subjected to something similar. Who'd lost his father to something similar, even if not at the hands of a mer-creature, specifically. Knowing how easy it was for even humans to be driven mad by the same circumstances. Hating the thought that there was anything so horrific he and Eridanys might have in common, both forced to resort to such evil while lost in the vastness of the sea. "Well—what were you doing so far out at sea? Sounds like it may have been your own fault, becoming a siren or whatever you say. Why tell me any of this?"

Thankfully, Eridanys didn't seem to notice Alba's sudden discomfort. He just chuckled, crossing his arms and leaning back against the edge of the counter. "I didn't merely *get lost* like some green sailor on his first voyage. I was banished from my kinship, here in Moon Harbor. And yes—out there in the great sea—in the endless loneliness, the hunger, the exhaustion, even I succumbed to the depravity of a siren. My song changed, allowing me to lure sailors like you for something to feast on to survive. I'm still a siren now, even after returning. And I would stay a siren even if I'd found my kin alive and well, whether they invited me back into the fold or not. Satisfied?"

"Why are you tellin' me this?" Alba asked again, though barely heard the words as they left him. His eyes remained on Eridanys' mouth, his eyes as they flickered over Alba's beat-up, muddy face. Alba didn't know how he felt hearing those words, either—except one thing. Pity. The smallest ounce of empathy, as someone who'd been compelled to depravity in similar ways.

He closed his eyes, exhaling through his nose and turning to address the crabs in the sink. Letting his thoughts roam, to weave in and out of the things Eridanys had told him, as vast as the sea itself. The merrow remained silent, like he wanted Alba to figure it out on his own.

"You said you wondered if mating with someone, even as a

siren, would allow you the same magic properties as the merrow with their chosen humans."

"Ah. You *were* paying attention."

Alba's frown dug deeper lines in his mouth, his forehead, enough that the mud chipped on his bruised jaw.

"So that... your partner only responds to your song. And so you can 'walk on land...'" His eyes flickered to Eridanys' very obviously already existing legs, crossed at the ankles where he stood. Recalling all his talk about traps that kept him in the water. Eridanys noticed, stretching one out and rolling his foot.

"*Protected shores*, I specified. On top of their traps, Moon Harbor has wards that keep unwanted merrow from climbing out of the sea."

"Unwanted merrow *and* unwanted sirens."

"*Unwanted* sirens is redundant, all things considered."

Alba huffed. "Well—out with it, then. All you do is speak in riddles. I'm more afraid of sayin' the wrong thing and lookin' foolish in front of you than I am of any siren's song you could sing."

"Afraid of *looking* foolish in front of me? Oh, dear Albatross—"

"I said out with it!"

Eridanys' hand found Alba's, taking it. Alba's breath caught, staring as the man drew it to his mouth, only a hair's breadth from kissing Alba's bruised knuckles.

"I want to mate with you. To make you my caller of the shore, just like merrow once did with the humans of Moon Harbor. So that you are only ever made weak by my own song, and you allow me to cross onto the shore, uninhibited by the warding bonds and traps alike that they have in their waters. Is that clear enough?"

Alba couldn't think straight. He couldn't tell if Eridanys' luring voice made his thoughts weave in and out to the point they were nonsensical, or if it was merely the outrageousness of the request.

Or—was it outrageous? If what Eridanys said was true, it would provide a solution to both concerns Alba had. To no longer worry about being lured by voices he didn't even realize were tempting him; and to allow Eridanys to join him the next time he returned to town, in case another of Josiah's men came looking for him. Like a feral guard dog on a leash, who would circle and snarl at anything that came too close while Alba went about both his and the siren's business.

"You already said once before that someone in town might recognize you," he argued anyway, though it didn't have much teeth. Seeking reassurance rather than a debate. "Aren't you worried about that?"

"I can be careful. Like I said before—I know the town. Well enough to hide from unwelcome eyes."

But Alba still didn't agree. Just gazed at where Eridanys continued to hold his hand, still hovering near his mouth, as if breathing in the smell of his skin.

"I wish to see what you saw in the trees," Eridanys insisted calmly, breath chilly against Alba's knuckles. "To determine for myself if it has anything to do with my missing kin. I want to see if I recognize them. Even if I don't—I want to know their reason for luring *you*, and whether or not they try again with me next to you."

"What, they won't be able to tell on their own that I can't be lured anymore?"

"Being my shore-caller will protect you from being lured by another's song, but not from any other tricks they may play," Eridanys said with a flicker of genuine warning, and Alba's blood chilled.

His hand touched Alba's chin, turning it to face him. He regarded every inch of Alba's face, muddy and bruised and swollen and ugly, as he himself once said, before his pale eyes skimmed up and down the rest of him in what felt like the same appraisal Alba always got from captains when new fishing contracts were assigned.

"You're exactly the type of man most creatures would love to play with."

Alba did not want to know what the hell that meant. He pulled from Eridanys' hand, but didn't step away entirely. Not at first, just glaring at the man's collarbones barely peeking out from beneath the open collar of his shirt. He ignored how his face, his ears felt warm as he braced himself to ask:

"If I say yes, what happens? I mean—how do we do it?"

"What do you mean, 'how do we do it'?" Eridanys said sarcastically. "Do you not know what I mean by 'mate with you'?"

"Not in the context of old human-merrow rituals! Of course not." He didn't mean to sound so shrill.

Eridanys' fingers ghosted over the nape of Alba's neck, making goosebumps flush down his skin.

"I'll sing for you when I'm ready. You'll come if it pulls you. Follow your instincts, and I will take care of the rest."

"That doesn't explain anything. You know that's not what I meant!" Alba insisted, closing his eyes and shaking his head. "I expect more than that, especially after you just got done telling me all about how sirens eat whoever they call to—"

"I also said they pleasure them, first."

He said it without a hint of teasing. In fact, as his eyes trailed up and down Alba for what had to be the dozenth time, his tone was entirely serious.

"Then—you intend to fuck me? Before you eat me?"

"I'm not going to eat you."

"Why should I believe that? For all I know, this is just some sort of game you like to play with your food—"

"*I'm not going to eat you,* sailor," Eridanys insisted with frustration, spoken through his teeth and grasping the nape of Alba's neck. Not forcefully, not to yank Alba back to look at him, but rather as a means of forcing Alba to meet his eyes. Alba did, held in place by the siren's hand, faces hardly a few inches from one another. He wondered how he must have looked beneath a layer of sea-mud. Did he look frightened? Apprehensive? Could

Eridanys see the hesitation, the uncertainty, the pure icy fear of having to admit out loud—he'd never fucked or been fucked by even a normal human man, before?

Perhaps he did, because he quirked an uneven smile suddenly, letting his eyes flit over Alba's face a moment longer before adding: "I suppose there's always the chance I'll get too excited, forgetting my own strength once I have you. Going mad with hunger enough to forget. Remembering how good you tasted the first time we met, knowing that I'd have to resist that temptation this time. I admit, every time your cheeks go red, I have to resist chomping down on you a second time. Wondering if your blood would be just as mouthwatering as the first, especially with me on top of you, writhing and gasping and begging for what I have planned—"

Alba's hands flashed out, smashing against Eridanys' mouth with wide eyes.

"Don't," he squeaked. A pathetic sound, tight in his throat, only making him flush hotter in embarrassment. "I—I just said, I don't want to play games with you. It isn't funny."

Removing his hands, Eridanys' smile underneath remained like he thought otherwise. Still, he finally let go of the nape of Alba's neck, settling back against the counter.

"I'm not going to eat you," he said one more time with finality. "There's still too much I want from you. Maybe I'll reconsider once our agreement is through, but—even then, I promise to make sure you enjoy it, first."

Alba moved like he was about to throw a punch, and Eridanys put his hands up in defense. His foxlike smile never faltered.

"I promise I'll treat you tenderly, sailor. Just come when you're called, alright? Don't resist me, this time. Who knows what I'll do if you don't come. I'm desperate enough."

"When?"

"When I'm ready."

"*When?*"

"Not tonight," Eridanys sighed, motioning to the pot of crab. "Eat. Sun's going down soon. Almost time to light the lantern."

"Don't start thinking you can tell me what to do."

But that only made Eridanys laugh, turning for the door. Alba hated how he straightened up in reaction, a sound leaving his mouth before he could stop it. Having to finish speaking when Eridanys turned with a raised eyebrow in question.

"You—You're leavin' me again?"

"Would you like me to stay?"

I don't care. Do what you want. It makes no difference to me. All things Alba nearly said on instinct, but never quite reached the back of his throat. He would never utter such a thing out loud —but the truth was, Alba wasn't eager to be left alone in that silent house again.

Glancing at the pot of crab, then back to Eridanys, he cleared his throat.

"I can't eat all this by myself," he said. "Don't want it to go to waste. I want you to eat some so you owe me a debt, and I can make you do chores while I'm tendin' the light."

Eridanys clearly didn't expect that. He hovered where he stood for a moment, like he was waiting for Alba to suddenly laugh at him for thinking he was actually invited. But Alba never did, and they stood there in silence.

Eventually, Eridanys' expression twitched, before returning to his seat at the table. Alba said nothing else, either, pulling a second plate from the cabinet and setting it alongside his own. Reminding him of the rare occasions when he'd share a meal with his mother, on those brief nights back home. Another pocket of warmth fluttered in his chest, and he smiled to himself, plucking crab from the pot and dishing them up. Enjoying the thought of having a companion there with him—even if that same companion's song would soon lure him into the sea.

CHAPTER 16

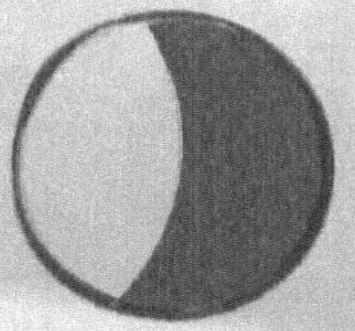

Eridanys did the chores Alba asked while Alba tended to the lantern that night, which, as always, Alba didn't actually expect. Which wasn't the response Eridanys wanted once Alba returned surprised to find the work done, pouting and insisting Alba trust him when he went about repaying debts.

Alba's continued disbelief only compelled the siren to stubbornly ask for more to do to prove himself, and Alba was happy to delegate some of the tasks he dreaded most. Not to mention—the more Alba kept Eridanys busy on the lighthouse rock, the more he wouldn't have to think about their conversation the afternoon prior. The more he could put off the anticipation, the anxiety about it. Hating not knowing when to expect what the man said would happen; preferring to go about his day as if they hadn't agreed to such things at all.

Despite his best efforts to put it out of his mind, though, Alba soon couldn't help but ruminate endlessly over what it would be like to—inevitably—give in to a call to someone like him. To be pleasured by a siren—like him. Suddenly acutely aware of the strength of Eridanys' arms, especially how they swelled beneath the weight of lifting and pushing a brick-laden wheelbarrow from the shed over the uneven, grassy terrain to the house.

He couldn't help but watch how the mer-man's shoulders and back moved beneath his shirt while laying bricks in a row along the crumbling garden wall, or the sight of his stomach flexing beneath the tiniest peek under his shirt when lifting his arms over his head. How he was both beautiful and handsome; how there was hardly a *rugged* thing about him, but that only made the strength of his movements more captivating to watch.

Alba knew what sex involved. He knew how to have sex. To an extent, he even thought he knew what to expect with Eridanys, considering he'd seen the man's cock a handful of times whenever he walked around naked right out of the sea. He was certainly better-endowed than most sailors Alba had caught sight of during his years sailing, but Eridanys' anatomy was, at the very least— *human.* At least so far as in his human form. He didn't want to think about how he might be mating with a merrow—a blood-thirsty *siren*—rather than a man.

Three days of calm, non-eventful cohabitation went by, weighed down only beneath Alba's own imagined apprehension. Distracted by the daily work, by tending to the lantern, by the slow progression of sea-mud healing the wounds on his face until he could almost convince himself the confrontation with Marco hadn't happened.

A part of him didn't want to mention it; a part of him wanted to ask. A part of him wished to pretend like he'd forgotten entirely; a part of him wanted to let Eridanys know that he was meant to go back into town for supplies in another day, and if they intended to mate before then, well—they were running out of time. God, how could he ever bring himself to utter such words?

But the following night, just after winding the weights for the last time before sunrise—a sweet hum found its way into the lighthouse from the distant sea, and Alba realized he would no longer have to.

His body responded before his mind knew what was happening, heart thrumming warmly in his chest and making his skin tingle. He touched a hand to his chest in confusion, a small, cold pinch of concern nipping at the back of his neck until he realized what must have been happening. It came with a rush of anxiety, instincts telling him to cover his ears—but just before he did, he stopped himself. No—that was what he'd been waiting for. He'd been warned. He'd agreed to not resist, to not hide away. He consented to being called, to following it. No matter what he would find on the other side.

Once he accepted his fate, forcing the nervous instincts away, the luring call draped over him a second time. Warm and inviting. Making his heart dance, wrapping him in a blanket then cinching a knotted rope at the base of his spine to pull. He stepped forward with its tug, exhaling a small breath and committing to it once more. Pushing the apprehension away. Deciding, even if it killed him, to trust that siren who claimed to still need him. Hoping it wouldn't come to that; hoping a siren was even a thing capable of being truthful.

What Alba didn't expect was how, once he gave in and let the song take hold of him entirely, it would be impossible to break free again. Especially once it melted what remained of his hesitation into nothing but sweet honey. Making his mouth water, lips parting and wishing to breathe it in. To taste the song on his tongue, wondering if it would coat his insides as deliciously as it caressed his mind. Deep and rich and melodic—invisible, all-encompassing hands groped at him, silencing his mind altogether, until only his most basic instincts remained. Basic instincts that knew only sensation, flesh—desire.

Alba barely exhaled another breath, and allowed himself to submit to it wholly.

Only partially aware of his movements, spirited away to a place far sweeter than any he'd ever visited, he left his cane behind. Hating how long it took to descend the stairs, he feared the song would stop before he could reach it. A song that knew him by name without having to call it, beckoning with a growing urgency that made his vision waver and his feet feel heavy. As if walking across the shifting deck of a ship in a storm; or walking in a dream where the earth was made of sand dusted over cotton.

He reached the bottom of the stairs and stumbled through the door. Out into the wind, sky still dark with sunrise a few hours still on the horizon. The start of rain pricked his cheeks like ice falling in shards from a glacier. He clung to the exterior of the lighthouse for a moment, straining his ears to listen over the incoming storm—wishing to hear its call again. Knowing it was there, sure it would ring out again for him. That song meant for him, only him—a song that meant someone, something was out there that wished to have him. Partially clinging to his wavering awareness of Eridanys—partially blinded by the heat growing in the back of his throat, his chest, behind his navel.

Using an arm to block the wind from his eyes, Alba stopped only long enough to strain his ears. To search the water thrashing with whitecaps against the weather, searching for a spot of moon on the surface who sang out to him. Soon the wind emphasized the sound, louder and sweeter than any fluted pipes ever could be. Carrying it to him, then swirling back and nudging him in the right direction. Toward the rocks slick with crashing ocean water, where he stepped closer than he knew better to go even on the clearest of days.

The moon was hidden behind a quilt of thick gray clouds in the sky—but a part of her found a way to pierce between stitches, swimming through the dark current. White and flowing like stringed opals under a light, shimmering with all the colors of the deepest parts of arctic glaciers.

Alba could do nothing but stare—that piece of the moon was the most beautiful thing he'd ever seen. Such a beautiful thing that sang to him, called to him, wishing to know him.

Alba knew that drop of moonlight in the dark sea, too—He knew Eridanys. He wished Eridanys would swim even closer. Just out of reach. Alba wanted to touch him. For the first time, Alba wanted to touch him all over, after so many days resisting every urge that bit at the back of his mind. Always keeping his hands to himself, sure he wouldn't have to that time. Eager to give in, eager to know and be known.

He didn't know how Eridanys sang so clearly with his mouth beneath the water—but then he rose slightly more, revealing the rest of his handsome, angular face, lips dripping with saltwater and moving with the sound of the song. Captivating, hypnotizing Alba no different than the turning lantern had captured the siren himself. Hooking around the thin angles of Alba's bones and drawing him nearer. A fish on a line. Eager to reach him, even knowing it might end in his own gasping and gutting.

Taking one step too far, Alba's foot slid out beneath him. Crashing backward onto the rock, waves swept over him instantly, dragging him into their embrace. On instinct, too drunk with desire to think, he inhaled—filling his chest with water that burned every inch of flesh it scraped against. It burned, it ached—but then cold hands found him. His arms, then his face—then something soft, smooth pressed against his lips, and the burning in his lungs faded.

Water spilled out from between his lips, summoned by the mouth pressed into his, drawing it back. Taking it for itself. Leaving Alba with a raw emptiness he wanted filled—filled, filled with anything he could be given.

Desperate to fill that void left within him, so much that his hands thrust out, grabbing the moon siren's face, cupping the curves of his jaw and kissing him back. Kissing him with inexperienced, desperate earnestness that would have been humiliating had he not been moon-drunk like an ocean tide sycophant following his goddess wherever she went.

"Mine's the first mouth you've ever kissed, isn't it?" Eridanys' melodic voice asked between their lips, and Alba barely managed to inhale a breath between it and the saltwater soaking him.

He didn't answer—he didn't want to admit it. He couldn't. Not to the thing that sang to him so beautifully, the first thing to ever desire him. But no answer was answer enough, and Eridanys pulled Alba closer. Kissed him possessively. To be the first to kiss him, touch him, devour him alive—and devour Alba he did, with hands and mouth and tail wrapping around him beneath the water, parting Alba's thighs against the rocks and gliding between them. Clawing at him, drawing the air from his lungs with every breath always on the verge of dragging him under. With such a hypnotizing voice in his ear, Alba thought he wouldn't grieve his own death if it was at the pale hands of the moon.

Pale hands pulled his shirt open, then tangled the hair braided down the back of his neck; a cold, pale mouth kissed along his jaw, then down his throat before biting at his collarbones. Alba's hands fought for something to grasp at, clawing at scaled flesh and bundles of muscle, back pressed into the smooth stone of the edge of the rocks as the strength of the sea pinned him breathless and gasping.

A tongue that felt warm only in such cold water swirled over his nipples just beneath the surface, teeth nibbling at his sensitive skin and summoning small gasps from his mouth. It left marks on him, and he shuddered as the beam of moonlight traveled lower to open the front of his pants. Mouth never pulling away, warm and cold and soft and sharp, tongue licking water from the skin beneath his navel, before sliding between his legs and making him buck. His hands found the siren's hair in the tide, overwhelmed with a rush of heat burning beneath his skin and gasping a lungful of sea spray, like kerosene sparking in his stomach.

He grasped Eridanys' silvery hair in two fists, but not to yank him away, not to push him deeper—only in need of something to anchor him in his body. The siren responded with sharp hands burrowing into Alba's waist, caressing the sensitive nub between his legs with wet lips, tongue traveling lower and teasing inside. Spreading Alba's legs open on either shoulder, gripping his thighs in sharp hands, moonlight eyes flickering up at him just beneath the water every time Alba writhed or clawed at him in overwhelm. As if wanting to see whether his prey enjoyed it, wishing to see how Alba's face contorted in the rush of pleasure.

Alba had touched himself plenty before, many times before

ever hearing Eridanys' song. In the dark, narrow confines of a bunk or a hammock while sailing in the north. Brief, rare stints of pleasure allotted to him on a ship crewed by men who had no business knowing what he looked like with his pants down.

An act that never brought much pleasure in the end, never left him breathless and smiling and warm in the cheeks like when people whispered about it. After climaxing, he would lie there in the darkness, staring at the wooden ceiling, listening to the creak of the ship. The voices of crew mates would waft around him, just far enough away that they wouldn't have heard or seen anything. Sometimes he would cry out of loneliness, misery, the rush of endorphins making him realize exactly how miserable he was and how badly he wished to go overboard like others before him. How that would be so much easier than what he was given.

When Eridanys teased him in the house, talking about how Alba certainly wouldn't be able to ignore his song, Alba had been intrigued. Even—curious. He'd wanted to know if that was true, he wanted to know how it felt to be called out to, knowing that was not something he was ever likely to get in his normal waking hours, whether in Welkin or on a northern fishing rig or anywhere else. There would never be anyone else to call out to him in desire, in affection.

Such fantasies had always been brief, passing fancies, never given enough time to fester into anything more. Knowing the danger of it, knowing his life and his mother's life would always take priority. He didn't deserve something like that, he would never have time for something like that. He would never be able to trust a stranger enough to give or accept something like love and intimacy.

Pinned against the rocks, grasped in the arms of the siren whose song sang against the nub of Alba's clit, savoring every taste of skin as the waves lapped and crashed against them—Alba finally knew what it felt like to shudder with pleasure. Real pleasure full of warmth and wine and a racing heart. With Eridanys' hands clinging to his flesh, as if worried the sea would taste him herself and whisk him away. Alba could even pretend the siren enjoyed it, too. He could even pretend Eridanys liked how he tasted, liked the feeling of Alba's skin under his hands. And while that pleasure was tinged with salty apprehension, not knowing which moment would be the one where he was finally dragged under or torn apart with sharp teeth—Alba never thought he was meant to know gentle pleasure, anyway. The way Eridanys clawed, grabbed, tore at him was all Alba could have ever asked for.

The hands bruising his waist pushed him back into the rocks again, then up, lifting Alba's lower half from the water. Exposing him to the cold air, the overcast sky. Alba collapsed onto his back, hands lashing out for anything to hold onto so he wouldn't slip back into the waves, finding Eridanys as he pushed himself from the water to follow.

The mer-man's eyes were bright even in the darkness, reflecting the occulting light of the lantern overhead whenever it swept by. Alba's instincts shuddered, blood running cold as everything told him to fear the creature licking its lips with such sharp teeth, but he didn't move. Just stared back at him, bare legs trembling, flesh raw and pink from the salt, from the onslaught of the siren's needy tongue. A hum emerged from the back of Eridanys' throat as if he could sense the nervousness, melting Alba's uncertainties back down to nothing again.

Using the indomitable strength of his long tail, Eridanys pushed himself fully onto the rocks, onto Alba. He smashed their mouths together once more, humming at the back of his throat like a purring cat.

"You will be made my caller of the shore," the humming, growling voice spoke between their mouths, making Alba's heart race. "My bride of the salted air, my brine witch. I will be your caller of the sea—your bride of the shore and soil, your mud witch."

He bit at Alba's lower lip, before trailing down his chin, his jaw, kissing the side of his neck where teeth once buried. Kissing

Alba's skin tenderly, trailing a long tongue over the faint scars that remained.

"Only my song will ever call to you—and I will hear when you call for me, from any edge of any sea."

Alba's hands trembled, wrapped around the back of Eridanys' neck as the words cascaded over him, through him, making goosebumps pucker his skin, breaths hitching with every curl of the tongue against him, as Eridanys' heavy body parted his legs and pressed closer. The weight of of him was crushing, suffocating, invigorating. To be pinned, held down, dominated by something that might let him live, might kill him—Alba only knew the unsatisfied swirling in his gut would soon tear him open, making him writhe and gasp, bracing for Eridanys to penetrate him with every grind of his tail between Alba's thighs.

The anticipation became all he could think about, sliding a hand between them, where he thought he might find the man's cock—but there were only flat, slippery scales. Alba groped further, until his fingers pressed into a dip in the muscles between his hips, slicing inside and summoning an animal sound from the man on top of him.

"Careful, sailor," Eridanys growled, and Alba nearly pulled his hand away in surprise, but Eridanys grabbed his wrist first. Smiling at him, darkly, intensely, then coaxing it back despite those words. "I don't like to be teased. Tempt me at your own risk."

Alba didn't know what to say, though didn't try to pull his hand back again, either. He touched his fingers to the slit once more, then pressed through the narrow opening, finding the inside as warm and wet as his own when turned on. Eridanys' breath caught, brows furrowing as Alba explored deeper, hypnotized by how the siren's expression shifted from focused to the briefest flicker of soft pleasure. A twitch that lasted only a moment before tightening again, Eridanys' lips parting with a breath as Alba's fingers explored further—finding the head of a swollen cock, dripping and slippery. One—and then two, straining to emerge where Alba might touch them more.

Alba didn't know how—he didn't know how to fondle a cock except by what he'd seen in brothels up and down the northern shoreline. But as the two heads slipped from the slit, Alba stroked one of them, letting his hand move how it felt natural. The growing hardness twitched against his palm, long and thick, textured with smooth scales and boney ridges beneath skin like that of his upper body. Soft but firm, warm and dribbling stringy pearls of pre-cum. His second cock was fleshier, softer, lacking the same bumpy exterior, but the size alone made it still intimidating.

Alba stroked the one in his hand, the siren's hips rolling in and out to gently thrust within his inexperience grasp. Circling his thumb over the tip, Alba watched Eridanys' expression with each movement, learning where he felt it most every time his lips parted for breath or his brows furrowed or his jaw clenched. Quietly enjoying that feeling of taking control of the arrogant siren for himself, even if just for a moment.

And only for a moment it was, as Eridanys soon grabbed Alba's hand, pressing it into the wet seaweed-caked stone beneath them. Breathing heavy, his opposite hand hooked under Alba's jaw, crushing their mouths together once more. Alba suffocated beneath the demands of it, before jerking his head to the side and gasping as the ridged cock rutted against him, filling him with another swirl of sweltering excitement. Eridanys' second cock lapped at him lower, teasing his rear and sidling inside slightly more and more with every roll of Eridanys' hips. Opening him slowly, stretching and spreading warm, slippery fluid inside that numbed any of the pain that might come once it finally couldn't wait any longer.

Eridanys' hands found the backs of Alba's knees, finally pressing him wide with all his weight behind it. Alba bit back a sound of surprise, then a gasp of discomfort as his hip jolted and a spark of pain bolted up the back of his leg. He pressed knuckles between his teeth as the ridged cock circled the sensitive folds of his skin, sliding between them before catching and slowly pushing inside.

Choking on another sharp gasp of surprise, of panic and then discomfort, Alba searched for the taste of pleasure beneath it, knowing there was honey to be had at the end of the first bite. He just forced himself to breathe, to keep the cries out of his mouth, only his fingernails digging into Eridanys' flesh as any proof of distress. Fingers that raked shallow lines up Eridanys' back, his arms, his shoulders; tangling in Eridanys' hair and pulling at the roots as every muscle in his body contracted. Forgetting the freezing chill of the water, the rocks scraping against his back, he felt only the swollen pressure of a cock buried between his legs, the other teasing deeper into his ass with each thrust.

Thrusts that started slow and controlled, allowing Eridanys to kiss him again, to bite at his shoulder, to push hair from Alba's face and command Alba to meet his eyes. But the moment Alba did, Eridanys' own face furrowed, and he pressed deeper. Harder. Pulling back and slamming in again, scraping teeth over Alba's lips parted in a gasp, practically folding him in half with hands still pinned in the crooks of Alba's legs. Using his entire body weight to bury himself to the root of his cocks, until both fully disappeared into Alba's body, until his stomach and hips slapped flush against the backs of Alba's thighs.

The rolling thrusts came hard and fast until Alba was drooling, whimpering, until he couldn't feel the pain of his hip or the rocks against his back, nothing but the crushing weight of Eridanys on top of him, the stretching, sweltering pressure of two cocks taking ownership of him. Splitting him where nothing else ever had, until he didn't know the difference between pleasure and pain, only that he—didn't want it to stop.

He wanted to be crushed, devoured, filled until he no longer felt a single thing. Until there was only Eridanys wrapping arms around him, pulling him close, pinning him as the thrusts continued, humming from the back of his throat again and melting the sharp, prickling edges of Alba's inside into wax.

Dominated until Alba's body was no longer his, all of it culminating higher and higher and higher with every slamming movement inside. Piercing him, filling him, tearing him open for the sea and sky to witness, lost in a swirl of pleasure and fear and pure delight. Until he clawed at Eridanys' body in return, opening his mouth and biting down on the siren's shoulder, making Eridanys hiss and wrench back.

"More, more—" Alba's voice trembled, fighting to keep Eridanys close as tears flooded from his eyes, washed away by the sea spray and rain. "Don't stop—I want you—to fuck me more, more—"

Alba grabbed Eridanys' face, kissing him. Kissing him hard and desperately, enough that Eridanys' lips shifted and his teeth drew blood from Alba's. The cut was quickly met with a searching tongue, all while the siren's hips dug deeper, hard enough to jolt Alba's body against the ground. Scraping the skin of his back. Feeling nothing except the all-encompassing sensation of being owned and eaten.

He drowned in his own gasping breaths, spirit barely clinging to his bones through hooks knocked looser and looser every time the siren's tail met the back of his legs—until it all culminated in an orgasm that wrenched his soul back into place, clenching every muscle until his bones creaked, back curving upward and mouth releasing a sharp, honeyed cry of release.

Eridanys laid a trail of kisses down the center of Alba's chest, before connecting with Alba's mouth once more, breathing life back into him, barely keeping him conscious long enough to whisper one last thing:

"I will protect you from harm, from the sea and on land, with this act. So be it."

Alba's tired heart fluttered. It warmed, it kissed at the inside of his ribcage in a different way than the warmth kissed between his legs. Matching heat dripped from him as Eridanys slowly removed himself. Warmth covering every inch of him, a blanket against the cold sea, the cold air. Enough that he could close his eyes, and drift away as safe as anyone could be.

Before he did, he extended his hands. Finding Eridanys' face through blurry eyes, he managed a weary smile without knowing why he did it, pulling the siren down to kiss him one more time before the exhaustion claimed him.

"Me, too," he responded. The words made Eridanys' breath catch, staring at Alba as if he'd made some sort of mistake, like he was never meant to utter the same sentiment in return. But if the siren said anything else, it was too late. Alba was already sinking into darkness more encompassing than the nighttime sea.

Chapter 17

Alba dreamed of hands touching him all over— gentle and fondling, between his legs and down his chest, combing back through his hair while lips pressed tender kisses to his cheeks, his temples, his ears, his neck.

He dreamed of hands sharp and tearing, grabbing and twisting him into whatever shape they pleased, shoving fingers into his mouth and drowning him beneath a constant stream of saltwater that choked him, that slowly turned him to salt from the inside out. Drenching him over every inch, enough that even upon waking—there was wetness between his legs.

The breath he inhaled was sharp, tugging the rest of his body to the surface with it. Quick and instant, he stared at the ceiling for a long while before ever realizing he was awake, eyes open. Only then did he exhale what was stored in his lungs, long and drawn-out and exhausted. He took stock of his surroundings, then his body, realizing with a silent grimace how every part of him ached. It was a wonder he wasn't discolored over every inch of skin once he lifted his arms to search for bruises.

Sitting up, he realized the wetness between his legs wasn't only a remnant of the dream, as fluids dripped from inside of him. His face rushed with hot embarrassment, leaping to his feet to rush for the washbasin beneath the window, only to collapse to his knees with a groan as a sore ache bolted up his spine. Christ—what had that siren done to him?

Finally regaining enough composure to remain upright, he gripped the edge of the washbasin, first throwing handfuls of water over his face before grabbing the hand towel draped over the side. Propping a foot on the edge of the bowl, he grimaced again at the sore, swollen redness more evident than ever once exposed, throbbing and hot from all the merciless abuse earlier that morning. Still vivid in Alba's memory as he gently wiped himself clean, biting his lip as even the slightest recollection made his heart race and his insides squirm.

Despite the roughness of it all—there was no regret, no resentment that laced the memories. In fact, his squirming insides even traveled lower below his navel the more he remembered, enough that he had to stomp his foot back to the floor and shove the images away before he made another mess of himself all over again.

His neck, shoulders, collarbones burned like he'd been bare in the sun too long, and Alba peeked at himself in the dirty mirror on the wall to see if he'd actually been torn open a second time. His skin was adorned with red spots, bite marks like collars of bruised crimson jewelry, and he had to trail fingers over them more than once to fully accept they were real and couldn't be wiped away. For a moment he wondered if that was all it meant to be claimed as a siren's favorite—but then, in the dim afternoon light, a tousle of silver in his messy red hair caught his attention. Running fingers back through it, his mouth dangled open in silent shock when strands as stark white as Eridanys' spilled from the hairline over his right ear.

A *caller of the shore*. That was what Eridanys had called him.

Alba touched the silvery piece of hair again, enchanted by it. How it shined slightly even in the low light, like the siren had implanted a handful of his own hair into Alba's scalp. A sign of ownership, most likely. A sign of warning to anyone who saw, perhaps. Alba was accounted for by something they wouldn't want to cross; something more dangerous than the image of merely a protective braid in his hair behind his ear. Something anything of the sea and anything of the land might know to stay away from.

It was enough to make his insides burn hotter, finally turning away and hobbling to the other side of the room. To yank on clean clothes—specifically a shirt with a high enough collar to cover the markings on his neck—and get to work prepping the lantern. To give himself anything else to think about, unsure how much more remembering he could take.

STEPPING out into the wind as the sun set, Alba squinted toward the water lapping against the rocks, surprising even himself when he smiled at the sight of a white moon-spot floating above the surface. It gazed back at him, just long enough to confirm Alba was up and alive, before plunking back down under again. Why did that make Alba chuckle? Why did his smile remain half-quirked all the way to the lighthouse door, all the way up the winding stairs with his cane in one hand and a book in the other? He must be going mad.

How would he ever explain what he'd done to his mother? What in the world would she say? Would she smile and congratulate him; would she sigh in exasperation, unsurprised her touch-starved sailor son had been so willing to open his legs for the first thing to call to him? Alba's face boiled in embarrassment for a handful of reasons, deciding right away that when he did eventually meet his mother again, there may simply be some things he would never share of his time in Moon Harbor.

Such circling madness continued through the night, constantly forcing himself to push away any sudden memories of the morning before. How it felt to be held so tightly in such imposing arms—how it felt to shiver and go numb beneath the cold, crashing waves. The taste of Eridanys' mouth, salty and sweet; how many times he nearly drowned during their ritual.

He didn't expect Eridanys to be there again when the next morning came, waiting outside the lighthouse door as Alba emerged. Scaring him enough that he screamed and had to bend over his knees to catch his breath. Eridanys laughed—a sound that edged too closely to casting a spell. The man even bent over to pick up the book Alba dropped, naked and dripping like every other time he'd only just emerged from the sea. Alba's eyes accidentally slid down his body to where the glamoured human-anatomy lacked the same impressive display as he'd come to know, quickly glancing back up again when he realized he stared.

Alba thanked Eridanys as the book was handed back, only to be interrupted when a mouth was suddenly on his. Stumbling back into the rough exterior of the lighthouse, Eridanys pressed into him, chest to chest and soaking Alba's shirt, a knee tucking between his legs. The book and his cane tumbled to the grass a second time as Alba instinctively butterflied his hands over Eridanys' chest, not pushing him away, not pulling him closer, just—feeling him. Feeling how the siren's heart pounded in excitement. How his face moved as Alba's hands traveled higher, to Eridanys' shoulders, then his neck, then to cup his jaw. Kissing him back before he realized what he was doing, caught in the rapturous sound of a song no longer being sung.

"Damnit," Alba finally gasped as a single sense of reality sparked in the back of his mind. "What—do you want?" He meant to say more, breathless with hands still on Eridanys' face, but the man was pulling down the high collar of his shirt and kissing under his ear, down the side of his neck.

"You. Again."

"Why—?" Alba couldn't believe it. He inhaled sharply, embarrassingly when Eridanys' thigh between his legs shifted, grinding into him, making his sore insides glimmer like sunlight. More sensitive than ever after everything he'd been through the night before. "N-not on the rocks again, though, right?"

Eridanys smiled—Alba heard it in his breath—pulling away to look at him before kissing the roots of Alba's hair where the silver strands grew. Not in affection so much as—possession. Alba was owned, accounted for by something of the sea, and Eridanys was clearly satisfied with knowing he was the one who placed the mark. It compelled Alba to rake fingers through Eridanys' hair in return, frowning as there was no ginger-red streak to match.

Eridanys kissed him again just as Alba noticed two rowboats on the water, headed in their direction. Inhaling sharply, he beat his fist against Eridanys' chest until the siren finally growled a complaint and pulled back. As soon as he did and Alba could grab his stubborn face and turn it, his demeanor changed in an instant. His arms around Alba's body tightened, as if he thought they were on their way to take him.

"It's probably Mr. Michaels to take me to town," Alba explained. Not wanting Eridanys to get the wrong impression. "You should get back in the water—"

But Eridanys ignored him, suddenly taking Alba's hand, scooping up his cane and book from the grass, and hurrying to pull him back to the house. Alba limped after him, snapping not to move so fast, only for Eridanys to growl in annoyance and turn to scoop him up in a single arm, instead. Alba's face flared hot, cursing and whacking him with closed fists again, all the way to the house where Eridanys finally put him back down.

"No, no!" he protested, smacking the man on the shoulder with his book. "I said go get back in the *water*, damnit!"

"And what if it's someone else come to beat you within an inch of your life?" Eridanys snapped, eyes still sharp, jaw still clenched. "You're not any good to me if you're dead. Not even a useful meal once your heart stops." He jabbed a finger into Alba's chest.

"Oh—we'll talk about *that* later!" Alba shoved the prodding finger away with his book, using his cane for another hit when Eridanys snatched the book away. "At least hide upstairs where no one will see you! I don't wanna to have to explain you to anyone either, you know!"

Eridanys' expression tightened, furrowing in every way to say he wished to fight about it more, but by then knew Alba was as stubborn as he was. He turned and stomped up the stairs, reaching the top just as the incoming rowboats clunked against the rocks outside.

Alba barely managed to rip fingers through his braid and re-plait it to hide the white streak, barely tying off the ends when a knock came to the door. Inhaling a deep breath, shaking out his hands, he made one final adjustment to the collar of his shirt before going to the door to answer, even managing a smile and a greeting and a believable show of surprise to find Eugene on the other side. Behind him, three other men made their way up the grass, not to the door, but in the direction of the lighthouse. Alba recognized one of them as someone who'd sat in the net-repairing circle on the dock the last time he went into town.

"Mornin', lad," Eugene said with a smile and tip of his cotton hat. Alba's racing heart relaxed just slightly at how normal it was, how the old man clearly didn't see a moonlit naked stranger running around the house hand-in-hand with his wickie. "Glad to see our last guest left you be. Assumed as much when the lamp kept gettin' lit—hope he didn't rough you up too much."

It took Alba a moment to realize Eugene was referring to Marco, barely managing an awkward smile and nod before he continued: "Thought I'd bring you your over-pay while the boys are getting things from the old lamp."

"The old lamp?" Alba asked as Eugene handed a rolled wad of cash over, leaning through the doorframe to look, watching as the others were indeed at the door of the retired larger lighthouse and letting themselves in. He remembered himself, then, jumping and stepping back. "Sorry, you can come in. Bein' out here all by myself has me forgettin' my manners, apparently." He barely heard the man's reply upon glancing down at the cash, only half surprised when it wasn't standard dollars there waiting for him, but rather dully printed paper with blue ink swirling around the corners, and what he swore had to be a peek at a mermaid under the rubber tie. "I thought the older sister was locked up for good?"

"Think I mentioned once that we store festivity goods in her belly." The man grinned, jokingly smacking Alba on the stomach and making him wheeze. Alba managed a polite, breathy little laugh in return. "If you're wantin' a ride back t'shore for supplies today, you'll be there with us 'til Thursday. New moon pulls the tide out too far for boats to leave the docks, so there won't be any activity in the harbor. Won't need to tend to the lantern 'til then, neither. If you wanna make a few extra bucks, some captains might need a hand gettin' bigger boats out to anchor at sea for the time, too. Gotta scoot them from the dock so there's no damage when the water shallows out."

"Oh—um, alright. Maybe. I'll come to town, though, sure," Alba wasn't exactly sure how to answer, though talk of the new moon's far tide reminded him of how high the full moon's king tide swelled in comparison. Apparently there were a lot of reasons the place was called *Moon Harbor*. He'd have to ask Eridanys if merrow magic had anything to do with it. "I'll grab some things and meet you by your boats. Do you need any help gettin' supplies from the old lighthouse?"

"Nah. Brought some of my biggest guys to do all the heavy-liftin'. You just mind your things and meet us out there." He pinched Alba's arm as he said it, a silent comment on how flimsy he was in comparison to other sailors who still wrangled fishing nets and giant crab pots day in and day out. Alba frowned, swiping himself away, which only made Eugene bark another laugh before seeing himself out.

Tucking the strange money into his pocket, Alba climbed the stairs to the upper loft. He nudged Eridanys back from where he crowded the passageway with head stretched out to listen to the conversation below. Only at the sight of claw marks in the railing did Alba realize how well Eridanys did resisting his urge to leap down the stairs and cause a scene.

"I'm gonna go into town with them, I think," Alba explained in a low voice, just in case any of the others were in hearing range. "God knows I could use a drink after what you did to me last night. Or ten. Oh—did you mate with me on the new moon as part of the ritual or somethin'?"

"The new moon isn't until tomorrow night," Eridanys argued. "And *no*, I could have mated with you whenever I liked. And I will continue to in the future."

"Apparently the low tide makes it impossible to sail in and out of the harbor," Alba ignored that last comment. "So they move all the boats out to sea before then... Why do you look so annoyed? You didn't already know that? You used to live here."

"I... knew that," he muttered, but averted his eyes as he did. "I only wasn't considering it in terms of sailboats, obviously... Traditionally, during neap tides, merrow would join humans on land to celebrate the new moon anyway, you know," he added, as if to prove it.

"You don't have to get defensive. I believe you."

"I'm not defensive," he practically growled. Alba still laughed under his breath.

"Whatever you say. Seems you get to continue that tradition this year, with the legs you can use on their shore thanks to me. You can't join me on the boat over, but if you wanna meet me on the other side, we can go see what's singin' in the woods together. Assumin' our little ritual last night worked like you said it would."

"It most certainly worked," Eridanys muttered, dropping heavily onto the edge of the bed as Alba went about finding clean clothes to pack. "Did they invite you to join them for anything else while you're there? New moon celebrations used to be quite the spectacle, with food and dancing and rituals."

"What kind of rituals?"

"Merrow worship the moon, so when she's grown tired and

fades from the sky, we dance and sing and make merry to draw her back out again. Making offerings to try and draw her back out again, gifts to show how much we miss her. How we noticed her absence. To remind her there are beings down here who would miss her beauty if she sleeps any longer…" He trailed off like such things were pleasant memories, and Alba said nothing to interrupt. Appreciating that rare, brief moment of contentment on Eridanys' normally harsh expression. "Makes me wonder if they've kept it up since my kin left."

"Seein' as it affects the tides so much… I have to wonder the same thing," Alba said with a tiny smile. "I imagine the townspeople would have their own reasons for wantin' to draw the moon back out again, considerin' she takes the sea with her when she goes."

"Hm…" Eridanys mumbled, like he hadn't thought about it that way. Like he was surprised at such a sincere response.

"And if they don't, well, you and I will just have to do somethin' ourselves, won't we? I'm sure we could make enough noise and offer enough attention to bring her back out, just the two of us. Does she also like licorice? I'll buy some in the general store with my first payment."

Eridanys didn't scoff; he didn't laugh or shake his head or mutter to himself in annoyance. He just looked thoughtfully at Alba for a long moment, like there was something else he wanted to say. Or he was waiting for Alba to add something else, something that would have been more expected than whatever foolishness he'd just rambled on about. Eventually the silence made Alba itch, and he tossed the bag over his shoulder with a change of clothes inside.

"Well—are you gonna join me or not?"

"I'll join you," Eridanys answered, shaking his head. "I'll join you! So stop asking. Just don't get into any trouble until I meet you, alright?"

"Where should we meet?"

"Where were you lured by the voices in the trees?"

"Erm—on the edge of the cemetery. But I don't think..."

"Then meet me at the cemetery. Tonight, before the sun sets."

"But—"

Eridanys was already getting back to his feet. He approached where Alba lingered at the top of the stairs, tugging on his braid before cupping the back of Alba's head to pull him in and kiss where the silver strands of hair were hidden beneath his natural red ones.

"You will not fall victim to the song of anyone but me," he reiterated. "So stop doubting my promise. Before I get annoyed."

Alba frowned, pulling away. Eridanys had indeed explained that already, but it didn't do anything to ease his nerves when reminded of how he'd been lured previously without even knowing it. Instead of arguing, he just closed his eyes and let out a breath.

"Wait here until we leave. Don't let anyone see you."

"I've gone this long."

Alba rolled his eyes, adjusting his bag. He offered Eridanys one last glance over his shoulder, before reclaiming his cane from the foot of the bed and making his way down the stairs.

CHAPTER 18

Across the water, Eugene surprised Alba when he offered a bed at his own home while they were in town, and Alba couldn't help but feel like it was some sort of trick while considering it. He agreed only once the man laughed and slapped him on the shoulder, assuring him there was nothing to worry about, neither him nor his wife would bite so long as Alba didn't give them a reason to. Alba just laughed awkwardly in reply. Not sure he wanted to ask what that could possibly mean.

The things Eridanys told him about new moon traditions between humans and merrow floated in and out of mind as he followed Eugene from the docks up the road, silently observing the broad range of decorations being set up around the town square as the people crowded around with more life than he'd seen since first arriving.

Embroidered tapestries, printed-paper art posters, endless strings of pearls and shells and woven seagrass were hung from doorways and looped around the neck of the dry mermaid fountain at the head of town. Handfuls of people sat in circles weaving baskets on their laps while chatting, discussing all the treasures and trinkets they'd found in months previous when the tide went out and gave them the chance to search the exposed mud. Things they hoped to find the following morning when they had a chance to go out looking again. Some even mentioned how the merrow would arrive once the sun went down, as if they still believed it. As if they only said so out of habit, or perhaps truly didn't know there was only one merrow left in their harbor.

Anyone who didn't know any better would assume they chattered about pretty shells and other gems—but Alba knew what they likely, actually referred to. Dropped merrow trinkets, treasures, abandoned by the kinship that once filled their harbor. His own curiosity tickled the back of his neck, wondering was sorts of things were hidden in the mud—but then the fluted pipes whistled as he passed by, and he pushed the thoughts away. Reminded of the spirits in the woods just a ways further up the road. Not wanting to think about how any of them might be able to see as he scoured the treasure graveyard just below.

The Michaels' home was a few blocks from the sea, as old as all the neighboring buildings surrounding it, sagging beneath its own weight and seemingly only remaining upright with the help of thick layers of brine and barnacles misplaced by the constant wind and impregnating the bricked facade.

Someone waited to greet them the moment they walked inside, as if eager to meet the wickie who'd survived the longest stretch of time tending to their light in months. It caught Alba off guard to be ambushed the moment Eugene invited him through the door, but he put on his most polite smile once he realized, even straightening up and trying to relax the rest of his posture like his mother used to always say when visiting neighbors on his nights back home. *You look like a feral cat being taken inside for the first time. Stop hunching like that. Why do you look so alarmed? Straighten up. Meet their eyes. You're a grown man, for god's sake. Stop acting like a salty sailor. I will not let you become an anti-social man who prefers the sea over people.*

Alba wasn't sure her efforts ever amounted to anything, all things considered.

He shook Phyllis Michaels' hand as she extended it to him,

just like he had everyone else who ever wanted to see him when he returned to Welkin. While Eugene was thick, sturdy even in his old age from all his years on the sea, his wife in comparison was barely a rod of a thing, though her handshake was firm as any he'd ever been on the receiving end of. She smiled at him with cheeks flushed pink, though something told him most of the color could be attributed to powder makeup. Everyone in that town seemed to doll themselves up as much as they could with pigments on their eyes, lips, cheeks.

"I kept wonderin' when I'd finally meet our newest lighthouse keeper," she said. Her voice reminded Alba of his mother's, calm and warm and naturally friendly. She even smiled like Edythe once did, and Alba couldn't help the immediate sense of endearment that softened his nerves. "Gene says you sailed some ten years before coming to work for us—a wonder you survived that long, considering that bright red hair of yours. And still so young! Such pretty blue eyes, too. You sure you weren't drinking saltwater while out on the sea, lad? Heard she loves blue eyes; might've spared you for it despite that hair."

"Phyl," Eugene grunted.

"I appreciate your hospitality, for lettin' me stay the night," Alba said, not sure how to respond to the rest of it. He was used to hearing such things, especially from the wives of other sailors, though never said as cheerfully as Phyllis Michaels did. Usually thick with apprehension, like they secretly prayed Alba wouldn't be assigned to any ship where their husbands or sons were also designated.

"*'Hospitality'*, hm?" Phyllis beamed, still clutching Alba's hand. "Fancy word for a wickie."

Alba cleared his throat a second time, managing another awkward smile. "I read a lot in my free time, ma'am. Plenty of it while tendin' the lantern, too."

"We need more men who are well-read," she winked, before nudging her husband, who made a gruff sound like in disagreement. "At the very least, to *read* at all would be an improvement."

"Stop houndin' the lad over his talk, Phyl," Eugene said, finally removing his wool cap and running fingers back through the thinning hair underneath. "Show him to his room, will ya? I gotta get the boys to start movin' boats out." He glanced back at Alba. "You have it in you to help out?"

Alba absolutely did not, especially with how his leg hurt like a bitch just from the hike up the road, not to mention he'd been ruthlessly attacked by a merrow on the lighthouse rocks just the morning prior—but he nodded, nonetheless. It was the least he could do. It would help time pass faster, anyway. A part of him was even curious to be out on the water when the tide shifted, to see if it really was as dramatic as Eugene had described.

Eugene nodded back, returning the hat to his head. "I'll find some boots and a rubber coat for 'ya, then. Dawson's old might fit you well enough."

Alba almost asked who *Dawson* was, vaguely remembering Eugene mentioning something about a son, but Eugene wandered off toward another room before he could. Phyllis waved Alba back around toward the staircase to the second floor, and Alba bowed his head before obeying. At the top, she led him down a narrow hallway with floors that squeaked with every step, pausing to pull the door of one room closed just before Alba passed, then continuing to another at the end.

"Sorry for the mess," she said while pushing against the door —though it took a little more ramming with her hip and a steady press of her hands on the wood to really knock it open. "This was my son's room up until a few years ago."

"Dawson, right?" he hazarded a guess, and Phyllis smiled at him with a nod, though said nothing else. Focused on tut-tutting the mess on the other side of the door, hurrying in as soon as the path was cleared to gather up anything knocked over by all her shoving.

Clutter piled from floor to ceiling in some places, filling nearly every corner and down one wall in a random array of boxes, bowls, piles of clothing, blankets, interspersed with shiny trinkets, photographs leaning against one another on the floor, fish netting and counterweights. When Phyllis apologized again, Alba told her it was no mind, appreciating anywhere warm to sleep for the next night or two. Whenever he spoke, she smiled warmly at him all over again, like merely having a young voice in the house was enough to make her heart sing.

"Does Dawson still live in Moon Harbor?" He couldn't resist further, dropping his bag on the bed as Phyllis hurried to clear more junk from it. "I've been givin' all my cigarette cards to Mr. Michaels, who said your son likes to collect them…"

"Oh, he did, did he?" She asked, and Alba sensed the slightest twinge of irritation. Small enough that once she turned around to smile at him again, he could convince himself he'd only imagined it. "Stays here mostly, but sometimes spends a night or two with a neighbor when he needs a change of scenery and they're feelin' sweet on him. Folk here love doting ever since he got sick, a miracle he hasn't been spoiled rotten. Sweet thing. You likely won't be runnin' into him anytime soon, though, so don't worry about a stranger sneakin' up on you in your sleep."

Alba smiled awkwardly, realizing he'd most definitely brushed up against the boundary of what would be shared about their son. He quickly changed the subject, asking about the decorations he'd seen on the street while following Eugene there, instead, and Phyllis seemed just as happy to join him in talking about literally anything else.

THE WORK of moving larger fishing boats out to sea by far wasn't the most difficult work Alba had ever done, but with the state Eridanys had left him in, it wasn't particularly easy, either.

His legs were sore, not even considering the crack in his hip. His thoughts were distracted, face and ears constantly going warm with every reminder, every random thought back to it. How Eridanys had kissed him again that morning with such eagerness. Even how the siren's face had changed while talking about old new moon traditions—Alba wasn't used to it. It shouldn't have meant anything, but he seemed keen on noticing everything Eridanys did since allowing the man to see him in such a vulnerable state. To *put* him in such a vulnerable state.

With every salt-soaked boat he helped navigate out of the harbor, Alba distracted himself by puzzling through all the ways he could ask about the history of the town, the harbor, if any of the sailors he helped had ever seen anything *out of the ordinary* while fishing; or even if any of them knew anything about any of the previous lighthouse keepers who Alba had already outworked just by staying as long as he had.

"That last one before 'ya was a real thing of gossip," the grizzled man said from behind the wheel, struggling to pick his words like he didn't want to say the wrong thing but was already in too deep. All the while not bothering to offer help as a swell tipped the boat and Alba nearly drowned beneath a falling pile of netting. "Rare to hear 'bout a lady tendin' a lantern, you know? Heard from a doctor years ago that there's somethin' 'bout how their feminine organs tangle up inside 'em if they stand too close to something always spinnin' like that. Tried warnin' her once, but she just smiled and said she wasn't plannin' on havin' no more babies anytime soon."

"The last lighthouse keeper—was a lady?" Alba asked, interest piqued even as the rest of him focused on gathering the nets back up. The sailor grunted again, adjusting the pipe in his mouth. "What was her name? You said people gossiped about her?"

"Didn't know 'er name, but... runned off, just like the rest. Kept t'erself," came the answer. "Gossip wasn't no more different than what they say about you, lad."

Alba frowned. "And what d'they say about me?"

The man's eyes hovered over the exposed black marks on Alba's arms, and Alba realized he should've known.

"Just that the sea takes a strange likin' to ladyfolk and gingers," he said. "How we should turn the next one away if they're one or the other again, or we risk the whole town goin' under."

Alba rolled his eyes, finally shoving the netting back into place. Still—his thoughts ran in a frenzy in the back of his mind as the boat puttered the rest of the way out from shore, churning over every one of those words. A lady tending a lighthouse... saying she wasn't planning on having any more children... Alba could even imagine the exact sort of smile that would have been on Edythe's face if the words had been hers. Biting back what she really wished to say in favor of playing vapid and silly, mostly just wishing to end the conversation so she could get back to her beer. It made him smile to himself. Hoping, maybe, it really had been her. God knew it would explain why Alba thought he found her handwriting in the keeper's log during his first week—a moment he rarely allowed himself to think about too much, else he might spiral into madness.

He almost asked the man to describe what the last wickie-lady had looked like—but then something else caught his attention in the nets he'd piled back in place.

Not unlike the damaged one worked by that circle of hands the last time he was in town, the netting on that boat was woven with silvery threads. Like the hair of an elderly woman, or rather —Eridanys' own moon-kissed strands. Similar enough that Alba couldn't help running a thumb over where the glassy pieces shimmered between the other fibers, trying to determine if they were intentionally woven in, or perhaps just tangled.

In a harbor once lush with merrow, and considering how much hair Eridanys alone had, Alba thought it wasn't unlikely that anything trawling the water might catch on loose strands lost in normal day-to-day. But despite such a simple explanation, he couldn't shake it. It nibbled at him, endlessly, no matter how far into the back of his mind he tried to tuck it away.

. . .

It was late evening by the time the work was finished. Alba was thrilled to finally be done—until that sorrowful song called out from the trees, and he paused to listen. Standing right off the side of the dock, he was the only one to pay them any mind, every other townsperson going about their business. As if they truly didn't hear it; as if they'd simply gotten used to it. He had to wonder which came first—the fluted pipes on their homes, or the pale faces singing in the woods.

Inhaling a deep breath, he checked the horizon over his shoulder. The clouds were thinner than they'd been that morning, making him think they might scatter no different than on the full moon. Offering a clear view of the sky where the moon would be nowhere to be found, to be beseeched and offered gifts in pleas to return, just like Eridanys described.

Making his way up the road, he had to stop and catch his breath more times than he was proud, having overdone it on the boats with an already overworked body. His hip throbbed like it barely clung into place by a thin strip of muscle, not helped by how the arm swinging his cane trembled any time he put weight on it. Only the thought of Eridanys waiting for him at the cemetery kept him going.

Reaching the top of the road, sweat dripped down Alba's face, loose hairs having to be pushed from his eyes in order to see clearly. He was glad for the emptiness of the grassy hilltop on the other side of the town, glad for the lack of salt-scatterers on his heels, thrilled for the lack of faces peering out from the woods. There was only crashing waves on the distant black-sand shores, birds from the forest, gulls crooning overhead. He took another moment to stop and breathe in the fresh air, letting it coat the inside of his lungs and quell his nerves. Unsure what made him so anxious to start—though spotting a hooded figure amongst the tombstones at the end of the cemetery footpath reminded him.

He knew it was Eridanys without having to see his face, embarrassed at how well he could recognize the man just by the way he walked, with a little too much elegance, but at the same time with hints of uncertainty like he wasn't quite used to propping up on two legs.

Eridanys moved among the grave markers like he was looking for something. He paused in front of each one as if to read the names, lips parting and whispering under his breath as Alba approached. If it hadn't been for his choppy footwork in the long grass, he might have even been able to sneak up him, but trying to handle his cane without losing it to the weeds was a noisy affair.

Once Eridanys spotted him, instead of saying *hello* or anything like it, he pointed at the headstone in front of him. "Can you read this?"

"Huh? Oh," Alba hobbled a little closer. "Uh, looks like *Abigail Parson.*"

"What about that one?"

Alba followed Eridanys' motion. "Miranda Deloitte."

"And that one?"

"Roland Sinclair..." he trailed off, raising an eyebrow. "You can't read, can you?"

"I can read just fine."

"It's alright if you can't. Doesn't bother me."

Eridanys scoffed, adjusting the scarf wrapped around his head to hide his hair and shadow his eyes as the sun barely peeked through the thinning clouds overhead. "I can read *fine*, but not human languages. My last partner taught me the English alphabet, but hardly more than that. Never saw a reason to ask. Always talked down to me when I tried, anyway."

"Sorry to hear that," Alba said. Eridanys threw him a sharp look, like Alba was on the verge of scolding him. Instead, Alba shrugged. "Readin's hard, 'specially if you don't learn as a baby. My mother taught me, but just enough to get by. Takes me weeks to get through even small books. Most folk I sailed with never learned how to read, neither, and plenty were smarter than any educated man I've ever met."

Eridanys didn't know what to say to that, like he'd never heard such words strung together in that order.

"I'm startin' to think your partner didn't treat you so well," Alba went on.

"I never said that."

"Didn't have to. Any other names you want to know?"

"No," Eridanys grumbled, then took Alba's hand, pulling him close then nudging him toward the trees. "I want to get this over with."

"What—you want me to walk back up there? By myself?"

"Don't know if they'll talk if they see me."

"Why not?"

Eridanys smirked. He nudged Alba forward again. "Don't think they'll be too thrilled to know I came back. Let alone alive."

Alba frowned. "Startin' to think your kin didn't treat you so well, neither..."

"Just go. I won't let them pull you in."

"I'm trustin' you." Alba's voice shook slightly, not realizing until the words were already out. He steadied his cane. "Don't take that for granted."

Eridanys was quiet for a moment, letting the words settle, before touching Alba's back once more. Not a nudge that time, but a simple, gentle touch.

"You can trust me."

Alba limped toward the mouth of the dirt path that lead into the trees, where the rope decorated with bells shifted in the evening wind. There was no song to greet him that time, to tempt him, and he wondered if it really was because he'd mated with Eridanys, or maybe just because they saw him coming. It did nothing to settle his nerves, fighting the urge to glance over his shoulder as he approached, wishing Eridanys was there with him.

He reached the gap in the trees, halting just before stepping through. Pausing for a moment, holding his breath, listening. Unsure if he was more unsettled or relieved by the silence. Finally, he cleared his throat.

"Hello," he said into the shadows, eyes flicking toward any

flash of movement. "I was here a while ago. You... drew me in with your song. Will you sing for me again?"

Alba thought he heard breaths. Perhaps a whisper, perhaps a soft giggle. It could have been the wind, or his own thumping heart playing tricks in his ears. Only when goosebumps flooded his arms, and a pale spot shifted behind a far tree, was he sure he wasn't alone.

"Are you a caller of the shore?" A soft voice cooed, gentle and alluring. Ghostly fingers suddenly touched the side of his head where the silver hair was tucked away, and it took everything in Alba not to lurch in surprise. "*Who is your caller of the sea, brine witch?*"

"Who else could it be? Who else is left?"

"Delphinus? Hydrus?"

"Cetus?"

"Circinus?"

Alba didn't answer. He couldn't. His ears rang as he immediately understood, every answer he sought striking like lightning with those teasing words alone. Confirming his first instinct all along.

"Then..." he croaked, trying to form a sentence in his mind, struggling to push it through to his mouth. "Then—you really are the merrow who used to live in this harbor?"

He jumped when echoing laughter responded, some close, some far off. More pallid faces blurred behind the trees, never lingering long enough for him to see their features clearly. Alba's heart thundered.

"You've been long from Moon Harbor, haven't you, child?"

"I'm not from—"

"But you smell of it."

He almost told them about his parents, words nearly spilling out of him as if pulled on a string. He barely bit them back, fighting to center himself back into his body. Recalling what Eridanys said, how mating would protect Alba from another song, but not their tricks.

"Why are you in the trees? Why aren't you in the water?"

"You have such lovely blue eyes."

"Who—"

"Those bloodstains on your skin—who do they belong to?"

"Come, let us get a closer look."

"Oh, sister, smell the salt on him. Whose call did you answer, child? Who did you mate with?"

"Oh—"

Alba's breath caught.

"They reek of Eridanys."

Silence fell. Hard and fast and sharp, cutting through Alba's flesh without leaving a mark. Leaving him trembling despite his best efforts, shivering in a sudden wave of icy cold air.

"Eridanys, the alm of the fata morgana... Does he really swim in our harbor again?"

"I was sure it was he we sensed."

"Why did he not answer our song?"

"He could not have crossed the sand without someone to call for him."

"Perhaps he answers now, with his new mate."

"Eridanys would never mate with such a red-haired wisp of a thing."

"Has he come to save us with a heart full of remorse?"

"Would you like to know what happened to the last human to call for him?"

"Closer, child, please, tell us more. Tell us of our brother returned from the sea-obscura."

More ghostly hands grasped at Alba's by his side, pulling on his cane, nearly knocking him off balance—but something else grabbed him from behind before he could be tugged a single step. Anchoring him where he stood.

The immediate eruption of gasps and hisses from the trees was deafening, making Alba flinch, only to be pulled back another step and tucked under Eridanys' arm. Protectively, firmly, as if there was still a threat of him being taken.

"He asked if you are the merrow who used to live in this harbor," Eridanys growled into the darkness. Bitter laughter responded that time. Apprehensive, suddenly, as if Alba wasn't the only one with chills at the sound of the command. "You will not deny my shore caller his answer again."

"Of course it is us, you wicked thing!"

"How dare you speak with such disdain, after everything you've done!"

"The sea spat you back out to repent for your crimes and set us free, you know it as well as we do!"

"Why else would you come back to this place that recoils at the smell of you!"

"Rotten creature! You brought this!"

Eridanys said nothing as the insults crashed over him, unmoving except to flex his hand on Alba's shoulder. Alba risked a glance up at him—but had to look away again just as quickly. The intensity of Eridanys' gaze would have turned any living thing to stone.

"Tell me what has happened to you," Eridanys said, ignoring all of their other calls. "Not so that I may save a single one of you, but so that I may thank whoever plucked your sorry souls from the sea to cleanse her of such vitriol."

Hissing, snarling answered.

"How dare you! Return to the fata morgana, you wretch! You were never a kin of ours."

"After we raised you, loved you!"

"You wish to see? Return to this place tomorrow in the mid-dark of the new moon and see what you've caused."

"See for yourself what you've done to us."

"Witness the consequences of your selfishness."

"See what they do to us while the moon rests from view."

"Perhaps the gods will finally take you once and for all—"

"Without a bone left behind to spit out again."

"And you, shore caller—"

Eridanys' hold on Alba tightened further.

"—Come bear witness yourself, see what this crimson-mouthed siren started. Come see why they did what they did to the blood you seek."

Eridanys gave no more chances for anything else to be spoken, sweeping Alba in one arm and pulling him from the trees. More snarling, biting sounds chased after them from the growing darkness, and Alba nearly turned to look, but Eridanys hissed at him, first.

"Don't," he whispered. "Don't spare them any more interest."

"My cane—"

Eridanys lifted it, clutched in his own hand. Tight, skin spread over the knuckles as tendons swelled through.

"You weren't in as right of a mind as you thought, sailor. Lucky I came when I did."

Alba snatched the cane back, finally managing to jerk himself out of Eridanys' arm. "I *was* bein' careful. You're the one who wanted me to speak to them by myself, anyway."

Eridanys didn't argue. Something about the new tense expression on his face told Alba he himself was conflicted about what he was so angry for, too, just gritting his teeth and glaring toward the sea as the sun set. After what felt like an eternity, the siren swung his arm back out again, scooping Alba by the waist and towing him back toward the town.

"You won't have to speak to them again," he muttered. "Good riddance."

"I'll gladly never speak them again," Alba huffed. "You, neither, if I could help it."

Eridanys surprised him with a sharp laugh, though it was sarcastic. "You say that so confidently, yet I felt how your heart raced the moment you realized I was behind you."

"Oh—fuck off! Let go of me!" Alba squirmed in the siren's strong arm, but Eridanys' grip remained firm, even laughing a bit more with the challenge of keeping hold on his thrashing companion.

"Don't fight so much, sailor. It gets me excited."

Alba groaned, giving in and letting the siren do whatever he pleased. Eridanys carried him until they reached the end of the cemetery footpath—but did so wordlessly. Not a sound leaving him as even Alba felt how the siren's mind suddenly drifted far away.

At the end of the path, he set Alba back down as the sky dimmed overhead, allowing stars to freckle against the increasingly dark backdrop in the absence of clouds. But even once Alba was free to walk on his own—Eridanys didn't continue. Not right away. He had his eyes turned upward, unmoving from where they huddled together alongside one the abandoned buildings at the edge of town. Far from any sound of the townspeople or their observing eyes, their excited chatter as they prepared for their new moon celebration the following night.

Alba didn't know when, exactly, his attention was drawn back from the stars to the siren standing next to him, but once his eyes lingered, Alba couldn't bring himself to pull away. No different from how he used to stare at the sky during long nights keeping watch on the deck in the middle of a dark sea, only the moon and her mantle of stars keeping him company, providing him any light to know whether his eyes were open or closed in such ringing emptiness.

Alba gazed as gently as he could at Eridanys, a child of the celestial goddess herself, not wanting him to be able to feel it. Not wanting him to know, to change how he stood or how his eyes traveled so carefully between every constellation as if he knew them all by name. Resisting the urge to ask if merrow also tracked the stars like humans did, telling stories and making pictures out of their shapes. He recalled the names mentioned by those voices in the trees, voices confirmed to be the siren's own lost kin. Names shared with the same stars Alba knew from books, the ones Eridanys tilted his chin to in front of him. Eridanys, himself, named after the river.

Alba soon realized, perhaps he was waiting for something. Something Eridanys would say, something he would do. Any movement that might hint at what the man was thinking, especially with what they'd just witnessed. All the things those faces said in the trees, mentioning constellations by name. Wondering if he searched for those stars in the sky, unable to help himself. But for as long as Alba looked at him, Eridanys never did anything except angle his face to the sky, as if waiting for her to spell something out for him directly.

"What are you—"

"Do sailors still use the sky to navigate?" Eridanys interrupted, making Alba jump. He hesitated, before biting back a wary laugh. Hoping the siren hadn't been reading his mind. "When I first told you my name, you knew it was from the stars."

"'Course we do. It's the most accurate map we got."

Eridanys didn't answer, didn't tease further, just continued staring up at the sky. Still waiting for its message to open up for him. Alba kept watching him, observing every twitch of his pale irises as they reflected the glowing white spots speckling the dark canvas. Without the moon to rival him, Alba thought he really was the most stunning thing to exist.

"The other merrow those spirits mentioned—they were all named after stars, too, weren't they?" Alba encouraged as casually as he could manage. Hoping Eridanys would tell him more. *Delphinus, Hydrus, Cetus, Circinus...*"

Eridanys still did not answer right away, but he nodded. Alba let him have his silence, not wanting to push any further if he truly didn't want to discuss it. Despite everything he wanted to know, both of Eridanys' relationship with those hissing things in the shadows and all the things they said to him.

Deciding just one more question might be worth the risk, he carefully added: "Will you do what they said? To go back tomorrow night, durin' the new moon..."

Eridanys considered it a moment, before closing his eyes. He exhaled a long breath.

"I'll have to think about it," he finally answered. "I still haven't decided... what I was even hoping to hear from them, once I found them. If I ever did. Let alone, especially now... whether or not I wish to care about anything they say. Or even the state they're in, how they got there... I..."

The silence that followed was as thick, as complex as Eridanys' expression, as the siren just continued gazing up at the stars. Waiting for his answer. To be told what he was meant to do next. Perhaps even what he was meant to think, to feel, like he'd never had the opportunity to do any such things for himself, before— like he'd always taken advice from the stars before deciding anything. Waiting for the moon to answer him, even as just the thinnest sliver she appeared as, before she'd disappear the following night. Perhaps too tired to respond even when one of her moonbeams from the sea needed guidance.

Alba didn't know what to say, either. The siren's words were heavy, enough that even he felt them as they left Eridanys' mouth. Alba only knew that wouldn't push it any further—only hoping that, perhaps by uttering the uncertainties out loud, it released some of the pressure of whatever had Eridanys' mind turning in such silence.

CHAPTER 19

ERIDANYS FOLLOWED ALBA SILENTLY THROUGH THE dark town, having waited long enough for most of the figures meandering about to retire to the bar or back home to their beds.

The siren kept the scarf pulled taut over his hair and face, turned low, doing his best to blend in with the darkness in a way that confirmed what he'd once said, that someone might recognize him. But more than that, Alba realized by the way he navigated even the narrowest of alleyways between buildings, that he was truly familiar with that place.

He must have once walked the streets with his human partner, where he was seen and known. Perhaps even by name. Even if not —someone may, at the very least, recognize him to be a merrow donning legs. And even if not then, should they spot him and Alba scurrying by in the darkness, they may wonder why someone who was clearly a stranger scowled so much at the decorations set up on the main road, mumbling to himself about all the things they did wrong. How some parts weren't meant to be on display until the following night. How they weaved grass in the wrong patterns and the silver flutes on the walls would drown out the ceremonial drums and clanging bells and singing should there be a single gust of wind—then how they shouldn't even bother, since human voices alone would surely be so ugly it would compel the moon to stay hidden forever. How they were missing some key tokens of appreciation for beseeching the goddess back, tokens always provided by the merrow when they joined the humans on land to dance and celebrate. How the whistling pipes were far too loud, when the night before the goddess disappeared was meant to be silent to allow her some of the peaceful rest she very well deserved before being summoned back again with raucous music.

Alba accidentally chuckled under his breath when the complaints grew more agitated, resulting in a snapped *"what are you laughing at?"* from the siren. That only made him snort and shake his head, swearing it was nothing and biting back further amusement. Telling Eridanys to make a list of all the things the people did wrong, that he and Alba would most certainly make up for it with their own private ceremony in the woods the following night.

Outside the Michaels' home, Eridanys stopped just before entering through the door. Inside it was dark, silent, hardly even the skitter of a mouse across the floor, but the man still went stiff as if he could sense something Alba couldn't. Alba gave him a long moment to say something, before reaching out to touch the back of his hand.

"You're actin' strange," he said. "Stranger than normal. Is everything alright?"

"Yes," Eridanys answered almost instantly, voice low. Stiff, unsure enough that Alba could tell it wasn't the entire truth. "Everything is fine."

"You're welcome to stay with me here tonight, if you'd like. If you promise to keep quiet and out of sight."

"Why?"

Alba frowned. He didn't realize it was a strange thing to offer, turning and flipping his braid. "I don't know. Nevermind, I guess. Go sleep in the cold sea all by yourself, like always—"

But Eridanys grabbed the back of Alba's jacket, mumbling about how Alba was the most stubborn person he'd ever met.

Alba didn't say anything, just stepped into the house while Eridanys' grip remained on the back of his coat.

He clung to it all the way to the stairs, then up them, then down the hallway, only releasing again once Alba stepped into his loaned room and held the door open for Eridanys to join him. Once again—the man stared inside, as if he could see something Alba couldn't. A ghost, a shadow, a threat lying low in the corners crowded with piles of forgotten belongings. Alba barely uttered a sound to ask if everything was alright again, but Eridanys snapped out of it, first. He stepped inside, practically yanking the door from Alba's grasp to close behind them.

"Did you visit town often when you had your human partner?" Alba could no longer resist the temptation once reassured that no one had heard or seen them sneak inside. He was in the process of shrugging his shirt off as Eridanys laid casually on the bed, arms crossed behind his head and gazing up at the ceiling with an unreadable look on his face.

"Not often," he answered. "But I see it's as miserable and rotten as I remember."

"Would the townspeople at least respond to you a little more positively than those merrow spirits in the woods?" Alba asked with a hint of sarcasm. Careful in choosing his words, watching Eridanys' reaction to see how he replied. Still not sure exactly what feelings the siren harbored after such a tense reunion—let alone the realization that everyone he'd ever known was seemingly trapped and haunting the land. "I can't imagine so, considerin' all the things your kin had to say..."

"No, I don't think so, either." Eridanys smirked, finally lifting his head to glance in Alba's direction. Watching as Alba shrugged off his shirt, folding it over his arm before undoing the braid in his hair. "What else did the spirits say about me? Before I joined you."

"Hmmm." Alba gazed out the window on the other side of the room, combing fingers through his hair, feeling every bump left behind by the plaits. "They said... they could smell you on me. Could tell I was a shore-caller right away. Said they also couldn't

believe you'd mate with someone with such red hair," he chuckled. "Nothin' much else."

"Hm," Eridanys hummed in what sounded like disappointment. Alba expected him to be gazing at the ceiling again when he
looked, but the man's eyes remained on him in the darkness.
Regarding him, his naked chest and back, the tattoos on his skin
and the black bloodstains that wove between them.

"Does that bother you?"

"What?" Alba asked, moving to untie his boots and finally
kick them off, next.

"That even they were shocked I would mate with a red-
headed thing like you."

"Not really."

"Why not?"

Alba shrugged. "I'm not so vain to think we mated for any
reason but you need somethin' from me. It was a decision made in
favor of gettin' what you wanted. For what both of us wanted, I
guess. I'm sure you've called out to and eaten plenty of folk who
weren't your first choice. I don't know."

Eridanys thought about that for a long time, before scoffing
like he was insulted. "Well—my relationship with my previous
partner was essentially a decision made for survival as well, if that's
how you'd like to think about it."

Alba wrinkled his nose. "Alright? I said I wasn't offended."

But Eridanys squirmed stiffly on the bed, before sitting up.
Muttering to himself. "How dare they imply they know what I
like or don't like. What I would favor or not. Do they think the
last one was my 'type'? When I wasn't with him by my own
choice, either. They don't know anything about me. Even while
with them, they didn't know a damned thing..."

"Listen, you really don't have to pretend I'm anythin' but—"
Alba attempted, but Eridanys sprung to his feet. He stalked to
where Alba stood with pants halfway off, grabbing his face and
kissing him with sudden forcefulness.

Alba managed a sharp gasp before his breath was stolen, stumbling backward into the wall as Eridanys pressed into him. Hard and demanding, as if proving a point to invisible voyeurs. Alba didn't know who; he—didn't care. He melted into Eridanys' mouth as quickly as they found each other, letting the man steal every other word he meant to say.

Despite his hands lacking their claws, his ears their webbing and his spine the sharp fins, Eridanys still consumed Alba like a starving beast on the rocks. Despite carrying him to the bed with two legs, despite there being only one cock straining against the fabric of his pants, Alba couldn't pretend he was having sex with a human man like any other. There were still those things about Eridanys that couldn't be separated from his siren nature, knowing it even if he'd never bedded down with anyone else before him.

It was the way he breathed, the way he kissed, the way Alba was sure a song purred from the back of his throat even if he couldn't hear it outright. Something that soothed his nerves, his entire being into the bed, pinned by something that would have torn him apart had it not had use for him. For a moment, Alba couldn't remember what that use was—hoping that just opening his mouth and legs would be enough to sate the bloodthirsty creature for another night.

He pressed himself into all of Eridanys' sharpest edges, beneath his skin and in his voice, wishing to be cut again. Just like the first time—a craving he hadn't expected, one he was eager to sate again; the taste of Eridanys' mouth crushed into his, a tongue sliding over his lips and invading his mouth while a hand slid up his shirt, down the front of his pants. Making him gasp and buck as fingers circled around the sensitive spot between his legs, yanking at Eridanys' own shirt in a desperate attempt to force it off over his head.

"There's nothing to hide behind this time," Eridanys said once his skin was bare for Alba to touch, trailing his tongue up the side of Alba's cheek and kissing where the silver hair grew from his temple. "No sea or waves or night—I get to see and touch every inch of you for however long I like."

Alba held his breath, cracking open his eyes long enough to search the low light for the man on top of him, taking his face and kissing him again. Bending his leg to press his thigh between Eridanys' in response, rubbing it against the growing bulge in his pants. He didn't want to think about that—about how much more vulnerable, visible he was there on his back on a bed, where people normally fucked each other. No different from two lovers, from a sailor and a whore in a brothel. He didn't want to think about how Eridanys would be able to see every piece of skin he'd been able to hide from unwelcome eyes his entire life, not realizing until that moment how the sea had acted as a curtain the first time they touched each other.

"My last human partner never let me do as I pleased," Eridanys went on, hands pushing Alba's shirt up, bundling it beneath Alba's chin and trailing his mouth down the center of Alba's chest. "I'll take my time learning what drives you mad."

"Fuck..." Alba sighed. He meant to add *'you'* to the end, but Eridanys' tongue stole his voice when it slid between his legs, making his back arch as an overwhelming, tingling warmth rushed to meet where the mouth tasted him. "Eri—"

Pale eyes lifted to meet his, making Alba's breath catch, quickly looking away again and crossing his arms over his face. A soft, laughing breath scattered against the inside of his thigh, before hands gripped his hips and forcefully flipped Alba onto his stomach.

He pushed himself onto his knees in an instant, surprised, but a hand found his back and shoved him back down again. He pressed a hand to the headboard in front of him, bracing for the sensation of something pressing into him, eager and apprehensive and anxious for that tight pain he remembered that came before the pleasure. When something soft, warm, wet found the folds of his skin instead, he jumped. Turning again in surprise, he was shoved back a second time.

Sharp hands dug pockmarks into his hips, keeping him from flipping over. Eridanys' eyes glowed in the low light as Alba still twisted his spine to look, only for his breath to catch and his arms to bend beneath him as a warm pleasure gently found the apex of his hips. Eridanys' tongue, long and slippery, teased between Alba's holes and all the sensitive skin surrounding them, made more intense by the way Alba couldn't move, couldn't writhe or pull away, forced to reckon with the overwhelming pleasure making his legs clench and tremble.

The tongue slithered in and out of him, circling his clit and his rim, and despite Alba's best attempts at keeping quiet, he couldn't hold back every gasp and bit-back moan. It was nothing like what he'd felt on the rocks the first time, nothing his own wet fingers had ever been able to find while alone in his hammock on the dark sea—and combined with the way Eridanys never took his eyes away every time Alba risked a glance, Alba couldn't help but find a sickening thrill in wondering if being eaten alive felt that good all the time. Feeling even closer to that creature taking a bloody bite from him than he had when they mated on the edge of the sea.

Before Alba knew it, his body burned hot, cold air from the cracked window practically turning to steam on his skin. He sank a little deeper into the nerve-wracking vulnerability of Eridanys taking ownership of him in such a way, tasting him with a coiling tongue, spreading him wider just to hear the sounds of surprise Alba made. And despite the agonizing self-consciousness that made every movement feel stiff and brittle, he couldn't help the pleasure that pitted like tangled rope in the base of his stomach, until he shuddered with each breath and even pressed his hips back in a silent plea for more.

Pulling away, Eridanys hooked an arm around the front of Alba's throat, draped over his back and pressing his chest and stomach into every curve of Alba's spine, leaving Alba to claw at him as fingers returned between his legs and he arched his head back with a gasp. With the siren's strong arm locked around his shoulders, leg propping between Alba's knees to open him further, Alba's mind only spun, sinking to his elbows and gasping as he was sure he'd been drugged—sure that siren's tongue was venomous, no matter where it tasted him.

"Good to know that stubborn exterior still melts with the simplest touch," Eridanys growled with a smile, pulling Alba upright, propped on his knees and pressed back into Eridanys' chest with the man's arm still bent around his throat. One, then two of the fingers fondling him crept deeper inside, making Alba jolt. "Which hole would you prefer I fuck first? Or would you rather I fill both at once, again?"

"F-fuck—" Alba attempted, but Eridanys' fingers slid deeper before he could utter another sound. They turned and twisted inside of him, stretching him wide before pulling out again with a wet sound, traveling further and teasing his ass next.

"I think I should tease you more before I decide—wouldn't want you screaming out for the whole town to hear, would I?" He edged a finger in, making Alba choke and bend forward, hands returning to the bed. "I think I'll start here, this time—you make such needy sounds when I play with it."

Through the haze of overwhelm, Alba glared at Eridanys over his shoulder with flushed, overwhelmed eyes. Something hard and ridged slid between his thighs, bumping over his clit and making him shiver with a hiccuping breath. Without the cold waves to numb him, Alba was more aware than ever of the size of it, the texture, having to bite his lip as it rubbed front and back against him and made his toes curl.

"Maybe I'll push it in while you're still tight and nervous," Eridanys whispered, leaning over once more until his mouth was close to Alba's ear. "Or should I ease it in slowly, until you're begging?"

"Just—" Alba bit the words back again, closing his eyes as Eridanys rearranged himself. The ridged cock slid up the back of his ass as a wetter, softer pressure kissed his opening instead, sliding gently inside an inch at a time as Eridanys coaxed it with his hips. Alba slid his hand down his stomach, between his legs in search, familiar with the sensation but not knowing exactly what it was. He found the siren's second cock pressing slowly into his rear despite still donning his human magic. "Ugh—"

Eridanys held Alba flush against his arched body, arm curving around Alba's middle as he eased deeper inside. His second cock was more flexible than the first, sticky and wet, though no less intimidating as it stretched Alba a little more with every roll of Eridanys' hips. Opening his ass wider while coating his insides with thick, slippery fluid, until Alba was sure he was going to split in two. Just gripping the pillow beneath him in one hand, the other bent back to grasp at Eridanys' shoulder pressed into the curve of his ribs. Needing something to keep him anchored, in his own body, as the pleasure mixed with flickers of pain, pressure, warmth and a sweet ache that had Alba moaning into his own shoulder pressed into his mouth. Wishing for something to occupy it, tongue pressing into his skin until he twisted his spine and cupped a hand behind Eridanys' head to pull him close. To kiss him as he dug deeper into Alba from behind, straining and stretching every inch of his upper body just to reach.

It must have caught the siren off guard, because he furrowed his brows, releasing a sharp exhale through his nose before threading his arm beneath Alba's, over his chest, cupping beneath his jaw and wrenching him closer. To kiss him harder like Alba wished, hips angling back before slamming deeper without warning.

Alba cried out in shock, nearly buckling forward had Eridanys not held him up. Getting only a brief moment to gasp as the world spun, eyes crossing and rolling back into his head as he swore the cock penetrated up the whole length of his spine. His muscles locked in on one another, hardly able to gasp as Eridanys pulled back and thrust in a second time. The overwhelm ignited over every inch of him, barely allowing him a single thought—

which was to demand Eridanys' mouth again. His only inclination while treading the all-encompassing feeling of being eaten from the inside out.

When he could no longer prop himself up, Alba collapsed into the pillow, biting down on the fabric as Eridanys made sure his hips remained upright for him to thrust his weight into. Leaning into him, bending Alba's spine until Alba groaned in discomfort, only to be met with a hand against the back of his head to press his face deeper into the pillow.

"You—were made to be fucked on your knees, sailor," Eridanys told him, gripping the headboard with the hand not pinning Alba into the bed. "Keep your ass up, just like that—*mmh*—A shame no other man ever knew you like this—your crew mates would have passed you around until every last one got a chance."

Alba wanted to glare at him, to scowl and hiss—but all he could manage was clutching at the pillows as he was filled and stretched and fucked like a sailor long neglected at sea might have done to him. Choking on every inhale as spit pooled in the back of his throat, flinching when a hand found the underside of his jaw again, arching his neck back, fingers invading his mouth. As the thick, wet cock thrust in and out until Alba was hardly more than shuddering flesh for Eridanys to twist and bend and enjoy as he wished. Forgetting every thought that came before it ever formed into something comprehensible. Hardly realizing what was happening even as Eridanys slowed, removing himself with a breath of satisfaction, then grabbed and turned Alba onto his back.

A thumb found Alba's mouth again, pressing inside and flattening against his tongue. "I should have fucked this mouth of yours first," he said, gazing down at Alba through eyelashes like he was hardly more than a meal to enjoy. "But your ass is too needy—begging for more by the way your hips are moving. I'm not even close to done with you."

Alba's lips closed over Eridanys' thumb, whimpering pathetically as the siren's opposite arm hooked under his hips and dragged him off the pillow, closer, spreading his legs again and angling himself with both cocks teasing both of Alba's holes. Easing forward and back to just barely part them with the tips, smiling as Alba writhed impatiently, cracking open his heavy eyes to gaze up at the creature on top of him. Unable to help rolling his hips slightly to tempt Eridanys back inside.

"Good," he encouraged, rising slightly on his knees and hooking a hand behind Alba's knee to bend him over himself, aligning himself and pressing both of his eager lengths inside. *"Ah —I don't want to hear you cry—when it's too much. You asked for this, didn't you?"*

Alba bit down on his tongue as he was penetrated with all of Eridanys' weight. His spine bowed beneath it, throwing his head back with a gasp as the ridged cock ground into him in tandem with the other. His hips bucked upward, then down again, kicking his leg out and nearly slamming a heel into Eridanys' shoulder had the siren not grabbed his ankle at the last second.

The sensation raced through his body like a bolt of rich lightning, only to crumple back down again with a whimpering, shuddering gasp as tears swelled in his eyes and his mouth dangled open in shock. Eridanys pulled back and pushed back in again, making Alba moan, hands extending blindly to clutch at him, searching for anything to hold on to, barely managing to bury fingers into the man's shoulders and pull him closer as hips slammed into him again, then again. Rocking Alba's body upward with every collision against the backs of his thighs.

Eridanys sank forward, pressing Alba into the pillows with his bodyweight, propped up with hands on either side of Alba's head and pinning him beneath the strength of his legs, his thrusts. Pushing deeper, Eridanys hissed for Alba to relax, but Alba was just trying to breathe against the hot pleasure taking root inside him.

Tears clung to his lashes before dripping down his cheeks, mixing with sweat and the flush of his skin. Through blurry vision, Alba saw exactly how the siren's cock burrowed into him, deep enough that barely the root of his shaft was visible through the curly red hairs beneath Alba's navel. He swore he could even see it pressing into his stomach from inside, making the muscles pucker as Eridanys pulled back and thrust in again. God—to see it so clearly, the size and shape, the texture, the realization that something so daunting was inside of him, inside both holes of him at once, using him, fucking him like he'd always fantasized some man one day would—Alba would have smiled if he wasn't so overcome with the aching pleasure of it all.

"Grip me harder than that," Eridanys grunted into Alba's ear, words laced with satisfaction. "I'm going to fuck you—until you can't take it anymore."

"Eri—"

Eridanys' hips dug into Alba again, harder and faster and with a demanding, merciless pace, as if desperate for more, desperate to fuck his captured sailor into oblivion. Hungry, starving, eager to quell his unmet hunger before ever unhinging his jaw to sink teeth into Alba's flesh. And all Alba could do was what Eridanys said—to cling to him, fingernails raking through skin and tangling up in hair, suffocating beneath the weight crushing him and the honeyed pounding of the ridged cock abusing his cunt, the slippery hardness burrowing hard and deep into his ass. Thinking nothing—except he thought every short breath might be his last.

"Let me hear you," Eridanys demanded in a low voice, thrusting faster as if to force it out. Alba flinched, throwing his head back and unable to swallow the gasp and small sound of overwhelm bubbling up the back of his throat. Gasping, writhing, clawing at Eridanys' arms, chest, shoulders for anything to hold on to, for anything at all to anchor him to solid earth as he was rammed into the bed with the same thrashing ruthlessness as furious waves against stone cliffs.

Eridanys clawed at the pillows behind Alba's head, clutching the narrow headboard until it rattled. As if despite it all, he still couldn't dig into Alba deep enough, fast enough—and Alba could only cling to whatever he could find for stability, with gasps and moans and pleas for mercy then pleas for more—not knowing if what he felt was agony or body-devouring euphoria.

Orgasms tangled in Alba's stomach, between his hips beneath the onslaught, making him cry out and claw at Eridanys still slamming mercilessly into him; drawing him closer and closer, before a deep, aching pain suddenly bloomed within his hip and back, just as his muscles tightened to finally cum.

Again, climbing higher and closer to the edge—only to be forced back again as the pain returned, hotter and brighter than before. To the point he thought he would go mad, real tears of frustrated misery spilling from his eyes as all he wanted was the release that kept coming so close.

He pounded fists against Eridanys' chest as if it was his fault, moaning pleas to his own body to allow him to experience that delicious sensation just once—but his body only rebelled further. His hip locked, a bolt of white-hot pain shooting down Alba's leg, up his spine, and making him scream through his teeth in surprise.

"Eri—danys!" Alba finally cried, smashing his hands into the siren's chest. "It—hurts! Just give me a second—!"

"I haven't finished with you yet—"

"Not your c-cocks, damnit!" Alba shouted, glaring up at the man with blurry, wet eyes. Eridanys stared at him for a moment, before actually sitting back, slowing his punishing pace.

Just slightly, at first, before settling further, all the while never taking his eyes from Alba as he did. Until the strokes of his hips moved long and slow, enough for Alba to catch his breath. It only resulted in more pained, overwhelmed tears pooling then spilling over his eyes as he groaned, pressing a hand to his hip in silent self-hatred, burning hot with shame and embarrassment.

"I—I like it," he tried to remedy nonetheless, though couldn't bring himself to look at Eridanys again. "It feels—it feels really good, I want you to keep—to keep fucking me, just like that, Christ Almighty—just—just—"

"Where?" Eridanys asked, catching Alba by surprise. Alba glanced up at him, briefly, distrustingly, and Eridanys rolled his eyes, slamming his hips forward again and pinning his cocks back deep inside. Alba threw his head back with a choked sound, before pitifully cursing the siren straight to hell. "I asked you where it hurt. Answer me."

"I..." Alba attempted to lift his head, but all the blood had rushed back beneath his navel—which only made the pain in his hip radiate hotter. His mouth went dry, suddenly wishing he'd just stayed quiet, but then Eridanys ground his dual lengths in and out again, making Alba shudder in new frustration. "In... in my hip. And every time I'm about to—about to cum, it—it won't let me. It all tightens up too much, that's all—but it doesn't matter, I only needed a second for it to relax—you can keep going, I won't bring it up again..."

Alba's face, his insides sweltered with humiliation. God—he'd never felt more pathetic, especially in front of someone who had no reason to do anything but laugh in his face. Who was Eridanys to care if Alba came? Even as Eridanys' hand slid down over Alba's hip, Alba only braced for him to grab and twist it, maybe to snap it in half along the crack already there.

"Am I making you feel that good?" He asked instead, trailing a finger down Alba's skin, shiny with sweat and trembling with every sensation, stomach clenching and rolling against the thick lengths still pinned inside him. "You want to cum so bad it's bringing you to tears?"

"No—"

"The other sailors really had no idea what they could have had in you, god help them," Eridanys went on with a playful smile. "The perfect holes between two trembling legs to take out all their aggression on. Clearly it's even your preference—rough and hard and demanding, until you're begging and crying..." he breathed, pressing down on Alba's hip before slowly pulling himself free.

Alba grimaced at the sensation, mouth hanging open with an unclaimed inhale of breath at the sudden rush of emptiness, left twitching and gaping once free.

Eridanys sat back with a sigh, combing fingers back through his hair before pausing to look Alba up and down. To regard every trembling, quivering inch of him, flushed red from the exertion and dripping with sweat, breathing hard and staring up at him in apprehension. His cocks remained erect, wet and twitching with want for release, and Alba could only wonder exactly what more the man would have to do to him before being satisfied. It was enough to make his toes curl, face going hot and averting his eyes. Not wanting to have to admit out loud, again, exactly how much he'd liked it—that feeling of being dominated, controlled, possessed. When it was by his own choice, Alba's blood raced with every instance of being owed, especially by something so greedy.

"Sorry," he said, hardly audible. He opened his legs again in invitation to continue, pressing his lips together when his throbbing hip made his leg flex awkwardly. "Say somethin'. Do something. Stop just starin' at me like that."

"I'm trying to decide what to do with you."

Another rush of shame, embarrassment, self-loathing soaked Alba deep enough that more nervous sweat bubbled on his forehead, dripped down his chest.

"You said it yourself," he muttered, still avoiding Eridanys' eyes. "You said you didn't want to hear me cry when it was too much, so I just—want to act like it never happened."

But Eridanys still didn't move. He just regarded Alba for a long time in silence. Only when Alba finally snapped around to swear at him did he frown, crawling forward and pushing Alba back onto the pillow. Alba opened his legs, spreading them over Eridanys' lap—but Eridanys grabbed one of his ankles, twisting him until he laid on his side.

He reclined behind Alba on the bed, pulling him close so every sweaty inch of Alba's back pressed flush into his chest. He still said nothing, sliding a hand between Alba's waist and the bed, hooking an arm around his middle and bending his hips. Fingering Alba's clit as he slid his ridged cock into Alba's ass, and then the other into his cunt. Alba moaned, eyes fluttering closed as he bit his lip and collapsed fully into the pillow.

"Is this better?" Eridanys breathed, hardly an inch from Alba's ear, hanging close as his hips rolled and reignited the pace. One hand found Alba's aching hip, the other continuing to tease his clit. Alba bit his lip and ground himself against the sensation, sliding the cocks in and out in the same motion, wanting to feel Eridanys pressed as deep as he had been before. "I have to make sure every time my mate cums, it's better than the last."

Alba groaned in a mix of exasperation and pleasure, bucking his hips against Eridanys' dancing fingers as the thrusting resumed from behind. But Eridanys was right—that new position eased the tight pain in Alba's hip. He could turn his head and bite back moans into the pillow, rutting needily against Eridanys' hand in the front, the size of him in the back, until the twisting orgasms rekindled between his hips. Eridanys cooed like he could sense them coming, deepening and quickening his thrusts until Alba couldn't breathe in line with the rhythm any longer.

Gasping and breathless, his hand stretched back and pressed into Eridanys' moving body, soon mimicking the same roughness, the same neediness and demand as before. The creeping pleasure leaked back into him, slowly at first then all over, catching in the pit beneath Alba's navel and tying golden knots tighter and tighter until finally cresting over, making him cry out in pleasure as his back arched and his insides coiled in release.

Clenching his teeth then sighing, gasping then shivering, clinging to the pillow beneath him like it was the only thing keeping him on earth, Alba swore he heard a soft chuckle escape the mouth of his partner. But when he looked, Eridanys' expression was mildly surprised. Like he hadn't actually believed Alba when he declared how much he liked it, like he'd really only let Eridanys fuck him so aggressively as a show of dominance.

"What are you doing?" Alba asked as Eridanys shifted, beginning to pull out. He reached back, touching Eridanys' leg, then the base of his shaft. Coaxing him back in again. "Don't stop. I don't want to stop. Not until... not until you finish, too. I want to know how it feels when you cum, too."

Eridanys said nothing; he hardly moved for what felt like an eternity, before gently pressing himself back inside.

"Is that so?" He asked, but the arrogance that time was different. Something about it felt uncertain, like putting on an act. Like he'd never been asked of such a thing, before. Never been offered.

Alba nodded in encouragement, then summoned the strength to roll his hips, moving up and down on Eridanys on his own terms a few times before the siren grabbed him and took control of the rhythm back for himself.

"I want to feel it," Alba sighed into the pillow, overwhelmed with the difference in pace, in strength behind the new resolve. More controlled, more—intentional. "Don't stop again 'til you cum inside of me."

Eridanys' hands flexed on Alba's body, though he said nothing else. Just did as he was told. As he was invited.

He fucked Alba with the same eagerness, but lacking the same aggression; with hitches in his breath, with arms wrapped around Alba from behind and hands that pressed flat against his stomach, as if to feel how the cocks moved in and out of him. Breathing against the nape of Alba's neck, sounds escaping the back of his throat in pleasured, stuttering gasps. Teasing Alba all over again until Alba came a second time, then a third—until, finally, Eridanys pressed himself fully inside, rooted into Alba's wetness, grunting and trembling as the cock in Alba's ass tensed and swelled. It knotted in place, leaking thick fluid that had nowhere to go but deeper, as Eridanys' teeth found the back of Alba's shoulder and sank deep enough to just barely break skin.

The swollen knot was enough that Alba learned how it felt to be filled, held in place as every inch of Eridanys' body clenched and squeezed against him. Biting back his own sounds of satisfaction, like he didn't want Alba to hear—like he hadn't expected to cum at all. But he spilled his pleasure into Alba with another few small thrusts, all of it slipping back out again once the cock finally released and Eridanys could pull away.

Alba's heart pounded with the sensation of the emptiness, the hot throbbing left behind, dripping with proof of Eridanys inside of him. Every inch trembled and buzzed and danced until he thought he might cry again, grabbing Eridanys face and yanking him down into a desperate, demanding kiss. Kissing him until he couldn't breathe—until he had to finally give in to the exhaustion clawing at his body to rest.

<h1 style="text-align:center">Chapter 20</h1>

Alba drifted in and out of sleep after the exhaustion took him. Lulled back to the surface of consciousness as something wet and gentle wiped the sticky, dripping residue from between his legs, not knowing if it was a wash rag or a tongue. Barely treading wakefulness as hands clumsily tugged clothes back onto his legs, over his head. Drawn gently under again as Eridanys collapsed into the bed alongside him with a deep exhale, shifting uncomfortably, elbowing Alba to scoot over, before finally sighing and pressing his body into Alba's from behind. Hardly any different than when he fucked him, only thin layers of clothing separating them that time. Even wrapping his arm over Alba's waist, though Alba wondered if it was only to keep himself anchored so he wouldn't fall off the edge.

Alba never expected to sleep so easily right alongside someone like Eridanys, let alone wrapped in his arms, held by that siren who'd been so rough and demanding and delicious only hours prior. Whose arm draping over him soon twitched and shifted as the siren himself drifted off, eventually traveling up to cup around the front of Alba's throat in a possessive, protective sort of way, like even fast asleep in that bed far from the sea, he still worried the tide might sweep in and take him. But the sensation of breaths against the back of his neck, inhaling and exhaling long and deep, lured Alba to follow suit after him. Even that possessive touch was comforting in its own sort of way.

Still, Alba knew he shouldn't let sleep come for him so easily, nudged back awake again and again with every sound on the opposite side of the door, from the street below, as humming song drifted in and out on the air and he didn't know if it was wind in the pipes or the spirits in the trees. Reeling him back to the surface of exhaustion again and again, drawling thoughts spinning endlessly in the back of his mind that he needed to be more careful. He should have been more careful. Anyone could have heard, anyone could have thrown open the door in the middle of what they were doing.

Only when he heard the sound of Eugene and Phyllis Michaels returning home from their early new moon celebrations, making their way up the stairs and to their own bedroom, did he finally relax. Sinking into Eridanys' body still pressed into him, clutching Alba tightly, possessively, protectively. Safe in that siren's arms. No one had heard anything at all—but even if they had, surely they would know better than to wake such a blood-thirsty creature as it slept.

THE SOUND of hands rifling through clutter drew Alba from sleep for the final time, pulled further by bright sunlight casting over him through the window. Cracking open his eyes, he groaned slightly, rolling over, then over again, searching for the pale demon making so much noise so early in the morning. As a lighthouse keeper, Alba didn't get many opportunities to sleep during a normal night, let alone to sleep in—and it seemed, as the mate of a siren, those rare opportunities would be just as fleeting even when the chance came.

"What are you doin'?" he asked, voice groggy. Eridanys' eyes barely flickered up from where he crouched on the balls of his feet like a wicked little thing, holding a bundle of loose photographs in his hands. Sunbeams only made his silver eyes more unsettling, piercing through them like pieces of foggy glass.

"Snooping," Eridanys answered, returning to his work. "There are interesting things here."

"Like what?" Alba sighed, finally sitting up. His hair was a mess, particularly matted in the back for the same reason as the warm, wet, throbbing ache between his legs, and he tilted his head away as his cheeks flushed. Eridanys didn't notice, busy browsing his discoveries as Alba worked to comb fingers through his hair.

He opted to not prod further, just watching, trying to figure out exactly what it was that caught Eridanys' interest with each item he picked up. A book he flipped through without actually looking; another handful of loose photographs he tossed to the floor; a stick of perfume he unscrewed, sniffed, and scowled at. It was amusing, strangely captivating. Alba even laughed softly a few times, earning a narrowed look from Eridanys in return, who clearly didn't like being watched. But did nothing to vocally protest, either, like he wasn't sure how to feel. Like no one had ever given him such attention in such a mundane moment, before. A shame—Alba couldn't help but be interested in everything Eridanys did.

As the sound of singing pipes slipped through the cracked window, Alba also couldn't keep other unspoken thoughts from growing heavier, previously tucked away, rekindled by the sound and the sight of the siren illuminated by the sun in front of him. Thoughts that drifted dangerously down the back of his neck into his throat, until he couldn't keep the repressed curiosity from bubbling over his tongue. Hoping their activities the night before had put his companion in a better mood to speak on it.

"Those spirits in the trees... they said somethin' about you being an alm of the... the fa... fata morgana...?" He started slowly, carefully. Eridanys didn't react outright, but Alba saw how the corner of his mouth twitch in agitation. Still, he continued: "I know what that means as a sailor, but for a merrow? What is it?"

"You still want me to explain the nonsense those voices

spoke?" Eridanys asked, though Alba sensed right away his aloofness was an act. There was a twitch in his jaw, like he'd been stirring through those things all night, himself, and the chance to speak them out loud was tempting.

"Humans have stories about people who go missing in the woods, don't they?" He went on despite the argument, like even he realized pretending he didn't care was a lost cause. "Those who vanish into thin air while fetching water, while traveling far from home. The details of the myths might be different depending on where you go, but... any town alongside the forest, the mountains, the moors, the sea has stories about people who disappear."

"Yes," Alba answered. Short and simple, not wanting to get in the way.

"Well—merrow have the same, of course. We can cease to exist in the vast emptiness of the sea as easily as a man might vanish into the trees—for more reasons than just being banished to be a siren, of course. It's why we tend to live in large kinshipped groups in bays or along shorelines, whether we make nice with local humans or not..."

Alba listened attentively, arms folded beneath him, lips parted slightly in interest. He always thought there was magic to Eridanys' normal speech as well as his song, and felt it tingling under his skin more than ever that morning. Perhaps because their previous night was still fresh on and under his skin, perhaps with the way Eridanys glowed like something angelic in the rare morning sun. Even Eridanys must have felt it, constantly averting his eyes from Alba's, then letting them float back, then shifting where he sat, doing something to keep his hands busy. Still always looking back to Alba again as he spoke. Like he wanted to see if the human on the bed really paid attention for as long as he talked.

"Merrow aren't meant to live on their own—which is why they become sirens when left to the whims of the open sea. That empty, lonely, infinite place where only sirens roam and hunt and seek corrupted kinships of their own—is called the sea-obscura.

Sailors call it the fata morgana, like you said. That hazy place on the horizon between the water and the sky, where ghost ships sail and rocky outcroppings trick sailors into thinking land is not far off... It's also where our gods and devils are said to reside. According to our stories."

"Even merrow have gods 'n devils?"

"Not like human ones," Eridanys smirked. "'Gods and devils', I say, for lack of a better term."

"Then you spent your time at sea with gods? Or devils."

Eridanys laughed under his breath. A small, but very real little chuckle. "I can't rightly say. You know how wickies like yourself go mad while tending to your lights? Many sirens go mad exactly the same. Who knows if they—erm, *we* actually see and speak with the gods, or if we're simply in a deranged stupor out there. Until we find something to eat, at least, and regain some clarity."

"You saw gods while out there?"

"Do you listen to anything I say?"

Alba laughed. "How long were you out there? In the sea-morgana."

"The sea-obscura," Eridanys sighed. "Who knows. There's no way to track lunations as easily as closer to land. Nowhere to write them down as they pass. Perhaps years."

"Did you find anyone to kin with while you were out there?" Alba asked. "Other sirens?"

"Plenty," Eridanys smiled. "But never for long. We crave kinship, but it's easy to drift apart again in a place so endless."

Alba nodded. He knew how that felt. He knew how easy it was to forget about land, about all the people on land on the other end of the sea. Out in the middle of dark nothingness—it was easy to feel like the only living soul breathing the air and knowing how it felt to be lonely. As if the rest of the world was only their imagination. A derangement, just like Eridanys said.

"Where did you sail?" Eridanys asked unexpectedly, catching Alba off guard. He never expected a question in return, resulting in him rambling right off the bat.

"Um, well—I spent most of my years up in the north. Sometimes whalin', sometimes fishin' on doggers, sometimes crabbing, sometimes ice harvesting. Spent some time in lighthouses here and there, too, or shipyards. Sometimes I'd be assigned to a ship a little more south where it wasn't so cold, but not by much. I've heard about places where the sun shines all the time and it's hot enough that you sweat all day, but... a part of me doesn't believe it. If those sorts of places are real, well, if I ever got all the way down there, I think I would melt, anyway. Like a frozen lake in the summer."

"I spent a lot of time swimming up north as well, you know," Eridanys teased with a threatening flick of his tongue. "Found there to be far more to eat with so many ships ice-breaking and whaling. I wonder if you ever heard me sing without knowing it."

Alba's face went hot. He shook his head. "No, I don't think so," he said. "I definitely would not be here if that were the case."

Eridanys liked that. He smiled a little too much, gazing at Alba a little too long as if imagining it. Alba averted his eyes, turning his gaze toward the growing sun through the window, letting it wash over his face. He felt Eridanys' eyes linger on him as he did, though he was sure he didn't radiate the same way the siren did in the brightness.

"You said you sailed for the Warren Company. Those are the men who keep coming after you, aren't they? That one called Marco, and the one before that. The already-dead corpse you tried to feed me."

Alba sank forward into the pillows, pressing his chin into one clutched beneath him. "Yes," he said with a frown. "I owe them a debt. Erm—no, actually. My father owed them a debt. A lot of money. Even when he died, they wanted it paid back, so they had me on their roster 'til I was old enough to be taken and made to sail in his stead."

"How much money? So much that you had to sail for so long?" Eridanys' tone soured. "Did you do any of it because you wanted to?"

"I don't know how much," Alba sighed. "I didn't do it because I wanted to, really, either…" Would he have if he'd been given the choice? He glanced back to Eridanys, again. An uncertain '*maybe*' ghosted in the back of his mind.

"What do you mean you don't know? It's your debt."

"It changed all the time," Alba murmured, stretching out his arms and letting the sun illuminate his tattoos and streaks of dark merrow blood between them. "And according to Marco, still accruin' debt as we speak. For all the days I'm missin' work at the fish market. For all the nights I'm technically rentin' a bed in that hellhole workhouse, even though I haven't been back in weeks." He sighed, combing fingers back through his hair. "They charged me for every meal I ate, for every new pair of boots or gloves, for every night I slept on the ship, every time I needed so much as a bandage. Not even countin' the piling interest and monthly allowance they gave my mother so she could afford to eat, since there weren't enough jobs in Welkin for her to earn her own way. I didn't—and never would—earn enough to make any profit. It was a losin' battle from the very beginning."

"Then what took you so long to…" Eridanys trailed off, pressing his lips together. Alba wondered what exactly made him bite his tongue, knowing right away what he meant to ask. *What took you so long to run away?*

"After I fell and hurt my leg…" he said, patting his thigh stretched out on the bed behind him. Grimacing after he flinched. "I just worked in the fish market, waitin' for a sign it was time to go. Didn't know if my mother was alive or dead by that point, since our house was empty when I got back. It was actually a telegram sent from this place that finally gave me reason to get away."

"Why would she be dead?"

Alba gulped against the lump in the back of his throat, but it didn't budge. "They told me from the beginning, if I didn't work, if I didn't perform to their standards, they wouldn't hesitate to kill her. That meant when I broke my hip and couldn't work anymore... Well. Didn't really matter the reason why I stopped workin'. Thought they'd give me more time to beg when I got back, but..."

He trailed off. His voice was beginning to tremble, and he had to remind himself—she wasn't dead. She may have even been tending the same lighthouse he did just before he arrived. She may even still come back for him; he may even still be able to find her once he finished what he owed to Eridanys.

"Once I got back to Welkin, even though she wasn't there, I just... had no idea what to do. I was just a kid when they grabbed me off the street. Didn't know about how to run away, how to get a job, how to find somewhere to live. How to even start makin' my own way. They did that on purpose, in case I ever got any ideas. Might be a miracle I made it all the way here in one piece."

It was bittersweet to recall, to relive every moment from when he first found the telegram in his box, to stabbing Josiah in the leg, to fleeing and somehow finding that place. Recalling how badly his leg ached without a cane to walk on, how he shivered in the rain, all those sailors who shrugged him off when asking for directions, constantly having to check over his shoulder. Knowing he was being followed, even if those looking for him didn't quite have his scent.

It made his heart race even there on the bed, reminded of how that first man found him on the full moon. How there had been others, and Alba had no idea where they went after that night. How even Marco had turned up in Moon Harbor, and even though he claimed it was only a lucky coincidence that they bumped into one another, Alba knew better than to believe that after seeing his father's name written in the town logs. There were no coincidences.

"... plenty of... the mud... need it to pay..."

Alba returned to reality, lifting his head to find Eridanys' eyes back on him.

"What?"

"I said there are treasures without number in the mud of the sea, if you need it to pay off whatever debts you owe."

Letting those words sink in, waiting for Eridanys to smirk before laughing in his face for believing it, Alba eventually cracked a weak smile.

"Yeah, sure," he sighed. "I don't think the Warrens will accept healin' sludge and strands of merrow hair, though. Even if they did, what I'd owe you in exchange would just make it redundant, don't you think? What good is payin' off one debt in exchange for another."

"You're already helping me solve the mystery of my kin. Not to mention shore-called with me so I can be here on land," Eridanys answered sharply, as if to reject his offer was an insult. "Perhaps, instead of killing you when this is all over, I'll bring you as many treasures as you need in exchange."

"Oh, you were thinkin' 'bout killing me?"

"At first, yes."

"But not anymore?" Alba chuckled. Eridanys didn't return the amusement, even looking embarrassed. Self-conscious, like he hadn't realized until that moment, either. Alba's smile softened.

"You really want to buy out my debt?" he asked, trying to draw the tone back to a teasing one. "What for?"

"Because I know the agony of owing a debt you can never pay back," Eridanys muttered, aggressively shoving the book in his hand back into the pile of clutter. "And you've gone this long without becoming as deranged and bloodthirsty as me. Perhaps I think..." he pressed his lips together. Still avoiding Alba's eyes, like even he didn't know what he was saying. Or why. "Perhaps I simply think it would be a shame if you ever did."

It caught Alba off guard, enough that he didn't realize he held his breath until he could hear his heart thudding in his ears. He didn't know what to say to such a thing—and hated how his heart raced so fast upon hearing it. Even more as the silence lingered between them, as if Eridanys actually wanted to know what Alba thought of it. Letting it linger, like he wanted Alba to know he meant it.

"Well…" Alba finally spoke. A part of him hated the silence. A part of him—wanted to know what other things Eridanys might say that would surprise him. "Your kin said if you wanted to know what happened to them, to go back at midnight tonight. Wasn't that it? So assumin' we stay on shore 'til then… We have all day, so… you'll have plenty of time to prove there are treasures in the sea," he said. Eridanys finally looked at him again, expression firm and unflinching and a mix of regret and apprehension. Alba motioned toward the window. "Come on, convince me. Show me where the treasures lie. In the mud right down there, where other folk are probably already diggin' and taking the shiniest things with the tide out as far as it is. Maybe then I'll sell you my debt."

Eridanys scoffed. He rolled his eyes, slumping back into his pile of things as a silent rejection of something so silly—but then Alba sat up and sighed, braiding his hair and pulling his jacket on for the day.

The siren scoffed a second time. Then groaned. Then straightened up, then rose to his feet. He grabbed Alba by the arm to yank him from the bed, towing him toward the door. Alba laughed loud enough to have to cover his mouth, and smiled all the way out of the house, moving quick and silently to not be seen by a single soul.

CHAPTER 21

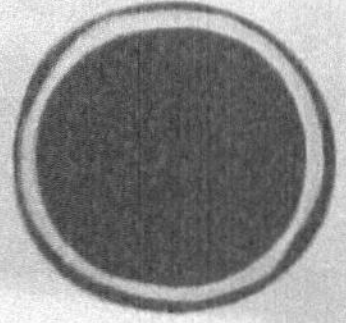

ALBA FOLLOWED ERIDANYS AROUND ON THE EXPOSED beach for as long as he could, far enough down from the main part of town that they could have been anyone. With the number of other townspeople digging around through the muck, no one thought to give them a second glance.

It was a strange ritual the more Alba thought about it, especially once seeing how many others searched the mud, like a there was something innately human about wandering the exposed seafloor in the warm sun to search for things otherwise unseen. Despite, according to Eridanys, the new moon being the time of merrow wandering onto the shore, it seemed humans still couldn't resist going out to meet them. Meanwhile, Alba couldn't help but let his gaze linger on distant silhouettes, especially those who wandered right up to the far water's edge. Wondering if they really were townspeople, or the drowned creatures who circled the lighthouse. He couldn't resist asking.

"The drowned souls who linger around the lighthouse—were there a lot of them when you lived here, too?"

"Of course. How else would I have known what they were in the first place?"

Alba frowned, nudging a rock over with the toe of his shoe.

"Did they also come up onto land to sing to the moon when the merrow did?"

"No," Eridanys grunted, distracted by turning over a large rock to search underneath it. "They were never so bold as they are now. Probably because there are no merrow left to scare them off."

"Is that why they don't bother me so much when you're there?"

Eridanys flashed a nasty, satisfied little smile, showing off his sharp teeth. A good enough answer.

The pale siren spent more time hunched on the balls of his feet mumbling and scouring the mud with his claws than he did upright. Intent on proving a point, on proving himself a fine mate that could provide treasures to his chosen person. Alba had never heard the man repeat his name so many times in only a few hours, endlessly seeking his attention with every additional discovery. *Alba. Alba, here. Alba, look. Alba. Alba. What do you think?* Always followed by an extended hand dribbling a few pearls, pretty shells, even sometimes what looked like lost merrow jewelry.

Alba grinned and thanked him each time, asking how he found them, wanting to find some on his own, too—but Eridanys always scoffed, shaking his head and hurrying away again like he preferred to keep all the glory for himself. That was fine, too. Alba much preferred the shiny treasures over the things he himself kept digging up—bones. A tooth. What he swore was a shiny ring on a decomposing finger, though too much salt had solidified in thick layers around the joints for him to really tell for sure.

When the uneven sand beneath his feet made his hip throb, Alba took a break on a rock jutting out from the exposed beach, letting his head dangle from his shoulders to stretch his back. Every part of him throbbed, once again for many different reasons thanks to the same siren that prowled the seabed, but having that chance to simply sit and watch the sand beneath his feet bubble, to listen to the receding tide, to glance up every now again and keep an eye on his mud witch searching for treasures, was a relief on every inch of him.

"Alba. What are you doing?"

Alba glanced up from where he'd nearly dozed off, blinking as another handful of pearls were offered to him. He took them with a tired smile, rinsing them in a small puddle alongside where he sat.

"Nothin'," he said, appreciating the offerings. Reminded of the strings of shells he'd found more than once on the doorknob of the house, the lighthouse, wrapped around a bundle of crab tossed over the rocks when he and the siren weren't speaking to one another. Wondering if they'd been gifts from Eridanys, too. Not sure it was worth trying to ask, thinking he already knew how Eridanys would scoff and insist '*no, of course not, what are you talking about?*' "Leg hurts from walkin' around, just wanted to take a break. These are really pretty, thank you."

Eridanys didn't turn away to continue searching that time, though. He gazed down at Alba with the slightest wrinkle in his nose.

"Even with your walking stick?" He asked.

Alba drew a circle in the sand with the end of his cane. "It's not magic. Someone did a real number on me last night, anyway."

"Why didn't you tell me?" Eridanys snapped, before pressing his lips together and exhaling through his nose. Calming himself back down. "That your leg hurt."

"Thought it didn't really matt—"

"How long until you learn to ask for my help? What about the next time when I don't notice and you get carried out to sea?"

"Carried out to sea?" Alba joked, making a show of gazing out to where the water was at least a hundred feet away. "Don't think that's really a risk right now."

"Last night you told me when your leg hurt," Eridanys went on stubbornly. "I expect you to do the same even when we're going about our business. Do you hear me?"

Alba sighed, swallowing back the instinctive rush of irritation that came with being told what to do. Especially in a tone like that —but it was a little too big to hold down entirely. "Is that really how you want to say such a thing to me?"

"What do you mean? Why wouldn't—"

"Try again," Alba said, tucking the handful of pearls in the pocket of his jacket. "Or I'm going to get annoyed."

Eridanys made a sound like he wanted more than anything to argue, before clapping his mouth back shut, puffing up his chest, crossing his arms before uncrossing them again.

"I—!" he barked, but gulped that back, too, finally managing a new approach: "I would like for you to tell me when you're uncomfortable! So that I can take care of you! That's all! Don't make me say it again!"

Alba laughed behind his hand, deciding that was good enough. Eridanys turned on heel, stomping off and kicking at a deflated clump of soggy seaweed before stomping back again.

"Please!" he insisted in frustration.

"Yes, alright," Alba assured, fighting back another laugh. "Thank you. And try not to take it so personally—askin' for help isn't my first nature. Had that beat out of me quick. Not even my second, I don't think."

Eridanys inhaled sharply through his nose. Alba didn't hear an exhale follow it.

"I want to know that you feel like you can rely on me!" The mer-man exclaimed with the same stilted discomfort. Clearly doing his best, all the while looking like he was about to pop. "You are my shore-caller and you will rely on me!"

"Christ, I said alright!" Alba barked a laugh, finally grabbing Eridanys' hand and yanking him down. The man obeyed, knees splatting into the mud in front of where Alba sat. "I will rely on you. Alright? You can rely on me, too."

Eridanys narrowed his eyes, mouth opening like he was on the verge of declaring he would never need Alba for anything like that —but, to even Alba's surprise, he stopped himself yet again. He averted his eyes, glancing down at Alba's leg with a frown, then turning and taking a seat in the mud.

"Thank you," he said flatly. Under his breath, like there was something to be afraid of with uttering such words. "I will sit with you until you're ready."

"You really don't have to—"

"I would like to be caring toward you," he interrupted, cutting himself short and pressing his lips together before adding: "I recommend you stop taking my offers for granted. Or else I might realize it's not worth the effort, just like with my..."

He trailed off, but Alba caught on. He shifted where he sat, adjusting his cane, waiting to see if Eridanys would continue. When he didn't, Alba nudged him with his knee. Wishing he would.

"You mean your last human partner," Alba urged gently. "Did he rely on you a little too much?"

"No." Eridanys' response came without hesitation. "He never asked me for anything. But for reasons different than yours. Even if he did, I wouldn't have wanted to give it. He only ever..." he trailed off again. Alba waited, then gently touched Eridanys' hair scarf, nudging it slightly from where a few strands of white hair were peeking through. Eridanys tugged it further at the thought. "He only ever took from me, without asking what I wanted. And I was expected to give it to him. I prefer to be asked, rather than expected..."

Alba thought he knew what that implied, but at the same time, there were so many immediate questions he wished to ask. So many things he wished to say, about how he knew how that felt, how he also hated being told what to do, how he'd spent his entire life never having a choice, either—but Eridanys already knew all of that. That was why he admitted such things at all.

"Thank you for resting with me," was all Alba could think to say in the moment, watching as Eridanys' tense muscles relaxed. Just slightly. Just enough to make Alba's heart thump, though he didn't know why. They sat in silence for a handful of minutes as the words caught on the salty breeze, sinking in, hooking into Alba in ways he didn't expect to linger in his bones for so long.

The only person he'd ever wholeheartedly trusted, relied on, felt safe asking for help from, was his mother—but without her there, Alba had felt the weight of being alone more than he would admit. There was something about not having anyone to rely on— and something about not having anyone to rely on *him*. His mother's reliance on him had been his sole reason for surviving for so long, and to suddenly go unneeded was like gravity had lightened its grip on his feet and he would lift off into the sky at any moment.

For Eridanys to say such things as wanting to be relied on, and for him to agree to rely on Alba in return, even a little bit—it helped Alba feel a little more anchored into his existence. Perhaps one day he would learn how to exist for himself and not anyone else, but—a part of him wasn't sure he was capable of leading a life like that, either.

"I hope you'll always tell me when you don't want to do somethin' I ask," he eventually added. Eridanys' head tilted slightly, just enough to glance his way. Alba didn't meet his eyes, prodding at a little crab emerging from the mud alongside the toe of his boot. "I'll even ask for more things in order to give you the opportunity, too."

Eridanys watched the crab scuttle back and forth, clacking its claws together at both of them in threat.

"Alright," he muttered. "I'll ask you for things more often as well. Even though there's nothing I think you could do for me that I couldn't do for myself."

"God. Close enough, I guess," Alba said, but laughed as he did. "How about you do somethin' about that crab for me? I don't like his attitude—*OH!*"

He practically screamed as Eridanys swiped the creature into his mouth in an instant, crunching down on it like a piece of rock candy. Alba grabbed his face in shock, before buckling over with laughter and having to hold on to Eridanys' shoulder for support.

Eridanys surprised him by chuckling, too—then laughing with him, a bright, musical, wholesome sound far more beautiful than any song Alba had ever heard.

Alba's pockets clattered with pearls and shells and other treasures lost to the sea and exhumed by siren hands. Soon, he even became obsessed with the look on Eridanys' face as he searched the mud, intensely focused with a little pucker in his lips, the smallest wrinkle in his nose, unblinking while scouring like an owl seeking a mouse on the forest floor.

Forced to wander further and further out toward the water, only the sound of the singing pipes reached them once far enough for Eridanys to heave Alba onto his back. Carrying him, not wanting to leave him too far behind, not trusting that the sea wouldn't suddenly swell forward and grab him by the ankles to steal. Alba asked if it was common for her to take shore-callers for herself; Eridanys said he would tell him, later. Not wanting to make him nervous. It made Alba tighten his grip on the man's shoulders.

But as time waned on, Eridanys' attention kept getting caught on the distant trees, glancing at them more often as the sun crept toward afternoon, then evening. Every time, Alba would say his name, tug on his hair, draw his attention back—until he couldn't, anymore. Until the sun sank to the horizon, and darkness consumed the town, and midnight was right around the corner. It wasn't until Alba suggested they return to shore that Eridanys finally released a long-held breath, as if he'd been waiting for permission. Demeanor betraying his words, his actions. Even he wanted to know. Even he wanted to see what the spirits in the woods meant when they'd invited him to *come and see what you've caused.*

It wasn't hard to melt into the darkness after crossing up onto the dark sand, where Eridanys hooked an arm around Alba's waist to hoist him up over the steepest patches of beach grass that would surely tangle his already unsteady legs.

It wasn't hard to disappear between the buildings where townsfolk clustered during their own new moon celebration, dancing and singing to music around a bonfire in the center of town, intermingling with wafting scents of roasted fish and bread and wild berry jams.

They slipped down a dark alleyway where no one would notice them, Alba keeping Eridanys' hand in his. Perhaps to help him walk easier, perhaps to avoid getting separated in the low light, he wasn't entirely sure. Eventually, they reached the cemetery, the edge of the trees where they'd had their confrontation the day prior. Eridanys' hand in Alba's tightened, as if silently seeking reassurance that he was still there. Alba squeezed it back, holding onto him tightly.

"Am I going to turn to salt?" He asked under his breath as Eridanys took his first step into the trees.

"Not so long as you stay with me."

Alba did exactly that, keeping a firm hold on Eridanys as they entered the woods. That time, there were no pale faces in the darkness to giggle and attempt to lure them, which meant they were on their own to figure out where to go. To figure out what the spirits meant to show them.

With one hand in Eridanys' and the other wielding his cane, Alba did the best he could to navigate the dark undergrowth without any way to see where they went, every now and again pausing to listen. To let his senses expand, wander, see if there was anything to draw him one way or another. There was only the distant sound of fluted pipes in Moon Harbor. The sound of Eridanys breathing steadily alongside him.

But something else made it hard to focus—as if the darkness didn't settle right. There were no wild things creeping between the plants, neither crickets nor mice in the leaves and pine needles beneath his feet. The wind hardly blew through the branches except at their highest points, as if even it knew there was something dangerous about being within reach of that darkness.

"Over here, brine witch."

Alba turned suddenly, just as Eridanys pulled him back on instinct. There, behind one of the trees, a spirit had come to see them. But only one, not flanked by a dozen others like all the previous times. Tall and thin, pale hair cropped short and rough, expression gentle, blank, eyes pale and empty. It glowed slightly, a muffled moon-beam not strong enough to even bounce off the plants around its feet. Eridanys' breath caught.

"Cepheus," he whispered, taking a step forward. "Is that you?"

The pale spirit's expression twitched with recognition.

"I'll take you to where they slaughter us. You'll witness another, tonight."

Eridanys' hand in Alba's flexed, about to say something, but the spirit interjected:

"Don't interrupt what you see. It's too late for them, anyway."

"What do you—"

The spirit called Cepheus turned, upright on two legs but floating through the brambles more than they walked. Eridanys remained rooted where he stood, held breaths coming back in sharp inhales, leaving Alba to take the lead.

Alba never let go of Eridanys' hand, either. Pulling him gently in pursuit of the spirit. Wishing he could ask where all the others were, why there was only one come to show them what the rest had been so eager to chitter about. His stomach knotted at the thought of it being a trap, of them both being lured into the vast darkness to be devoured or to, perhaps worse, wander aimlessly for an eternity like the rest of them—but then the spirit came to a stop up ahead, and melted into the shadows without another word.

Alba held his breath at the small clearing that opened ahead of them, smelling thick of salt and iron and moss. Strings of pearls, shells, and bells dangled from the trees, barely disrupted by the nearly-nonexistent air gliding past.

Months' worth of partially-melted candles encircled the outer edge, white as snow and leaking melted wax across the earth with every previous session they burned. And in the center—an altar of salt piled nearly as high as Alba's knees and as long as he was tall, pure white and donning lines drawn into the surface with fingers. Swirling, runic markings interspersed with shells and pearls and other treasures of the sea, no different from the ones in his own pocket.

"Don't," he whispered when Eridanys attempted to step forward. The man conceded with a frown, returning to the shadows just as Alba swore he heard footsteps approaching from the other side of the darkness.

At first, he thought them to be more spirits—but those figures cloaked in white were as living and corporeal as he was. They walked on two legs, with heads bowed and a platform held between them. On it, a bundle of something wrapped in canvas fabric, reminding him too much of how they used to haul expired sailors off ships into port for the undertaker. But those approaching the circle didn't step like tired sailors disposing of their dead—there was something purposeful about their movements. How they took the same steps in tune with one another, how they hummed under their breaths, how the same salt-scatterers Alba knew tossed handfuls of the mineral along behind the procession.

Instinctively, Alba put out a hand to nudge Eridanys slightly further into the shadows, kneeling behind a bush and pulling the siren down with him. Together, they watched as the canvas-wrapped bundle between the figures was slowly lowered to the grass. The two leading at the front kneeled in front of the piles of salt.

Hands emerged from wide sleeves beneath the folds of the robes, moving in line with one another to gently tuck into the pile of salt and reveal something beneath.

Bones. Dried flesh. Pale, snow-white scales. Swathes of silver-white hair, crusted with salt like frozen drops of water on spider webs.

Alba's ears rang. The world around him crept to a halt, only those in the clearing moving as he felt disconnected from the earth. Just staring as his mind raced, trying to—understand. Trying to make sense of it, to rationalize what horrible thing played out in front of him. With such ease, such natural movements of the people involved, as if it was nothing to shock them.

Next to him, Eridanys was silent, motionless, forced to remain in the shadows as the cloaked figures removed knives from their dressings and proceeded to cut the long-deceased, preserved merrow into pieces. Flaying it like Alba used to flay fish at the market. Picking up every single scale dislodged in the process; cutting the impossibly long tresses of silver hair and tucking them away like reaping wheat during harvest. Dismembering what remained of skin clinging to bone, bundling pieces into grotesque bouquets then tucked into baskets set in a line behind them, as other robed figures went around the circle to light the candles one by one. All the while—a pale spirit watched from the bushes only a few yards away. Unblinking. Unmoving. Resembling the very thing those people desecrated.

When the remains were fully picked and tucked away, not a single strand of hair, scale, tooth, fingernail missed—Alba realized what was wrapped in canvas behind them, just before they unfurled the fabric and removed the fresh creature to be laid within the gap in the salt.

A second merrow—as pale, white-haired, moon-kissed as Eridanys right next to him, equally soft and flushed with life, skin and tail glistening in the circling candlelight as if plucked from the sea only moments prior to being brought.

Breaths shuddered in and out of it, slow and even not unlike the occulting glow of the lighthouse lantern. Its eyes were covered with a blindfold, the mer-creature doing nothing to fight back, to even move despite clearly still alive, mouth hanging slack and body limp as its limbs were rearranged to fit within the gap left by the one that came before it.

The cloaked figures hummed as they worked, those kneeling directly over the merrow singing in low voices with words Alba didn't know. A silver knife was produced, and Alba had to look away, not wanting to see. Next to him, Eridanys watched every moment, unblinking, compelling Alba to glance back as well. Not wanting to shy away when Eridanys had no choice.

The shining blade was drawn over the merrow's throat, stirring only the weakest sound of gargling breath from the creature's mouth as it otherwise remained motionless. Unaware of its own impending death—enough to make Alba's heart squeeze in nauseated pity.

Black blood spilled in a necklace of obsidian over its pale skin, dripping into the grass and staining the pure salt surrounding it. The robed figures continued singing as they did—a comfort to the dying creature, perhaps a beseeching of whatever gods might be watching, surely to plea forgiveness for something so horrible. Made worse when the knife was then held over the merrow's chest, hovering, waiting for its breaths to shallow and slow—then plunged into it in time with what Alba was sure would have been its last breath.

The shine of the blade diminished as it crunched through bone, slicing down its center before hands slid inside to butterfly the ribs open. Alba pressed his hand to his mouth, dropping his cane. When the hands burrowed into the merrow's chest to scoop out its still-beating heart, dropping it into a basket—Alba stumbled backward. Pine-needles crunched beneath his feet, but no one noticed over their humming song. Eridanys remained where he was, still clinging tightly to Alba's hand. Keeping him from going further, resisting Alba's own silent plea to get far away from such an evil sight.

Before spreading the salt over the body, using a knife different from the one to slit the merrow's throat and open its chest, another figure drew a long, precise line down the center of their tail. A silver tool like a potter's rib was inserted beneath their scales, scraping thick curls of shimmering white fat out from between the skin and muscle.

With it came a distinct minty-sweet aroma—and a wave of spinning, nauseating recognition crashed into Alba like a tidal wave. He finally jerked his hand free of Eridanys', not caring that he might crumble into salt, just wanting to get away. Wanting to escape that smell, the understanding, the realization of it all coming together in a single thunderclap echoing in his ears.

The unique oil used to fuel the lighthouse lantern. Its pearlescent sheen, its distinct aroma, its texture similar to whale fat. Even Alba wasn't innocent—even his own hands cannibalized a part of those poor creatures. How many merrow had been used to fill the lighthouse basin that he scraped chunks from every night to light the wick and smooth the gears?

Alba turned and stumbled into the darkness, keeping his eyes closed as long as he could, wandering blindly until he couldn't hear the singing chorus, the sound of scraping fat from meat any longer. Only then did his mouth open, sick spilling out of him in pitiful, groaning heaves of his insides. Clutching his head, his stomach, he crouched alongside a tree and fought back tears that burned the backs of his eyes.

He wished to do more, wishing to scream and claw at his mind until he couldn't remember what he'd seen. To claw at his mouth, to rip out his teeth and throat and tongue as it tingled and tasted of salt and rust and blood and stringy meat.

Forced to recall memories pushed so deeply away he would never have to be reminded. The nature of sailing in the north, where there was no way to know how thick the ice grew, whether a ship would be able to pierce through it; never knowing if one would end up stranded and starving in the freezing cold, forced to find food where it fell. Where it fell and closed its eyes to sleep and never opened them again, to be cut into pieces and boiled in salted water and choked down by mouths desperate to live.

Forced to find food, to choke down the meat of a man he'd

bunked alongside, only then understanding that what happened to his own father wasn't an act of depravity so much as desperation, turning men into animals relying on survival instinct alone—

"Albatross."

Alba tensed. He held his breath, pressing his palms into his eyes before finally opening them to the darkness. Not having to search for long before the moon offered a beam of light to gaze upon. No—not the moon. The moon was nowhere to be found, nowhere to witness her own kin in the sea pulled apart by human hands beneath the canopy of the trees.

It was Eridanys standing over him, expression flat, empty. In his hand he held Alba's abandoned cane, though didn't offer it. Instead, he knelt down to join Alba in the grass, overlooking the far-off town at the base of the hill, the sea as dark as the woods without the moon's light.

Alba nearly asked what he was doing, then nearly apologized, then nearly got back to his feet to pretend like nothing was the matter at all—but the words caught when he saw the faint flicker of tears in Eridanys' eyes. Barely visible in the low light of Moon Harbor; shining like specks of snow on his lashes.

Alba hated himself for not knowing what to say. Not knowing anything to say, not even a whisper, a sound of acknowledgement or apology. All he could do was put his arms out, pulling Eridanys into an embrace. It felt so small, so pitiful, but Alba held him tightly even in the silence, hoping it would be enough. Eridanys leaned into him; he exhaled a chilly breath into Alba's hair, embracing him back. Holding him for a long time, breathing him in, eyelashes tickling the side of Alba's neck where the siren pressed his face against his shoulder. When Alba attempted to pull away, Eridanys squeezed him tighter, drawing him closer.

"Not yet," he whispered. "Will you—do something for me, and—stay a little longer. Please."

Hardly a sound. Embarrassed to say it—or perhaps never

knowing he knew how to. Alba pulled him tighter, practically clawing at him. Holding the back of Eridanys' head, the center of his back, trying to pull the man and everything he was into his chest.

"Yes," he whispered. "Yes, Eridanys. I will—I'll stay with you until you're ready."

Eridanys' face disappeared back into the crook of Alba's neck, body shuddering with every inhale as if he cried without tears. Like he didn't know how. Alba wouldn't rush him. Alba would wait for as long as Eridanys needed.

CHAPTER 22

After witnessing it in the woods, it was impossible not to notice, to fully understand, how each and every part of the merrow were used in the isolated confines of Moon Harbor.

The shining scales that decorated the homes, the streets. Shells dangling in long clattering chains and garlands over doorways, strung with silvery braids. The equally silver hair woven intricately into their fishing nets. Shimmering droplets of the moon embedded in carved woodwork around doorways and windows, around the edge of rowboats, tied into the same garlands that sagged heavy with shells and polished glass after the new moon celebration in the street. Shimmering powders on the peoples' eyes. Pieces of white fish-skin used as bandages on wounds. Minty-sweet fat used to fuel their lighthouse.

"It's no wonder I was alone when I returned."

Eridanys' words struck Alba like a punch to the chest, standing next to him on the edge of the town while the rest of the inhabitants slept beneath a dark sky catching early light of a rising sun. He couldn't stop his hand from reaching out to take Eridanys', squeezing it. Eridanys held it tightly, refusing to let go again.

"When we first spoke to them on the edge of the trees, I..." he continued, trailing off like he forgot himself, then closing his eyes and forcing himself to finish: "I didn't think they were dead. I thought perhaps they'd been cursed to stay there, or were choosing to hide because of something that happened with the people. I never thought... If I'd known, I wouldn't have been so..."

"You didn't know," Alba reiterated. He squeezed Eridanys' hand again. Not sure what to say, next. Not sure if Eridanys needed comfort, or someone to silently listen, or something else. He could only open his mouth and see what words came next.

"You should destroy this town," he whispered. Eridanys' eyes flickered to him in question. "The sea would listen to you, wouldn't she? Summon the water high enough to wash through every house. Up every street, so every stolen part of your kin can return to where they belong."

"But then you'll leave, too," Eridanys mumbled. Like he didn't mean to say it out loud, a thought he didn't know he'd ever have until that moment. Not unlike all the times he asked if Alba's leg felt alright, the words were spoken in uncertainty. Unsure why he felt that way, why something like that would eat at him in the first place.

He squeezed Alba's hand once more, like he thought Alba would vanish in that moment with the mention of it. As if he realized then, just as Alba did, that their agreement had technically come to an end. They'd found Eridanys' kin; they learned what happened to them. Perhaps that was why Alba didn't crumble to salt the moment he released Eridanys' hand during the ritual the night before. The siren's curse had been lifted.

But Alba didn't acknowledge it. Neither did Eridanys. They just stood there in silence, looking at one another as the wind whistled through the town, through the fluted pipes, making the distant waves crash and froth.

"Won't you leave, too?" Alba finally asked. "Without your kin here. Surely you won't stay?"

"And you?" Eridanys asked instead of answering. The words

rushed out of him. "You'll go searching for your mother somewhere else, won't you?"

He sounded almost panicked. Alba just watched him for another long moment, before finally turning away. His heart raced. He didn't know. *Yes. No. Not yet. As soon as possible.* He—didn't know.

"Not today," was all he could think to respond. "I have to figure out where to go, first."

"She might have left a clue somewhere," Eridanys insisted. Alba nodded.

"I think so, too. Maybe even in the lighthouse, if she really did stay there before I did. I'll take a few days to look, I think."

"I'll stay with you," Eridanys added. Alba looked at him again, finding how the siren's eyes had never pulled away from him for a moment. "I'll keep the drowned souls from bothering you until you go."

Alba managed a weak smile. "Alright," he said. Grateful for those words. Unsure what else to say. Unsure how to put the sudden squeeze of his chest into words, only knowing they sounded an awful lot like *'come with me.'*

THEY WALKED the length of the black sand until cliffs got in their way, then crossed onto the exposed mud slowly soaking through with returning seawater as the tide crept back to where it belonged.

Eridanys invited Alba onto his back when the ground grew too slippery for him to walk with his cane, and Alba wrapped his arms securely around Eridanys' shoulders. He closed his eyes, listening to the sound of the encroaching sea and overhead gulls gliding by. The muted sun rose to tease the darkness away, distant clouds crowding the horizon with the return of Moon Harbor's constant rain.

"Do you know what they were singin'?" he asked as they reached the far edge of the lapping water, where Eridanys set Alba down just long enough to strip off his clothes so they wouldn't be ruined when his legs combined back into a tail. He pulled Alba back in place over his shoulders before answering, stepping into the water toward the lighthouse in the distance.

Alba didn't know exactly when the man's glamoured legs formed back into a tail, but sensed the shift in force against the water. He steeled his arms around Eridanys' neck, hiding his face in the man's hair against the cold spray.

"It was a song of blessing," Eridanys answered after gathering his bearings. "Thanking the gods for their benevolence, praying for more, showing humility to those who may have been harmed in the giving of a gift."

Had he not already been pierced to the bone with the chill of the water, Alba's blood would have gone cold.

"And which god would believe that, exactly?" He spat, partially from the bitterness in his gut, partially against the saltwater infiltrating his mouth. Eridanys didn't answer right away, suddenly coming to a stop and treading water. Alba felt the swaying of a strong tail moving effortlessly below him, making him shivering in intimidation.

"Would you like to see?" Eridanys asked over the waves. They were just within reach of the lighthouse rocks, making Alba frown.

"Don't you dare take me to your sea-obscura—"

Eridanys laughed, shaking his head and patting Alba's arm wrapped around him. "No, not that far. Hold on tight, sailor. I think a morning spent in the merrow baths sounds refreshing."

"The what—?"

But Eridanys was already grabbing Alba's cane and his own spare clothes, tossing them at the nearest clump of grass beneath the lighthouse, before adjusting his trajectory and cutting back into the heart of the water.

Still clinging around his neck, seawater swelled relentlessly over Alba's shoulders, especially once they skirted past the breakwater of the harbor and into rougher seas. He felt every catch and release of the strong muscles of Eridanys' shoulders and back, straining his own arms with every pull forward. Eridanys' partially-webbed fingers reached up to grasp briefly at Alba's arms encircling him every few minutes, as if checking to see if he was still there. As if Alba didn't weigh enough to be sensed any other way.

The water dipped further in temperature as the clouds swept in faster than Alba expected, swallowing up the brief sunlight offered by the new moon. The sea appeared equally furious as it rushed back toward the shore, waves angrily beating against the jagged rocks of the cliffs, deafening with every crash like banging war drums. Alba watched the flaring whitecaps as each wave smashed and curled over itself, sensing how Eridanys' strokes moved in time with each one.

Despite the sea's thrashing, Alba never felt a moment of anxiety, even though everything in his instincts insisted otherwise. Eridanys' tight body, the shifting of his muscles, the clear show of strength with every passing moment, would have eased a sense of calm into even the most frightened of swimmers.

They continued down the rocky shoreline until the jutting stone grew into terraced cliff sides, like steps used by giants to crawl onto land. Eridanys came to an unexpected stop, bobbing up and down over a swelling wave that proceeded to crash against the stone cliffs a few hundred yards away. Alba pulled away from where he barnacled against the siren's back, but even then nothing stood out to him.

"There's a cave lagoon on the other side of those cliffs," Eridanys said, using a finned finger to point. "If you look closely, you can see where glass windows set in the stone reflect the clouds. Just there, to the left of that little tree on the edge. Do you see?"

Alba squinted, but siren eyes must have been better than human ones, because he saw no glass window in the stone nor any little tree clinging to the edge of the rocks. Eridanys might have also been teasing him, for some reason or another, and Alba nearly accused him of such before Eridanys touched his arms again. That time, holding them tightly. Locking them into place.

"The only way in is through an entrance beneath the surface, about a dozen feet down. You'll have to hold your breath, but it shouldn't be too long. Especially not for a seasoned sailor like you, right?"

"Wh-what?" Alba gasped. "No! You're not gonna fool me like that—"

"I'm not fooling you," Eridanys insisted, allowing incoming waves to draw them closer to the cliffs, keeping back just before they were smashed with the force of a fully-sailed ship. "You're just going to have to trust me."

Alba didn't answer, he didn't know how, just tightening his arms until he was nearly choking the siren.

"Don't you dare drown me," he threatened into Eridanys' ear. "I'll haunt you for every day you're still alive."

"Promise?"

Alba scoffed—barely getting another chance to suck in a final breath before the sea decided for him. A giant wave crashed overhead, thrusting Eridanys under.

Alba nearly lost his grip, grappling to keep his armfuls of Eridanys' shoulders, not wanting to be slammed against the rocks and split his head open. Eridanys' hands grasped at him in return, locking Alba securely in place, wiping all his apprehension away in an instant.

Alba held his breath for as long as he could, taught how to balance his lungs and his panic from all the previous times he'd gone overboard—but diving down then navigating into the dark cave Eridanys described took longer than he expected. The freezing water didn't help, the effort required to cling to Eridanys didn't help—and he nearly choked down a lungful of water against his will, had they not suddenly ascended like a bolt and burst through the surface into a pocket of air.

Gasping, he still inhaled some water despite his best efforts, immediately coughing as his eyes snapped open. Searching in every direction of where they'd emerged, the sight left him breathless in a different way, mouth dropping open in awe.

A cathedral of stone and moss, crawling vines carpeting the domelike ceiling and reflecting off the bluest water Alba had only ever seen trapped in the deepest reaches of northern glaciers. Birds chittered between the rock and the greenery, a handful bathing in smaller pools along the walls that fed into lower bowls, stepping down and down before spilling into the main basin where he and Eridanys had surfaced. Waves from the other side of the stone crashed against the rocks, gallons of water spilling in through man made holes in the face to fill the basins and tumble into the pools below. It smelled of fresh water and verdant greenery Alba had always associated with home, since there was nothing like it in the north. The rush of familiarity was so strong it nearly brought tears to his eyes.

Somewhere on the other side of the fog of his amazement, Eridanys chuckled, splashing a handful of water into Alba's face.

"Taste it," he said. "It's fresh."

"Fresh? How?" Alba mimicked in disbelief, skimming his fingers over the surface before cupping some to drink. Eridanys wasn't lying—the water was crisp, even slightly sweet, like something straight from the heart of the mountain. As he scooped another mouthful, his eyes followed where Eridanys next pointed to the stacked bowls where the birds bathed themselves.

"Merrow magic in those bowls. Filters out the salt. Usually it's gathered later for ritual spellcraft, or to trade with humans who need it for their own magic, but, ah, you can see where it's been spilling over the edges and building up after being neglected for so long."

Alba nodded in curiosity, then had to grapple for the nearest ledge of moss-covered stone, not anticipating how sore and exhausted his arms were from clinging to Eridanys' through the open waves. He lost his grip the moment he tried to pull himself from the water, groaning as he emerged again with a cough. Eridanys laughed, watching as Alba struggled to heave himself up a second time, finally placing his hands within the curves of Alba's waist to lift him out of the water with ease. Alba just crawled on his hands and knees over the soft moss before collapsing face-first into it with a relieved sigh.

His tense muscles finally relaxed, fully unraveling and leaving every inch of him trembling in both exhaustion and the chill of the air. He only lifted his head again at the sound of the siren splashing back beneath the surface, finding his moonlit companion gone. It compelled him to crawl to the edge of the rocks, mouth hanging open in another flush of awe when he realized exactly how deep the caves stretched beneath the pool.

Every inch of the submerged cavern was intricately carved. Archways, columns, balustrades swirled with sea-inspired motifs, walls were adorned with carpets of sea-grass and barnacles, tapestries of carved stone mosaics decorated with painted pigments and shining abalone shells. A city beneath that dome of air where Alba gazed from, a separate realm from his own where merrow and sea-monsters lived and lurked. For the most part it sat unmoving—until a single streak of moonlight caught his eye, racing in and out of openings in the stone, between columns, under and over archways at a speed Alba never would have imagined before meeting Eridanys. His siren moved so fast, especially in the deepest reaches of the water where no tide could pull back on him. To witness it was equally unsettling as it was mesmerizing.

Once Eridanys vanished through an entryway in the stone and didn't emerge for a few minutes, Alba was finally able to break his attention away and back to where he'd been left on a bed of moss like the siren's dinner. Searching the walls and high ceilings of that domed cavern, the carvings were far less adorned, but he spotted some the closer he looked. Managing to get to his feet—stiffly, without his cane to help him—he limped carefully over the thick mossy surface to see for himself.

Lines like ocean waves swirled in and over one another; sea life and shells; strings of pearls were interwoven with lines that could have been the tide or endless locks of merrow hair. Alba followed them down the length of the wall, smiling to himself when the images eventually spilled into a larger genre scene interspersed with characters, with a story.

A pack of merrow in the sea; peeking out from beneath the surface; offering a handful of shells to a human on the docks; intermingling, merrow in the water and humans on the shore, hands held in a circle; an abundance of fish brought by the permanent residence of them in the harbor, where humans could fish and eat with plenty; a human and a merrow intertwined with one another on an altar as a circle of onlookers smiled and raised their hands in celebration; a funeral procession that ended at the edge of the water beneath a full moon, where the deceased was tossed into the waves and reborn with a tail and moon-kissed scales...

Alba's fingers hesitated on that final piece of the tapestry, something about it making his heart squeeze, though he didn't know what exactly the emotion was. The image was both foreboding and wistful. To be reborn as a merrow after a human death.

He couldn't help but think of his mother, wondering if she once put her hands up in celebration while a human and merrow mated with one another on an altar—perhaps to become callers of one another. Did she exchange shells and pearls with the merpeople off the edge of the docks, too? Did she know those same merrow were being cut open in the woods on the new moon, harvested like fruits from the earth?

There was no painting of that horrible ritual anywhere on the wall. Did the merrow even know what the humans did with their kin in the dark? When the moon wouldn't be there to see? When the new moon was supposed to be a time of celebration and dancing and singing out for the moon to wake from her rest, like Eridanys once told him? What those cloaked figures did in the woods—even Eridanys had been shocked. Even Eridanys had shed a tear at the realization of why his kins' spirits were trapped in there. They'd even said something to imply it was his fault, that something he did was the reason—but what did they mean?

"Something caught your interest?"

Alba jumped, turning quickly just as the siren heaved himself up onto the edge of the mossy stone, shoulders and arms bulging with the weight of himself. His long white tail remained intact, draped in the water as the wide, opalescent fins at the end waved lazily above and below the surface.

"What is this place?" Alba asked, pushing his disquieting thoughts away. "You called them merrow pools, but they look more like some kind of flooded ruin?"

"Ruin?" Eridanys asked, taking a moment to comb fingers through his long, wet hair, like every siren did in old human drawings. Beautiful and mesmerizing, as they were always said to be, as if it was Alba's first time seeing him. "Not *human* ruins like I know you're thinking, no. These are merrow-made."

Alba nodded. Sailors told stories and sang songs about mer-peoples' palaces beneath the sea, though Alba only ever thought them true as much as his mother insisted. He couldn't resist pointing to the series of carvings depicting the merrows' history with the town, a silent question as Eridanys' eyes skimmed each part with furrowing brows. As if having to remind himself after so long at sea, and not being particularly thrilled about it.

"What of it?" he mumbled, turning away with fingers still in his hair, braiding tiny plaits and pulling pieces from where they tangled in the strands of pearls. His tail splashed in agitation a few times. "A honeyed story told in drawings where everyone is smiling and cheering. You of all people know how easy it is to depict something terrible as something beautiful with enough color and flowers and grinning faces."

"Sure," Alba answered. He bit his lip, deciding to pick his battles and returning to where Eridanys sat on the edge of the rock. There were other things to see, after all. He didn't need to spend so much time dwelling on parts that would only sour his siren's mood.

Unbuttoning his shirt, kicking off his boots, Eridanys watched Alba undress with an eyebrow raised in question. Alba stripped off his trousers and underwear last, pulling his braid loose from the plait before sucking in a deep breath and stepping off the edge into the crisp, clean water. Without the salt to burn his eyes, he opened them in the dull light, sinking as far as expelling the air from his lungs would take him. Wanting a closer look at the stunning formations below.

Unsurprised when a moonbeam suddenly circled then swam up alongside him, Alba smiled, pointing down at the rest of the cavern eagerly. Eridanys followed his finger before nodding back, expression curious. He then reoriented himself, and Alba couldn't resist reaching out to touch his tail, not expecting the siren to startle like a cat. A flurry of bubbles erupted from Alba's mouth as he burst out laughing, having to throw out his arms and kick back to the surface again to cough and catch his breath. Eridanys followed, peering at him with his eyes narrowed in agitation.

"I know you're a fast swimmer," Alba said, breathless and wiping spit from his chin. "Could you take me to the bottom to get a closer look? Then back up again before I suffocate? I wanna see."

Eridanys cocked an eyebrow before lifting his head slightly more to expose his mouth.

"There is much more to see than your tiny lungs would be able to hold."

"We'll make more than one trip," Alba insisted. "Just show me your favorite spots. You're obviously familiar with this place. C'mon. Humor me. Oh, unless you really aren't as fast as I thought…"

Eridanys' hand lashed out, grabbing Alba's wrist with a tight smile. "Alright, sailor. How long can you really hold your breath?"

Alba barely had a chance to inhale through a sharp laugh, before Eridanys dragged him under.

Chest-to-chest, the siren held Alba securely in place, meaning all Alba had to do was wrap his arms around the back of his neck to remain upright. He kept his face hidden in the crook of Eridanys' neck as they descended, the growing chill of the water making his cheeks burn, only pulling away once they balanced out again. Blinking open his eyes, another small wave of bubbles escaped Alba's mouth at the up-close sight.

Embedded with flakes of silver and gold, iridescent scales from more fish than Alba could count, shining abalone shells, opalized stones and crab shells, the mosaic was larger than he was, depicting what he thought might be the merrow's creation story. Some mythological figure, a scene he would be sure to ask for an explanation of the moment they returned to the air.

A finned goddess encircled by the moon and all her lunations in a crown behind her. A flock of moon-white merrow encircling a massive whale-like creature with another halo of moon phases behind its head, fins extended and raining down fish and shells and silver over them. A bountiful offering from a god to its people; and in it, nowhere were there any humans to take part—until Eridanys took Alba's hand, flattening his palm within the center of the whale's crown, where his fingers were surrounded with silver riches and beams of moonlight.

He turned, meeting Eridanys' eyes. Even in such low light, the siren glowed like the moon herself; brighter than the mosaic, more stunning than even the goddess depicted there. It left Alba breathless, even more than the water that refused him air. And such a beautiful, breathtaking thing—was looking right back at him, as if there was a chance in the world Eridanys could ever think the same of someone like Albatross Marsh.

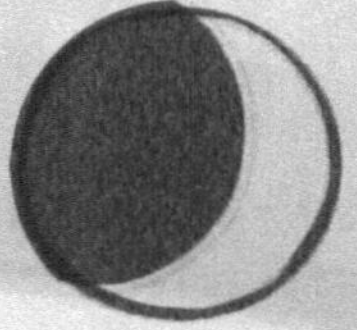

CHAPTER 23

Just like the day prior, Eridanys was determined to find and offer Alba any pretty thing he dredged up from the mud at the bottom of the pool. Alba, who sat on the edge of the moss and combed merrow oils through his hair until it shined, smiling every time that piece of the moon appeared beneath him again with more treasures to offer. Long strings of pearls, pieces of chipped glass mosaic, a dusty-pink scallop painted around the edge in shining gold.

When even Eridanys grew tired from all the effort, he sat against the edge of the rocks as Alba offered to comb aromatic oils through his hair, too, strangely thrilled at the opportunity to touch something so perfect. Already softer than silk and shinier than silver, the oils made hardly any difference in what was already so lovely, and Alba made sure to express it out loud every time he thought about it.

Eventually the compliments ensured Eridanys' ego got the better of him, taking Alba to kiss him. To open his shirt, then his pants, to pull him over the moss and spread his legs and devour him in exchange for all the musing over how beautiful and perfect and handsome he was.

Alba didn't complain—he even liked gripping that flawless

hair in his hand as his toes curled in the loamy moss and his back arched in pleasure. Left gasping and grinning after Eridanys' tongue was finished with him, closing his eyes and listening to the waves crashing against the opposite side of the rocks, the birds seeking solace in the bowls on the wall, the sound of the siren's tail lazily waving back and forth in the water. If he could, he might stay there forever.

"When we had that mating ritual on the rocks... was it the same thing as that?" Alba asked, pointing to the depictions on the wall.

"More or less," Eridanys answered, crossing his arms over the edge of the moss to rest his chin on the backs of his hands. Alba sat up to see him better, sitting so close to one another that the siren's cheek brushed against the side of his leg. "Back then, it was an affair of everyone to come and watch. To oversee the marriage between land and sea, shore-callers and sea-callers."

Alba frowned. He absentmindedly squeezed the water from his hair as Eridanys spoke, not liking the thought of it, though he wasn't sure why at first. Was it the idea of mating with someone while a crowd of onlookers watched? Or—was it more the thought of Eridanys doing such a thing with someone else for everyone to see?

"Does it interest you that much? Merrow lore."

Alba turned back with an eyebrow raised, like his response would be obvious. Clearly not to Eridanys, however, who gazed at Alba with a blank expression, still resting his chin on overlapped arms. Waiting for an answer. It made Alba self-conscious, not sure he'd ever get used to being stared at like that. It made him ramble.

"Well... apart from simply wanting to understand what I've gotten myself into, I think learnin' things about the merrow, especially the ones who used to be here... it helps me feel closer to her. Erm, my mother. Like it gives me somethin' to look forward to, as if I'll finally have somethin' other than sailing to talk to her about when I see her again. Not so much stories about people circlin' and watching a merrow and a human mate, let alone how I ended up doing the same thing, but different, but—um, well... Her stories about mermaids and mermaid magic and them granting wishes were all I had that Josiah Warren hadn't tainted, for so long..." he trailed off, before closing his eyes and sighing. Eridanys' fingers found Alba's hair, beginning to braid it, as if he could sense the growing frustration. "I wish it had all been as sweet as that. But like you said earlier, reality is hardly as lovely as the stories told about it."

Eridanys' fingers slowed, before forming another plait and running it through again. Alba bit his lip, adding: "I'm... sorry. About what became of your home. Even if it wasn't as perfect as my mother used to describe. I imagine it was at least better than what it turned into."

"Don't be," Eridanys replied after a moment. He paused for a long time, before continuing. "I didn't know what to expect when I came back. It's not unusual for relations between merrow and humans to sour after so many generations, but—I suppose I never expected what actually happened. And I still... can't imagine how it degraded so far to become what it did..."

"Then, what we saw in the woods last night—was not a common ritual between merrow and the townspeople," Alba commented, less a question than an acknowledgement. Once again choosing his tone carefully.

Eridanys smirked, and Alba was relieved he sensed the sprinkling of sarcasm.

"No. Not that I was aware of, at least."

Alba didn't know how to say it—but couldn't hold the question back any longer, either. Eridanys would either answer, or he wouldn't. But Alba couldn't stop himself. "When you first approached your kin in the woods—they implied, erm, that it was... your fault, what happened to them. Do you know...?"

"I've been thinking about that as well," Eridanys admitted with a frown, responding more readily than Alba expected. "I'm sure they're referring to the circumstances around my banishment, but... apart from that, I don't know. Whatever lead to what we witnessed last night was their own doing. Whether they would admit it or not."

"You didn't tell the townspeople to use your kin's body parts for earrings and fishin' nets?"

Another smirk, once again to Alba's relief. "I did not. I don't think I would have been that creative."

"What..." Alba trailed off, unsure again. "What were the circumstances around your banishment?"

Eridanys' expression did not crumple into disdain or anger; it didn't smirk or chuckle, either. It remained blank, which Alba hadn't considered might be the worst sort of reaction to receive. He almost added that Eridanys didn't have to talk about it if he didn't wish to, but the siren exhaled through his nose, closing his eyes and shaking his head.

"I refused to obey a command my human partner made of me. One thing lead to another," he answered simply. Clearly not willing to talk about it in its entirety—at least, not yet. Still, Alba wouldn't take those simple words for granted. He wouldn't bother Eridanys to say more. He nodded in understanding.

"I'm sorry your last partner did not treat you well."

"Don't be," the siren muttered, reaching up to touch the side of Alba's face with his hands. "I much prefer my new partner, anyway. He's much more submissive. Both on his feet and on his back. His blood was warm and sweet, too, as a virgin."

"Oh, stop it," Alba groaned, knocking Eridanys' hands away and making him laugh. "Virgins do *not* have blood any different from anyone else."

"Perhaps you're just special, then," he amended. Alba rolled his eyes, throwing out his leg to shove Eridanys back into the water. The siren went with a sharp laugh cut off by the water, leaving only a ring of bubbles and a thrashing tail as he fought to right himself again beneath the surface. Hair clung to his face and down his chest when he re-emerged, still laughing. A sound Alba realized might be more powerful than any song ever would be.

Turning his eyes down as his cheeks flushed, Alba finally got back to his feet. He searched for his clothes before any needy blood could color his cheeks and inspire Eridanys to do such distracting things with his tongue again.

"Should we head back?" Alba asked while pulling his freezing-cold slacks back on.

"I have a gentler way of getting you out of here," Eridanys answered, crossing his arms over the ledge once again and watching Alba's every move. "The lagoon extends that way. Opens up at the river a little bit into the trees. We can walk back."

"A reminder I don't have my cane. Someone threw it in the grass by the lighthouse."

"It's implied I was going to carry you," Eridanys said with a sarcastic smile. "Seeing as I carried you all the way here, why wouldn't I also carry you all the way back? By sea or on land."

Alba hated how his ears went hot at the offer, not to mention the way Eridanys said it. He just focused on the buttons of his shirt, pulling on his boots, then finally returning to the water to slide back in. Eridanys swept him up the moment he did, and Alba took hold of him in return, careful not to pull his hair or bend the line of finned spines up his back as he positioned himself securely like the first time.

Eridanys carried him across the length of water in the main atrium, then ducked beneath a partially-submerged archway to emerge in a room on the other side just as tall but not nearly as wide around. Alba still gawked at the height of the spires, charmed by the sound of rain and wind through trees closer than ever.

"Did everyone in Moon Harbor know of this place?" he asked. "Or was it only other shore-callers?"

"Only merrow and their shore-callers," Eridanys confirmed. "I'm sure the townspeople knew *of* this place, not unlike many of our other secrets, but at least while I was here, very few were allowed inside to bathe and fuck one another."

"Oh—did they?"

"Fuck each other? Constantly. These walls used to ring out

with the sounds of merrow-human orgies at almost all hours of the day."

Alba's ears burned again. "Oh," he whispered. "Sounds fun."

Eridanys hummed with a little smile, as if disappearing back into those memories. Alba didn't like the little pang of jealousy that struck him again, not wanting to think about his siren pleasuring or being pleasured by anyone else—but he pushed the thoughts away as quickly as they came.

"They would have all liked you very much, you know," Eridanys went on, as if he knew. "The way you sound. The way you taste. Whimpering and writhing under the hands and mouths of a dozen other merrow, I wonder how long you would have been able to stand it before begging for mercy..."

"And you would've let them?" Alba snapped back, blood turning his cheeks red as he pulled on Eridanys' hair. "You would've been fine with that? I don't believe it."

"Hmm," he considered, chuckling with every tug of his hair. "I would have. But only once."

"What?"

"To give them a taste. So they always thought about what they were missing while I fucked you alone in front of all of them."

"S—" Alba choked. "Stop it. No you wouldn't have."

"Guess we'll never know."

"Well, I think..." But Alba's argument trailed off when something caught his eye in the next cavern, crawling up the cave wall. A rope, fed through a series of iron loops hammered into the stone. He might not have thought anything else of it, had he not then spotted a second one. And on the other side of them, a third. A fourth. Whatever it was—they were casually swimming right into the center of where all four lines met at the ceiling.

"Eridanys, wait—"

Something clicked overhead—followed by the rapid hissing of ropes through metal eyelets. Like the mouth of a beast from below, the seabed suddenly rushed up to meet them, finding the bottom of Eridanys' tail and crushing it into Alba's legs, before slamming into them from all sides. Water spilled in a deafening torrent as the net tore them from the water and hoisted them impossibly fast into the air, momentum nearly slamming them into the ceiling where the hoist was nailed into the stone.

Crashing down again into the apex of the hanging net, Alba was crushed beneath the weight of Eridanys' body and writhing tail. He clawed at Eridanys' scales in a desperate attempt to pull himself free and take a breath, even only a small one, just enough that he might not suffocate so quickly.

Eridanys fought to right himself in the awkward grounding, finally managing to grab Alba under the arm and wrench him upward. Alba clawed after him, finally pulling himself free, wiping his sore nose from where the siren's tail had smashed and made it bleed. He was relieved to find Eridanys equally unharmed —until his hands smeared through dark blood staining moonlit scales. He gasped at the lacerations criss-crossing Eridanys' tail, cut by the rough fibers of the rope.

He turned quickly back to Eridanys, looking him over one more time. Worried he might have missed something else. Eridanys just looked at him with the same intensity as always, as if on the verge of asking if Alba had planned it, if he was behind their sudden capture—but Alba's clear concern must have kept the words at bay.

Another *click* rang out through the cave, and both froze. Alba held his breath, searching in every direction, trying to anticipate what else could possibly leap out to get them when they were already twenty feet in the air—and then he saw it. A lantern unwinding like a lighthouse counterweight from another mechanical hoist on the ceiling, descending until it bobbed on the rope at their eye-level. Already illuminated, it smelled of freshly-struck kerosene soaking a wick. He and Eridanys both stared in silent apprehension, Alba's mind racing trying to figure out what, to figure out why, *who.* Eridanys had once mentioned traps laid around the harbor—could that have been one of them? But why didn't Eridanys notice it?

Alba turned his eyes to search the ceiling, then to examine the rope netting up close. The woven fibers couldn't have been any older than a few years. They lacked the same silvery fibers as all the others he'd seen used for fishing. New alarms pricked the back of his mind, making the hairs on his arms stand on end.

"Alba," Eridanys whispered. Alba snapped back to look at him, breath catching when he saw a faint glow forming in the backs of the siren's eyes.

He followed where they stared, finding the dangling lantern again—just as the heat of the wick warmed a metal plate encased inside, beginning to turn. Encircling the light, gradually, then slightly faster as the metal softened and relaxed. Around, around, around—occulting the glow.

Alba had come to memorize the exact pattern of Moon Harbor's lighthouse characteristic—and it took only a handful of rotations for him to know, the pattern was exactly the same.

He moved before realizing, snapping around and smashing his hand over Eridanys' eyes before they could gaze a moment longer. Eridanys' own hands flew up to claw at Alba's on instinct, hissing like an animal in warning, but Alba just shoved his hand back and pinned the siren against the netting.

"Stop!" he exclaimed, voice cracking. "Please, just—it's alright. It's alright, Eridanys. It's—it's like the lantern in the lighthouse. I don't want it to hypnotize you. Not again. Alright? That's all. Just trust me."

Eridanys went silent, though his attempts to tear Alba's hand away diminished. Breathing heavily, Alba swallowed back on the nervous lump in his throat, forcing himself to ask: "Are you alright? Are—are you still with me?"

"Y-yes," Eridanys answered. His voice trembled in a way Alba didn't expect, a way that pulled on the frayed edges of his soul like the sound of a frightened animal might. He held Eridanys' face a moment longer, before gently sliding the pads of his thumbs down from Eridanys' eyebrows, over his eyelids, trailing off his lashes onto his cheeks.

"Keep your eyes closed for now, alright?" he said. "Just in case."

Eridanys' hands grasped at Alba's wrists, as if Alba was his only anchor. As if a reminder of the nightmare of being hypnotized was enough to petrify him the moment he realized the risk of it happening again. Alba's mouth dangled open with want to say something, something comforting, but he didn't know.

"It's..." he tried, anyway. "It's gonna be alright. I'm gonna get you down, so don't worry. Just trust me, alright? These ropes aren't anythin' special, I just need a way to cut them... Ah, hold on."

He patted around his clothes, sighing in relief when he found the gold-painted clamshell brought to him from the bottom of the pool was still in the pocket of his slacks. He turned it over in his palm until it nestled as comfortably as any other gutting rib ever had on the deck of a tilting ship.

"Keep your eyes closed," he reiterated, flexing the shell in one hand and ghosting his fingers over Eridanys' eyes with the other. "The shell you brought me, I think I can use it to cut the ropes. If it breaks, will you go down and get me another one sometime?"

Despite everything, Eridanys smiled wearily. "Of course."

Alba's grasp trembled with having to balance on wavering legs while pulling himself up to where the net dangled from the hoist. Gritting his teeth, he summoned everything he had, stretching his arm through one of the gaps in the netting and gliding the scalloped edge of the shell up and down the thinnest frayed fiber he could find. It was a grueling, miserably slow task, enough that he had to stop and catch his breath more than once. Each time, Eridanys' hands lifted to clutch him around the waist and support him upright, and Alba's heart raced with determination to keep his siren out of harm's way.

He worked the scallop over the ever-fraying rope again and again, back and forth, fingers going numb the harder he pressed with every slice—until eventually, the weight on the thinning rope made it groan, then creak, and Alba barely yanked his arm back before it snapped.

Crashing back to the water, it knocked the air from Alba's lungs, and he was grateful for the haste with which Eridanys wrapped him in strong arms to draw him right back to the surface again. Gasping and coughing, Alba managed a pathetic *'thank you'* as Eridanys searched him all over—but both of them fell instantly silent at the faint sound of approaching footsteps.

Eridanys barely glanced over his shoulder, before sweeping Alba toward a dark corner of the pool behind a cluster of rocks. Alba kept his mouth clamped shut, attempting to silence his sporadic coughing, swallowing back every twitch of the muscles at the back of his throat. He didn't care if there was a mouthful of water still in his lungs—he knew he didn't want to be found by whoever set that trap.

Four men stepped from the shadowy passageway at the end of the cavern. Alba recognized them all to be people from the town —but the one at the front he knew best of all. Eugene Michaels, with his cotton hat and a cigarette hanging from his mouth. Looking perturbed at the sight of an empty net floating lifelessly on the surface of the pool, lacking whatever prey it originally snagged. The others drew the failed trap to the shore, and Eridanys' breaths stopped just as Alba's did.

The men knelt down alongside the netting, picking it up and observing it all over. With the slightest flicker of light through a gap in the ceiling, Alba realized with a terrified thud of his heart— there were white scales from Eridanys' tail embedded in the fibers.

"Knew there was at least one more," Eugene grunted, pulling a handkerchief from the inner pocket of his coat to pluck up each individual one, like gathering coins from a web. "Knew the marks on that wickie were merrow-stains, too, goddamnit. Actin' like he didn't know nothin' about them in this harbor. Goddamn lyin' Warren sailors."

Alba's heart slammed harder in his chest. Eridanys' arm around him tightened.

"You think it's that one who did in Dawson?" Another man asked as Eugene finished gathering his collection of scales, twisting off the kerchief into a makeshift pouch and tucking it back into his coat. "Sure he's the only one left, isn't'e?

Eugene didn't answer. He just stared, silent and motionless, at the water. Alba had never seen such an intense look on that man's face—one no different than a captain staring down a storm on the horizon. Certain he could outsmart it.

"Dawson say anythin' to you 'bout where he might be?" Another man asked. Eridanys' held breath faltered, cold against the back of Alba's neck. Eugene closed his eyes and pressed the handkerchief containing the scales to his forehead.

"Dawson still hasn't said a thing," he muttered. The rest of the men shifted uncomfortably, before one offered apprehensive apologies.

"Sorry to hear that, Gene. Maybe next time. He's lookin' more like 'imself every month, can't need much more now."

"Should we check the other nets around town?" another asked, lighting his own cigarette with the stiff movements of someone irritated to the brink of their sanity. "Might've caught 'im somewhere else. Clearly he's not gettin' far if this one cut him up bad enough to graze scales."

Eugene considered it for a long time, before nodding.

"Yeah. You and the boys go check the other traps."

"What about you?"

The man turned back to the water. Gazing across it as Alba, even from that distance, watched the thoughts turn behind his eyes. Contemplating a storm on the horizon, one only he could see, one only he knew.

"Think I might go pay that wickie a visit."

"The one stayin' with you?"

Alba's heart pounded faster. Eugene flicked his cigarette into the water, finally turning to leave.

"Haven't seen 'im since last night. Must be back at the lighthouse," he answered. "Better go check on him—and see if I can jog his memory 'bout how he got those bloodstains."

CHAPTER 24

IT MUST HAVE BEEN AGONY FOR HIM, THE SALT SOAKING his wounds, but Eridanys swam fast and hard against the stormy sea on the other side of the cliffs. That time with Alba in his arms, pulled into his chest, one arm holding him in place while the other cut through the water in tandem with his whipping tail. As fast as he could go, racing Alba back to the lighthouse, having to get there before Eugene Michaels did.

Reaching the rocks, Eridanys tossed Alba up onto them with surprising roughness. Alba splatted into the mud, rolling over himself before scrambling back to where the siren had collapsed halfway onto the rocks. Eyes closed, breathing so hard his body rose and fell like its own heartbeat.

"Go on," he growled as Alba asked if he was alright, giving a sharp look. "I'm fine, just go. I'll get healing mud from the seabed—"

"But—"

"I said go!" he snarled, pushing Alba away.

"A-alright!" Alba's voice trembled. He stumbled back, nearly slipping in the mud again. "Just—come back soon, alright? Once the old man leaves, please come ba—"

"Get going, sailor!" the siren commanded, and Alba turned to race for the house.

Through the door, Alba went straight up the stairs to strip off his wet clothes for dry ones. He rinsed the saltwater from his hair before toweling it off, beginning to braid it over one shoulder when a knock came at the door—and everything went still around him.

He'd made it in time. Everything was going to be fine. Nothing had changed from before, he had no reason to worry, to be nervous about Eugene Michaels. He could talk his way out of telling the truth about his stained skin just like the first time—but then Alba caught sight of his hands, realizing his palms and fingers had been stained with the blood from Eridanys' tail.

Downstairs, Eugene Michaels invited himself in, calling out for him. Alba barely heard it. There was only the quickening thunder of his heart in his ears, the thunder of the storm on the house, and the trap door of the storage room rattling on its hinges for the first time in weeks.

There was nothing he could do. He couldn't hide. He was trapped—he was trapped, and he couldn't hide. He was cornered on a fishing boat in the middle of a dark northern sea with nowhere to run. He was trapped, but—but—there was always a way out. There were always lifelines to cut and bodies to shove into a raging sea if he had to.

But before that—he had to relax. He knew how to act. He knew how to blend. He knew how to disappear despite standing right in front of someone.

"Mr. Michaels?" he called down the stairs. "Just a moment!"

He finished braiding his hair.

"I was tarrin' the roof just before the storm hit... tryin' to get the muck off my hands."

He splashed around in the water basin below the window. He looked out of it for a moment, hoping to see Eridanys' moon-spot in the water, but there were only angry waves. Angrier than he'd seen in a while, as if they knew one of their merrow had been tangled in a net and torn apart.

Descending the stairs, he offered Eugene Michaels a small nod in greeting. The man nodded back, holding up the cane Alba had forgotten about in the grass. Alba smiled in embarrassment, not bothering to make up an excuse, taking it back and noticing how the man's eyes flashed to his stained hands right away. Eugene's mouth even opened slightly as if to ask what happened, but Alba had already given him a reason. A reason that would be strange to question. Alba didn't want to give him enough time to think of another way to make his accusation.

"What can I do you for?" he asked, grabbing the kettle and filling it with water from the sink. He moved with intention, placing it on the stove and lighting the wood underneath. Eugene watched in silence as he did, taking a seat at the table. "Must be pretty important if you rowed all the way out here in this storm. Came on fast, didn't it?" The wind howled overhead as if on cue, whistling through hairline cracks in the windows. "Might have to go out and secure the shutters if it rages any bigger. Want some tea?"

"The missus was worried about you," Eugene finally answered, returning to the same old man Alba had known since first arriving in Moon Harbor. "Since you didn't come back to the house last night. She was real excited, wanted to introduce you to our son."

"I caught a ride with the sailors goin' out to fetch their boats on the water," Alba lied with ease, though the mention of Eugene's son made his nerves pluck. He paused just long enough for the kettle to whistle, setting out cups and teabags as he added: "Sorry, should've said somethin'. Didn't want to bother you any more than I already was."

Eugene chuckled. He thanked Alba for the tea, taking a single polite sip, before returning the cup to the saucer.

"Was hopin' I might ask if you'd remembered anything from how you got them marks on your arms," he said. Getting straight to the point—but Alba was prepared. Enough that he didn't flinch, that he could act surprised in a way that didn't immediately give him away for the wrong reasons.

Pouring his own cup of tea, he glanced down to where his sleeves were rolled up to reveal the discoloration. His eyes grated over the matching stains on his hands again, too, knowing the man didn't believe his excuse for those. Exactly the same in color, the slight iridescence of them. Alba couldn't think of a single way that conversation could possibly end without some truth coming out, whether on purpose or by accident, and his nerves spiked.

"Afraid not," he finally answered, taking a seat at the table across from the man. "Though I promise I've been scourin' my mind for it. Makes me uneasy not knowin', too, y'know—"

"Those markings come from spilled merrow blood, lad."

Alba's heart thudded. Eugene said it with assertion, like he thought it would be enough to frighten the truth out of Alba that easily. Alba's mouth even dropped open slightly in surprise, and he did his best to play along. The right sort of surprise. Not the kind that would give him away too quickly, even if it was inevitable. He pretended to look up and down his arm again, as if seeing the markings in a different light.

"Oh?" he asked.

"There's at least one in our harbor, I'm sure of it," the man continued, hardly a moment of pause from when Alba's voice stopped. "If you've been philanderin' with it behind my back, you'd be wise to tell me now. I won't play any games with you."

"I really don't—"

"Don't you lie to me, lad!" Eugene snapped, and Alba stiffened. But instead of filling with fear, like the man clearly intended, Alba's expression hardened. He wasn't going to be intimidated through a raised voice—and that man should have known, no sailor alive was afraid of a little shouting.

"I'm afraid I don't know what you're talking about," he said flatly.

"Listen close to me, Alba," Eugene said, pointing a finger in emphasis. "I know you know. I know you've seen it. I'm tellin' you right now—that merrow, the last one livin' here, killed my boy. Dawson deserves to know Eridanys has been taken care of when he finally comes-to again."

"What?" Alba choked, not sure which part exactly it was in response to. Eridanys—? Eugene's son—? "'Come-to?' But you just said—"

"Merrow magic fills every inch of the harbor here, but none as powerful as they themselves," Eugene said matter-of-factly. He touched his hand to his chest. Alba's ears rang. He thought back to those hands pulling a still-beating heart from that merrow in the salt. "For months, I've been collecting their magic to help my son heal. But there isn't much left. Please, lad, help me. What better odds do I have to bring my son back than to feed him the heart of the one who killed him?"

Alba had to brace against the edge of the counter. Eugene used such vague descriptors, but Alba knew what each and every one of them meant. Harvesting body parts from the merrow the night before. Admitting to having done it for months—long before Alba ever arrived. There was no question where the merrow went. Why their spirits were trapped in the woods—even why they blamed Eridanys for their gruesome fates, if him killing Dawson Michaels started the horrific cycle. But with that confession—Alba thought he at least better understood *why*.

When Alba didn't respond fast enough, or the way Eugene hoped, the man's expression firmed again. He took off his hat, dabbing sweat from his forehead, running a hand back through thinning white hair.

"You came here lookin' for your mother, didn't you? How's this, then. You tell me where the last merrow is, I tell you where she is."

"You—!" Alba gasped, lurching forward. His mouth dangled in shock, staring at the man, crushed beneath a thousand emotions at once. Not knowing which words to choose, feeling more like he might be sick than anything else. "Then—she really was here! The whole time!"

"Aye. Never should've come back to this place, but we'd never forget Edythe Marsh."

Alba stared at him. Knowing what he wanted to scream, doing everything in him to keep it back. To keep calm. To not be too impulsive with his reaction, to keep the situation under control as much as he possibly could—as much as possible while his patience thinned with every passing word.

"Your wife know too?" he asked. "She know, too? That I'm her son? Who else? Everyone?"

"Yes, lad. 'Course she did. We all did. Quite the topic of gossip when you first came to town. Look an awful lot like your pop. Sorry to hear what happened to him. Awful shame what the sea does to men lost on her."

Alba ignored that offer of condolences, hating how he didn't know if they were genuine or just more acting. How he suddenly didn't know how much of Eugene was a lie, how much was sincere, especially after being shown so much kindness since arriving. That man who'd helped him from the start, who extended so much patience and offers of normalcy, even letting Alba sleep in his home. Hating the bitter taste of learning everyone already knew and lied to him, too. The whole town knew who he was, why he was there. Hiding it from him as he chatted with them on the docks and searched their town records and helped move their boats out to sea when the tide receded. How much did they know about what came of the merrow, too, then? How many knew exactly what went on in the woods the night before, when the moon wasn't there to see?

"Why hasn't she come to see me?" Alba asked, sounding like the plea of a child.

"Haven't told her you came, yet."

"Why—!" His voice cracked, only barely keeping the emotion back.

"Didn't know if we could trust you, 'course. As a Warren sailor 'n all."

"You—Tell me where she is."

"Not until you tell me—"

"I said *tell me where my mother is!*" Alba shouted, slamming a fist on the counter. Behind him, the trapdoor in the store room whipped open before slamming shut again. Even Eugene jolted, eyes flashing to the door then back to Alba, a wave of rage crashing over his expression.

"Playin' games with me, boy?" he accused, rising from his chair. Alba stepped back on instinct, but didn't cower. He straightened up further, clenching his jaw, gripping the edge of the counter in a desperate attempt to keep his rioting emotions under control. "You and that wretched creature—he'll bring you nothin' but misery! Listen to me, you don't know nothin' 'bout the sort of magic that resides here. One song and they own you—"

"I know plenty 'bout songs of the sea," Alba said back. "I don't need you lecturin' me on things I learned first-hand. Now —tell me where my mother is, and I won't throw you anywhere you might get a lesson, yourself."

Eugene put his hands up. Considering Alba's offer, eyes flickering between where he white-knuckled the edge of the counter, and the storage room door that rattled with the banging hatch on the other side.

"Alright, relax," he said, voice calm. "I'll take you to 'er. She's hidin' away in a cottage right outside of town. Let's go there and have a chat, hm? She'll tell you. 'Prolly scold you right for believin' anything a merrow says, too."

A shrieking bellow emerged from the depths of the hatch, wailing like a foghorn warning, a throat filled with water and warbling like a flute notched wrong. Alba was nearly able to ignore it, too overwhelmed with the rush of adrenaline at the mere mention of his mother being safe, being somewhere nearby, of him having been within reach of her the entire time. He was almost able to ignore the sound of the haunted waters frothing and calling out to him from the other side of the storage room door—but beneath the whistling wind of the storm, the crashing waves, the howling of drowned voices in every direction, Alba heard something else.

The clanging of a turning lantern. Just like the first time he arrived at that house, a sound he'd grown used to hearing, one that melted into the back of his mind until it hardly existed. But that time, standing there, he heard it again—louder than ever. The clang of a turning lantern he hadn't lit in nearly three days.

Always in such a hurry, with that bone in your teeth. His ears rang. Eugene turned back to him, wondering why Alba had stopped following, but Alba was unraveling the lie with a thousand realizations all at once.

Things he'd known from the start, but never let fester for his own sanity—the notes in the lighthouse keeper's log in his mother's handwriting; the boat captain who admitted to a woman tending the lighthouse before him. Even the simple fact that— Edythe Marsh would have never sat and waited obediently in a cottage on the edge of town. Whether or not she knew Alba had come looking for her—his mother was not the type to rush, but she would never allow someone to tell her to *wait*, either.

"Where is she?" Alba asked again. Eugene scowled, shaking his head, but Alba remained where he stood. "My mother's not the type to sit and wait to be told what to do, even in a place like this. You're goin' to stop lyin' to me now, Mr. Michaels."

Eugene dragged a hand down his face, growing more agitated, looking Alba up and down before licking his lips.

"The Warrens have a long history in this town, you know," he said. Alba's heart thumped. "Saw how Marco dealt with you, too, when he was here. Must be worth a lot to 'em, hm? They're a ruthless lot, 'specially with their contracts."

Alba said nothing. Eugene brushed himself off, then returned to his seat at the table. He sipped at the cooling cup of tea set for him.

"I have their inquiry address in the harbor office, you know. Sure they'd be glad to get a telegram from me, lettin' them know one of their lost sailors washed up in my harbor. May have even killed one of their own." His eyes lifted to meet Alba's once more. "You feed that man to your hungry siren too, lad? Sure bet Mr. Josiah would like to hear all about it, if he's anythin' like his brother Herman. Think he'll go easier on 'ya if I tell him your siren probably liked the taste of your mother just as much? She never was a strong swimmer."

Boiling water tore over Alba's skin like acid, but he barely felt it. He felt only the impact of smashing Eugene Michaels' head with the copper pot, like a strike of lightning up his arm with every slam and clang of metal against hard skull bone.

Even when the man grunted and tumbled from the chair, putting his hands up and begging Alba's name, Alba couldn't stop—he threw himself on top of the man and drew his arm back to hit him again. Something inside of him finally snapped, bent far too long beneath a growing weight, breaking open until he couldn't stop it, finally split open with one final threat on his mother's life for Alba's submission.

Years of abuse and anger and fear and intimidation, helplessness and submission, bowing his head and giving thanks for the scraps he was offered; stowed-away frustrations of coming close but falling short, a peaceful life baited but never given; biting back, keeping his temper, obedient and silent and docile.

He slammed the hot kettle again, and again, until the man's round head was as concave as the pot that bludgeoned it. Until there were no more pleas from him, only the gurgling of lungs attempting to inflate through the flakes of bone and splattered blood that remained of his mouth and nose. Only then did Alba sit back, returning to his body, staring down at what remained of Eugene Michaels for what felt like an eternity—before stumbling backward into the wall, dropping the pot with a deafening *clang*. The house plummeted into echoing silence.

Screaming—horrified screams rushed him, all around him,

making his insides curl and tangle, hands flying to his ears to try and block them out. Only after the sound beat into him until the world spun, did he realize they were his own. Screaming, sharp and haggard, choking on spit building up in the back of his throat, slicking his hands through blood up and down his arms, screaming and clawing at the crimson on his skin as if the old man's blood would stain him like merrow's stained like ink.

Alba screamed until he could no longer breathe, until tears clogged his vision and spit foamed at the corners of his mouth and snot dripped from his nose and all of it finally closed up his throat. Sobbing and crying and banging his head against the wall at his back in a desperate attempt to wake up, *wake up,* it wasn't real, he hadn't just done that, Eugene Michaels had not made those threats, he'd not put those thoughts into Alba's head, those images, Eugene Michaels of all people had not just compelled Alba to beat him until he was nothing but flesh and blood and viscera on the kitchen floor—

Moon-white hands suddenly grasped at his, and Alba jerked away with another shrill gasp. Not wanting to be seen, not wanting to stain Eridanys with what he'd done. But Eridanys pulled Alba's hands from his face, demanding to know what happened, if Alba was alright—thinking the blood on his arms and drenching the front of his body was his own, as if he didn't see the bubbling lump of flesh on the floor right in front of him. As if he couldn't smell the iron in the air and taste the rust on his tongue.

Alba just wailed, sobbing, crying, shaking his head, it wasn't his fault, he didn't mean to kill him—it was an accident, he didn't mean to, he didn't want to, that kind old man that would row him to and from the lighthouse, whose wife was back home waiting for him, who had been the only one to show him kindness since he arrived, who offered him sanctuary in a world that never did anything but hunt Alba down—

Eridanys pulled Alba in, kissing his burned hands with a cool mouth. He pressed a hand to the back of Alba's head, pinning him into his shoulder, stifling his cries and willing him to breathe. *Breathe, take a breath. You're alright. I believe you. It was an accident. You didn't mean to hurt him.*

"He—he said—!" Alba choked, shrill and unfamiliar to himself. "He was threatening me—! He said he was going to—! I didn't know—what else to do, but why did I—Why did I—! I didn't have to kill him, I didn't have to—!"

"Easy, sailor," Eridanys whispered. "What did he say to you, Alba?"

Alba finally grabbed at Eridanys' arms, his shoulders, his chest. His hands left streaks of red and pink across the siren's skin, in his hair, but Alba couldn't wipe it away no matter how hard he tried. It only made him shake worse, losing any remaining grip he had on himself.

"Did you eat her?" he begged. "Did you eat her? My mother, tell me, god, did you—?"

"No," Eridanys said. Instantly, like swearing an oath. Alba's head dangled forward, screaming one more time in overwhelm, but that time allowing Eridanys to slide closer. To hold him, to pull Alba into his chest and wrap arms around him. Protective. Safe. Guarding.

Eridanys turned to lean back against the wall, pulling Alba into him. Alba curled into the the siren's wet chest like a child, skin smelling of salt fresh from the sea. Through blurry eyes, he could see angry, swollen red marks criss-crossing Eridanys' legs where they'd been razed by the net in the cave—and he sobbed all over again.

Like a child, like a frightened animal. Everything hurt, inside and out. His hands, his mind, his eyes, his tongue, his chest, his hip. It all ached as everything he'd ever built to protect himself finally wore away, beaten through after years of cold nights and bitter loneliness and salt and clenched fists and harsh realities. Until every inch felt as desecrated as the copper pot, held together only by two arms wrapped around him.

Chapter 25

Alba didn't know when he fell asleep, only that it was there on the floor in Eridanys' arms. Exhausted, wordless, eyes just cracked enough to know whether it was day or night. Aware of only the feeling of Eridanys beneath him; fingers stroking his hair; a gentle, comforting hum singing from the back of his throat in a language Alba didn't know. One that numbed him, soothed him, enough that eventually the shuddering cries ceased and he was able to drift.

Eventually the arms holding him in one piece lifted him from the floor and carried him to his bed. They laid him on the mattress, carefully stripped off his bloody clothes, then tucked him naked under the blankets before leaving him to rest. Whispering one last reassurance that he would be back soon.

Before sinking away, Alba heard the sound of dragging across the kitchen floor below. Something heavy, something wet, something that made the trapdoor rattle and slam on its hinges until fed. Only once it splashed into the frothing water did the house finally fall silent again, and Alba drifted away imagining the foamy water tinged pink with torn flesh.

The state he sank into was hardly sleep, passing through the floor while his body clung to the bed, dangling by hooks as he tried to flee the taste of rusty, metallic blood in his mouth. The vibrations of metal in his hands with every striking blow. The wet, cracking sound of bone pulverized by copper. But no matter how deep he dangled between sleep and wakefulness, he still shuddered back awake at the sensation of cold water dripping against his skin.

Sprinkling his arm, then his cheek, summoning him back into his body. Alba sleepily pushed the blankets aside to welcome Eridanys into the blankets with him, not caring that he was soaking wet. Knowing he slept heaviest, deepest, most restfully when by his side.

But it wasn't Eridanys' moonlit form standing next to the bed once Alba opened his eyes. Instead, he was met with the dripping, inhuman silhouette of one of the drowned humans of the sea.

Choking on a gasp, Alba bolted upright before kicking away into the wall. He barely managed to call out Eridanys' name, voice raspy and hoarse, bracing for the creature to put out its hands and tear him open—but the drowned corpse didn't move. It just gazed at him with hunched features, a rat's-nest of muddy hair tangled on the back of its head, once-pale skin discolored from rotting in the sea, peeling from bone where not already exposed. There were no eyes in its sockets, only black depths, but Alba knew right where it stared. At him, at the merrow bloodstains on his arms.

It smelled of old fish and brined mold clinging to the beach; the smell of something washed up and just starting to bloat. A fresh death, still wrapped in seaweed and partially devoured by the salt of the waves. The rotting corpse gazed at him, dribbling dark ooze from a long cut in its throat, seawater spilling from the gaping hole that had to be its mouth as it eventually attempted to speak.

"Ah... Ah..." it rattled, sound bubbling at the back of its windpipe as if full of water it couldn't vomit up. It repeated that sound again and again, unable to utter another syllable, before lifting a

lanky, dripping arm to point. A gnarled, rotting finger extended toward the stairs, followed by another attempt to vocalize.

Only then did Alba realize what it wore—a dissolving linen shirt, pants, suspenders littered with barnacles and mold. No different from what he wore on any day while tending the lighthouse—enough that the initial fear in his chest unclenched slightly. His heart raced no slower, however, a quiet thought ghosting in the back of his mind, questioning once again where all the previous lighthouse keepers had actually gone.

"What?" he managed, though it was hardly more than a breath. The thing gargled out another sound, before stomping a bony, rotten heel into the floor. *Bang, bang, bang, bang*, no different from the slamming of the storage room hatch.

Alba sat up slightly more, holding the blanket to cover his nakedness. He swallowed back the buzzing nerves keeping his throat tight.

"You—you drowned in this harbor, didn't you?" He attempted again, pausing when his eyes flickered back to the clear cut over the drowned's throat. He pressed his lips together. "I—I don't know how to help you, I'm sorry—"

"*Ah... Ah...*" it interrupted, pointing again. Alba shifted on the bed, opening his mouth to try and compel it to leave a second time—but the drowned soul lifted its opposite arm, gently touching Alba on his nose. The smallest tap on the end, the smallest motion that made his heart burst. His mother used to do that when he wasn't listening. To compel make him pay attention. *This is important. Look at me and listen.*

Dread filled every inch of him. He stared at the creature, seeing only rot and flesh reclaimed by the sea, but something told him to obey. *This is important. Look at me. Listen.*

Alba sat forward, shuffling slightly to the side to carefully move his feet over the edge of the bed. Never taking his eyes from the creature, all while it never took its nonexistent eyes from him. Never lowering its arm pointing toward the stairs.

"Are you gonna hurt me?"

The drowned soul touched the tip of Alba's nose again. *"Ah...
Ah... Ah..."*

"A-alright," Alba finally answered, voice trembling. "I'll
follow you."

Hurrying to dig a pair of slacks from the clothing chest at the
foot of the bed, Alba's mind spun at another reminder of how
similar the clothes he pulled on were to the ones clinging to what
remained of the corpse. White shirt, cotton pants. Common,
sensible clothes for any wickie working long hours.

Alba didn't bother with shoes. He didn't bother to braid his
hair, didn't bother to find a jacket. He could barely find enough
mental clarity to walk upright on two feet as the creature finally
lowered its arm and moved with an uneven gait toward the stairs.
Alba followed, though kept his distance. Seeing every time the
drowned glanced over its shoulder to check if he was still following. The movement was so human, enough to squeeze Alba's
heart each time, every time they would have met eyes had it had
any left.

At the bottom of the stairs, Alba followed it toward the door,
but not without first glancing into the kitchen. For what, exactly,
he wasn't entirely sure, until he spotted his cane on the floor by
the table. Otherwise, the house was empty. Dark as the stormy
night outside.

Eridanys was nowhere to be found, and neither was the body
of Eugene Michaels. The only proof it hadn't all been a horrible
dream was the dark pool of blood on the floorboards, one that
matched that left by the first man Alba had killed there, with a
long smear of where he'd been dragged to the storage room. Just
like Alba had imagined while drifting off. He nearly asked if that
drowned soul had been the one to request it, if it had been one to
feed on it, perhaps even the cause of the hatch's incessant banging.
Hoping it wasn't leading him out into the storm to push him in,
next. Unsatisfied with its previous offering.

Outside, Alba had to put his hand up to protect against the

piercing rain falling nearly horizontal against the wind. The drowned soul didn't react except to waver on its feet, scraps of skin and hair and clothing tearing away and vanishing into the night sky with every gust. Alba expected it to lead him to the water—surprised when, instead, it turned toward the lighthouse.

As they made their way closer, Alba's heart thumped in surprise when it bypassed the working lighthouse for the larger one, silent and dark as the unlit lantern right alongside it. Standing tall with its boarded up windows and towering brick exterior—though for the first time, Alba listened. Truly listened. He heard it. The clanging of a turning lantern, despite both towers sitting unlit.

At the old lighthouse door a few feet ahead of him, the drowned soul wavered on its balance again, before digging a rotting hand into one of its pockets. It removed a keyring that whipped and clacked against the wind, fresh blood bright and smeared on the silver.

"Alba!" Eridanys' voice called suddenly over the storm, and Alba barely turned just as the man ran into him, grabbing his shoulders to steady him. "What in god's name are you doing out here? You have to get back—"

But Alba grabbed Eridanys' arm with one hand, pointing with the other at the drowned soul who didn't have the dexterity to insert the key into the lock, a rhythmic metal sound chiming out every time they missed and pulled back to try again.

Alba expected Eridanys to snarl, to growl and lunge at the creature—but he stood still. Staring at it, mouth dangling open slightly as if wishing to say something. His hand on Alba's shoulder tightened, before loosening slightly, then releasing him. He placed a hand on the small of Alba's back—and encouraged him to continue. To meet the drowned at the door, together.

"Let me," Alba said as they approached. The creature wavered on its feet again, turning to look Eridanys up and down first, then to where the siren's arm clung to Alba around the waist. The holes where eyes should have been stared for what felt like an eternity, even as Alba plucked the keys from its skeletal hand—gently, so carefully—to unlock the door, himself. He felt as the drowned's eyes traveled back to him, all while Eridanys' hand remained on his back.

By then Alba knew better than to believe anything Eugene Michaels had told him, but there was still the slightest confusion when the door to the retired lighthouse opened and no boxes of supplies lined the walls like he once claimed. He grabbed a lantern hanging by the door and lit the wick, extending his arm into the rest of the room to look closer, but still found it empty of everything except dust.

The rhythmic clanking of gears turning a lantern high above them was undeniable. It gave Alba goosebumps, not waiting before fully stepping inside to bypass the wind and know it for sure.

There was no reason for a retired lighthouse's unlit, untended lantern to turn. And in the belly of that tower, there was more than just the sound of the turning light—the air was hot, reeking of burning fuel that Alba had since learned to be made from merrow fat. It was humid enough to make him break into a sweat. Turning his head up to look, the stairs winding up to the top were maintained, the upper floor was even clean and organized. He didn't have a chance to ask what the drowned soul meant to show him, finding it already at the base of the stairs and starting its way up.

A stomach-turning sense of betrayal and further confusion filled Alba to the brim as he climbed behind it, Eridanys on his heels only after promising to keep his eyes downturned from the light.

None of them said anything as they made the journey, even Alba's weak hip keeping quiet, numbed from all the adrenaline pounding through his veins like fuel of his own. Wanting to see. Wanting to know why Eugene Michaels would have lied to him about something so mundane; wanting to know the extent of every lie that man had ever told him, especially after witnessing first hand how skilled he was in telling them on the spot. Claiming to never know Edythe from the start; then saying she hid in town; then implying Eridanys had already eaten her.

Alba knew Moon Harbor was a place built in isolation, secrets, people who preferred their privacy—but he never imagined what it would all come to the longer he stayed. Had Eridanys never cursed him to remain, he never would have learned any of it. Eridanys may have fallen into one of the town's traps. His heart may have been stolen for Eugene's son; his hair would have been woven into fishing nets to lure better catch; his scales ground up into eyeshadows and pinned into earrings; flesh and fat melted down to fuel the lighthouse every night. It was enough to make Alba flare with rage, squeezing Eridanys' hand harder.

"Ah..." the drowned soul stopped at the base of the final ladder into the lantern room above. Alba stopped alongside it, before glancing at Eridanys, who placed a hand on Alba's back again on approach. The faintest occulting light glowed through the cracks around the hatch leading up, enough to make Alba's blood pound hotter.

"Ah..."

Alba turned back to the drowned soul, not sure what to say, let alone why it wanted him to know the retired sister's lantern still turned behind boarded-up weatherglass. The soul gazed at him once more, then surprised him as it lifted a hand to touch his cheek, as if appreciating the sight of him. As if envious of the warmth of his skin, the flesh on his bones and the life in his eyes. Alba didn't pull away, letting it regard him how it wished, sensing its loneliness as pale-blue lips parted with what remained of its mouth, and it attempted to utter another few sounds.

"Is there something else you want to show me?" he asked, unsure, watching as the soul lifted a gnarled hand to gently touch what remained of its once dark blonde hair, raking fingers through it and ripping something free. It extended it toward him, and he was hesitant to accept whatever it'd just pulled from its body—but then the lantern light illuminated the hairpin pressed into his hand. Alba dropped it to the floor with an echoing clatter.

Alba knew it. He knew the pearls that lined the outer edge, the silver plate pressed with the image of a mermaid in the center. Bought with his pittance of an allowance one day at a shop in the north. Sent by mail. Worn by Edythe Marsh every time he visited afterward. Her favorite hairpin, missing from the house when he went back to it in Welkin. His first clue that she'd gone somewhere on her own accord.

The drowned soul in front of him held it in her hand, long decomposed by the sea. Having long become one with the salt that ate away at anything that once made her human.

"Mama?" His voice shook. The drowned soul's pale mouth cracked into a weak smile, and Alba's world crashed down around him.

He lunged with his arms out, embracing her with a rocking gasp. He clung to her as his body broke down into trembling breaths, clawing at what remained of her, too shocked to know if his fingers raked through rotting flesh or seaweed or barnacles.

Not caring, wishing he could properly hold her to make up for all the time he spent never realizing. Never realizing—she'd been right below his feet the entire time. Rotting away in the sea, alone, unnoticed, cursed at by him, repelled by Eridanys who kept the hauntings out. His mother, his mother, who had been there waiting for him from the beginning, just like she always promised. His mother, long dead and dissolving, who wrapped what remained of her arms around Alba in return.

"I'm sorry it took me so long, god, I'm so sorry!" he begged, pulling her closer, hating how cold she was, how she didn't wheeze and laugh with every squeeze of his arms, how water sloshed around beneath her skin and gurgled at the back of her throat. "I got your message, I promise I came as soon as I could! I'm sorry I didn't get here in time—I'm so sorry to leave you alone for so long—! After all this time—I still couldn't—I couldn't save you..."

The drowned soul let out a sound like a relieved sigh, nestling herself into Alba's embrace, pressing her face into the crook of his neck as if able to feel his warmth. To smell the sweat on his skin, to sense his heart beating alive and fast in his chest. Alba could do nothing else but silently cry, pulling her closer, closer, until his fingertips broke through brittle bone like eggshells. Just wanting to feel her warmth, wanting to feel what he always did after coming back home again from sea to hug her.

"Ah..." she murmured against his shoulder. *"Ah... lba. Alba."*

Alba wept until he couldn't breathe, every inch of him shaking as he clung to the remains of his dear mother who had never lived a gentle, peaceful day in her life. He grieved every moment he'd ever lost with her, every moment ever taken from him. He grieved what he'd come so close to having, how close they'd both come to escaping misery to perhaps find peace somewhere far from where all the pain existed. He'd come so close— only to lose her, and all of it, right at the very end.

Another hand found his back. Warm, protective, comforting.

"I think she may be the same soul who attacked me the night we met," Eridanys said. Alba didn't move, but his mother did. She trembled, slightly—and it took a moment for Alba to realize, she was laughing. It was enough for him to pull away, cheeks red and wet with tears and seawater. Boney hands lifted to try and wipe them away.

"You swam me back to shore," he said. Each word hiccuped as he fought to regain his breath, only for it to catch again when his mother's lifeless lips lifted into another weary smile. She nodded. More hot tears swelled in Alba's eyes. "Was it you always bangin' on the trapdoor, too?"

She nodded again. That time, Alba managed a weak, breathy chuckle of his own, finally wiping his own eyes.

"You were loudest when I first got here... then the night that first man showed up... then again when Marco came... and again when Mr. Michaels was there..." he said, not sure to who, not sure why, but every additional understanding was a comfort. "You kept tryin' to warn me..."

Edythe Marsh nodded along. Her stiff blue mouth cracked upward again. Alba didn't realize he smiled back at her, until it faltered upon glancing down to the cut on her throat. He reached out to touch it, but a decaying hand snapped up to grab him before he could.

"What happened to you?" he asked weakly. "Mama, who killed you?"

She turned to Eridanys. Alba snapped to look at him, too, but Eridanys threw his hands up before he could be accused of anything. Only Edythe's surprisingly strong grip still on Alba's wrist kept him where he was. She and the siren looked at each other for a long time, before Eridanys' eyes traveled down her face, to her lacerated throat, to the front of her shirt. He reached out to tuck a finger over the collar, tugging it slightly to the side.

There, in what little remained of her flesh, were markings similar to the ones drawn in the pile of salt that covered the merrow during the new moon ritual. Alba stared at them, then back at his mother.

"When?" he asked. Despite lacking eyes or the flesh in her cheeks to properly express herself, Alba could see exactly what look she gave him. Like every other time he asked something that was obvious, something she expected him to figure out on his own. It didn't take much scouring of his memory before the answer struck him. As obvious as she implied.

"The full moon."

She nodded. The telegram really had reached him only a few days too late.

There was so much more he wanted to ask—but Edythe's decaying form was beginning to tremble. Shedding water and skin and hair at a more rapid pace. Alba thought it had to be because she'd been out of the water too long, throwing out his hands and beginning to say something about returning—but she grabbed and stopped him, first. She held his hands, looking at him, then at Eridanys, offering him a nod of acknowledgement. Eridanys nodded back, saying nothing.

"Mama, please," Alba insisted. "You have to get back to the water. Here, I'll carry you—"

But she shook her head. She touched the tip of his nose once more, then lifted both hands to scoop a few pieces of hair from under his ear. Braiding it, just like she always used to before they parted again. A promise it wouldn't be the last time.

"*Sa...fe,*" she uttered. Still smiling weakly, even as the skin on her face went taut, then sloughed heavy. She took one of Alba's hands, then reached for one of Eridanys', and tucked them into one another. Alba could only stare at her.

"Please—" Alba croaked. "There's still so much more I want to say, please don't let yourself go yet, mama—" but Alba was running out of time, and Edythe appeared intent on letting the clock go.

Alba couldn't wonder if she was in pain, if existing as a corpse was agonizing, overcome only with his own selfishness and childish neediness. Needing his mother. Wanting his mother, to know she was safe. Happy. Taken care of. He wasn't ready to let go of her, yet—not after so many years existing only for the sake of taking care of her.

But Edythe, the mother she was, knew better than Alba did— and knew better than to linger when it would only draw out his own agony. She'd never been one to baby him, she'd never been one to give him everything he wanted.

She took his face in all that remained of her hands, and kissed his forehead. She kissed his cheeks, one after the other. She kissed the tip of his nose. She offered him a gentle, loving smile—before her fragile legs finally buckled, and the rest of her tumbled to the grated floor with an explosion of water and a *thud.*

Alba screamed, throwing out his hands to catch her, to put her back together, but Eridanys grabbed him first. He pulled Alba into his chest, holding him there as Alba pressed hands into his mouth to stifle his cries, trembling, choking on breath as the sound of what remained of Edythe Marsh sloughed through the grates and dribbled to the floor down below.

"It's alright Alba, it's alright," Eridanys insisted again and again. "She can finally rest; she's finally resting. Drowned souls only cling nearby when they have something left to do, something they meant to do while living. She passed on knowing you were safe. She's finally at rest."

Alba's silent weeping slowed to hiccuping gasps, still shaking, held tightly in Eridanys' arms as he stared at the pile of flesh, bones, seaweed, barnacles, soggy clothing on the floor. Nothing recognizable that remained of her, only parts of the sea that held her together well enough to walk when she needed to. Nothing left for Alba to gather into his hands and piece back together in the shape of her. Edythe's soul only clung to that rotting corpse long enough to make sure Alba was alright—and then she could finally release the hooks and the heaviness of something so rancid.

Alba could find comfort in that—at least, one day, he'd be able to find comfort in that.

But in that moment, he felt only the pain of knowing he'd never find her once he finally left Moon Harbor; he'd never return home to find her waiting for him again. He'd never get to tell her about everything he'd done and seen; he'd never get to tell her everything about Eridanys.

"I should've recognized her sooner," he whispered. "She tried to get my attention so many times."

"I don't think she held it against you," Eridanys insisted. "She probably knew you'd be hard to get through to. Did you get your stubbornness from her?"

Alba pulled away, just enough to look up at him. To narrow his puffy eyes, practically glaring and inciting Eridanys' eyes to narrow right back again. The siren smiled as he did, though. Gentle and reassuring, a face Alba wasn't used to seeing on someone normally so sharp around the edges.

"There's a reason she brought us here," Eridanys went on,

tilting his head toward the ladder into the lantern room. "Come, let's see."

Alba nodded, wiping his eyes, his nose on his rain-soaked sleeve and pulling away. He offered one last glance to the pile of remains on the floor, carefully shuffling around them so as to not step on a single drop. Also wanting to know what Edythe was trying to show him. Something important enough to die for.

Wiping his eyes and nose one more time, Alba motioned for Eridanys to step back so the rotating light wouldn't catch him. Eridanys obeyed, turning around and shielding his eyes with his arm.

"Call out if you need me," he said.

"I will," Alba answered, setting his cane aside and reaching for the ladder. Sucking in a deep breath, he shoved the hatch open.

Blinded by the lantern as he stepped through the hatchway, Alba threw a hand out to protect his eyes. He blinked through the passing glow, attempting to regain his sight in the amount of time it took the slow-moving light to come back around again.

Not wanting to risk Eridanys getting caught in its sweep, he crawled up onto the covered grating even before he could see again properly, closing the trap door behind him with a muffled *clang*. Down below, Eridanys called out to ask what was up there, and Alba rubbed his eyes, blinking a half dozen more times before he was finally able to turn and look.

Stumbling backward, he fell to the floor with a gasp. Eridanys called back sharply to ask if he was alright, and Alba quickly shouted back *"don't come up here!"* the moment the ladder creaked with Eridanys' weight. He was fine. Alba was fine—but didn't know how he would ever describe the sight in front of him.

He couldn't count them at first. Too much hair draped the floors, the walls, like spider webs on the verge of encasing him like a fly caught in a trap. Making him hesitate to move his feet. Barely closing his eyes or even lifting his hand to block the lantern light that swiveled.

Four. There were at least four, dangling upside down from

nets hooked to the ceiling, no different from the one that'd nearly caught him and Eridanys in the pools behind the cliffs. Four merrow dangling upside down, heads facing the rotating light, eyes empty except the glow of the glass drum devouring any thought they may have. Many covered in gruesome scars left behind by the same ropes that cut into Eridanys. Moonlit tails tangled in knots, making the woven ropes strain beneath the weight. Hardly breathing—hardly showing any signs of life, except an overwhelming need to watch the rotating glow for every moment it rotated and blinded them all over again.

"Oh... my god," Alba whispered once the words finally came. Eridanys demanded a second time to know what Alba saw, but Alba still didn't know how to explain.

He didn't know how to describe something so horrible without Eridanys storming his way up and putting himself in the same danger as those dangling, unmoving, hypnotized in the nets. Alba had no idea for how long they must have been there, only that, even as he approached to get a closer look, there wasn't a breath of response. Not a single flicker of acknowledgement as he moved his hand in front of their eyes, reminded of the one sacrificed in the woods. Even when Eridanys had been mesmerized by the smaller light, there was still a part of him aware on the inside—a part of him that knew it could follow Alba out, down the stairs, all the way back to the house where he could close his eyes and rest. But those there, hanging in their permanent nets, were hardly more than breathing shells of who they used to be.

Alba's mind raced, heart pounding hard and fast enough that his hands trembled. He wound them together, wringing them in apprehension with what to do, what to say to Eridanys down below, even debating whether or not he should say anything at all. Even if there was a way to stop the lantern from turning, even if there was a way to take the captured merrow down, away from the light, would it make any difference? Would they ever return to their own minds, depending on how long they'd been catatonic like that in the first place? Perhaps there was only one way to find out—though even it would take some time.

"Eridanys," he called. "The basin of fuel down there, how full is it?"

Alba listened as Eridanys crossed the grating to look.

"Nearly full. Probably a few day's worth."

Alba nodded to himself, thinking they must have refilled it the day before the new moon—then realizing, like a punch to the stomach, exactly where they'd gotten the merrow for their ritual. His voice trembled as he called out next: "Are there any release spigots on the bottom? Probably locked with a bolt or a key?"

More silent searching, before: "Yes. There's a turn valve under a metal cage."

"Do you still have Eugene Michaels' keyring that my m-mother gave us?" His voice hiccuped at the reminder. He closed his eyes, focusing on a breath and listening as Eridanys searched.

"Yes. One of them fits. Should I turn it?"

"Well..." Alba didn't know. He didn't know what to do, didn't know if it would make any difference even if the light turned off. "Well—before you do, I... I should tell you what's up here. So you can decide for yourself, whether you wanna..."

Another pause. "What's up there, Alba?"

Alba closed his eyes again. He turned back to the four merrow in their nets, never knowing there was an uninvited visitor in their midst. Realizing he stood in one of only a handful of empty spots where he was sure the sacrifice from the new moon had likely hung only a few days prior.

"It's... your kin," he finally explained. More silence from below. He waited another moment before continuing. "A few of them, at least. Maybe... maybe even the last of them. They're... in nets, like the one that almost got us in the pools. The light in here is turnin', and they're all captivated by it, just like you were that one time—*No!*" Alba lunged when Eridanys attempted to shove his way through the trap door, throwing his weight on it. "Eridanys, no! Stop! You can't, the light—!"

"Let me see them!" Eridanys snarled, vicious and bloodthirsty. "Let me see them, Alba!"

"No! Just—wait a second!" Alba shouted back, banging his fist against the metal until it rang out loudly through the whole lighthouse. "I'm not lettin' you anywhere up here 'til the light's out! If you turn the valve and let it empty, it'll die soon enough."

Eridanys didn't answer out loud, but rather with the banging rattle of feet on the grated floor; then a brief twisting of metal, a key in a lock, and the sound of warmed fat guttering out and splattering to the floor below.

"Alright," Alba said after a moment. "That's why I wanted you to decide. But with how much oil is in there, it might take a day or two to drain. Then another day before the light finally burns out."

Eridanys muttered something in reply, and Alba banged on the hatch again in threat.

"Don't you curse at me!" he snapped. "It is what it is! But I'm not lettin' you up, no matter how much you complain."

"Then come back down," Eridanys growled. "I don't like you being up there by yourself, either."

"You better not try'n force your way in when I open this door."

"I *won't*, damnit! Get back down here!"

Alba huffed, scooting backward and testing the gate. When Eridanys kept his word and didn't try to shove through, Alba shimmied his way down, but not before casting a final glance at the merrow still dangling. Entirely unaware of his visit. A few more days wouldn't do any more damage to them than already done.

"Give me the keys," he said upon closing the hatch overhead, barely casting a glance to the spigot and seeing his siren had nearly torn the entire piece off. With the keyring in hand, Alba searched through them before finding the one he was looking for, using it to lock the trap door closed so Eridanys wouldn't get any ideas while Alba wasn't looking.

Eridanys' expression creased in annoyance, but he said nothing, only stepping forward to grab Alba off the ladder and scoop him into his arms. Alba didn't complain, just gripping the keyring in one hand and putting his arms around the back of Eridanys' neck. They made their way down the stairs. Out the door. Back out into the storm, where the fluted pipes on the side of the house wailed deafeningly against the wind.

Chapter 26

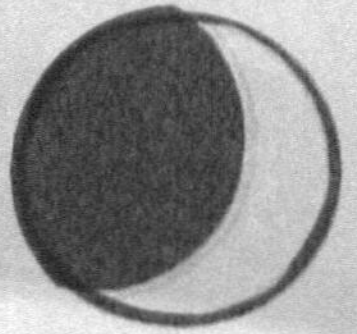

The first three weeks of sailing after being stolen off the street had been the most harrowing of Alba's life. Not knowing where he was or for how long; not knowing when or if he'd be able to go back home; not knowing what his mother thought, or if the Warrens had done something to her while he was away. For the briefest moment, a part of him even wondered if she'd sold him to sail in order to pay their debts, and he hated himself every day after for ever allowing it to manifest at all. Edythe Marsh was all Albatross Marsh had in his entire life; she was his reason for living, and in many ways, he was hers. In many other ways, against both of their wills.

The thought of his mother no longer being there to give Alba reason to live was, perhaps, the only thing possibly more harrowing than those first few weeks had been.

Staring at the ceiling from his narrow bed, cramped alongside his siren companion, Alba thought of nothing except how all those times he ever felt lonely could not hold a candle to the grip true loneliness had on his heart. Lungs. Insides. Running his soul through its fingers like raking through hair, unraveling him piece by piece, again and again as he came back together every time a noise or a breath or a whispered word forced him back to the real world. Only to spiral and sink again the moment the silence returned.

"What did you do with the body?" he asked, referring to Eugene Michaels. Unable to take the quiet any longer, unsure if Eridanys was asleep or awake.

"I gave him to the sea," Eridanys answered, not an ounce of weariness in his voice. Alba wondered what he thought about in the silence for so long. "Figured she would know what to do with him."

"You didn't eat him?"

"Wasn't appetizing."

Alba meant to chuckle, or tease a little bit, but couldn't summon the strength. He stared up at the ceiling for a long time again.

"Before I killed him, he admitted to usin' merrow parts for their magic. I think he was one of the robed people we saw the other night."

Eridanys nodded.

Alba inhaled quietly through his nose, holding it. "Those marks on my mother's chest—they matched the ones on those salt piles."

"Yes."

"I think they killed her, too."

"... Yes. I do, too."

"But why?" Alba's voice cracked. He shifted uncomfortably on his back. "She was one of them. She grew up here. Why would they kill her?" He thought of how her name had been scribbled out of the town's register. Finally having an idea of why. Wishing he didn't.

"I don't think it was personal," Eridanys said. Thoughtfully, not like he was tired of Alba rambling. Alba waited to see if he'd say anything else, only letting out a held breath when he did. "She said they killed her on the full moon."

"Yes," Alba breathed. "But I don't think she knew it was gonna happen when she tried to get me to come. They must have killed all the previous wickies on the full moon, too. That was always when they disappeared."

"All of them except you."

Alba closed his eyes. "Probably just because they didn't know where to find me..." he trailed off, recalling that night. How a group of shadowed men huddled around the door as he was disposing of that fresh corpse. It made his heart sink, vomit burning in his throat as he swallowed it back. He crossed his arms over his face, forcing himself to keep it together. Realizing— perhaps they'd tried.

On the heels of that sickening understanding, something else emerged in the back of Alba's mind. A vague memory of something he'd seen carved into the wall of the merrow pools. He searched the mental image, eyes still trained at the ceiling as his heart thumped, then sank, then twisted.

That image of the funeral procession beneath a bright, round moon. Throwing the deceased into the sea, where they became a merrow. Where they became—exactly what Eugene Michaels had been trying to trap, so desperately, knowing Eridanys was the last one. Was it possible—those people were killing wickies every full moon, thinking they would create new merrow to turn around and sacrifice all over again on the new moon...?

Closing his eyes, he was going to be sick.

"Fuck," he croaked. "Fuck, fucking Christ... fuck this place. *Fuck* this place, *god*, why, why did she have to be from *this place?* I could've had a second chance..." Pressing his palms into his eyes, Alba held his breath, watching colors spot the darkness under the pressure. Unsure why he said it, not realizing it was even out loud until the end. "I was almost given a second chance... If I'd only left Belmar sooner... If I'd only run away sooner... I could've made it in time to save her. I could've made sure she was happy. Maybe had a normal life. I could've taken care of her until she grew old, like a son is supposed to. We could've... had a normal life."

"Hardly normal," Eridanys mumbled. Alba's tired, swollen eyes cracked open to scowl at him, unsure if the siren's uncertain smirk was charming or annoying. "I would have still put my eyes on you and failed to ever look away again. I would have still made you mine any time I spotted you. From any shore."

Alba wanted to smile. Even a tiny bit. Something about that made his heart beat once, twice, at a higher note than all the others.

"I don't think she would've let it be that easy."

"I would have charmed her into letting me have you."

There it was—Alba managed the weakest little laugh. "I don't know. She was always keen on tricks of the sea."

Eridanys surprised him when his hand slid under the blankets, taking Alba's and holding it.

"She sensed it on me," he said. "That I would take care of you when she was gone."

Alba pressed his lips together. He let those words hover, to envelop him, closing his eyes and blinking back another rush of tears as if he hadn't already cried enough. "You don't mean that."

"I mean it."

"Only out of guilt."

"No." Eridanys squeezed Alba's hand. "Since I made you my caller of the shore, I was determined to keep an eye on you."

"But not because you wanted to."

"You never listen." Eridanys sat up, perching on a bent elbow and frowning down at Alba stubbornly. "I'm trying to tell you that I've come to care for you more than I anticipated. Perhaps I didn't intend on staying with you long at first—"

"You also thought about killin' me."

"I did. But not anymore."

"You care for me enough to not want to kill me?"

"Yes. So I suggest you stop arguing before I change my mind."

Alba managed another weak laugh. "I'm not very easy to love. You may still wish to kill me anyway, one day."

"Only time will tell," Eridanys answered, sarcastic smile remaining. "Until then—let me stay with you."

"I don't want to stay here."

"Neither do I. We'll go somewhere else. Anywhere you want." He laid back down, crossing his arms behind his head. It took up most of the pillow, forcing Alba to shimmy down slightly, sighing and resting his head on Eridanys' chest as there was nowhere else to go.

"I don't know anythin' about goin' places by land."

"Neither do I. We'll figure it out together."

Alba drew a line up and down the center of Eridanys' stomach, watching the muscles flex as they were teased. He wanted to ask if Eridanys meant that; if he knew exactly what he was saying. Alba then wanted to argue that he was not usually someone who needed constant comforting, or coddling; he did not usually speak openly about his fears or his feelings, let alone show them for anyone to see. Alba was as reclusive as any siren out in the vast sea, unsociable, unapproachable, preferring simplicity and silence over excitement. But—all at the same time—the thought of parting ways with his own siren made his heart race nervously. Whether he feared being alone, or he feared the thought of leaving Eridanys all alone, he didn't know, but—

His finger drew a circle around the base of Eridanys' chest. He couldn't help but be reminded of the merrow in the woods, under the dark sky. Its chest cut open, its still-beating heart pulled out. That rush of fear and anger at the thought of the same thing, one day, happening to Eridanys while Alba wasn't there to protect him. The same flood of emotions grasped at him, silent and intense. But before he could answer, there was something else he wanted to know, first.

"Your last human partner—his name was Dawson, wasn't it? Dawson Michaels."

Eridanys' breath caught. He sat up slightly again, then slightly more, propping himself back on his elbows as Alba turned his head to look at him. Finally, the man nodded.

"Yes," he breathed. "My last shore caller was Dawson Michaels. Eugene Michaels' son."

"That's why you acted strange when we slept in their house."

A muscle twitched in Eridanys jaw, but he nodded.

"Mr. Michaels said you... killed him. His son. Is that true?"

Eridanys reached out to run fingers through Alba's hair, as if to comfort him before answering. Like he thought the truth would make Alba push him away and race out the door. But Alba just watched him, unmoving.

"Yes," he finally answered. "Yes. I killed him."

"But he deserved it."

The words made Eridanys pause—perhaps by the way Alba said them. A statement, not a question. A reminder.

"Yes," Eridanys repeated. "I had to kill him in order to survive."

"Was he going to hurt you?" Alba asked, placing his hand in the center of Eridanys' chest. "You once said you were banished because you refused to do somethin' he asked."

Eridanys pressed his hand against Alba's, until every inch of Alba's palm and fingers were flush against him. Enough to feel his heartbeat, strong but anxious.

"Yes," he said again. "I... I once told you how our presence here brought more fish than the people could eat."

"I remember."

"Well—because we were partnered to one another, Dawson thought he could do whatever he wished with me. Had all these ideas about merrow magic. One day, he told me I would be leaving on the next boat out to sea. To work as a ship hand in order to see if my presence would draw more fish into the nets even outside of the harbor. But I'd seen drawings in his study, things he'd sketched—drawings of merrow tied off to the bows of ships. Hardly sailing on them like he described to me. Bait dangled over the water. When I refused to go..." he hesitated, blinking up at the ceiling, then closing his eyes with a frown. "... he tried to force me. Tied me up, threatened to kill me. Tried to throw me onto a ship in the middle of the night when everyone was asleep. But I escaped—and I killed him." His fingers in Alba's hair paused, eyes going dull as he recalled the memory. "Tore out his throat with my teeth. We both fell over the side, and I drowned whatever life was left in him. It sounds cruel, but—I felt like I had no other choice. But killing one's own shore-caller is a terrible sin —so I was swiftly banished."

Alba's hand flexed against Eridanys' chest. Wishing he could reach inside to caress the racing heart in his ribs and comfort it.

"Didn't you try and explain that to your kin? Why did they still...?"

"They didn't believe me," Eridanys said, like it was the first time he'd ever said it out loud. He took Alba's hand on his chest, squeezing it, then kissing it, then placing it back. "They knew how strained my relationship with Dawson was from the start, since... since I never wanted to be mated to any shore-caller. From the beginning, I never wanted any of it. It was forced on me; expected of me. I tried more than once to get out of it over all the time we were mated. So when I killed him, especially so violently, they wouldn't listen to anything I had to say. They didn't care what my reasons were."

Alba stared at him. Feeling how his siren's heart pounded harder. Seeing how Eridanys wouldn't meet his eyes, as if confessing such a thing still filled him with shame. It only filled Alba with anger.

"He deserved it," he said. Forcefully. Insistently. Eridanys offered a self-conscious smile in return, fingers returning to push hair from Alba's eyes. Alba's gaze remained on where his hand pressed to Eridanys' chest. His fingers twitched. He forced himself to take a long breath, to ease the fury back. Not wanting to raise his voice, to speak too intensely, in any way that might imply he thought Eridanys was wrong for the shame he felt when recalling the memory. Only when Alba's own pounding pulse slowed did he speak again.

"Mr. Michaels said Dawson is still alive. Recoverin', even, with the use of merrow parts. The heart, specifically, I think, which we saw them takin' from that merrow last night. He tried to convince me to tell him where you were, said it was '*better odds to save him by feedin' him the heart of the one who killed him'..."*

"Dawson Michaels is dead," Eridanys said with certainty. "I don't know what that old man thought he was doing—but it wasn't resurrecting his son."

Silence hovered once more, and Eridanys shifted where he sat. He didn't meet Alba's eyes for a long moment, before starting again:

"Does that bother—"

"Let's leave," Alba interrupted. He sat up, touching Eridanys' face—then kissing him. Kissing him long and hard and breathlessly, pressing their foreheads together when he finally pulled away again. "As soon as the sun comes up, let's leave. We'll take that old man's boat to shore and we'll walk until we can't anymore."

Eridanys stared at him, breathless, before pulling Alba in and kissing him again. Again and again and again, until Alba didn't know where he ended and the siren began. Taking note of each and every part of him—vowing to protect him from harm, just like he once did on the rocks.

He dreamed of the moon. High and bright overhead, swollen and drenching the trees encircling him in blue light. Draped over the body of Edythe Marsh on her back beneath a pile of salt, eyes glazed over and reflecting the celestial body in the sky. Her throat gaped open, staining the salt covering her with crimson, soaking into the grains, melting into water that lapped over her until fully submerged. Laughter, music trilled from the trees around him, deafened by the roaring of ocean waves growing from the blood-red water swirling at his feet.

Come see why they did what they did to the blood you seek.

Alba woke with a sweating gasp to the sound of dishes clinking in the kitchen below. Stirring, his body felt heavy as if pumped full of sea clay, cracking at the joints as he groaned and stretched his arms long, trying to nestle his soul back into the exhaustion of his muscles.

He assumed Eridanys was down getting into something he shouldn't be—but then the siren in question mumbled in annoyance at Alba's shifting body, putting out his arms and pulling him close. Pinning him, as Alba just stared at him with wide eyes. If Eridanys was there in bed, still, then—who was in the kitchen?

"E-Eri!" he hissed, shaking the man, then grabbing his face and squeezing. "Eri, wake up! I think there's someone downstairs."

"Just your imagination," Eridanys muttered, attempting to roll over, but Alba grabbed him by the ear and yanked him back.

"God!" Alba hissed, deciding against it and shoving Eridanys back into the pillows. Kicking off the blankets, he climbed over his companion, hurrying to pull on a pair of pants. Eridanys grappled for him instantly, intent on pulling him back into the bubble of warmth they'd created, but Alba bypassed his hands with ease, hissing at him to *"stop, cut it out! Someone's downstairs!"*

His heart pounded, unable to imagine who it could possibly be, unsure whether he should be reaching for a weapon or not. But whoever it was hadn't come looking to bludgeon him in his sleep—and might not even know he was up there. Pausing at the top of the stairs, he listened for a moment longer to see if he could tell whether it was more than one intruder, before clearing his throat and politely calling down: "Hello?"

No answer came. The sound of rattling dishes continued. Alba's heart pounded, but he knew he couldn't allow anyone to roam around the house, the lighthouse, anywhere—especially with the bloodstain on the kitchen floor. Especially with the clear voice of another man falling out of bed with him. He gulped, straightening his back, and slowly descending the stairs into the kitchen.

"Oh," he choked at the bottom. In the briefest cast of sunlight through the constant cloud cover—the faint silhouette of someone familiar stood at the empty sink. An empty sink, yet clattering with the sound of dishes, though it grew slightly fainter to the ear as soon as Alba saw her. Her, her, he knew her—it was his mother.

At the very least, what remained of her. Her ghost. Her spirit. Slightly translucent with a faint glow, looking like herself again. Her healthy, human, living self, except for how Alba could see through her. Dressed in a plain work shirt and slacks, hair pinned back with the same clip she'd handed to him the night before in the lighthouse, before falling to pieces. He'd tucked it safely into the inner pocket of his jacket, alongside where he kept her original telegram. He knew that personage hadn't stolen it, but he couldn't help the sharp pinch of worry that it might be gone when he went looking for it again.

Perhaps it should have startled him more, but—in a way, he was relieved. To have one more image of her as she was to be his last, instead of what she'd become beneath the sea. But that relief didn't last long, as he took a few steps closer, fighting the misery that came with how she never turned to look at him. Never smiled at him, acknowledged him. He realized—she might not even know she was gone. A residual spirit, a piece of her that didn't know any better, imprinted on that house. Trapped there.

His relief at being able to see her one last time gave way to nausea, and then anger. Knowing she'd satisfied what kept her soul there already, the night before, even confirmed by Eridanys. Settled the moment she collapsed into nothing but water and seaweed and rotten clothes, she should have passed on. For her spirit to still linger, even as just an echo—it meant there was something else. Or, worse—that something was anchoring her soul in that terrible place.

Alba's eyes lingered on how full and long her hair was in that spirit form. How, as a drowned soul, one side had been roughly shorn away. At the time, he thought perhaps it had been cut when her throat was—but touching the tiny braid left in his own hair by her dying hands, he had another idea.

"Is that...?" Eridanys asked upon finally arriving downstairs, trailing off as Alba put his hand out toward his mother—and she vanished with the tiniest flicker of light in an instant. Gazing down at his fingers, Alba let the thought ruminate for a long time, before looking back at his companion.

"I don't think we can leave yet," he said. Still touching the braid left by his mother. Her protection spell; a promise that he would always find his way back home should he ever get lost at sea.

Despite it all—he couldn't move on until he knew for sure, there would be no part of Edythe Marsh left behind once he was gone.

CHAPTER 27

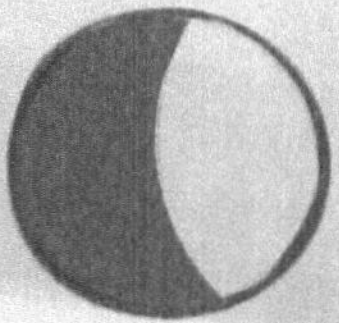

ALBA'S ARMS CLENCHED TIGHTLY AS HE PULLED THE water with every sway of the oars in his hands, watching as a moonlit blur floated in and out beneath him in pursuit. A lazy predator dragging a recovered corpse along behind him, the faintest trail of red on the water as he did as Alba asked. Following all the way back to shore, wanting to know what Alba had in mind.

It wasn't the first time Alba had been tasked with telling someone their loved one had died at sea; though that time, instead of feeling grief as the family member fell to their knees and screamed and begged to know what happened, if their child had any last words, anything at all Alba could say to comfort them—Alba felt only a heavy, brooding curiosity as Phyllis Michaels looked at him blankly, put out her hands to take the damp cotton hat he held, and offered him barely a nod of understanding.

"Told 'im not to go out in such a harsh storm," she mumbled. "Sea's been looking for any reason to swallow him up for years, now. Was a miracle he lived this long, I think."

"What do you mean?" he couldn't resist.

It wouldn't be that easy, he knew as much, but would have regretted it if he didn't at least try. Phyllis just shook her head, sighing and turning to the fireplace mantle to place the hat next to Eugene's picture.

"I'm sorry for your loss," he went on. Not wanting to appear rude, hoping she would continue. There was something else Alba wanted to know, hoping she'd tell him without him having to ask. A question that burned in the back of his mind all morning while rowing to town.

Curiosity stemming from the funeral procession he'd once seen on the wall of the mermaid baths. Another question of why his mother's hair had been cut when killing her. Wanting to know whether or not there was a reason her spirit lingered like all the merrow in the woods. Wanting to know if cutting hair was a common practice when any person in Moon Harbor died—not just wickies and carved merrow.

"Don't be, lad," Phyllis sighed, adjusting a photo of Dawson Michaels alongside the others. Alba's eyes lingered on it, realizing it was the first time he'd ever seen the man's face, his soft features and pretty blonde hair. Reminded of what Eridanys told him the night before. Feeling nothing but resentment toward that person, glad to know he was long dead, too. "Some things are expected, especially when you cheat dealings with higher powers."

Alba's mouth opened. He almost asked. He almost asked more, but stopped himself. He didn't want to draw attention to himself over the markings on his arms, again. He didn't want to mention the things Eugene said to him about Dawson before Alba smashed his head in, either.

"Will you hold a funeral?" he asked. "I'm happy to help however it be."

"Thank you, dear." Phyllis turned back to him with a weary smile. "Without any body to put in the ground, we may at least hold a ceremony. I'll speak with the others in town and see what we can gather together. I'll send someone for you once we decide how to proceed. I do hope you'll join us. Eugene spoke fondly of you from the very beginning."

Alba's smile twitched. He forced himself to think of his

mother, of all the things Eugene said to try and trick him in his last moments, not wanting to get lost in his own confused grief and guilt.

He left Phyllis Michaels with a few final words of reassurance:

"Perhaps his body will turn up soon. The sea is cruel, but not merciless."

Alba sat alone on the end of the dock, empty of fishing boats as the doggers of the town dragged nets through the water out on the horizon. A little wobbly from all of the imbibing he did immediately after meeting with Phyllis, as he'd gone far too long without a drink and a cigarette. Both at once revived every dying part of him in an instant.

Nursing a remaining half-bottle of whiskey in his lap, Alba's feet swayed back and forth, watching the dark water below as the sun reached late-afternoon and another thick collection of storm clouds formed on the horizon. They brought another bitter wind, though the smell was fresh and salty and crisp as ever. He inhaled as many lungfuls as he could, cleansing the tobacco from his lungs before inhaling another deep drag and doing it all over again like a ritual. The world was a little sweeter on the nerves with a buzz on the blood.

When a piece of the moon flickered into view beneath his feet, Alba grinned, opening his knees to get a better look. Eridanys slowly ascended to break his face through the surface, offering Alba a sarcastic, naughty little smile.

"How did the widow Michaels take the news?" he asked. "Her husband's body has already washed up on the black sand beach, as you requested."

"Wonder how it ever would have gotten there," Alba laughed warmly. He swished the alcohol in the bottle in offering, and Eridanys opened his mouth, allowing a string of the amber liquid to be poured over his tongue. It made Alba smile bigger, made his insides twirl and itch with the sight. Lips wet, liquid dripping down his chin. Glancing over his shoulder, there was no one on the street behind him—and Alba couldn't stop himself from sitting forward, hooking a hand under the back of Eridanys' head, and pulling him into a kiss. Tasting the whiskey and salt on his lips, his tongue, wishing he could have a moment longer to enjoy it. But even a little drunk, he knew better than to risk being seen with the last merrow of Moon Harbor.

"What was that for?" Eridanys asked with a little surprise.

"I just like you," Alba answered. "You and your mouth. That's all."

"You..." Eridanys' expression remained the same, but he opened his mouth again when Alba sloshed the bottle back and forth in offering. Alba wasn't sure why he said it, or why he said it *like that*—but his tongue betrayed him, adding:

"Will you help me row back to the lighthouse? I think I want to like you a little more."

Eridanys gazed up at him for a moment longer, before smiling and diving back into the water. Alba laughed, stumbling to his feet, then to where his stolen dingy was tied off. Tripping into it with another cry of amusement, the boat pulled away from the dock without him ever having to touch the oars. Something had already taken hold of the rope to tow him where they could be alone on the lighthouse rocks.

CHAPTER 28

Eridanys lunged from the water the moment Alba stumbled onto the beach grass, making Alba shriek with drunk laughter as he tumbled onto his back, pinned by the soaking wet siren. Flattened into the dirt, clawing at Eridanys' strong back and kissing him until he had to gasp for breath.

"Like this," he moaned, sliding his hand down to where the man's skin became scales. "Fuck me like this."

"What—right here for any sailor to pass by and see?" Eridanys purred, pushing hair from Alba's eyes before trailing his tongue up the side of his throat. "You want them to watch? To ask themselves—how long their wickie has had a strange man locked away in his house to fuck as he pleases?"

Alba pulled at Eridanys' hair as the weight of the tail rubbed between his legs, biting his lip before sitting up and turning his body, catching Eridanys off guard and rolling him onto his back. Straddling the siren's waist, Alba stared down at him through half-lidded eyes, already flushed.

"No," he said. "Not a man. A siren. Like this—I said I wanted it just like this."

Eridanys' hands found Alba's hips, looking at him like he'd just uttered something nonsensical. Like he never considered it to be an option outside of the initial mating ritual—let alone something his partner might want. It only made Alba more eager to kiss him again, tangling fingers up through his hair, running his thumbs over the sub-dermal lines on his face, pinching at the webbed fins where human ears would have been.

"Are you sure?" Eridanys asked between their mouths, but Alba was already rolling his hips against the dip beneath the siren's navel.

"Why wouldn't I be?" Alba kept Eridanys' face in one hand, sliding the other between them. Doing what Eridanys had done to him so many times, the small things that made Alba's blood bubble sweetly. Teasing his nipples, his chest, the slit between his hips where Alba knew the siren's members were tucked. "Let me do what I like, this time. If you want me to."

"I—" Eridanys' brows furrowed, fingers digging into Alba's hips as Alba's fingers inserted slightly into the slit. "I want you to."

Returning his hands to Eridanys' chest, Alba pushed him back into the grass. Eridanys watched him with hesitation, putting his hands out to grasp at Alba's arms, though not with any force. Like he needed the touch to be sure nothing caught him by surprise, clearly intimidated by the thought of someone else taking control from him. But he said nothing else, and nothing about his body-language implied he'd changed his mind, so Alba did as he said he would.

Undoing the front of his pants, Alba rose to his knees just enough to slide them off, which Eridanys took as invitation to grasp the skin of his thighs directly. Alba smiled at him, tossing the pants away before opening his legs over the siren's chest, then coaxing Eridanys' mouth to taste him. Eridanys' eyes flashed in understanding, eagerly gripping Alba's hips and pulling him closer. Closing his eyes and lapping his tongue over the sensitive nub between Alba's thighs and making Alba shiver.

Alba moaned softly, biting his lip and bending forward to plant his hands in the grass over Eridanys' head. Eridanys' fingers dug into his skin deeper, summoning more hiccuping breaths to tumble from Alba's mouth as he rolled his hips slightly, breath catching with every slide of the tongue beneath him, inside him. With every glance down to Eridanys' handsome face, half concealed beneath his body, eyes closed and lashes fluttering.

Encouraging Alba to ride his tongue like he would a cock, Alba obeyed, using Eridanys' lewd mouth like a personal toy designed to make him moan. Grinding against him for as long as he liked, until his legs trembled from the effort, from the rising delight in the base of his stomach. Bringing himself right to the edge before pulling back again, not ready to finish. Not wanting to reach it, just yet. Not while such a staunch awareness of how empty he was swirled in the pit behind his navel, wanting more. Craving to be stretched and filled.

Pulling back as the itching need grew too unbearable, Eridanys attempted to hold Alba down, still busy with his task, but Alba pulled further. He took Eridanys' hands, pinning them into the grass over his head and breathing heavily.

"Can I keep going?" he said. "Doing whatever I like."

Eridanys smiled hungrily, licking his lips. "I think I like being used by needy sailors like you, after all."

That made Alba flush more, but he shook his head to wipe the embarrassment away. He focused on the present, on the moment, on how much more he wanted so badly, searching for his discarded pants and using them to tie Eridanys' wrists together over his head, all while the siren purred with each touch.

Sitting back on Eridanys' stomach, Alba took in the sight of him, like drinking in a tall glass of sparkling wine. Face flushed, mouth and chin wet from where it'd tongued every inch between Alba's legs. Eyes sharp and directed right at him, like an animal playing along, knowing full well it could break free and do whatever it wished whenever it wanted. The muscles in his strong arms strained slightly against the binding, flexing his shoulders and chest in a way that made Alba's skin flicker slightly hotter. Even after seeing it so many times before, submitting beneath it, a willing victim to it, there was something so dangerously captivating about him—and Alba couldn't help but smile selfishly to himself. A perfect siren, all his. Eridanys was all his.

There on the wet, muddy grass just out of the water, sprinkled with rain and the waves rushing the rocks, Alba was no different from any other sailor enraptured by the mere sight of something so beautiful—except that that one, specifically, would never sing to anyone else ever again. Alba wanted to give him good reason, wanted to taste every inch of him, for once. To make Eridanys feel as desired as he did Alba, even without a song from the back of his throat.

He kissed Eridanys first, tasting himself on the siren's lips. Trailing his mouth down his chin, then his jaw, Alba bit at his collarbones and licked saltwater from the dip between them. He circled his tongue over Eridanys' plum-colored nipples, eyes flicking up when he felt the man's breath hitch beneath him. Biting at them, pinching them with his fingers, Eridanys did his best to keep the clear pleasure off his face, still saying nothing, though Alba could feel how his heart raced, tail clenching and writhing slightly beneath him.

"Do you like being touched here, too?" he asked, and Eridanys barely grunted a *"yes"* in reply. Flushed, frustrated, Alba found himself captivated by the sound. No luring song needed.

Alba took his time. Kissing Eridanys' skin coated in salt and rain; trailing his fingers over every bump of muscle down his stomach, biting back another smile as the siren moaned breathily even as Alba's fingers trailed over the slitted gills behind his ribs. He licked the divot of his navel, before trailing kisses across where soft skin met shimmering scales, watching Eridanys' expression change as he dipped his tongue into the erogenous slit surrounded by the scales like diamond coins. Tasting salt and mint, holding either side of the base of the man's tail while sinking his tongue deeper inside and tasting the pre-cum dripping from the growing lengths inside. Reveling in how Eridanys' breath caught so often, how he pulled against the bindings on his wrists, muscles in his chest and arms stretching and clenching in ways that drove Alba mad.

Easing fingers inside, Alba pressed against the wet, shuddering wall of the pocket, smiling as both cocks swelled out under the pressure. It was his first time seeing them up close, and he didn't hesitate to slide his hand up the length of the one spotted with hard ridges, then the softer one erect beneath it. Both already dripping with stringy pleasure, more pearls forming on their tips. Swollen and twitching, eager for more, eager to be used however Alba pleased.

Stroking the bottom cock with one hand, Alba trailed his tongue over the tip of the harder ridged one, watching Eridanys' face again before taking it into his mouth. He slid his tongue up the length, then swirled it over the tip, expecting the same salty, watery taste as before, but not the underlying sweetness. Like little drops of honeydew swelling from the slit at the head, making him wish for more. Compelling him to close his mouth over it fully, running his tongue around and pressing it into the opening that leaked such sweetness.

Eridanys finally couldn't bite back his moans, throwing his head back, arching his spine and rolling his hips to edge deeper into Alba's mouth. Alba let him, still stroking the second cock and never taking his eyes away, watching the siren's expression tense and loosen, the muscles in his stomach doing the same with every turn and draw of Alba's tongue. Pulling the length as far back into his mouth as he could, Alba held his breath and enjoyed the sensation, how it shifted and bumped the back of his throat every time Eridanys writhed in pleasure.

The serpentine muscles of his tail moved like rippling waves beneath him, rainy light reflecting off the moon-gray scales like shimmering mica in beach sand. Alba's hand not working the second cock trailed down to feel it, to fully understand the strength of the beast churning beneath him, clearly resisting every urge to twist and slam Alba onto his back in the grass. Like it took everything in Eridanys to let Alba continue as he pleased, even at his agonizingly slow, worshipping pace—but that only excited Alba more.

The fact Eridanys resisted all of those animal urges in order to give Alba what he wanted—the fact he enjoyed it enough to bite back the instinct to take what he wanted sooner. It made Alba sink lower, taking the hard, ribbed cock all the way to the back of his throat until it nearly choked him, swallowing against it, letting his throat flex around the tip as Eridanys bit back another moan.

"That's it," Eridanys exhaled in a rough breath, and Alba lifted his eyes to find the siren smiling indescribably at him. Thrilled but nerve-wracked. "You like how I taste, don't you, sailor?"

Alba slid his tongue up the bottom of the length, slowly—torturously slow by the way Eridanys' expression warped—sucking on the tip again before pulling away. More breathless than he expected, face hot.

"Yes," he said, voice hoarse from the penetration in his throat. "And you like how I use my mouth, don't you?"

Eridanys's smile twitched like he almost burst out laughing, throwing his head back again and bending an arm over his face. "God—Neptune save me, I will gut any man who ever lays a hand on what's mine."

Alba laughed, crawling back up Eridanys' body to kiss his chest again, then his mouth, not expecting how demanding the siren grabbed and pinned him there the moment he could. Caught within his bound arms like a fish in a net, Alba kissed him with all the same eagerness, sure that had his teeth been any sharper, he would have left gashes in Eridanys' lips.

He settled himself between the two cocks as their mouths fought for dominance, grinding back and forth over them without sliding anything inside. He pressed his hands flat to Eridanys' chest, moaning softly as the dual members stimulated him on both sides, enjoying the feeling of Eridanys' entire body clenching in response. How his already dripping cocks throbbed harder, how every time they caught the edge of near-insertion before popping free again, a low snarl of disappointment and growing tension rumbled from the back of Eridanys' throat. But Alba took his time, enjoying himself, enjoying the feeling of teasing something otherwise so demanding, so harsh and domineering and quick to take whatever it wanted. Teaching his siren how to be patient. But most of all—how to be pleasured by someone else's hands and mouth.

When he did invite Eridanys inside, Alba used only one of the cocks to start, biting his lip as it spread his hole open while the second cock rubbed deliciously up and down his clit with every sway of his hips. It soon grew harder and harder for Alba to keep his voice down, to bite back any sound more than a sharp moan or a gasp, muscles quivering as Eridanys' cock pressed deep into his stomach, making his heart stop and start again.

Reaching the edge of his willing patience, Eridanys' hips dared to move on their own, suddenly thrusting upward into Alba's body and making Alba jolt, crying out in delight and losing the rhythm of his movements as a rush of sparkling overwhelm injected his muscles.

Hunching forward, bracing against Eridanys' body again, Alba could only moan and gasp as Eridanys buried his hips up inside a second time, claiming the movements for himself and fucking Alba from below without the need of hands or anything else. Filling Alba to the brim and making his toes curl every time the muscled tail coiled and Eridanys' skin slapped against the backs of his legs, while simultaneously stroking his clit with the bumpy ridges of his second cock.

When the thrusting from below unexpectedly slowed, Alba cracked his blurry eyes open in question, world spinning in an overwhelming haze. Before he saw Eridanys' face, he heard his voice:

"I feel your leg clenching," he said, like a warning. Alba nearly asked what he was trying to imply, but then the strokes into him resumed, slow and careful, rolling in and out like rhythmic waves against the beach. "You have to tell me if it hurts."

In his spinning mind, Alba didn't know what Eridanys meant. His body felt fine, more than fine, on the verge of ascending into the sky—but as he settled back in, a dull throb made itself known in his hip, striking down the length of it in a quiet, buzzing hum. Not yet pain, but a pinched nerve prepared to complain. He grimaced, pressing a hand to his hip and shaking his head. Hating how Eridanys could sense it before even he did, as if he could feel every shift in Alba's weight, how he sat, how he unconsciously adjusted his posture without even knowing it.

"I guess... you'll have t'hold me in place," he said, struggling at first to even find his mouth to speak. Sitting forward, he groped around over Eridanys' head to grab the knot of the slacks keeping the siren's wrists together. Pulling them free, he wobbled as clawed hands immediately found his hips and balanced him back upright. Before sitting back, he met Eridanys' eyes again, realizing the smile on his face must have been pitiful by the way Eridanys laughed at him.

"Are you enjoying yourself?" he asked, initiating the pace once more, knocking what few thoughts Alba had loose all over again. Alba wavered upright before sinking down to recline chest-to-chest with him, biting back a moan as the second cock finally caught on the edge of his cunt and invited itself inside.

"Yes—god, yes," Alba sighed, shivering in pleasure before lifting his head just enough to kiss Eridanys for what had to be the hundredth time. He bent his back and moved his hips in time with the siren's thrusts, pressing them deeper, squeezing both members every time they buried inside of him.

"Eridanys," he breathed, struggling to find the words again, voice stolen by the siren driving him mad with every movement. "Oh, Eri—Eridanys, that's... oh, god, you feel... so good, it's..."

Eridanys' hand cupped the back of Alba's head, holding him without dominance, almost with a sense of tenderness, keeping him where he was. To see Alba's face, to watch every shift in his expression. His opposite hand remained on Alba's hip, holding it, squeezing gently every time the muscle throbbed or tightened in discomfort. Sensing it, even before Alba could.

"Alba... " Eridanys whispered, like he wasn't sure he was allowed to. Like he only did it because Alba said his name, first—but then the sound came again, and again. *Alba, Alba,* like the taste of it on his tongue complemented the pleasure sparking in his blood.

Alba opened his hazy eyes again, unable to help the overwhelmed smile that stretched his sore lips. It was the first time anyone had ever said his name so intimately—so full of emotion. Gentleness, tenderness—nothing he would have ever expected from a mouth lined with such sharp teeth.

"I'm going to c-cum, I think," he said, biting back a whimper that chased it. Eridanys pulled him closer, kissing his hairline where the silver patch grew. Tasting the salt and sweat on Alba's skin, holding his lips there.

"Cum for me," he whispered, making Alba shiver. "I want you to cum for me, Albatross, my prince of the sea."

Alba groaned, but his breath continued to hitch until his arms wound around the back of Eridanys' neck and he cried out with every new thrust. Stimulating him sharper and deeper, making him tighten and release. Eridanys held him in return, quickening his pace, pressing as deeply as he could, teeth trailing over the skin of Alba's shoulder.

"You feel so good, Alba—" he said between gasps, words spilling out like he never expected them. "I want to be the only one—who ever says your name, inside of you, knowing you, Alba, *Alba.* My caller of the shore—*Mine,* only mine—"

The coiling pit in Alba's stomach tightened for the last time, and he threw his head back with a cry as the sensation ricocheted through the rest of his body. Hot and cold at the same time, like lightning and the stabbing pricks of ice water on skin. Cutting off his breath, clutching every muscle in a vice grip as his insides tightened in vain against the cocks penetrating him, wishing to both push them out and hold them in place.

Alba hardly bit back a shriek of delight as Eridanys' fingers found his clit in the midst of it all, teasing and swirling a thumb over the nub already swollen and used, summoning another shuddering cry of pleasure to choke from Alba's clenched body.

When his muscles finally released again, Alba slumped over Eridanys' shoulder, caught in his arms and held close, a cool mouth littering gentle kisses up the side of his neck.

"God—god—How could the sea ever let a demon like you onto the shore with the rest of us..." Alba shuddered, wrapping his arms back around Eridanys' body.

Eridanys chuckled under his breath, holding Alba with continued, surprising carefulness, brushing hair from his damp forehead.

"She didn't let me go without a fight, as a matter of fact," he answered. "And she will be very envious to learn I have given myself to a sailor who can use me whenever he likes." He kissed the center of Alba's chest. "However he likes."

"Oh," Alba sighed. "How did I get so lucky?"

"Not luck," Eridanys teased, stroking in and out a few more times before finally pulling free. Alba groaned once he was left gaping, a part of him tempted to arch his back and slide the man's cocks right back in again. "I told you once before—If you hadn't chosen me, first, I would have simply stolen you away to keep for myself. To use whenever, however I like."

His fingers trailed delicately over the black stains across Alba's chest, the thinner streaks over the front of his neck, the smallest tendrils that curled slightly under his jaw. It made Alba shiver, pushing Eridanys' hand away. Something about the tenderness of that touch, specifically, was more overwhelming than all the others, and Alba's heart raced in a different way.

"Does it have to be only one or the other?" Alba asked. Eridanys' eyes searched him like he wasn't sure how to answer, like that was never something he considered. Frowning, Alba reached for Eridanys' ridged cock again, rising on his knees and sliding it back inside with a small sound. Eridanys' arms around him tightened. "Can't we—use one another equally? Own one another equally?"

"Can we?"

Eridanys' expression was almost unsettling, making Alba worry he'd said the wrong thing, or—just kept planting ideas the siren never thought possible. He just took Eridanys' face, holding it, kissing him, riding him in the way he'd learned he liked. Slow at first, then faster as the man's breaths caught. Fucking himself on Eridanys until Eridanys grabbed his waist and fucked him in return, met with Alba's own movements until they matched in tempo and Alba's mouth dropped open with another wave of squeezing, rising pleasure.

"Just—like that," he said, voice cracking. "Again—You're going to make me cum—again, Eri, *mmh!* At the same time—I want to c-cum at the same time."

Eridanys' sharp nails dragged down Alba's back, his jaw clenched, muscles tightening to the point his thrusts lost rhythm. Feeling desperate, close to the edge. The whole time, he stared at Alba, seeing him, observing him, his eyes, his mouth, every movement of his face. All over again, always looking for a lie, or a trick, or perhaps simply waiting for him to take back everything he said —but Alba just kissed him again, pressing their mouths together even as another orgasm rocked through his body, followed shortly by Eridanys pinning himself deep between Alba's legs and locking him there by the waist. Releasing inside of him, enough that it spilled out and dripped down Alba's leg. Leaving Alba breathless, dizzy, sweaty and flushed as he finally pulled away again. Wanting to see Eridanys' face as he came, for the first time.

Eridanys' expression clenched harder, brows knitted and teeth locked—before melting into one of pure, innocent, thoughtless bliss. Every inch of him, his hard exterior, the guard he always kept up, the gnashing of his teeth even when fast asleep on the bed by Alba's side—sloughed off like crashing waves from a breakwater.

When that softness remained even once his eyes opened again, searching for Alba still hovering over him, Alba couldn't help but wonder—if there was more to it than just the physical release. As if there was something else—unseen, unspoken. Especially when the siren's mouth lifted into a weak smile, then pressed a gentle kiss to Alba's chest. Breathing out Alba's name one last time, like a prayer.

CHAPTER 29

Three days passed since Alba spoke to Phyllis Michaels and Eridanys dragged Eugene Michaels back to shore. Three days of returning to a normal routine, Alba thinking he might otherwise go mad. Not wanting to bring any more attention to himself from the town, even spending nights in the lighthouse tending to the lamp.

Doing chores around the house, cleaning the cistern, making repairs, searching passively for any other signs of his mother's brief stay as a way of keeping the grief from eating him a little too much. Asking Eridanys if he could do anything about the other drowned souls in the water, convinced they were the other missing wickies, wanting to know if there was any way Alba could set them free, too. They kept their distance from Eridanys, he'd said, but would still try nonetheless.

Three days until the lantern in the retired lighthouse finally stopped turning, and Eridanys could join Alba at the top to witness what Alba had described to him. Where he stood in silence for a long, long time, staring at what remained of his kin who never came-to again after so long beneath the influence of the turning light. Four pairs of eyes reflecting the occulting glow even once it had long died; unresponsive, unmoving, hardly breathing. When Alba finally nudged Eridanys to ask what he was thinking, Eridanys jumped, like he'd forgotten Alba was there with him. He offered Alba a weak smile, though it didn't last long, especially once he turned back to the others.

"I'll bury them," he said. "There's a sacred site on a small island a ways out to sea. While the town buries Eugene Michaels and you search for what's keeping your mother here—I'll bury the rest of my kin. Then you and I can finally leave. Without any ghosts to follow us."

Alba squeezed his hand. "Alright," he said. "I think that sounds good."

It was three days until someone came to the lighthouse looking for Alba, telling him there would be a funeral for Mr. Michaels at sunset. Alba thanked them, doing his best to keep his breathlessness to himself. To cover the marks on his neck with the collar of his shirt, sweeping his hair one direction to cover the white streaks. In the washroom, his siren waited impatiently in the tub for him to return, swishing his tail over the edge and smacking it against the aluminum in warning. Alba pretended like he didn't hear it, assuring the messenger he would be there, thanking him for coming, closing the door once the man turned and made his way back to the boat tied off on the rocks.

Returning to the washroom, he scolded Eridanys for being so stubborn, kicking off his slacks and climbing back into the tub to take his face and kiss him. Opening his legs to continue what had been interrupted. Knowing it would hopefully be the last time anywhere near that godforsaken place.

Eridanys helped Alba to shore, where they exchanged a silent look as Alba tied the boat off. A look of thanks, a look of *'see you soon'* and *'be safe.'* Alba pretended to work on the knot the whole time he watched the moonlit siren swim away, until there was nothing left to see.

He'd already helped bring down the four merrow from the lighthouse to lay in the grass, accessible for Eridanys to carry out to where he intended to bury them. Alba hoped it gave him some closure, hoped it meant he could finally let go of the idea of Moon Harbor, just like Alba had once he realized his mother was no longer there waiting for him.

It was strange not having Eridanys alongside him after so many days in such close proximity. Especially after how easy it'd become to touch him, kiss him, as natural as ice melting into water; how it felt to sleep in his arms in a shared bed, warm and safe and exhausted as a chilly tongue licked drops of sweat from his temple and the side of his neck depending on how they got there. How Eridanys wanted to taste every one of Alba's breaths whenever their mouths connected, to steal every one of his heart-beats even once they were finished. Even once Alba was left used up and hardly able to move, left vulnerable to the creature who talked so often of how good he smelled, how badly he wished he could have another taste while kissing the faint scars left on Alba's shoulder by his own teeth.

A part of Alba wasn't sure he would decline if asked—there was something erotic about knowing his blood coated the tongue of something so sharp and strong and deadly, who craved it so badly, so much that he would resist simply because the tempta-tion was exciting enough.

None of those thoughts were appropriate to have while Alba searched for the end of the funeral procession, already winding its way slowly through the town, up the inclined road toward where he was a little too familiar with the location of the cemetery.

Merging in with the rest of them, he kept his cane close as to not trip any of the surrounding mourners, searching up ahead to spot Eugene's simple pine coffin supported on the shoulders of four men. The same four men, he knew, who'd once followed Eugene into the merrow pools where they hoped to have trapped the last of their prey. He wondered what they thought about losing their leader to that very same creature—despite it never being confirmed. Alba was sure there were whispers. A stormy sea might kill a man, smashing him against rocks until he was beyond recognition—but even the sea wouldn't do to someone what Alba had done with the copper pot.

Alba being the reason for the old man's untimely death was part of the reason he was so eager to join. But more than that, the reminders ruminated endlessly in the back of his mind, every little thing he wanted to keep his eyes sharp for. Unique funerary rites; Eugene's hair being cut, perhaps braided and given as an offering to his widow. A part of Alba even wondered if they'd hike all the way to the cemetery, only to lob his box over the cliffs back into the sea, like he once saw depicted in the merrow pools. Whether or not it was a full moon, Alba wanted to know how far Moon Harbor's beliefs went—and if they really had been killing wickies to try and create new merrow for their sacrifices.

"Is that Dawson Michaels' ex-fiancé there? With Mrs. Michaels at the front," someone passing nearby asked the woman next to her, and Alba's attention traveled up to the front of the line once more where Phyllis Michaels walked.

Alba hadn't noticed it before, but the gossiping birds alongside him were right—there was someone else there with her, a hand on her back, leaning in slightly every now and again to whisper reassurances and words of comfort. Dawson's ex-fiancé— Alba remembered Eugene saying something about him, mainly that he'd been nothing but trouble for both Dawson and the town, how he'd left after Dawson *fell ill*. Alba couldn't help but wonder if *falling ill* was an easier way of saying *was attacked and killed by his merrow companion.*

"Ah, no, that's his younger brother, I believe. Took over the family business when he died. And here I thought they'd forgotten all about us since striking rich."

"Remembered enough to take our fish every month, at least," another added.

"Seems that one still keeps in contact with Phyllis."

"So kind of him to come all this way for the funeral," the whispers continued.

"Yes, so kind of him to use a sprinkle of wealth to come back to visit us," another grumbled. "Maybe one day all the men they took will come back, too, with all the money they promised to send from their adventures on the sea."

"Oh, stop it, Ellen. No use in holding grudges after this long. Our men were likely taken by the water the moment she got her hands on them, after all we've done to her..."

"Shh," another hissed, and Alba felt eyes travel to him. He pretended not to notice, pretended to be wallowing in his own silent, stoic grief.

He pretended not to notice the people noticing him, just like the people pretended not to notice the clear singing from the trees. Ringing out louder, more intensely than he'd ever heard before, as if the sight of the entire town making its way up the hill excited the trapped spirits for good or for worse.

Their song intertwined with the whistling flutes on the buildings, one occasionally overtaking the other depending on the wind. As they reached the top of the road and turned down the path toward the cemetery, only the wailing ghosts of sacrificed merrow landed on Alba's ears. He knew it had to be the same for the rest of the townspeople, knew there was no way every single one of them could just pretend not to hear it—though no one turned. No one paid any mind to the apparitions in the trees— and Alba thought he finally understood the purpose of the musical pipes. To build up their immunity to any song at all, whether mundane or crafted by the sea.

Only one head in the procession turned, and it was the stranger walking at the front with Mrs. Michaels. Proof that they'd come from the outside, they had no idea what to expect of such a strange little town. Alba could only guess how tightly Phyllis clung to that man's arm to keep him from answering the call and sprinting into the woods.

Having to eventually stop and rest his leg on the journey to the cemetery, Alba missed the start of the eulogy and words offered by kin and friends, but those things didn't matter to him so much. He only wanted to see if they cut his hair. If they tossed him into the sea. If they carved markings into his body.

But when he arrived at the burial, encircled by townspeople all whispering and quietly weeping, there was no ceremonial hair cutting. They lowered Eugene Michaels into the earth just like every other burial plot around them; dressed in plain clothing like any other sailor who never knew or cared for particularly fine things. The man was, as simply as any other, nailed into his coffin and lowered into the wet ground with nothing more than his wool hat and nicest shirt to take to the other side with him.

Alba knew he stared as the body was lowered, though wasn't sure of the look on his face as it went. Only that his brows were furrowed, hand clenched hard on the head of his cane. Flushed with hot frustration, confusion, uncertainty—disappointment. Knowing it might yet be another day before he and Eridanys could leave. Another day, another week, who knew if they ever actually would escape Moon Harbor, that place the both of them seemed destined to end up no matter how they got there.

He decided to offer Phyllis Michaels a look and a nod of acknowledgement, apology, at the very least before turning to make his way back down the road, to escape that crowd of mourners. But the moment Alba glanced up, he made eye contact with the newcomer standing across the grave from him—and everything in him went limp.

Josiah wore a fine black suit. His dark brown hair was nicely combed back, shiny with pomade and as flawlessly held together as the rest of him. Even the thin beard on his face was neatly trimmed, perfectly outlining the way he smiled across the coffin lowered slowly into the ground, hand-over-hand with fraying ropes. Smiling at Alba. Turning him to ice, making him wish to vanish into the rainy mist floating just above the green grass of the cemetery floor.

Dawson Michaels' ex-fiancé... his younger brother...

Alba took a slow step backward. Josiah's eye twitched slightly in reaction—a predator eyeing his prey about to bolt. Alba's instincts told him to wait, don't move, stop, *stop—!* but he was already turning. Pushing through the crowd gathered at his back, rushing through them and not caring that he made a scene.

How long had Josiah known where to find him? From the very beginning? Since Marco never returned to Belmar? Did Eugene Michaels send a telegram long before making his threat? When did he first spot Alba in person? Just in that moment, over the face of the coffin? During the procession? Alba knew it would happen, eventually—he knew it was only a matter of time before Josiah Warren came looking for his lost little ship rat—and the instant he did, Alba knew nothing except the need to get *away*. To run, run, get somewhere safe, far away, safe, far away—

His instincts told him to run for the road—and he did, at first. But then his feet took him down through the center of town. Not in the way out, the same way he first arrived, no longer cursed to crumble into salt once he left the sound of the sea, where he could run until his legs gave out beneath him, until he ground the crack in his hip all the way down to dust and there would only be dragging himself by his hands to go any further. Instead—he ran to the sea. He ran to the docks, jumping to the black-sand shore, racing down it. Losing his footing, clawing at the grains and kicking them up in a storm as he pushed himself back to his feet again, throat sore and cold and cut by the salt in the air and the rain hitting him.

"Er—Eridanys!" he cried out once too tired to run any farther. There would only be cliffs, soon, with no more beach to follow. "Eridanys! *Eridanys! Please!*"

He didn't know if Josiah would follow him all the way there, especially while the funeral continued. He didn't know when Josiah would come to collect him, either in that moment, in a few hours, a few days, even—but he would come. He would come himself, or someone else would appear with a dozen hands to grab Alba and steal him off his feet just like the first time when he was a child—and Eridanys would never know what happened to him. That grim reaper would come for him just like every other time, killing Alba on the spot or dragging him back to Belmar where he would never get another chance to escape again. Josiah would make sure of it. He would break both of Alba's legs; lock him in the workhouse attic or send him back out to sea where there was only water in every direction and no one to hear him.

"Eridanys!" he screamed again, desperate, searching the waves, water stirred up by an incoming storm. *Please, please,* he wanted to see a streak of moonlight coming for him—Alba wanted to be safe. Alba wanted to be somewhere he knew he was safe—

The moon answered. No—his siren answered. Eridanys heard him. His guardian sown from the night sky shimmered beneath the water's surface, and Alba threw himself into it. His feet sank into the mud, tide nearly knocking him down had arms not flown out to catch him. Eridanys emerged with a gasp of surprise, grabbing at Alba with wide eyes, touching him all over in search of an explanation for his panic.

Alba didn't know what to say, didn't know how to explain, just threw his arms around Eridanys and clung to him. He was safe there, safe, safe, *safe,* even right there on the beach where anyone could see. Where even Josiah would see, Alba knew he was safe so long as Eridanys had him.

"What happened?" Eridanys repeated, growing more demanding the longer Alba took to respond. A hand scooped his wet hair over his shoulder as he still refused to let go. "I'll take you back to the lighthouse—"

"No!" Alba trembled, shaking his head, clinging tighter. "No, no—he'll find me there, they'll find me there—"

"Alright," Eridanys answered, as if he immediately understood, without another word. "I'll take you somewhere else. Somewhere no one will think to look for you. Hold on to me tightly, the sea is rough."

Alba did as he was told. His shaking arms locked like vices

around the back of Eridanys' neck, pressing his face into the siren's strong shoulder as they turned against the water.

He only had the courage to crack his eyes open again and gaze back toward the shore a single time—but wished he hadn't. Hardly more than a silhouette on the misty black shore, Josiah Warren watched as Alba was carried away by the last merrow of Moon Harbor.

Chapter 30

Eridanys said little while he worked, dredging sea mud and clay from the bottom of the lagoon. Alba watched in silence from where he'd been left off to the side, with promises of safety. *No one will find us. Just stay right here and calm down.* Not sure how long he'd been there, exactly, sitting motionless and out of the way. Just watching as the siren gathered his clay and brought it back to the surface, smearing it with intentional movements over the bodies of his kin laying silently in the grass on the opposite shore from where Alba sat. Only a few yards away. Easily within calling distance, though the reach felt impossibly wide.

Alba sat with knees pulled into his chest. Watching without seeing, ears ringing, constantly glancing toward the far mouth of the cove in search of ships looking for him. Knowing they would be looking for him, even as a storm brewed on the air. They might already be turning the lighthouse over. Would they find the other merrow missing when they did? Did Josiah know what to look for? At first Alba was sure he wouldn't—but the gossip from the funeral procession wouldn't leave him alone. *Is that Dawson Michaels' ex-fiancé there? No, that's his younger brother... Took over the family business when he died...*

Pressing his hand to his face, Alba held his breath until his thoughts blurred and the world spun.

That place Eridanys took him, which Eridanys had called a sacred site to bury his kin, was only just big enough to be drawn on a map as an island. Though even then, a drop of ink might have exaggerated its size.

Just large enough for cliffs and trees to grow, grass and wet ferns carpeting nearly every other inch of the stone and soil emerging from the sea. Barely out of view of the mainland shore, the sister lighthouses only just visible from the mouth of the lagoon. Though in the dimming light of sunset and the thick fog rolling in, even they were barely more than shadowy fingers emerging from the horizon.

Another incoming storm violently churned the sea around them, loud enough to be heard even within the safe confines of that cerulean pool, though never reaching where Alba sat on the edge of the moss pulled in tightly on himself. Shivering from all the times waves crashed over them on their way there, trying to convince himself again and again that not even Josiah Warren was mad enough to try and sail during such a thrashing squall.

The lagoon sat at the end of a narrow channel of sharp, rocky cliffs at the mouth of the island, secluded within an embrace of trees and walls of stone in every direction. Fed by a dribbling waterfall swollen with endless rain, protected from the wind enough that even tired seabirds nested in pockets of the stone, terns and laughing gulls and, to his chagrin, even a pair of albatross clacking their beaks together and throwing their heads back to trumpet words of affection to one another.

On the other side of the pool, the five remaining merrow of Moon Harbor gathered, though only one moved about with life. Diving down to the bottom of that pool again and again, water clear enough that Alba could watch every movement. Eridanys, who searched for specific patches of mud and scooped them into his hands, dragging them back up and spreading it over every inch of one body or another. Rarely speaking, and only in whispers to his fallen brethren when he did. Alba didn't like to look—the merciful cuts across each of their throats, spilling thick black blood into the grass, were enough to make his stomach turn.

He didn't want to know if there was a reason Eridanys chose that method to put them out of their misery. He didn't want to know if there was a connection between it and how Edythe was killed, like mimicking some merrow ritual. Alba was tired of rituals, sacred sites, merrow magic, symbolism. He was tired of all of it.

Eridanys covered his kin to toe in the mud, leaving only their faces exposed above a muddy line drawn along the shape of their jaw. He finger-painted different markings on their cheeks, dots and lines and symbols Alba did know, but even from the distance recognized as similar to those drawn in the piles of salt on the new moon, then carved into his mother's rotting skin. The siren added more markings into the layer of clay covering the rest of their bodies last, swirling motifs like waves, birds and shells, pearls, ancient languages of the deep.

At its core, while the sight made Alba's stomach churn, he also couldn't deny the process was something serene to watch. The solemnity with which Eridanys did it, the careful and intentional movement of his hands, his fingers, even his expression remaining flat. Despite Alba knowing how Eridanys felt about his kin, he still offered them respect in death. One final extension of familial reverence, even to the people who'd once wronged him so terribly.

Once finished, Eridanys disappeared back into the pool, swimming all the way to the bottom where he spread his hands over the patches of disturbed mud. Like a painter smoothing the pigments on his palette, erasing any sign anyone had ever been there.

He remained down there a moment longer, unmoving, floating and staring out toward the channel that lead to the sea. Alba almost felt guilty for watching so closely in such a private moment—but then Eridanys' head turned to where Alba sat.

Looking for him, too. Alba hunched slightly more into himself, but still didn't look away. Embarrassed. Selfishly hoping his siren would come to meet him.

Eridanys did. Extending his arms, his tail unfurled beneath him, ascending in a strong, fluid motion right to where Alba sat on the edge of the water. Alba finally let his tense body unfurl, making room for Eridanys to break the surface between his knees.

He slid up to touch Alba's face and kiss him without warning, leaving Alba breathless, needing an extra moment to compose himself. Eridanys, meanwhile, slathered one last handful of rich mud over Alba's hands, and Alba watched as the stains on his palms from the siren's blood washed away in the water with ease. When Eridanys moved to spread it further up Alba's arms, Alba stopped him. Not sure why; having come to know the blood stains he donned as well as the tattoos in his skin.

"Are you alright?" Eridanys asked after rinsing Alba's skin for the final time. He kept one hand on Alba's face, the other propped alongside his hip on the grass. Alba nodded, before motioning with his chin to the other side of the pool.

"Are you finished?"

"Yes." Eridanys glanced over his shoulder to his kin. "Now we let them rest where they lie. As the tide rises and fills this lagoon, it'll wash over them, carrying away the mud and clay, and eventually, taking the rest of their body out to sea. To nourish the mud with their magic, for any merrow who may come next. Deep enough that no human can find and poach any part of them."

Alba nodded. Something about that was comforting, even to him. He cupped a hand around the back of Eridanys' head, combing fingers into his wet hair, the pearls interspersed throughout the strands.

"Despite everything they did—I think this was admirable of you."

Eridanys smiled wearily, bitterly, like he wasn't sure how much he agreed.

"I have been thinking again about how... I don't know what I hoped would happen when I returned. What it was I hoped to find," he muttered, swaying slightly as his tail moved beneath him. "First I thought it was to show them I was still alive, as if it would prove I was more than they ever thought; that I never needed them, I was capable of surviving on my own on the outside despite everything they ever taught me... To prove it was possible for someone to live, even thrive outside of their protection. Maybe someone else in the kinship would see me and realize they didn't have to stay somewhere they didn't belong, as well. I had changed like they said I would—but I only resorted to the violence I did because I had no choice." He went silent, furrowing his brows as he thought about it more. "You once said... the reason you didn't run away sooner was because sailing was all you ever knew. That that was done on purpose, that keeping you from learning how to live elsewhere was the best way to keep you compliant. I think merrow teach their young the same way."

Alba squeezed the nape of Eridanys' neck in encouragement. Eridanys exhaled through his nose.

"Even once I came back and realized they were gone, then learned they were all dead, then even how they died, I... I didn't know how to feel. Was I happy? Was I angry? Did I feel vindicated? But to be vindicated would mean I was vengeful from the beginning—and I don't know if even that was true. When I was banished, I was angry, but more than that, I was..."

Eridanys shook his head, a muscle in his jaw clenching.

"Confused. Ashamed. Determined to prove I didn't need a corrupt kinship to survive. I do not forgive them for casting me out, but—" he clenched his jaw again, before the tension in his body relaxed, as if finally letting go of something invisible clinging to his back, weighing him down. "I do not think... they deserved to suffer like this. I never wished them peace, or happiness, but—I never wished them pain, either. A part of me always even wished they might realize their cruelty, learn from it, come looking for me, or at least welcome me back if I ever returned. Another part of me wished to forget they ever existed, to live as if I'd never had a family at all Either way, perhaps all I ever wanted was peace."

He glanced over his shoulder again. Watching his deceased kin, adorned with burial rites given by his own hand; the hand of a merrow wrongly cast out, forced to become something unrecognizable and full of rage and violence, who still offered such tender reverence to those who'd done him wrong.

Looking back at Alba again, Eridanys surprised him with another calm smile.

"I never expected to find that peace in the companionship of a wickie, instead."

Alba rolled his eyes, but pulled Eridanys into him. Kissing him. Deep and tender and full of affection and apology and a silent promise.

"I'm sorry I called to you in the middle of—"

Eridanys kissed him again. "You never listen. I told you before —I will drop everything with one call of my name." His expression softened, tracing fingers from Alba's temple back through the silver strands of hair behind his ear. "You're my shore-caller. I will always come when you call, no matter where or when. From any shore."

"What if I can't reach a shore to call from?" Alba asked. He didn't mean for it to sound so frightened, hating himself. Hating how he'd felt like nothing but a pathetic, whimpering child for days, made weak by the world after so many years hardened into something that could withstand it. As if meeting Eridanys was his final undoing.

"Then I will beseech the sea to rise high enough for me to reach you," Eridanys said without hesitation. "And I think she would listen."

Alba furrowed his brows. He squeezed his eyes closed in embarrassment, letting his head droop before shaking it.

"I'm sorry," he said again. "At the funeral—he was there. Josiah Warren was there. I just panicked, I didn't know what else to do..."

Opening his eyes, he gazed down at where Eridanys' skin turned to scales from his stomach to his hips. He reached out to touch them, feeling the bump of every shiny piece like coins beneath his fingers.

"I think... Herman Warren was Dawson Michaels' ex-fiancé. The one who left after you killed him." He finally met Eridanys' eyes again. "Did you know that?"

"That they were fiancés? No." Eridanys frowned. "I know Herman Warren spent some time in Moon Harbor—but not the reason, or his business, or even for how long. Especially not that sort of relationship he had with Dawson. Most details like those were kept from me on purpose. What in god's name is his brother doing here?"

"Everyone was sayin' he came to pay his respects to Mr. Michaels," Alba muttered, touching Eridanys' stomach again, then his chest, as if feeling the siren's heartbeat would relax him. It did. "But I think... he finally came lookin' for me. Maybe Phyllis said somethin' when she invited him to the funeral. Marco said Josiah had no idea he was here when he came—but who knows how true that was. Maybe Eugene told him a long time ago, since he was comfortable threatenin' me with the same thing right before I killed him..."

His hand on Eridanys' chest closed into a fist. He squeezed his eyes shut again, inhaling a deep breath and letting it loose through his nose. Controlling it, keeping his composure despite the nausea in his gut.

"I don't know how I'm supposed to find whatever is keepin' my mother's spirit trapped if he's in town," he went on, voice cracking again. Hating himself again. Reaching up to touch the tiny braid left by Edythe's hands in his hair. Full of exhaustion and disappointment and frustration, all the way to his fingertips. "I can't just leave her here, but I... I don't know what to do."

Eridanys said nothing, just touching Alba's face, stroking his cheek with a hand designed to tear rather than gently caress. Alba leaned into it, closing his eyes once more. Trying to find even the briefest moment of rest there against it.

"Let's destroy this town..." Eridanys said, repeating the comforting words Alba had once said to him. "*'Summon the water high enough to wash through every house, up every street, so every stolen part of your kin can return to where they belong...'*" He pressed his forehead to Alba's, closing his eyes, placing both hands on either side of Alba's face. "So every part of your mother can return to where she belongs, as well. To wash her out to sea, so she may be set free from this place."

"How?" Alba asked, leaning into him.

"The king tide on the full moon," Eridanys told him. "When the moon is strongest—when merrow traditionally make their pleas to the goddess. I'll call out to her, no different than you called out to me from the shore. I'll plead with her to raise the tide even higher, to wash every part of this cursed place back into the sea."

Alba wanted to cry, but he wouldn't. He wouldn't cry again, no more, not again. Instead, he hooked his hands over Eridanys' wrists where they still held his face, hoping to steal his surety. His faith, his confidence.

"Alright," he said. "Alright."

"Until then—we'll leave," Eridanys went on. "We'll disappear before anyone can find you. We'll stay somewhere safe, warm, new, somewhere on land. And return when it's time. To cleanse this shore and her forest of all her sins."

"Alright," Alba said hoarsely. "Yes, alright—I'd like that. God, I'd like that."

He kissed Eridanys again; he kissed Eridanys again and again, finally wrapping his arms around the siren and pulling him out from the water. More and more, longer and hungrier until hands pulled at clothes and mouths skirted from lips to find other wet places to worship. Alba and his siren, who would always come no matter which shore Alba called from—who Alba would always answer no matter which part of the sea beckoned his name in return.

ALBA SLEPT SWEETLY WRAPPED IN ERIDANYS' arms among the moss and trees and incoming lapping waves of the tide; where the chill could never find him, even without blankets. Where discomfort was far from him, even without the comforts of a bed. He was warmed by the trailing remains of the man's hands and mouth and body pressed against him until he was moaning and gasping; comforted into a deep sleep by the mere proximity of him with eyes closed and arms pulled into his body. Safe in Eridanys' arms. Safe in the arms of his merrow-siren love.

Perhaps that was why he never stirred, until it was too late. Until Eridanys jolted upright with a hiss and a snarl, throwing himself over Alba just long enough for Alba to rush back to life with a gasp.

Everything moved too fast for him to react—moved too fast for him to think, to respond, until Eridanys was already being tied with ropes, face down in the moss, biting and snarling, whipping his massive tail like a wild animal, six men required to pin him.

Until more hands were on Alba, throwing him down and smashing his face into the earth until he tasted blood. Cursing at them and thrashing, he kicked his legs in an attempt to break free, only to gasp and go still when a knife found his throat.

"Easy, lad," a gruff voice cooed. "No use making all that noise, now. No one's gonna hear you. Just go easy now, come on. That's it."

They bound Alba's wrists, then his ankles, leaving him on his side to watch as Eridanys was finally subdued by the others. From boats tied off on the lagoon, other silhouettes searched the opposite shore for the merrow corpses already reclaimed by the sea like Eridanys once described, shouting in frustration to one another as tensions grew. Watching them search, one other figure smoked in the darkness, only the pinprick of the end of a cigarette visible. Alba knew who it was without having to see his face.

Josiah saw Alba looking. He dragged long on the cigarette before flicking it away and approaching. Alba stiffened, bracing as Eridanys growled, low and threatening. Unblinking as he watched the man approach, then kneel down in front of Alba—and the siren tore through the ropes binding him, flaying open the chest of the nearest man before lunging off his coiled tail with all the speed and strength of when he was in the sea.

With teeth bared and claws spread to strip flesh from Josiah's bones, Alba could barely gasp a syllable of Eridanys' name before Josiah turned, burying a knife into the siren's ribs. Summoning black blood to bubble around the edge of the blade, spilling from the wound the moment it was yanked back out again. Despite it, Eridanys still slashed his sharp nails, missing Josiah's throat but ripping trenches through his cheek. Josiah shouted, clutching his face and stumbling back, barely dodging another attack and slamming the knife into Eridanys a second time. Sending the siren back to the dirt.

"Eri—!" Alba cried as Eridanys collapsed with a strained grunt, clutching his ribs but still stretching his neck to search for Alba only a few feet away. Others rushed Josiah, disarming him, calling him mad, snarling that they needed to keep the merrow alive, *damnit!*—but Josiah just watched where Alba and Eridanys stared at one another on the ground. Where Alba didn't know what to say, paralyzed by the sight of his siren's nose and lip bleeding dark blood, Eridanys' eyes wide and pupils dilated in a frenzy. Searching until they met Alba's, where he snarled something Alba didn't hear.

Not a threat—maybe a command. Maybe a declaration of some sort—but Josiah planted a foot against Alba's back before Alba could respond. Pressing weight down, crushing him, bowing his ribs, saying something to get Alba's attention, but Alba didn't hear it, either. There was only Eridanys; Eridanys' strained, terrified expression, straining harder in pain and panic as men rushed to bind him a second time. Tighter, using more rope, barely managing it as Eridanys snapped teeth and thrashed his strong tail in response. Then dragging him away over the grass even as he continued to fight, a thick pool of black blood left behind. Smearing over the dirt, the rocks, staining the beach as he was carried to one of the boats.

The regret of saying nothing, only able to helplessly watch as it happened, was like a knife in Alba's own ribs.

"So glad to see you again, Mr. Marsh." Josiah knelt down in Alba's line of sight, forcing Alba to look at him by curling a finger beneath his chin.

Alba snapped his teeth down on it hard enough to feel the bone crunch, earning a slamming fist to the side of his head like a disobedient dog. It made his ears ring, but he still managed to laugh, not knowing if the blood on his tongue was his own or Josiah's.

"I've been searching everywhere for this godforsaken town, you know," Josiah went on, grinding his teeth together. "Ever since I found some very interesting drawings in Herman's lockbox. Even Marco wouldn't tell me, despite running him ragged for so many years to get him to talk. But once your mother ran off, and you took off after her—I went to see where she came from. Saw it on her papers. Knew if I found her, I'd find you, and I'd find Moon Harbor. But, as it turns out, I didn't need you at all— Moon Harbor came for me first, when Herman's old father-in-law croaked."

Josiah grabbed a handful of Alba's hair, craning his head back and forcing him to meet his eyes. Alba strained against the burning pain of his scalp, but still managed a weak smile with lips painted red with blood. Reveling in the sight of four bloody gashes disfiguring the man's face, dripping thick and wet down his cheek and into the grass.

"You really are more trouble than you're worth, aren't you, Albatross?"

"And here everyone says you're the smartest of the Warren

boys," Alba spat. Josiah pressed the end of his cigarette into Alba's hairline, making Alba jerk backward.

"I knew it the first moment you were plucked off the street like an alley cat, Albatross," he ground out. "You, your damn mother, your damn father—your whole family, nothing but a pack of freeloaders from a useless little town. Though after seeing it for myself, I have to say, it's no surprise how easy it was for father to lure the lot of them out to sail for him. Your father could've actually done something for himself, you know, had he not died so easily. Wonder if his meat tasted as weak as the rest of him when they ate him up north, too. You should know—is it true dead men taste like pork?"

Alba snapped his teeth again, but Josiah pulled back fast enough to avoid them that time.

"As much as I don't want to be responsible for you anymore —that pet of yours is a siren, isn't he? Don't look so surprised— I've been reading Herman's notes for a long while, now. I also know a siren will attract fish as well as any merrow ever would, and I know they need fresh meat to survive. Hopefully he'll be hungry again soon, though I can't say skin and bones like you will satisfy him much." He released Alba's hair, patting his cheek before squeezing his face. "You can consider your debt paid with your life, Albatross. Go on, fellas, give Alba something to help him sleep on the trip back to town. Talk to you again soon, seabird."

"Bastard!" Alba shouted, twisting and attempting to kick away the faceless shadows that suddenly encircled him. Fighting and cursing at them, he snapped teeth at their hands, their fingers —but an oar cracked against the back of his head, and the world tumbled into darkness.

CHAPTER 31

ALBA KNEW THE GRATED FLOOR BY HOW IT SCRAPED against his hands. It thrust a mouthful of adrenaline down his throat, landing like a rock in his gut and wrenching the rest of his body awake in an instant.

Jolting upward, he leapt to his feet with the slamming nerves—only to stumble as the world turned, tripping back to his ass with an echoing crash against the metal. He was in the lantern room, just like he first thought. The one he knew so intimately, the one he'd worked every night for just over a month. But that wasn't what alarmed him right away—it was the fact he was alone. There was no sign of Eridanys anywhere, not even his blood. Not a single piece of hair. No one but Alba and the giant glass lens.

He forced himself to stay calm, as impossible a feat as it felt. He bit down on his tongue to center himself in his body, to focus. Breathing hard through his nose, he quickly searched the perimeter of the room for any other sign of what had happened since they were found on the island, though it came up nearly as empty. Even the view through the weatherglass didn't offer any clues, as there were no more boats tied off to the lighthouse rocks than a single dingy banging against the edge. Moon Harbor looked no different in the distance. There were not more boats crowding her docks that he could see from so far away.

His cane was missing. The hatch leading down into the rest of the tower was locked. His head throbbed, the back of it caked with dry blood.

Finally, Alba called out in case anyone could hear him below. Not caring if it was one of Josiah's men or someone else. A part of him just wanting them to know he was awake. He was alive. And if they wanted to shut him up, they would have to come and do it themselves.

Come early afternoon, someone did. They commanded him to step away from the hatch, unlocking it and climbing up with a gun brandished to keep Alba in check. Alba obeyed, even putting his hands up before they had to ask. Knowing it was one of Josiah's men the moment he laid eyes on them, needing no other introduction. Letting them think they were intimidating, imposing enough to explain Alba's instant submission to whatever they said, whatever command they made. Perhaps not knowing how familiar Alba was with the Warrens, with Josiah, with how the man worked. Alba did not submit because he felt small—but because he knew how to outwit Warren muscle better than they could imagine.

Alba would submit until he could leave the lantern room. And then, until he could leave the lighthouse. Until he could step out into the fresh air, to see if Josiah was anywhere nearby. To find out if there was a reason he didn't kill Alba right away. Alba had ideas. He had assumptions. But all of those implications depended on one other thing: Whether or not Eridanys was still alive somewhere, too.

The man who came to collect eventually lead Alba down the stairs, out the door, through the wind and sharp rain back to the house. Inside, Josiah did not turn to look at him amongst the other four men crowding the small kitchen table, but Alba kept the disappointment off his face. Just observing how they helped themselves to what little supplies he'd had left in the fridge and cupboards. The men, meanwhile, only glanced at him in return. Just long enough to acknowledge his arrival, before one waved a hand, giving Alba a curt: *'Well, get to work.'*

TENDING to the lantern had always been grueling, only made more so in that state of limbo. Not sure where Eridanys was, let alone if he was dead or alive. Not knowing where Josiah was, what he was doing, when he would be back, except for the vaguest ideas Alba could cobble together from eavesdropping on conversations held between his babysitters. Occasional talk about whether or not there was enough food to last *'another couple of days'* until Josiah *'was ready to leave.'* How one hoped to get the job done early, wanting to be back in Belmar by the end of the week. Talking amongst one another about how the tides in Moon Harbor were said to be stranger than anywhere else, especially when the moon was at its biggest; making one of them grumble about how he didn't like being in such proximity to such barbaric pagans, making the sign of the cross as he did.

Enough sprinkled conversation for Alba to puzzle-piece together a certainty that Josiah would be back soon enough, and whatever he had planned had its own reason to need Alba. Perhaps only to collect his debt, the one he himself said Alba would pay off with his life—but even so, Alba would be ready. Until then, he would behave. Just like in the north, just like in Belmar, in Welkin, while Edythe Marsh was still held as collateral for his obedience. Alba would behave. *Always in such a hurry. Take the bone from your teeth. Good things come to those who wait.*

In the early morning of the third day, Alba spotted something entering the harbor from far out at sea. When sunrise came, he used a palm-size spyglass to search, recognizing the ship in an instant—an ancient wooden vessel with canvas sails, the size of at least three small fishing boats combined. A flagship of the Warren company, designated by the mermaid carved into her bow. The same one whose mast Alba fell from, breaking his hip and ending his life as he knew it only a few months prior. Like Josiah thought himself funny.

The sight of her made Alba's stomach sink, then turn over itself. Enough that he bent forward and nearly puked. Feeling her deck swaying beneath his feet, smelling the crisp northern air, with white-knuckled hands clinging to the netting of the mast. Waiting for the captain to call up to him. How he only had to hold fast a moment longer, a moment longer, before someone would surely call for him to come back. He remembered how cold his hands had been, stiff and calloused and as fatigued as the rest of him from a long day of pulling nets from the rough sea. How the call never came, never came, never came, before a wave did. Crashing over the ship and knocking Alba loose, sending him tumbling like an angel tripping from heaven to the hard deck below.

Josiah knew what he was doing, calling that ship in. Alba hoped to express his amusement to the man sooner rather than later.

ANOTHER DAY PASSED, and Josiah's men took Alba across the water to the town to gather supplies. They left him on a bench by the docks with a chaperone as they went about their business, not wanting him to walk around freely. Not wanting to risk him making a run for it and vanishing for a second time.

Alba had no intention of going anywhere. Not without knowing where his siren was. And especially not when the towns-people gave him the looks they did—as if, should they get the opportunity first, they would gladly strangle him before Josiah ever could.

Word must have spread. Not only was Alba in a relationship with the last merrow of their harbor, but also possibly behind the death of one of their most respected members of the community.

Alba just kept his expression blank as they passed, even as they cursed him under their breath, eyes flitting between him and the man sitting alongside him as if searching for a way to take out their anger without being seen.

Alba focused his attention on the work being done to Josiah's ship. The ship that ended Alba's life. Being so close to her again after so long was bittersweet, knowing it was unfair of him to blame her for what happened, though even the briefest of glances up at the height of her mast made his world spin all over again. But after only a moment more, those memories were no longer the reason he stared.

Workers clustered around her bow. Hammers chiseled into the carved mermaid, and only when one of her arms snapped off and tumbled into the sea without a flinch from the artisans did Alba realize what they did with her. Chipping her away, laying the bow bare. Reminding him of something Eridanys had once told him, something Dawson Michaels once wanted to try. *I'd seen drawings in his study, things he'd sketched, drawings of merrow tied off to the bows of ships...*

"No!" Alba leapt to his feet, only to be grabbed by the arm and shoved straight back down to the road. Still, Alba shrieked, screaming and threatening the man like spitting blood through teeth, crushed beneath his weight and tied-off with rope looped on his belt just in case of that exact thing. But even as they bound Alba tight again, crushing the air from his lungs until his eyes bulged and every breath came in a wheeze, Alba just kept thinking—

If anything—if anything—

Eridanys was still alive—and Alba might even know where they were keeping him.

Once Alba knew what he needed, it wasn't hard to watch the men laze about the house while doing his own tasks. As they played cards, made a mess of the kitchen or the sitting room or bedroom loft, smoking pipes and drinking alcohol brought over by the crateful by a dingy. Watching and waiting, just like his mother always told him.

Waiting until the opportunity finally came, when just enough of them were dead-drunk on the couch, reclined on the rug in the sitting room, none the wiser to the wickie who gently prodded around in their pockets for a ring of keys he wasn't supposed to know the purpose of.

Once he had them in hand, Alba didn't waste a moment. He braved the stormy, mid-afternoon wind, hurrying past the house, the younger sister tower, to the retired lighthouse at the far end of the row. His siren was inside. He had to be. He had to be. Alba was sure of it. If not—

He didn't want to think about what he would do *if not*.

"Eridanys?" Alba asked upon stepping inside and closing the door behind him. The floor was coated in a thick layer of solidified fatty oil, shimmery and white and smelling sweet and minty. Remnants from when they'd emptied the basin only a week prior, though the lantern overhead turned with rhythmic *clanks* again. Refilled. Rotating with a purpose, Alba knew. He just had to keep his nerves under control.

Footprints clustered in a path from the door to the bottom of the stairs, a few spots smeared where someone must have slipped, other trails demonstrating something heavy being dragged. The faintest streak of black blood spilled over top. Alba didn't waste a moment longer, hurrying for the stairs and throwing himself up them.

Just like the first time while guided by the drowned soul of his mother, he didn't feel the ache in his leg, or the exhaustion that came with climbing the circling incline so fast. Even faster, that time, knowing if he was right, time was of the essence. If he was right—Eridanys had been victimized by that turning light for days. Alba didn't want to be too late. He would never forgive himself if he was too late. He wouldn't let Josiah live it down if he was too late.

"Eridanys?" he asked again upon reaching the top of the stairs. Breathless, hoarse from the effort. "Eri? Please—say somethin'."

There was no reply, at least not from the voice Alba hoped to hear—but a faint scratch of something against the top of the hatch made Alba jump. He scrambled for the keys, nearly dropping them in his hurry. He climbed the ladder and unlocked the hatchway into the room above—but it barely moved. He checked the lock again. It should have opened, Alba was sure.

He rammed his shoulder harder against the underside of the metal. It gave way slightly that time, with a telling bounce on the other side, and he realized with a jolt in his chest—Eridanys was on top of it. Unresponsive except for small, rapid breaths, unable to lift himself upright to allow Alba through.

"Eridanys!" Alba gasped, shoving his arm through the narrow opening, partially to prop it up, partially to touch him. To brush the back of his knuckles against the siren's cheek. "Eridanys, I'm here, just—! Just hold on a second, alright? I'm gonna try and roll you off. Just hold on. Keep your eyes closed."

Gritting his teeth, Alba rammed the hatch again, then again, and again, managing to nudge Eridanys away slightly more every time. When he finally won out against the siren's weight, sweat dripped down his face. The light blinded him in an instant as the hatch flew open and slammed against the floor with a deafening *bang*.

Alba didn't hear it; he didn't feel the burn of the light on his eyes. He saw only his siren, his caller of the sea, his companion, lying limp on the floor. Stained with his own blood, wounds festering like congealed black ink on his stomach; eyes barely cracked open, a faint occulting glow in the far reaches of his irises; his chest rising and falling in frantic rhythm, like a fish trying to breathe on a dry dock. His silver hair draped in a tangled mass around him, tail chained off to the weatherglass, once-sharp fingernails worn down into bloody nubs. Beneath where he lay, claw marks were carved into the wooden boards. Signs of the siren's futile attempts to escape, to carve his way out, until he could do nothing but collapse and wait for death.

"Eri," Alba cried, throwing his arms out, grabbing Eridanys' face and turning it toward him. Tucking his eyelids closed, brushing messy strands of hair from his forehead, pulling him close to shield him from the light. "I'm right here, come back to me. You're still alive—thank god, you're still alive, I was so worried. Close your eyes, rest for a moment. I've got you."

Eridanys' face twitched slightly. Alba thought perhaps he was trying to smile, or whisper something to him, and he leaned in closer to hear it—but instead of speaking, Eridanys' hand lashed out, grabbing Alba's shirt and yanking him close. Sharp teeth snapped down on the side of his neck, and Alba bit back a scream, digging his fingers into Eridanys' shoulders and choking on every breath as pain surged through him. Still—he raised a hand to gently comb through the back of Eridanys' hair, staring at the ceiling and fighting to keep the discomfort out of his voice.

"Y-you must be hungry," he rasped. "It's alright—it's alright, t-take what you need, yeah..."

A part of him was prepared to die like that, despite all of his attempts to stay alive. He wouldn't mind—to die saving the person he'd come to care for so much, he wouldn't mind at all— but then Eridanys' grip on him softened. His sharp, burrowing teeth shifted, drawing out of Alba's flesh, replaced with a swirling tongue that licked over each crescent-shaped row of bleeding marks. He lapped up the blood that spilled out, before his mouth found Alba's suddenly, and Alba tasted the metallic sting of his own blood on the siren's lips.

The way Eridanys kissed him wiped away any possible disgust, kissing Alba with the same devouring intensity of the teeth in his shoulder, as if it took everything not to eat Alba in a single bite. Kissing him hard and demandingly, hungrily, but at the same time —with desperation, with a type of thoughtful tenderness Alba didn't expect. Like he truly didn't think he'd ever see Alba again, like he thought Alba wouldn't come for him.

"I'm sorry it took so long," he said breathlessly between their mouths, as Eridanys' lips never stopped pressing into his, muffling the words. "I came as soon as I could. I promise."

Eridanys still said nothing, just kissing him. As if his mind shuddered beneath the blinding glow of the lantern, unable to find the words, unable to recall how to speak. Saying everything he needed with his mouth on Alba's, lips forming the words he needed without ever uttering a sound. Spelling out his gratitude, his own relief in how he devoured Alba's existence with every breath passed between them.

When he finally pulled away again, Alba was nearly disoriented, closing his eyes as Eridanys pressed their foreheads together.

"My sea prince," the siren finally whispered hoarsely. "My caller of the shore. I thought just of you to keep my sanity."

Alba kissed Eridanys again, wrapping arms around him, holding him close. Wishing he could drag him from that floor, down the ladder, away from the turning light that drove his siren to near-madness. But Eridanys was too weak, Alba was too weak, and—he didn't know where they would go from there. There was no way for Alba to get Eridanys down the stairs by himself, let alone to free him from his chains, let alone to drain the fuel basin a second time.

When frustrated tears finally broke over his lashes, he attempted to squeeze them away, but Eridanys noticed. He sighed, using his thumbs to wipe them from Alba's cheeks before they could drip all the way down.

"There's enough salt in the sea," he whispered. "Don't add to it with tears, Albatross."

"I don't know what to do," Alba's voice shook all the same. "What the hell am I supposed to do? I can't help you—I can't even help myself. I don't know what in god's name I'm supposed to do now... I couldn't save my mother, I couldn't save myself—

and now I can't even save you, after only just getting you. After just finding somethin' else to live for."

Eridanys wiped more tears from Alba's eyes. Alba hated it—hated how subdued his normally frenzied, bloodthirsty, angry, stormy siren was. He hated knowing why he acted the way he did, hated thinking of how much pain he must be in from both the swollen wounds in his stomach and the whirlpool in his mind. Alba hated how he could see the glow lingering in the back of Eridanys' eyes despite how he spoke, he hated how there was the slightest slur in every word.

"I wish to live for you as well," Eridanys said breathily. "It's going to be alright, Alba. We'll still find a way—to have a life together."

His voice weakened the more he spoke, drawing out, every effort exhausting him. But that weak smile never left his face, the soft shape of his eyes never hardened or even flickered from Alba's. Not for a second. All Alba could do was fight his tears, fight back the emotions, hating himself and everything he'd ever been, everything he'd ever allowed to happen to him—

But then he thought of his mother. His father. How they'd suffered in all the same ways he had—but weren't to blame. It all stemmed from the same person—the same family, the same sailing company, the same debt, the same town, the same reasons. All of those things—that ultimately left Eridanys there, draped weakly over Alba's lap, barely able to hold his head up.

"I'll kill him," Alba said, voice trembling with rage. "I'll gut him like I should've gutted him the first time. I never should've bothered stabbin' him just in the leg—I should have plunged that goddamned knife into his chest! Into his goddamn head! Over and over, so I would never have to worry about him ever fuckin' again!" He took Eridanys' face, breathing hard, blood boiling hot with new life. He kissed his siren one more time. "The next chance I get, I'm going to kill him. I have to, if I want a life with you. I'll tear his throat out with my own teeth if I have to—and if there's anythin' left once I'm done, I'll throw him to you, and you can make a fine meal out of the rest."

Eridanys' smile remained weak, tired, but aware. He bared his sharp teeth in emphasis, and Alba hooked a thumb into the crook of his mouth to really see all of them.

"You'll get your revenge on the Warren family right along with me," he reiterated. "We'll enjoy the taste of him together."

"We will." Eridanys continued smiling. "Won't waste... a single piece."

Alba knew he couldn't stay much longer, both as Eridanys struggled to keep his eyes open, and knowing his chaperones would eventually notice their keys missing. The sun would rise, and Alba had to be back where they could find him.

Unable to do anything else, he pulled the cuff of his sleeve over the ball of his thumb and wiped his own blood from Eridanys' mouth and chin. Not wanting anyone to know their feral siren in the old tower had already been fed.

"Promise you'll live long enough for me to save you," Alba whispered. "I heard them talkin', they said Josiah wants to leave in a few days. I think he might be waitin' for the full moon—which is when you and me were gonna destroy this town, anyway."

He offered Eridanys a small smile, though by then the siren's eyes had closed, head resting on Alba's lap. He combed fingers gently through Eridanys' hair, undoing as many tangles as he could. "I'll take care of everythin'. All you have to do for me, for now—is keep your eyes closed against the light."

"I will," Eridanys answered. Slurred, drunk on his own exhaustion. Alba just kept stroking his hair, until he was sure Eridanys fell into a peaceful sleep.

Alba would be back. He would do something. He would help him. He would save him. Eridanys would get his chance to find a new home with someone who loved and cherished him, far from Moon Harbor where there were only bad memories and new nightmares.

Alba, who hadn't been able to save his mother. Who would

fight tooth and nail to protect what else he'd come to care for, the only thing he had left. No matter if it left him wild and mad and deranged with bloodlust like a siren banished out to sea. He already knew what flesh tasted like on his tongue, by nature of the life the Warrens had forced him to lead—and he wasn't afraid to sink his teeth into it one more time.

Chapter 32

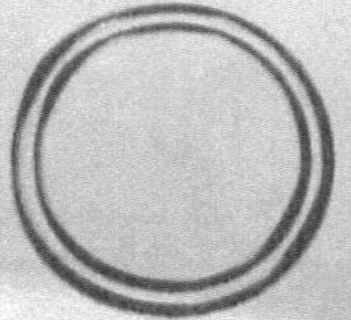

Alba watched the full moon creep closer every night while tending to the lantern. Taking notes in the tender's log, scribbling lines on pages opposite the ones written by his mother. Instead of lists of supplies, he made lists of things he wanted to see once they were free. Experiences he wanted to share with his siren, places to go, things to eat, ways to get there. *Climb a mountain. Dance at a festival. Ride a train. Walk through the desert—and see if such places are actually as hot as I once read about.*

The night before the full moon, Alba wrote one last page. A manifesto of the everything he'd seen, not sure if he would leave it behind to be discovered by the next wickie, or perhaps something he would take with him once they went. He wrote about how the people of Moon Harbor used merrow magic for themselves, and all the things he'd realized were just harvested parts—the hair woven into their nets to lure more fish; the scales used as wound bandages; earrings and makeup pigments and adornments in their homes; shawls draped over the oldest of them, perhaps to extend their wavering life; still-beating merrow hearts claimed to revive the dead. And those were only what he'd seen with his own eyes.

He wrote about the wickies who came before him, particularly the ones whose notes and names were recorded in that same log book. Explaining what he thought happened to them, based on what he'd seen of their drowned corpses haunting the lighthouse rock, as well as the murals in the mermaid caves. *'I think they killed wickies on the full moon and threw them into the sea hopin they would become new merrow, since they were runnin out of merrow native to this harbor. Including my mother, Edythe Marsh, who was born in this town. I think they (under instruction of Josiah Warren) will try and do somethin similar to me tomorrow night, when the full moon comes again.'*

Closing his eyes, Alba breathed in deep to keep his nerves at rest. The thought made his heart want to race in anxiety, finding reassurance in the simple thought of—if they attempted to do to him what they'd done to his mother, he might see exactly how they kept her spirit trapped there in that town. He would see what she saw in her final moments. He might see exactly what he needed to finally put her to rest.

Even if he couldn't—destroying the town would hopefully do the job for him. He still didn't know how they would, but—he would not leave Moon Harbor until there was nothing left of it to mourn.

ALBA WAS ALL TOO convincing when the men came to gather him the following night, acting surprised and caught off guard and confused, fighting back against them with everything he had, knowing they'd overtake him with ease. His only moment of genuine bloodthirst came when he laid eyes on Josiah waiting on the docks across the water, face bandaged where Eridanys had raked claws through his cheek. Appreciating the sight of his ship missing the mermaid on her bow. Prepared for a replacement.

The reminder alone was enough to make Alba lunge, nearly getting within reach to shove him into the water where he'd be crushed against the dock. It earned him a punch to the stomach, buckling forward with a grunt, reminded not to be so impulsive. He would get his chance to kill Josiah Warren, later.

There was no way for him to anticipate where the people held their full moon rituals, half-expecting to be led to the same place he witnessed the ritual on the new moon. The townsperson who guided them as the sun set carried a single lantern, draped in a black robe that shadowed their face, a polished sickle swinging from the belt on their waist. They constantly glanced over their shoulder to where Alba walked silently on their heels, two of Josiah's men behind him, constantly nudging him along with the end of a shotgun.

The ache in his hip made the hike to the cemetery on the hill agony, but Alba kept it from showing on his face. He just watched the lantern as it swung to and fro on the pole, lighting their way through the deepening dark. From the forest to their right, a sorrowful song hummed in pursuit of them, and Alba knew if he turned to look, a gallery of moon-pale faces would be watching the procession.

The cloaked figure didn't take the path into the trees like Alba expected, instead passing down the length of the cemetery to another worn trail leading over the side of the hill and snaking down toward the shore. At the end of the long, winding path, illuminated by the bright moon in the clear sky, a finger of dense forest jutted out into the sea, dissecting the black-sand shore just before the cliffs blocked the horizon.

"Is the merrow ready to be delivered to the new harbormaster?" the lantern-bearer asked with a brief pause to look back at them. A silent warning that they wouldn't continue further until they got the answer they wanted—and an unintentional announcement to Alba, loud as ever, that the townspeople had been told something very different from what Josiah actually meant to do that night. Alba nearly said something, but held it back. It wasn't his business what lies Josiah was spreading.

"Yessir," one of the men behind him answered. "All trussed up and ready for whenever we're done here. You'll get your magic fish, don't fuss about it. Go on, then, or this'll take all night."

The lantern-bearer's eyes lingered on Alba for a moment, before turning to continue. Alba followed, still without a word, not sure if he was amused or annoyed that the people had apparently fallen for the first lie they were told. After everything Eugene had said about the Warrens' long history in their town, they really should have known better.

Limping miserably by the time they reached the base of the path, the outcropping of trees extending onto the water greeted them, a garland of pearls and jingling bells hanging across the entry just like the way into the forest at their backs. Down a corridor between the rich-smelling pines, a small clearing opened up, grass bedded down and loamy with a shallow blanket of water as the moon's king tides flooded it with every wave.

The trees encircled a standing wooden slab like a mantle of witnesses. In the dark, it was hard to see what exactly was carved into the altar, how the stones were arranged in the dirt beneath their feet, how many cobwebs crisscrossed between the branches encircling them with how often they trailed over Alba's cheeks and arms. But there was one thing he did see—in the light of the single lantern, the altar was soaked a deep plum-red from long-spilled blood, proof of the previous wickies cut open before being tossed into the waiting waves lapping right up against the base of it. Previous wickies, including Alba's own mother. It was enough to make his knees weak, falling to one of them just to be yanked back upright again.

The lantern-bearer approached the altar, setting the pole carrying the light into a designated slot in the earth. They pulled the sickle from their belt, sliding the flat side of the blade up and down the edge of the wood as if polishing it with the old blood stored within the fibers.

Behind him, Alba heard the sound of shuffling fabric, then the strike of a match. He smelled the rich scent of tobacco, glancing over his shoulder just as one of the men stepped away from the other. Approaching the robed figure while taking a drag from his cigarette. He interrupted the person's movements, saying something Alba couldn't hear—before lifting his foot and punting them into the waves.

Hardly a second passed before a flash of bright moonlight lunged and thrashed beneath the water. Alba held his breath, staring, unblinking, at the churning froth, seeing the exact moment the foam tinged pink, then bright red, then went still again.

"The hell'd you do that for, jackass!"

It made Alba jump, stumbling back a step as the man behind him stomped forward, waving the shotgun around and grabbing the coat of the other in anger. "It's gotta be hungry enough to eat the damn wickie!"

"Look, there's an arm floatin' up. See it? Thing didn't eat the whole guy." He glanced back to Alba, the second one following suit. "S'not like he's too big of a meal, either. More like a dessert."

"We was supposed to spill 'is blood on the damn altar so the folks think they got their witchcraft done," the second man continued to argue, growing more agitated. "I'm half a mind from cutting your own neck on it so Josiah doesn't come'n chew me out once he starts gettin' angry telegrams from these twats."

"No god-fearin' man's gonna be standin' by when witchcraft's goin' on," the other spat, sucking on his cigarette again before claiming the shotgun and turning to Alba. "C'mere, wickie."

When Alba didn't move, the man grabbed and dragged him closer. He chuckled upon gripping Alba by the nape of the neck and pointing into the water, dark and lapping at the edge of the grass, sometimes high enough to kiss their feet with the unpredictable tide.

"See 'im?" he asked. "That's that merman you've been spreadin' your legs for. What's a fish cock in the ass feel like?"

A frenzied, moonlit creature thrashed beneath the surface, leashed in place by something Alba couldn't see through the darkness. Knowing it was there by how stilted the movements were.

But Eridanys' snakelike silhouette was undeniable, and the strength with which he churned the depths into bubbling foam was enough to strike another apprehensive bolt of fear into Alba's heart.

God—with how blindingly fast he tore the previous person apart the moment they hit the water, Alba could only pray Eridanys would use his eyes before doing the same to him.

"Maybe he'll let us watch and see 'fore he eats you up," he man continued, leaning over Alba's shoulder. Close enough that Alba felt the end of the gun against the small of his back, the heat of the man's breath on his neck.

He closed his eyes, preparing to be pushed, to face whatever remained of his siren's self-control—but a king tide suddenly swelled in fast and hard, crashing against the rocks with waves tall enough to soak the trees and knock all three of them off their feet. It sucked Alba in first, and he inhaled a mouthful of air just as his head cracked against the rocks and the strong tide turned him over himself.

With his arms tied behind his back, Alba could only kick his legs, releasing what little air he could from his lungs to search for the bubbles and figure out which way was up. Something clawed at him from below, knocked away with a slam of Alba's heel. He fought to climb through the water, straining his legs and propelling himself upward as if hooked by a line.

The moment he broke the surface, coughing and spluttering, Alba barely managed a sharp *"Eri—!"* before the same hands that'd grabbed him from the depths yanked him back under again, a knee smashing into his cheek as one of the men fought to remain on the right side of air, using Alba as a life preserver. Alba kicked his legs, thrashing against him and his weight, fighting to knock himself free before he actually did drown—until a streak of silver tore from the darkness like an arrow, slicing into the man and ripping him from Alba's shoulders.

Alba frantically kicked his legs harder, breaching the surface again with something akin to a death rattle, barely managing a breath before having to dunk under once more as another wave swept over. It carried him toward the rocks that time, as if wishing to do him a favor—slamming him against them, but far enough over the lip that he was able to grind his knees into the stone and anchor himself. Just enough to cling to it as the water flooded back out, letting him sink, melting into the stone and grass, water-logged like a heavy canvas sail.

Coughing and gasping, he managed to clear his sore lungs just enough to finally inhale a shaky, scratchy breath, knowing he couldn't lie there and recuperate for long. He didn't know if another wave would come. He didn't know if another of Josiah's men would grab his ankle and drag him back under. Knowing it was their job to kill him, whether through Eridanys' hunger or to simply drown him and lie.

But when Alba finally gathered his bearings enough to strain his head around and look, the water was silent. Motionless, except for the waves. Even they seemed to have taken on a new state of calm, barely lapping against the rocky outlet. Skimming over the grass as if wishing to caress Alba's cheek pressed into the earth.

When a dark mass suddenly bobbed back to the surface, Alba jumped with another haggard gasp, only to hold it once he saw the gaping mercilessness of the man's missing arm, the way his head lolled in the water with only the finest tendon in his spine keeping it attached at the shoulders. Releasing his held breath with a deep shudder, Alba managed to sit up with a small grunt, watching as the fresh corpse once again disappeared into the darkness. Pulled by invisible hands—though Alba knew.

None other emerged. There was no movement for what felt like an eternity—before the moon of the deepest depths shimmered into existence, and Alba's breath caught for a different reason. Sitting forward, he watched in heart-racing anticipation as the whiteness grew closer, sharper, nearly within reach, finally crossing the threshold of the sea to lift himself on strong arms and press a kiss to Alba's mouth.

Alba pressed back into him relentlessly, straining against the ropes keeping his arms behind his back, wishing to hold him, to knot fingers in his hair and pull him closer, to kiss him and kiss him and kiss him forever. Eridanys gave Alba exactly that without having to be asked, hands finding Alba's hair, his face, drawing him impossibly close until there was hardly a breath between them of their own. Kissing him with lips and a tongue that donned the same taste of rust as when they'd kissed in the lighthouse.

Eridanys was the one to pull away first, and Alba nearly tumbled face-first into the water with how far he leaned into it. The siren produced the ceremonial sickle, and Alba released a short breath of gratitude, turning enough for the ropes binding him to be cut. He sighed in relief once free, rubbing his wrists before properly throwing his arms around Eridanys, the both of them tumbling into the water and emerging once more with mouths pressed against one another.

"Come on," Alba finally encouraged, breathless, grabbing Eridanys' arm. "Will you swim me back to the docks?"

"Unfortunately I cannot, sailor." Eridanys' smile was uneven, unsure. He gently swam Alba back to the rocks, heaving him up onto them again. "It's chains keeping me here. Nothing I can break out of, either, despite how hard I've been trying."

"O-oh," Alba whispered, feeling like he'd just been kicked in the chest. His thoughts raced, he—had to figure something out. He still had time. He could do something. He had to do something. They were so close—and he didn't want to lose another chance at the only thing he wanted.

"Albatross."

Alba jumped, turning quickly. From the darkness—that voice. It took him a moment, but he was sure of it—the voice of his mother.

He scrambled for the nearby lantern lying on its side and only just clinging to life. Allowing the kerosene to soak back into the fabric wick, he waited for it to reignite before pushing himself to his feet. But even with the added light, there was nothing there when he searched. Not even Edythe's residual spirit wandering between the trees. Nothing, no one, only the blood-soaked altar.

The lantern's glow spread over the discarded shotgun, and Alba raced to gather it up, checking to find both shells inside still dry. He turned back to Eridanys as a thought raced to his tongue, stopping short when something else caught his attention in the light.

All around him, the trees dripped with the sound of rain from the tidal wave that soaked them, clumps of foliage and cloth and rope dangling from their branches—or so he first thought. One closer look and Alba realized, knotted in the branches were strands of braided hair.

Eridanys asked what was wrong, but Alba didn't know what to say. There, right there, tied up on the branches around where other wickies had lost their lives on the red altar soaked with blood—exactly what he'd been hoping to find.

What he hadn't anticipated was the number of them. More than the ones he knew by name from the entries in the lighthouse keeper's logbook. There had to be dozens, even a hundred of them, ranging in every color, every texture, length, age. A long record of humans losing their lives where Alba stood, saturating that wooden pedestal with crimson—perhaps even long before Moon Harbor ever had any merrow living in their waters.

Alba didn't know what it meant, who the rest of them could have possibly been sacrificed to, let alone why—but it filled him with anger. Trembling enough with fury that the lantern-light shuddered in his grasp.

All of those people killed—how many were consenting? How many cried and begged and were dragged against their will? How many slit throats and bodies thrown into the sea for her to eat, and how many of those were with the agreement of the sea all the same? Too many were already forced to endure her against their will—Alba included. Eridanys included. His mother in death. His father in life. And the sea was always required to take them, to treat them no different from any others, even if she very well knew how much they feared her and her waves and her storms.

How many unwilling souls did she draw into her depths from Moon Harbor alone, nothing more than an ancient, wild thing driven to mad derangement, bloodlust, no different than a siren banished into vast loneliness?

Alba glanced back at Eridanys, his merrow turned siren, forced to kill on the sea to survive. He thought of himself, who once threw a man into the waves for the sake of his own life, and, in turn, his mother's. He thought of his father, who froze to death in the north, bodily remains picked off by sailors-turned-vultures else they meet the same end—no different from Alba forced to pick the remains off someone else succumbed to the cold, decades later.

His mother, who ran from the sea she loved so much only because she was told it wouldn't be forever. It would be for her own benefit, the Warren Sailing Company would take care of her and her new husband and their eventual child. Tricked, trapped, forced to her end by the one thing she always dreamed of seeing again one day, by the same people she always thought would embrace and protect her if she ever returned.

Killed to fulfill the bloodlust of a town driven to derangement by their own greed for magic; magic harvested from creatures driven mad by their own self-virtue; self-virtue that drove a merrow to gut his own caller of the shore, rather than be strapped to a Warren ship as a lure for fish, for wealth, for profit, to line the pockets of the same people who preyed on Edythe and Edward Marsh with promises of the same—

I'll kill him, Alba thought. He meant to say it out loud, but if he opened his mouth, he would only scream.

He turned back to the trees, to the hair hanging from their branches, immortal reminders of the cruelty of that town and how its people fed into the parasite that was the Warren Sailing Company. Alba hated it—he hated all of them—and for a town full of people who thought they could own the magic of the sea and take everything from her to benefit themselves—he would force them to plead with her for safe harbor.

With a sweep of his arm, the lamp crashed against the high branches of the nearest tree. Glass and kerosene burst into a thousand pieces, scattering heat and sparking flaming children where they landed. Their hunger quickly took root, eating at fresh wood shielded from waves by thick clusters of pine needles; growing hotter and hotter until even the wettest of branches didn't stand a chance. Where the seawater soaking them bubbled until it boiled, spewing steam and thick smoke that replaced the fog that carpeted the land every night except the two where blood met the air.

Alba watched the fire burn until the sweat on his face edged on boiling with it, waiting for the satisfaction to come, the satisfaction that would allow him to turn and leave and walk away and be done with it all—but it never did. It wouldn't come. Not until Josiah Warren's blood smeared over Alba's hands like that of the wooden altar.

Turning back to Eridanys, the siren gazed up at him in silent intensity. Alba stared back, lips parted slightly in consideration, before crouching on the balls of his feet. He adjusted the shotgun in his hand.

"Show me your chains."

Eridanys narrowed his eyes, but dipped beneath the water, situating himself in a way that exposed the end of his long tail. It strained against the taut pull of the metal links anchored to something in the shallows. It didn't matter what—Alba didn't hesitate. The moment Eridanys flashed the shackle into view, Alba pressed the gun into the crook of his shoulder and pulled the trigger.

He was no sharpshooter, but he'd spent plenty of time perched on icecaps with fellow sailors, shooting empty crab shells tossed into the air to cure their boredom. Alba could aim well enough to not blow off Eridanys tail, hoping to, at the very least, weaken the chain links enough that the siren could lash his way free.

He didn't know whether he was successful at first, as Eridanys immediately thrashed back under the surface and tore back out again to curse at him—but Alba put his hands out, taking Eridanys by the face and kissing him. Eridanys' sharp teeth grazed the skin of his lip, his surprised anger snuffing as he wrapped arms around Alba in return, nearly pulling him back into the water with the embrace. Alba kissed him until the flaming heat on his back made sweat build and soak into his shirt, inhaling breath after breath between their mouths laced with saltwater and his siren's skin.

"Find a way out of the chains," he said. "I know you can. And then—we'll meet again before sunrise. I promise."

"Alba—" Eridanys attempted, but Alba pressed fingers to his mouth, before closing his eyes and pressing their foreheads together.

"There's just one more thing I need to do," he whispered, taking the shotgun in his hand again. "Just one more thing. Stay somewhere safe until I call for you. Please. You only have to do me one more favor, ever again."

Eridanys' hand found the back of Alba's head. Fingers tightened in his hair, and he was pulled into another rough, desperate kiss. Alba returned it, using the sensation of Eridanys' mouth to numb the growing fear in the back of his throat.

"Call for me," Eridanys said, like a command. "Call for me the moment you need me, Alba. I'll come."

"I know," Alba whispered. One more kiss, that time gentler. A promise. "I'll see you soon."

Eridanys had no chance to respond. Alba was already pulling away and limping into the mantle of burning trees.

CHAPTER 33

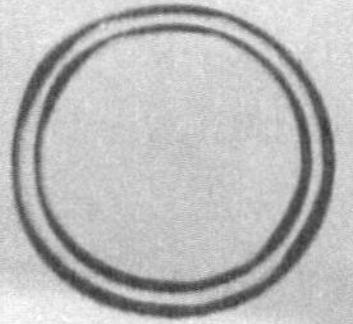

Smoke filled the town before Alba made it to the top of the hill. Carried by a tidal wind blown from distant ocean horizons. Propelling Alba forward with the flames, swirling constantly around him as if to clear the air before it reached his lungs. Circling him as he stood at the mouth of the cemetery, overlooking the town painted orange against the darkness as fire spread.

He wanted the burn of woodsmoke in his lungs; he wanted it to burn his eyes and nose and throat and chest—he wanted to burn all over. He wanted to glow like flames, like the blinding light of a lighthouse lantern, so they would all see him coming. So Josiah Warren would see him coming and know—he was a death knell to run from. He was a rocky outcropping that would tear anyone who came too close into pieces, leaving nothing behind but scattered bone and flesh for seabirds to pick at.

Using the shotgun as a makeshift cane, Alba limped to the road leading into town. The thick smoke swelled high enough to block out the stunningly bright moon, and people took notice. Pointing, gasping, shouting about a fire just as Alba reached the end of the road, some rushing up the street past him, some back into their homes, others toward the swollen sea where they thought the water would protect them. Faces Alba had come to know in passing, rushing by as if he didn't exist.

A cluster of Warren sailors huddled around the side of one of the buildings, speaking in low, rushed voices as they stared up at the growing smoke, clearly anxious as they kept glancing down the road. Waiting for permission to go from the man they were loyal to, finding comfort in a single shared cigarette passed between them.

Alba approached with the shotgun tucked in the crook of his arm, asking outright where he could find Josiah. When the first man took one look at him and barked a laugh, Alba lifted the gun and pulled the trigger. It knocked him back, summoning screams of alarm from the others, scattering like rats as Alba tossed the empty gun away. He claimed the newly dead-man's own firearm from the road to replace it, stealing a handful of bulky ammunition from his pocket in the same motion.

Turning, Alba cornered one of the remaining dogs as the others escaped, who threw his hands up, cowering, declaring *"He's at the Michaels'! At the Michaels' house!"* before frantically shoving Alba away and racing up the road with the others.

Alba's ears rang, shoulder sore from the kick of the blast as he popped the barrel of the new shotgun open to check the shells inside. He then wasted no more time, turning to head in the direction he'd once followed on the heels of Eugene Michaels.

With his limp growing heavier with every step, the shotgun returned to supporting his stride. He stumbled every time someone shoved him out of the way, racing from the flames spreading over beach grass and licking at their homes. Sparks caught on sails flapping on docked boats, devouring every salt-soaked board.

Alba walked toward it, the glow, the heat that made sweat build on his face and burned his eyes. Dragging himself forward, heart pounding as he imagined it. Josiah sitting across the table from Phyllis Michaels, drinking tea and eating dinner. Perhaps discussing his brother Herman, perhaps discussing her son Dawson. That house where he and Eridanys had slept side by side in a cramped bed after fucking one another into the pillows—all the while Alba never knowing what other terrible things the siren may have been subjected to beneath that same roof. It was enough to make Alba's vision blur, flaring bright and hot as the flames, on the verge of combusting himself.

The front door glimmered with merrow scales pressed into the plaster around the entryway. Alba reached it just as it opened —Josiah on the other side, half a movement from stepping out to see what all the noise was about. He met Alba's eyes—and ducked an instant before Alba pulled the trigger, blasting a hole through the side of the doorframe where his head had been.

"Bastard!" Alba shrieked, firing another shot that decimated the staircase railing into splinters. Racing inside after him, Alba popped out the spent shell-casings and replaced them with a quick motion. Like his mother once taught him in the woods outside their house.

Just inside, Phyllis Michaels lunged at him from the sitting room. Alba knocked her back with his elbow, before yanking on the trigger and sending her backward, next. Ears ringing, he stared at where she writhed on the floor, clawing at the old rug and dragging herself toward a nearby trunk, pulling it over on top of herself. Inside, a merrow-hair shawl tumbled out, stained instantly with her blood as she attempted to pull it over herself.

"Good-for-nothing... wickie..." she moaned. "Should've killed you while you slept... like I meant to... Knew you were fucking that—damn merrow... A good-for-nothing... salted tramp, just like your damn—mother..."

Alba approached. He kicked the trunk away, taking a handful of the shawl and wrenching it from her hands. She turned, staring up at him with wide eyes, chest splayed open and bleeding over the rug where she lay.

"Did you offer my mother a place to stay, too?" he asked

breathlessly. "When she first got here. Did you all welcome her back?"

Phyllis' eyes darkened, but a blood-splattered grin split her face.

"Of—course," she choked. "We—were happy to have her— back again. Little—Edie Marsh—a stupid bitch, ever since—she was a little girl. Always talkin'—'bout how she was goin' to find a better life—somewhere else. Came back anyway. Was a real— delight—seein' the shock on her face when—we dragged her to the altar. Never cried or begged—'til she felt the sickle on her throat." Her smile spread wider, eyes bulging. "You have your father's—ugly red hair, you know. But her eyes."

Alba pulled the trigger, decorating the side of the couch and hardwood floor with her last splatter of life. Making his ears ring, making his world spin, vision bright and throbbing and wavering in and out as his hands were and weren't his with every twitch of his finger on the trigger.

One more. Only one more, making his tongue roll over in his mouth. Like a hungry churning deep in his gut, satisfied with every pull of the trigger. Squirming in anticipation as he popped the empty shells from the gun and replaced them one last time.

Over him, that home barely standing beneath the weight of the sins carried out in its belly groaned, earth below begging to be cleansed where no amount of salt scattered by white-clothed hands could burn the evil away any longer. Only fire, only fire, like traveling preachers used to call out on the street as he and his mother hurriedly passed by. Alba had been baptized by them as a baby, promised fire and brimstone if he didn't worship their book —but god had never done anything to save him from the devil that came calling when he was thirteen.

He didn't need god where even salt couldn't cleanse wicked- ness—he would bring his own fire. He would take care of the devil, himself, with the flames of cast-off souls and a shotgun in his hand.

In his search, Alba was forced to reckon with the full extent of the Michaels' involvement in the butchering of the merrow of Moon Harbor. Hidden off the kitchen was a room with ceramic floor tiles stained black with blood; pastel wallpaper splattered like a pen whipping ink. A faded black and white photograph of Eugene standing with a smiling crew alongside a dazed merrow dangling like a fish on a line behind them. Crude drawings of merrow anatomy pinned to the walls. Scribbled notes of the healing capabilities of their skin, teeth, bones, hair woven into pretty white shawls. Journals logging each and every one of them caught and when. How long they wasted away in the old light-house beneath the turning light. Exactly how many still-beating hearts the man fed his son in hopes of saving him.

Alba destroyed that room in a wild burst of rage, even knowing the approaching flames would devour far more than he could break and tear. Wanting the fire to know exactly what deserved to burn most.

With no sign of Josiah on the bottom floor, Alba made his way to the stairs. Adrenaline helped dilute the ache in his hip, but he still dragged his shoulder along the wall as he climbed.

Moving slowly, listening with every step, he was aware that whenever the wood creaked beneath his feet, Josiah would hear him. Josiah would anticipate where he was, where he came from. It didn't matter to Alba—even if the man hid from him to avoid the gun, eventually the fire would come and consume them both.

As he reached the top of the stairs, something creaked behind the one door Phyllis hid from him the night he stayed. Alba moved for it. Nudging it open with his foot, he raised the gun to his nose, holding his breath as he took in the room. The distinct, sticky stench of decomposition struck him first, a miasma almost heavy enough that he had to cover his mouth.

The glass in the window frame cracked against the heat from the neighboring building alight in flame; mold grew in dark clusters along the head and baseboards on the walls, bed neatly made and recently slept in by the glass of water on the nightstand. And in the corner—a single figure sat stark upright, unmoving in a chair, facing partially toward the bed, the door. Soft blonde hair was brushed back, silvery pigment brushed over his closed eyes and cheeks dusted with far too much rouge, lips stained red with lipstick lovingly drawn on. He wore fine clothes, finer than any others Alba had seen in town, silk vest buttoned up over his chest, high collar masking dark bruising on the front of his throat, silver cufflinks reflecting firelight over his wrists. A merrow-hair shawl was draped over his legs, and Alba's blood ran cold when his eyes lingered on the cards spread out neatly in front of him. Cigarette cards, including the ones he'd shared with Eugene.

Eridanys' previous caller of the shore. Dawson Michaels—or at least, what remained of him.

Despite the clear attempts at making him look young, lively, merely sleeping peacefully in his chair—the closer Alba crept, the more the pallor of Dawson's skin was undeniable. His hands were porcelain white, fingernails gray and sunken; he hunched unnaturally, hardly reclining in the chair as much as he was propped up by the arm rest. He did not move, not even to breathe, not even to twitch, even as the window finally shattered from the heat and flames curled up the wallpaper.

"He was even more beautiful in life."

Alba jerked around, raising the gun as Josiah stepped into the room behind him. He held a ragged fishing knife in his hand, eyes wide, wild, directed at Alba with bloodlust shining in them.

"How much did your mermaid tell you?" he went on, pausing just long enough to get a good look at Alba, his posture, how he held the gun, as if trying to determine whether or not he actually knew how to use it.

Alba adjusted his grip, knowingly, to prove himself a threat. Josiah's mouth twitched.

"I was young when they got engaged, but I remember being stunned by the sight of him. I remember how shocked I was that my brother would ever want to marry someone from such a run-down shithole as this—But the second I saw him, I understood." Josiah's eyes flickered to Dawson, the briefest little look, as if even as an adult he couldn't believe it. "Dawson's theories on using merrow to lure fish was supposed to make our family wealthier, enough that we wouldn't need anything like steam ships even now. Even in death, Herman wouldn't tell anyone what happened here, what he and Dawson were planning—and it took me years of scouring his things to get even the smallest understanding.

"He was so secretive—so possessive of his lover's work. Didn't want anyone claiming it as their own, even after he'd died. Even Marco kept his secrets—apparently even visiting this place every now and again to continue recruiting sailors behind my back. Selfish and stupid, all of them. Dawson, my brother, Marco, every half-wit in this town who chopped up every last merrow living in their harbor." His jaw clenched. "Except one. That last one of yours. After I'm done with you, I'll truss him up like a prized catch and he'll bring me more acclaim than Herman ever deserved. I'll feed disobedient sailors to him when he's hungry, and come back to this place every few years to see if all of Moon Harbor's murdered wickies actually turned into merrow like these idiots always prayed. Maybe I'll find you again, then. Unable to sing with your throat slit. Just like your mother."

Alba pulled the trigger, but Josiah barely moved out of the way. He lunged with the knife bared, slamming Alba back onto the bed, wooden feet scraping across the floor as Alba used the gun as a shield against the knife. His arms shook beneath Josiah's weight, the pressure of the knife hovering over his eye almost too much to hold back. His saving grace was a rafter cracking in two overhead, one side tumbling down and smashing against Josiah's back, knocking him to the side and allowing Alba to kick him off fully.

Josiah's knife slipped, clattering to the floor as Alba managed to throw himself over the opposite side of the bed, falling to his knees then scrambling away as Josiah lunged. Alba tumbled backward into where Dawson sat, knocking the corpse loose to topple to the floor. It hit with a weighty *thud*, still soft and pliable as the day he died.

Cold, clammy, lifeless—*dead*. Dead all along, despite the merrow hearts. Despite all the blood spilled by Eugene Michaels and everyone else who listened to him. It filled Alba with bitter, toxic fury as black as the blood staining his arms, ears ringing loud enough to deafen the rest of his thoughts, leaving only his emotion to drive his instincts—and he kicked himself back into the wall, lifting the shotgun to blow the head off of Dawson Michaels' dead body.

Josiah let out a horrified sound behind him, but the sight filled Alba with euphoria. Staring at the thick, congealed remains splattered over the floor at his feet, he choked back a sudden bout of laughter as he couldn't help it. That person who had been dead for years, who resembled Alba in age when Eridanys tore his throat out, who Alba knew so little of—except that he'd done nothing but mistreat the siren he'd come to care so much for. The merrow-turned-siren who Alba would cherish and love and grow old with despite it all, in spite of it all.

Josiah lunged for Alba's gun, surprising him with the speed and dazing him when the butt of it collided with the side of his face in the power struggle. Stumbling back, Josiah pulled the weapon into his shoulder, and Alba threw his hands up on reflex, despite knowing both shells were already spent. Once Josiah realized it, himself—he reeled the shotgun back, smashing it into Alba's head before Alba could dodge away.

Josiah grabbed him next, wrenching him from the wall to shove him to the floor, smearing Dawson's remains with Alba's back as he pinned him and smashed fists into his face.

Alba barely had the strength to put his hands out, a useless attempt at defending himself as they were easily knocked away. Instead, he lashed his arm out to where Dawson's remains slumped alongside him. Scraping fingers through the stringy viscera, he shoved a handful of the rot into Josiah's face, grinding it into the man's mouth until he felt teeth graze his knuckles.

Josiah bellowed out in disgust, buckling over and choking, gagging on the taste, allowing Alba just enough time to kick him off and drag himself away—toward where the serrated fishing knife had skittered beneath the bed.

Stretching for it, grappling at the handle, he barely scooped it into his hand just as Josiah grabbed him by the back of the shirt and yanked him back out again.

Hands found his throat, pressing into it, choking him—and he threw his arm in an arc, slamming the blade into the side of Josiah's neck. Deep enough that blood instantly waterfalled out, drenching Alba's hand and soaking down into his sleeve—though Josiah didn't react right away. Too overcome with his own adrenaline, his rage, he only tightened his hands.

Beneath strained gasps, Alba shoved the blade to the side, cutting through the clenched muscles of the man's neck and summoning more blood to gush from the opening. Splattering him with crimson hot enough to nearly burn his skin, pouring in a curtain over his chest, his arms, his face, into his mouth until he choked on it when finally able to gasp.

Josiah finally pressed a hand into the wound, gargling, wheezing. Staring at Alba without moving, as Alba managed to pull himself free. The man found the bloody knife on the floor where Alba dropped it, lashing out with it, breaths growing raspy as he still never took his eyes from Alba stumbling away from him.

"Just die already!" Alba screamed, and the corner of Josiah's mouth quirked in response. Alba's final plea for relief, for respite, to be free of the weight suffocating him since the day he was born. The yoke around his choking neck, the burden on his back, exhausted until exhaustion was all he knew. Just wanting relief— just wanting a chance to breathe. To take the life he'd lost through his fingers again and again and again, that time refusing to let it go, clinging to it with all he had left—a life that would start only when that man was dead.

He grabbed the shotgun off the floor. Josiah attempted to say something, to taunt him, to cut him with the knife—but Alba smashed the butt of the shotgun into his head. Josiah crumpled to the floor with a grunt, and Alba hit him again. Again and again, bludgeoning his skull until there was hardly anything left. Until the man was faceless and inhuman even with air still in his lungs, as faceless and rotten as Dawson's corpse, as Eugene and Phyllis Michaels' corpses, as all those people sacrificed to the sea on that bloody altar. As faceless and rotten and inhuman as Alba had become since first stolen off the road, just a sailor, just a body, just two arms to heave nets from the sea—only just realizing he had a face to be seen at all when Eridanys held it gentler than he ever deserved.

Only when the shotgun fell from his grasp, slippery with blood, did Alba finally stop. He sank into the gore at his knees, breathing heavy, jaw hanging slack before clenching tight. A wailing, tearing emotion whirled in his chest, growing tighter, higher up his throat, before finally spilling out of him—except instead of a scream, it was splitting laughter. A shriek of amusement, erupting so hard from his chest that he buckled forward, wrapping arms around himself as more vomited out of him, no different than the cries of dread while kneeling in Eugene's splattered viscera. Making every inch of him shake, gasping and trembling and shrieking with laughter to the point he couldn't breathe, until the blood spilling from his nose and split lip dribbled over his tongue and down the back of his throat where it mixed with Josiah's splattered over him.

Alba laughed until tears filled his eyes, burning and blinding him; until he didn't know if mirth or agony howled from his lungs. He hardly felt any difference between its hands around his throat and how Josiah had clutched him. Choking him, suffocating, making him bend and hunch and gasp until he was sure his heart would split and erupt out of his chest.

His hands clawed at the thick, hot blood painted across the floor, at the lifeless flesh within reach, smashed into unrecognizable oblivion. He raked fingers through it, squeezing until handfuls of minced entrails squirted between his knuckles, laughing again when he realized why it was so familiar. That old, frozen memory of having to eat to live. Forced to eat his own kind by the demands of the man who laid faceless on the floorboards, only a few feet from being devoured by fire. Whose generational greed resulted in Alba's father being cannibalized in death; in Edythe being digested by the salty sea; in Eridanys forced into depravity to feast on others until his song warped into something predatory.

Alba scraped handfuls of indistinguishable innards between his fingers. He choked back another bout of laughter, a decade of crushing anguish, and buried a handful of the last remains of the Marsh family curse into his mouth.

USING FURNITURE, door frames, the walls to support himself, Alba limped from the room. Down the hallway, the stairs. Slowed by the pain in his leg, his blurry vision through eyes nearly swollen shut, how hard it was to breathe. Moving to put one foot ahead of the other by the sound of fire devouring the house's wooden bones, until they groaned and crackled with bowing insides.

The world warped and smeared around him, thoughts dragging into a trickle, every movement requiring more effort than the last. Requiring him to blink through growing sweat dripping from his brow into his eyes, infiltrating his mouth and mixing with the blood on his tongue.

The door still hung open as he reached the bottom of the stairs. He could see the street through it. Empty, silent, except for roaring flames turning that town to ash. He thought he could hear the sea close by, as if the king tide swelled higher than ever before. Searching for its sacrifice. Seeking the human blood offered to sate it every month prior, as if it hadn't been given enough.

Alba followed the sound, hoping it would ease the dryness of his mouth. The cracked dust in his lungs. The hot blood searing his skin.

The moment he stepped into the nighttime air, he collapsed to the road, cobblestones baked and warm from the heat of the fire.

"Eri," he mumbled, closing his eyes as exhaustion crept over him. Heavy and sticky and making it impossible to keep himself above the surface of thought. "Eridanys... I'm here."

The sound of water trickled closer, a king tide seeking its sacrifice, reaching as far as it could with blood-stained fingers, snaking between cracks in the cobblestones. It found Alba where he lay, just like the sea always did when he thought he'd left her reach. Dark and muddy, made black by the soot of the burning town, tinged pink with blood. Growing. Swelling.

Gliding past him to continue up the street, spilling into open doors and sweeping debris away with it. Offering Alba only a passing greeting before continuing on its way, intent on other things than simply drowning him.

Alba closed his eyes again, resting against the cooked ground, waiting to be carried away like the rest of the crumbling houses. Not fighting as the tide swelled higher. Draping over his hands, his legs, his back, until it infiltrated his mouth and washed away any remaining blood caked against the back of his teeth. Rising until it lapped over him, kissing the split skin of his hands, his face where Josiah had beat him—before a wall of water suddenly crashed over the town entirely, sweeping Alba into its grasp before he had even a chance to call out one more time.

It swallowed him whole, turning and tumbling him like a doll trapped in a whirlpool, and all he could do was brace for the moment he slammed back into the earth. Smashed into a crumbling building. Was skewered through the chest.

But the moon found him first in the darkness, swirling within that smoke and ash-stained water as black as the stains on his skin. The moon with its familiar hands, its firm grasp that held Alba protectively, pulling him into its chest and holding him close.

Alba wrapped his arms around it in return. Not sure he would actually feel anything if he did, not sure how much of the moon's glow was his imagination, or death coming for him—but Eridanys was solid. Eridanys was flesh and bone, and Eridanys was holding him. Holding him where Alba knew—he was safe. Anywhere Alba was with Eridanys was safe.

A flutter of bubbles escaped Alba's lungs, catching on his nose, in his eyelashes. Any that clung to the curve of his swollen lips were swiftly kissed away by the siren who held him, before he sank peacefully into the dark sea that always wished to take him.

CHAPTER 34

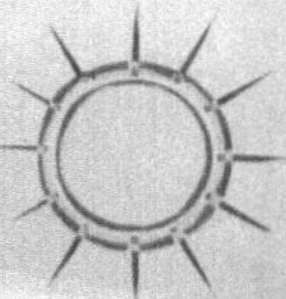

THE SUN TOUCHED HIS FACE. THE SUN HE SAW SO little of, for as long as he could remember, was there to greet him as his ghost crept back into his body one drop of blood at a time.

But it wasn't the sun he wanted—it was the moon. It was the moon, her shine, her glow—and once his eyes cracked open, even through the blurry haze, Alba got his wish.

His moon was right there next to him, waiting for him to wake. Then touching his face once he stirred, chilled and comforting, compelling Alba to lean into it. Wishing to disappear into its soothing gentleness, to strike the heat that burned on and beneath his skin away.

Eridanys. Alba smiled, blinking until he could see where they were. Overhead, he recognized the ceiling of the lighthouse lantern room, eyes sore and stinging terribly.

Only when he tried to speak did something crumble on his skin, realizing how almost every inch of him had been smeared with the harbor's healing clay. It made him chuckle, weak and breathy, though he still didn't fully relax. Not yet. Not until his hand reached out, touching chilled skin again, fingers trailing down and arm, finding a bent knee, then a stomach slathered with its own muddy bandage. It stoked Alba back to life slightly more, forcing himself to lift his head, then sit up. To properly look into Eridanys' face, where all he could do was sigh in relief. His piece of the moon, there, smiling at him.

"You're alright," he said with a wobbly smile. "Thank god."

"I promised I would come for you," Eridanys answered. Touching Alba's face, his hair; the streak of silver, the tiny braid still intact beneath his ear. "No matter which shore you called from. No matter how far, I said I would beseech the sea to rise high enough for me to reach you. And that—"

"She would listen," Alba finished for him, emotion burning in the back of his throat. He closed his eyes, cupping his hand around the nape of Eridanys' neck and pressing their foreheads together. Listening to the sound of the sea on the other side of the weatherglass. The gulls calling to one another. Eridanys' calm breaths. Calm, safe, peaceful.

"What happened to it?" he finally asked, memories hazy, but clear enough to know exactly how the high tide rose to collect him. "What happened to the town?"

Eridanys nodded his head toward the window. "Take a look for yourself, sailor. See all that's left."

Alba gulped, suddenly apprehensive, but crawled slowly to the window. His breath caught as he looked, witnessing what remained of Moon Harbor and her clusters of buildings. At least, where the clusters of buildings once sat, flattened into a streak of burnt sand and debris and only a few skeletal remains poking through. The shore that was once the color of merrow blood had been pushed up the hill, warping the line of the beach, swallowing half of what had once been the land. Reclaimed by the waves, left destitute. Not a soul wandered her beaches, and what remained of the streets were hardly more than faint lines cutting divots through the nothingness.

"It's gone," he whispered. "It's really... gone."

"Just like we said," Eridanys reminded him. Alba turned, gazing at the man for a moment, before laughing sharply. He threw himself into the siren's arms, clinging to him as something nearly lost. Something he loved and could keep, unlike so many other times. Alba's merrow, his siren, his caller of the sea, his companion, who he would keep close until he took his last breath.

Alba would be able to keep Eridanys by his side, to start anew, to have a life, to have a home, to have someone to take care of like he always wished.

"*I love you,*" he whispered, pulling the man closer. "I love you, I love you. I want you, I want to be with you, anywhere else than here."

"I'll go wherever you are," Eridanys responded, breath tickling the hairs on the back of Alba's neck. "With you I'll always stay, Albatross. Prince of the sea."

Eridanys carried Alba down the winding stairs, where a blanket of seawater flooded the lighthouse floor. The lighthouse floor and the entire island outside of it, enough that, at just the right angle, it felt as if they walked on the surface of the sea. Alba slid off Eridanys' back to feel it for himself, smiling and splashing his feet over the soaked beach grass and even laughing as minuscule fish skittered around where he stepped.

In the keeper's house, Alba didn't have much he cared to salvage, except his coat and the possessions tucked safely inside. Hoping it still hung on the hook where he'd left it, and hadn't been scrounged through by Josiah's men while they stayed. It was thankfully where he expected—though his heart sank as he burrowed a hand into the pocket to find his mother's hairpin missing.

Nearly crying out for Eridanys, not sure what else to do, the sound caught in Alba's throat when a seabird suddenly squawked at him from the kitchen table. The albatross clutched the pin in its beak like some kind of cruel irony, though Alba wouldn't hesitate to throttle his own namesake to get it back. He threw up his hands, lunging and tossing his jacket with the same finesse as unfurling a fishing net over the open sea. The bird anticipated the assault, spreading its wings and trilling at him before sweeping through the front door, ignoring Alba's threats, then pleas, as it went.

He chased it out as fast as his aching leg would let him, searching high and low as the bird took off like a shot into the sky. Eridanys witnessed none of the theft as it happened, distracted by something over the edge of the flooded rocks. Alba could only wave his hands, calling out for the bird to *give it back, it was his, it was all he had left!*—yelping and ducking when the bird suddenly swooped down, nearly taking his head off.

"Damn you!" he shrieked, grabbing a soggy handful of mud to throw, falling far too short.

Eridanys called out to ask what was wrong, and Alba turned to tell him—only for something to *plunk* in the water at his feet. He scrambled for it, scooping the pin into his hands and glaring at the bird as it swooped down over him again, before skimming the water to land a few yards away. A second albatross joined it, clacking their beaks together in affection like long lost lovers finally reunited. Alba just scowled at them, securely tucking the pin into his braid at the nape of his neck and going to see what had Eridanys so preoccupied.

"Oh!" he exclaimed, spotting it instantly. Flooding the harbor for as far as he could see, lazy pearl-white jellyfish swayed with the tide. Bumping unawares into one another, sometimes tangling tentacles or getting snagged on the rocks. When Eridanys scoffed and stepped forward to pinch one and throw it back out into open water, Alba had to fight the instinct to grab and stop him.

"Didn't it sting you?" he asked, grabbing the man's hand in concern. Eridanys just wrinkled his nose.

"It did. Not very grateful, are we!" he shouted, making Alba raise an eyebrow. Eridanys sighed, then smirked, running fingers back through his hair. "You know how humans believe lost sailors become seabirds to fly back home? Merrow believe the same—but jellyfish. Worthless, brainless jellyfish..."

"Then...!" Alba grinned, before laughing. "That means all your kin were washed out to sea after all."

"Suppose so."

"They're not going to keep us from leaving, are they?"

"I don't think so." Eridanys flashed Alba a mischievous smile. "I'm not above eating the death-spirits of my own kin. They should anticipate as much and stay far out of my way."

Alba laughed again. Eridanys spotted the pin in his hair, then, smiling and complimenting it, running Alba's messing braid over his fingers.

"That suits you," he said. "Glad you get to keep that reminder of her."

"Me, too," Alba smiled back, taking Eridanys' hand and squeezing it. He offered one last glance back to the seabird who'd stolen it at first, chuckling as it continued dancing with its partner between nuzzling and tapping beaks. Touching the pin in his hair again, the smile faded slightly as his heart skipped a beat. *You know how humans believe sailors lost at sea become birds to fly back home?*

Stray tears dripped from his eyes, leaving streaks in the healing mud on his face. Eridanys noticed before Alba did, brushing the back of a knuckle over his cheek to catch one.

"Oh—" Alba jumped, quickly wiping them away, though more only followed behind. He couldn't stop them. "I know, I know, the sea already has enough salt. I don't know why..."

Eridanys stopped him before he could smear the rest away. Regarding Alba for a long time, his smile never faded.

"Especially here, in this harbor—she has not had nearly enough salt from tears of joy," he said gently, eyes flickering up to where the birds circled one another. "Cry all you like, Alba. So she can have a taste of it for the first time in a long time."

Alba did—he cried. He cried, then smiled and laughed and threw his arms around Eridanys, knocking them both to the flooded earth where Alba held him, then kissed him, then laughed more as Eridanys turned him onto his back to kiss like he really meant it. Soaking Alba through with saltwater that, for the first time, embraced him back like he was as much a part of her as Eridanys was.

Alba cried and kissed his siren for as long as he liked. Never once feeling a single tug in his belly, nor the constant pull of somewhere to be, something to do, someone to wait for. All he wanted was right there with him.

Alba was in no hurry. He had all the freedom in the world.

Acknowledgments

My partner, my cover artist, my companion, my caller of the sea, Mo, without whom the first seeds of A BONE IN HIS TEETH never would have been planted. Knowing there's a hundred thousand more where that came from, I'm so excited to see where our stories continue to take us.

https://morlevart.com/work

Twitter: @morlevart

Instagram: @morlev_art

My beta readers, blurbers, and peers who provide so much emotional and mental support throughout the unwieldy process that is writing a book, especially when things feel a little too heavy to keep going.

My readers, new and old, who show me so much kindness and give me so much motivation to publish the best work I can. I have so much in store for the future, I hope you'll stick around.

Anyone who has ever left a rating, review, or spread word of my books to friends and family, I will never be able to put into words how much I appreciate you, and how such small things help indie authors like me so much!

About the Author

Kellen Graves (they/them) is a queer indie writer and artist from the Pacific Northwest, where they live with their partner, two cats, and crystal collection. They also enjoy digital illustration, photography, collecting planners, and disappearing into the ocean.

You can find more info about this release and upcoming releases, see their art, and connect by following Kellen on social media or checking out their website.

Twitter: @skellygraves
Instagram: @skellygraves

skellygraves.com
skellygraves.carrd.co

* 9 7 9 8 9 8 8 8 0 7 7 2 8 *